MEXICAN FOLK NARRATIVE

FROM THE LOS ANGELES AREA

PUBLICATIONS OF THE AMERICAN FOLKLORE SOCIETY

Memoir Series

GENERAL EDITOR, WM. HUGH JANSEN

VOLUME 56   1973

Mexican Folk Narrative from the Los Angeles Area

Introduction, Notes, and Classification by

ELAINE K. MILLER

PUBLISHED FOR THE *American Folklore Society* BY THE
UNIVERSITY OF TEXAS PRESS, AUSTIN

Library of Congress Cataloging in Publication Data

Miller, Elaine K   1937–
    Mexican folk narrative from the Los Angeles area.

    (Publications of the American Folklore Society.
Memoir series, v. 56)
    Tales in Spanish.
    Revision of the author's thesis, University of
California, Los Angeles, 1967.
    Bibliography: p.
    1. Tales, Mexican—Los Angeles. I. Title.
II. Series: American Folklore Society. Memoirs,
v. 56.
GR115.M52   398.2   72-5206
ISBN 978-0-292-74143-0

DEDICATED TO

those who told the tales and opened

a whole new world to me.

CONTENTS

Illustrations of informants, following p. 202

1. Lola Cruz
2. Luis Cruz
3. Tecla Rocha
4. Isaura Benicia
5. Hugo Massa
6. Amalia Hernández and Elisa Contreras
7. Inocente Rocha
8. Rafael Gudiño
9. Alicia Salinas
10. Candelario Gallardo

The following work is a revision of my doctoral dissertation, completed in 1967 at the University of California, Los Angeles, in the Department of Spanish and Portuguese.

I became interested in folklore while a graduate student in Spanish at Indiana University and decided to continue my graduate study at the University of California, Los Angeles, where I could combine Spanish and folklore and do fieldwork among the Mexican-Americans of Los Angeles. There was at that time very little recent published material available from urban Mexican-American communities, and Los Angeles seemed to be relatively unexplored in the area of Mexican folk narrative. At the time of this writing, to my knowledge, the situation remains essentially unchanged. There is no large published collection of Mexican folk narrative from Los Angeles.

The nature of my work is essentially that of *collectanea*—a documentation of the folk tradition present among the Mexicans in the Los Angeles area. There is an obvious need for more specifically theoretical studies, and, therefore, while that is not within the scope of this work, I do hope this collection may eventually be of use toward that end.

I would like to acknowledge those people whose assistance and support was of especial value to me in carrying out this project. For the guidance offered me in their capacity as members of my doctoral research committee, I am especially indebted to Professors Stanley Robe and Shirley Arora of the Department of Spanish and Portuguese. Professor Wayland Hand, chairman of the Department of Folklore and Mythology, very kindly made available to me the material in the Archives of the Center for the Comparative Study of Folklore and Mythology, at UCLA. To all these people I am appreciative of the opportunity to have shared information and impressions, based on their extensive experience in folklore research and fieldwork, which helped me to formulate this project.

Finally, I wish to acknowledge those who told the tales.

Brockport, New York

INTRODUCTION

The Geographical Area

The material presented here was collected between March 1966 and July 1967 in and around Los Angeles, California. The areas represented are the two towns of Santa Paula (pop. 15–20,000) and Oxnard (pop. 50–60,000), both about fifty miles up the coast from Los Angeles, and the urban Los Angeles areas of Culver City, Santa Monica, Venice, and West Los Angeles.

These areas are on the west side of Los Angeles, which has an estimated Mexican-American population of 30,000. This figure represents a small percentage of the total Mexican-American population of Los Angeles, which is generally acknowledged to be around 1 million, or 10 percent of the overall population. In the entire state of California, Mexican-Americans number about 2 million, once again representing 10 percent of the total population; and of these 2 million over 80 percent live in urban barrios. These statistics are part of a larger picture that places the total Mexican-American population of the United States at around 8 million, making this group the second largest ethnic minority in the country.

The Informants

In my fieldwork, I did not attempt to work with a representative number or portion of the thirty thousand Mexican-Americans who live on the west side of Los Angeles. I spoke with some seventy-five to eighty and recorded material from forty. In the selection of informants, no attempt was made to control, or to draw conclusions based upon, such factors as age, sex, place of origin in Mexico, or length of residence in the United States. The background of the informants is varied and as widely diverse as is the make-up of the Mexican-American population of the Los Angeles area. The areas of Mexican background represented by the informants include ten states: Chihuahua (1), Federal District (1), Guanajuato (3), Guerrero (1), Jalisco (9), Puebla (1), Sinaloa (3), Sonora (1), Yucatán (1), and Zacatecas (5). One informant was from Arizona.

The informants' length of residence in California at the time of the interviews ranged from ten days to sixty years.

Their ages, too, covered a span of sixty years, the youngest being twenty-four and the oldest eighty-four. The following distribution resulted: nine informants in the twenty-to-forty age group, nine in the forty-to-sixty group, and nine over sixty, including two informants in their eighties.

The predominance of women over men informants is probably due to the fact that most of the collecting was done during the day, when the men were most often not at home.

Collecting Procedure

I made contact with informants in a variety of ways: in one area, through the neighborhood priest; in another, through the local representative of the Poverty Program; and in another, through the membership list of the Guadalupana Society. In each instance, however, it was a question of receiving a name and an address, knocking on a door, introducing myself, and explaining my interest and my purpose. On some days, in the absence of specific leads, I would simply set out to canvass a two- or three-square-block area in a predominantly Mexican neighborhood, hoping to discover in the process a potential informant or two. The result of such efforts was always unpredictable. I did no written advertising of any sort and made no personal appearances before large groups to explain my project, nor did I offer payment for collaboration.

In about five months of actual collecting I had gathered a corpus of around 160 narrative items collected from forty informants; 82 narratives from twenty-seven informants are represented in this collection.

A tape recorder was used, with the informants' knowledge and permission, to record all material, and the narratives were transcribed from the tapes and are presented here exactly as the informants gave them, with the exception of those minor alterations noted in the section containing linguistic notes.

The Informants' Attitude toward the Material

In my search for folk material, I found most of the people with whom I came in contact to be quite friendly and receptive to the idea once they understood what I was doing. Some were really quite delighted that I was interested in their experiences, beliefs, or stories, and somewhat surprised to find that I was familiar with such things as *duendes*, the *llorona*, and *ánimas*. They often asked to hear their stories played back and showed obvious enjoyment of them. One informant, an excellent tale teller, was so pleased at having his stories recorded that I was moved to leave with him, on a subsequent visit, a copy of several recorded tales.

I did, of course, encounter many people who were unable to give me any information at all, either because of "not remembering" any stories or experiences to tell, or because of outright rejection of the material. Some examples of skepticism or rejection met with on the part of the informants can be found in the sections on the *llorona* (see No. 41), *duendes* (see pp. 140–159), and the *nahual* (see p. 160 and No. 58). There was only one instance of unwillingness to cooperate unless paid for the information, and this I felt to be very much due to the influence of the informant's son, who held out the hope of some financial gain from his father's stories of his experiences with Pancho Villa.

I think it is accurate to say that there is an undercurrent of belief on the part of these informants that the types of incidents narrated here are things that happen in Mexico and not in California or the United States. Of the sixty-two legendary narratives presented, only seven are located outside of Mexico: five from California, one from Arizona, and one from New Mexico. The five California narratives (26, 27, 28, 29, and 30) all deal with ghosts; the story from Arizona (39) tells of an encounter with the *llorona*; and the narrative from New Mexico (60) is a version of the *mal hijo* theme. In casual conversation, several informants spoke of people who thought they had heard the *llorona* here, but it was never very emphatically affirmed. One informant told me very definitely that the *llorona* appeared only in Mexico, while others, obviously, felt that people could have encounters with her in Los Angeles. Once again, although the number of examples is limited, an interesting pattern emerges: the ghost story is the one seen by the informant as the least bound geographically, or perhaps culturally, to Mexico.

It can also be stated definitely that legendary narratives are more widely exchanged than are traditional tales. Of the forty informants who recorded, only two had a repertoire of tales. Legendary material, very closely related to belief and therefore more effectively integrated into daily life, seems to persist with a naturalness that escapes the tale. It is, so to speak, functional, for it deals with what the informant often regards as reality, phenomena that may really be operative in his life. The tale, with its primary function of entertainment, has come to be replaced by other forms of entertainment; and this process is likely to happen quickly in a modern, busy society, such as that which faces the Mexican who comes to live and work in Los Angeles.

Documentation Procedure

The narratives presented here are classified and documented according to the following standard tale and legend reference works: Antti Aarne, *The Types of the Folktale*; Ralph S. Boggs, *Index of Spanish Folktales*; Reidar Th. Christiansen, *The Migratory Legends*; Terrence L. Hansen, *The Types of the Folktale in Cuba, Puerto Rico, the Dominican Republic, and Spanish South America*; Oskar Loorits, *Livische Maerchen- und Sagenvarianten*; J. Qvigstad, *Lappische Märchen- und Sagenvarianten*; Jacques Sinnighe, *Katalog der Niederländischen Märchen-, Ursprungssagen-, Sagen- und Legendenvarianten*; and Stith Thompson, *Motif-Index of Folk-Literature*.

The documentation immediately following each of the tale and legend texts is presented in the following order: first, the identification of motifs or tale types, in order of appearance, according to the various indices used; and, second, the alphabetical listing of references to parallel versions. Motif numbers from the *Motif-Index of Folk-Literature* are cited without reference to Thompson.

Besides the many published collections that were consulted in order to cite parallel versions of the narratives, mention should be made here of the usefulness of the Archives of the Center for the Comparative Study of Folklore and Mythology at the University of California, Los Angeles. Additional unpublished material that proved quite useful, much of which has since become available in published form, was made available to me by Professor Stanley Robe from his own extensive collection of Mexican folk narrative.

Linguistic Notes

In transcribing the texts presented here, first consideration has been given to readability; therefore, it is not intended that any text be regarded as a phonetic transcript.

Some nonstandard forms have been included, but they are, in general, only those forms which are either readily identifiable or of especial value in indicating the speech level of the informant. Wherever there is a possibility of confusion the item is clarified in brackets immediately following. These items together with other nonstandard forms are included in the Vocabulary. (See Appendix 3.)

Two blanket statements may be made about the speech of these informants: (1) All are *yeístas*. Both *ll* and *y* represent [y]. The sound [ḻ] is not present in their speech. (2) All use the *seseo*; *s*, *z*, and *c* followed by /e/ or /i/ are all rendered [s]. The sound [ɵ] is not present in their speech.

Only those nonstandard forms representing either phonemic or morphological variation are transcribed as spoken by the informant. Phonetic variations, for the most part, are not represented, for their very great frequency and widespread occurrence would detract considerably from the important goal of readability of the text.

Two extremely common speech characteristics reflected in the texts are more conveniently mentioned here than listed in their numerous individual examples in the Vocabulary.

1. The inflected forms of the verb *estar* are very frequently

rendered as follows: *está* [ta], *están* [tan], *estaba* [tába], *estaban* [tában], *estamos* [támos], *esté* [te], *estén* [ten], *estuvo* [túbo], and so on. Such pronunciation is indicated by the written forms *'tá, 'tán, 'taba, 'taban, 'tamos, 'té, 'tén, 'tuvo*, and so on.

2. The second person familiar (*tú*) verb forms, terminating in *-aste, -iste*, are quite often rendered with an analogical *s*, thus giving *-astes, -istes*, as in *presentastes, trajistes*.

The following items represent those speech characteristics which have not been reproduced in the texts, but which should be pointed out as fairly common occurrences in the speech of these informants:

1. Final /s/ as an indication of plurality may occasionally be rendered [ø] or [h], as in *años* [áŋo] or [áŋoh].

2. Final /d/ and also intervocalic /d/ may occasionally be rendered [ø], as in *usted* [usté], *acabado* [akabáo], and *le dije* [le íxe].

3. Intervocalic /b/ may be rendered [ø], as in *iba* [ía], and in *aventaban* [abẹntá:n].

4. /rl/ is not always realized as [rl]; occasionally it appears as [l], as in *verla* [béla].

5. /e/ before stressed or unstressed /a/ or /o/ is often rendered /i/, i.e., [j], as in *golpeado* [golpjáðo], *golpeó* [golpjó], and *peleonero* [peljonéro].

6. The lexical item *luego* is quite often given as [lwo] or [lo].

Abbreviations Used in the Documentation

AFAA	*Antología folklórica argentina (para las escuelas de adultos)*. Buenos Aires: Consejo Nacional de Educación, 1940.
AFAP	*Antología folklórica argentina (para las escuelas primarias)*. Buenos Aires: Consejo Nacional de Educación, 1940.
AFC	*Archivos del folklore cubano*. 5 vols. Havana, 1924–1930.
AFCH	*Archivos del folklore chileno*. Santiago.
ASFM	*Anuario de la Sociedad Folklórica de México*. Mexico City.
AUC	*Anales de la Universidad de Chile*. Santiago.
AVF	*Archivos venezolanos de folklore*. Caracas.
BAE	*Biblioteca de autores españoles*. 71 vols. Madrid, 1846–1880.
BATF	*Boletín de la Asociación Tucumana de Folklore*
BIF	*Boletín del Instituto de Folklore*. Caracas.
BTPE	*Biblioteca de las tradiciones populares españolas*. 11 vols. Seville-Madrid, 1883–1886.
CFQ	*California Folklore Quarterly*
FA	*Folklore andaluz*. Seville, 1882–1883.
IJAL	*International Journal of American Linguistics*
JAF	*Journal of American Folklore*
NMFR	*New Mexico Folklore Record*
RCHG	*Revista chilena de historia y geografía*. Santiago.
RF	*Revista de Folklore*. Bogota.
RFC	*Revista de folklore chileno*. 9 vols. Santiago, 1909–1923.
SFNM	*Spanish Folk Tales from New Mexico*. Memoirs of the American Folklore Society, no. 30.
SFQ	*Southern Folklore Quarterly*
TFSP	*Publications of the Texas Folk-Lore Society*
UAHB	*University of Arizona Humanities Bulletin*
UCAAE	*University of California Publications in American Archaeology and Ethnology*
WF	*Western Folklore*

I. Legendary Narratives

Religious Narratives

Folk narrative of a religious nature is represented by a large body of traditional legends about virgins and saints with which most Mexicans are familiar. Knowledge of such stories, if not officially propagated by the Church, must inevitably be a by-product of the very real role that religion plays in the life of the Mexican, whether as a matter of sincere personal conviction or as a product of inevitable cultural impact.[1]

Aside from the traditional legendary lore about saints and virgins, religious references of another sort can be found scattered throughout narratives that may or may not be predominantly religious in nature. The opportunity is often taken to incorporate into these narratives elements or incidents that reflect attitudes toward the Church and the priesthood. Considering all the material presented here, irrespective of category, it may be useful to draw together such examples and observe the patterns they present, thus lending an additional perspective to the consideration of religious material as it occurs in folk narrative.

Legends of Virgins and Saints, Nos. 1–9

The narratives included in this section have to do with miraculous origins and appearances, the attributing of special wishes to images and the manner in which these images are believed to make known their will, the lifelike qualities the images are often believed to possess, and miscellaneous miracles attributed to the images.

The first two narratives relate the miraculous appearances of El Señor del Encino and La Virgen de San Vicente. The Mexican novelist Agustín Yáñez writes the following account of El Señor del Encino, which roughly parallels that of Narrative 1 presented here:

[1] As pointed out by C. G. Loomis, saints' legends were once the "only officially sanctioned body of material for popular consumption" ("Legend and Folklore," *CFQ*, 2 [1943], 279).

Quiere la leyenda sacra otorgarle milagrosos orígenes: el haberse aparecido
a un leñador borracho que daba malos tratos a su mujer y convirtió su vida
el día que tratando de hacer leña de un encino, descubrió al Señor.[2]

[The sacred legend attributes to this saint a miraculous origin: that of
having appeared to a drunken woodcutter who treated his wife badly and
who changed his ways after finding the image of the Señor del Encino in an
oak tree he was chopping up for firewood.]

The didactic element, of central importance in the Yáñez account, is
not expressly stated by the informant of Narrative 1, although the detail of the habitual drunken state of the woodcutter may imply it.
However, the details of the miraculous discovery are sufficiently intriguing to make a good story out of, without the informant's adding
the didactic element. The contrast in emphasis between the novelist's
summary and the version from oral tradition is also appreciable in the
details of the development. Whereas in the former the cutting down
of the tree is a natural function of the man's occupation, the latter
makes it the outgrowth of mysterious happenings almost from the very
beginning, through such details as the fatefully repetitious knocking
off of the man's hat and the bleeding of the branch when he cuts the
branch off in anger. The dramatic build-up, although brief, is effective. It is as if El Señor del Encino were asking to be found, an element
of fate and dramatic tension that contributes much to the story.

This same type of legend is discussed by Efraín Morote Best in his
classification of Peruvian religious legends. A man sets about to chop
wood, sees that the tree bleeds, and so decides that a holy image
should be made of the wood.[3] There is a basic difference, however, in
that the image is not actually found intact in the wood, as was El Señor del Encino, but rather is carved out of it. One of the images mentioned by Morote Best, about which the legend is told, is El Señor de
la Misericordia de Marcabalito. In a popular version of a Mexican legend about this same Christ image, El Señor de la Misericordia, he is
found already formed in the wood of the tree,[4] a situation more closely paralleling that of El Señor del Encino in Narrative 1.

<hr>

[2] Agustín Yáñez, *Yahualica*, pp. 93–94.

[3] Efraín Morote Best, "Dios, la Virgen y los Santos (en los relatos populares),"
Tradición (Cuzco, Perú), 5, nos. 12–14 (1953), 81–82.

[4] Stanley L. Robe, *Mexican Tales and Legends from Los Altos*, pp. 517–519.

The recounting of the miraculous appearance of a portrait of La Virgen de San Vicente [V263] in Narrative 2 stands in humorous contrast to that of El Señor del Encino. The tone is one of skepticism, for which possible explanations may be sought in both the personality of the informant and the nature of the material itself. All the information offered by this informant is characterized by an attitude of good-natured, humorous skepticism, as may be observed by consulting the other narratives collected from her. A categorical rejection of the material, based on rational evaluation, would not be of much value to present here; that, however, is not the attitude of the informant. She can perhaps be seen as representing a transitional stage in the process that may eventually lead to such rejection. She is comfortably familiar with the folk material she relates; it seems an integrated part of her life experience. But because of exposure to more "modern" ideas and a different way of life, she has become skeptical. The details she relates are interspersed with her own humorously quizzical reflections about the credibility of it all.

The incident she narrates is a relatively recent one (she places it in the 1940's) and for this reason one might look to the material itself for some insight into the skepticism. There is a natural inclination to view miraculous appearances as things of a past era, not likely to happen any more. Time lends credibility; the acknowledged existence of El Señor del Encino predates the Virgen de San Vicente incident by over a century.[5] The informant, therefore, finds it a very compelling possibility that the woman simply painted the image on her wall the night before announcing the miraculous appearance; without specifically stating so, she also suggests an ulterior motive by adding that the woman made a great deal of money out of the incident. ("Se hizo rica con la Virgen que se apareció allí.")

Narratives 3, 4, and 5 have to do with the attributing of certain lifelike qualities to religious images [D1620] and the interpretation of various mysterious phenomena as expressions of the will of these images to remain in a specific place [D1654.8.1]. Alexander Krappe deals with such a phenomenon in a chapter on local legends in which

---

[5] Yáñez, *Yahualica*, pp. 93–96.

he refers to "stories of holy images that laugh, weep, sweat, bleed, nod, and return to their old places when once removed."[6]

La Virgen de Talpa of Narrative 3 is known as a sweating image. In an article entitled "Popular Medicine, Customs, and Superstitions of the Río Grande," published in 1894, reference is made to this common type of story of the "virgen que suda," or the sweating image of the Virgin, a concept that the author links to the old idea of the sweating Buddha. He mentions also a pamphlet entitled *La novena de San Ramón*, which makes reference to other sweating images;[7] in an earlier article he writes of The Madonna of Agualeguas, "la Virgen Suadanda [*sic*]," as a specific example.[8]

The informant gave a fervently enthusiastic description of the perspiration-soaked face and garments of La Virgen de Talpa, most emphatically affirming the truth of it as something she had seen with her own eyes; she then gave a final reassurance that, although it may be difficult to detect now since the image has been placed much higher up, it was most dramatically visible when it could be seen up close.

In Narrative 4 the same informant tells a legend about another image of La Virgen de Talpa that protested against being moved from Talpa by miraculously reappearing there after each attempt to move her. Legends of this type, about images returning to where they want to be, are mentioned by George Foster[9] as being very common. Also, the work already cited on the classification of Peruvian religious legends lists several examples of it under Type 17: "las imágenes que salen de sus camarines, abandonan los templos y andan por calles y caminos, casi de modo habitual."[10]

The inclination to attribute lifelike qualities to this Virgin, who would leave her footprints in the dust and whose arrival was always announced by the spontaneous ringing of the church bells, acts as impetus to the legendary anecdote that the informant goes on to relate. The presence of the blister on the Virgin's cheek is explained as the

6 Alexander Krappe, *The Science of Folklore*, p. 78.
7 John G. Bourke, *JAF*, 7 (1894), 129–130.
8 Bourke, "La Virgen Suadanda [*sic*]," *Scribner's Magazine*, ca. 1894.
9 George Foster, *Culture and Conquest: America's Spanish Heritage*, p. 161.
10 Morote Best, p. 98.

result of a nonbelieving captain's attempt to disprove her lifelike qualities by placing his lighted cigar against her face. It is curious to note that the legend, as it is told by this informant, now stands as a simple explanatory one, minus any didactic element of proof or disproof of the qualities in question.

Another version of the incident (not included with texts), related by a Mexican Roman Catholic priest from Oxnard, California, may be offered in comparison. He attributes the act to a priest who, having heard rumors of a belief that La Virgen de Talpa walked about and would at times go to visit her sister La Virgen de San Juan, felt he could in this way prove the falseness of such beliefs about holy images. His account is as follows:

En cierta ocasión el señor cura, oyendo los rumores que se escuchaban y queriendo oponerse a cualquier tradición ligera, dicen que estando la gente reunida les dijo: —Hijos, ¿por qué andan inventando cosas que no les constan? ¿Por qué andan inventando historias? Miren. Esta imagen no es nada más de una sustancia, de una preparación de maíz molido o de algún otro material, y no como se dice que es viva. Y miren, hijos. Les voy a probar. Con su cigarro quiso quemarle la mejilla. Actualmente la imagen tiene una pequeña mancha que parece como una ampolla seca. Esa es la narración de la ampolla de la Virgen de Talpa. Que sea cierto o que no sea cierto, ¿quién sabe quién pueda aclarar eso? Es lo que se cuenta.

In a work entitled *Historia de Nuestra Señora del Rosario de Talpa* there is the following discussion of the mark on the Virgin's cheek:

La creencia más popular y generalizada lo atribuye a una quemada. Unos afirman que [lo hizo] el Ilmo. Sr. Obispo Ruiz Colmenero, primer Mitrado que visitó este pueblo en toda su historia en 1649 y que conoció la Sagrada Escultura poco después de la milagrosa renovación; otros dicen que fue un párroco, quizá el Pbro. Br. D. Pedro Rubio Félix, que fue el primer clérigo testigo del milagro; unos terceros culpan a un simple sacerdote y no falta quienes digan que fue un revoltoso, Rojas, quien conociendo el origen milagroso de la celestial Señora "para probar si de veras estaba viva le pegó un cigarrillo encendido en la mejilla produciéndole la quemada que luego originó la mancha o lunar."

Esto creyeron y cantaron millares de peregrinos y personas piadosas en aquella sencilla estrofa de las arcaicas alabanzas de la Virgen de Talpa que dice:

> "El Cura quedó
> bastante afligido,
> muy arrepentido
> cuando te quemó."[11]

The author goes on to state the opinion that none of these explanations is at all likely, for such profanation of either the temple or the holy image could not have occurred and that, furthermore, close examination reveals no traces of a burn. He considers the mark to be "una cosa propia y natural de ella" (a natural mark).

Of the four persons mentioned by Carrillo Dueñas as those to whom the act is popularly attributed, the last two are represented in the two accounts presented in this collection. Narrative 4 refers to "un capitán incrédulo" (a non-believing captain), a parallel to the "revoltoso" mentioned above; and the above account given by the priest refers to an unnamed priest, the "simple sacerdote" who is also the subject of the verse. These last two, the anonymous priest and the rebel, as opposed to specific figures in the church hierarchy, would be logical choices in the popular development and transmission of this legend. Aside from the fact that names are likely to be forgotten anyway, the simple parish priest and the rebel, in their very anonymity, provide the legend with greater flexibility. It might perhaps be difficult to explain such an act on the part of a bishop, with all the weight of authority granted him; and the conclusion arrived at, whether it be irreverence on his part or proof of the nonmiraculous nature of the image, would be less appealing to the popular mentality.

C. G. Loomis, in his article on Christian saints' legends, observes that a "communal didactic urge is the initial promulgating force for the dissemination and preservation of the rich treasures of the basic materials of folklore."[12] This didactic urge as felt by the devoted masses would most logically be directed toward strengthening, not weakening, any belief held and toward taking advantage of any opportunity to indulge the very basic wish to view miracles as possible. The verse referring to the repentant priest reflects very well this pop-

---

[11] Manuel Carrillo Dueñas, *Historia de Nuestra Señora del Rosario de Talpa*, p. 364.

[12] Loomis, p. 279.

ular attitude. Likewise, the version that attributes the act to a non-believer permits a conclusion that is satisfying to the underlying didactic urge. His nonbelief condemns the act and serves to enhance the aura of holiness about the image, while at the same time specifically refraining from stifling belief in a miraculous quality.

It has been stated that Carrillo Dueñas, the author of the history of La Virgen de Talpa, did not feel that any of the legendary explanations of the mark on the Virgin's cheek were acceptable. He terminates his discussion of the topic by citing an explanation that he personally feels to be more credible and that will serve here as a link between this legend and the one following, which tells of the Virgin's miraculous renovation. A bishop whom he consulted on the subject was of the opinion that the mark was simply evidence of the worn condition of the image prior to the miraculous renovation. This explanation, too, is not devoid of miraculous implications, for it is implied that it was the Virgin's will to retain this small reminder of her former condition: "... me contestó que él personalmente creía que el mencionado lunar fuera simplemente una mancha que tenía la Sagrada Imagen desde antes de su milagrosa renovación, la misma que quiso conservar como un vestigio, como un recuerdo de lo que era antes."[13]

An account of the miraculous renovation referred to here is given by the same priest who told the story of the mark on the Virgin's cheek. It is said that the image, when it had become very old and worn, was set aside to be burned and its ashes distributed on Ash Wednesday as was the custom, when it was suddenly and miraculously restored to its original splendor. The informant relates: "Dicen que el señor cura tenía la imagen ya arrumbada en un cuartito para quemarla, bendecir las cenizas, y distribuirlas el miércoles de ceniza si es que le hacían falta las cenizas de palma. Y que cuando fue por ella ... para quemarla encontró todo el cuarto iluminado, resplandeciente, y la Virgen renovada."

A published version of the miraculous renovation of this image parallels the one told by the Catholic priest, except that the image was to be buried instead of burned.

---

[13] Carrillo Dueñas, p. 365.

Celebrados los festejos [la festividad de Santiago y de la Limpia Concepción de Nuestra Señora, Septiembre de 1644], el Sr. Cura Félix encontró que los talpenses conservaban en su pequeña capilla algunas imágenes de Nuestro Señor Jesucristo y de la Santísima Virgen, en pésimo estado de conservación. Por considerarlas causantes de indevoción, y quizá por cierto refinamiento estético, ya para irse al lugar de su residencia, dispuso que en la Sacristía fueran enterradas esas imágenes, ajadas por las manos corrosivas de los años.

El 19 de Septiembre de 1644 los naturales principales del pueblo, mayordomos y priostes, decidieron se cumpliera el mandato de su párroco. A una india tenanchi, de nombre María, hija del cantor Francisco, fué a quien primeramente se le reveló el grandioso suceso.

Al tratar de tomar en sus manos una imagen de la Sma. Virgen del Rosario, carcomida y rota, un resplandor vivísimo la deslumbró; su azoro fué inmenso, y no pudiendo resistir la impresión, cayó sin sentido.[14]

The priest from Oxnard, used here as an informant, speaking as a member of the Roman Catholic clergy, stated very emphatically that the Church does not encourage the attributing of lifelike qualities to the holy images. It does seem, however, that the popular inclination to do so, based in part on a real desire that it be so, would easily survive without any instigation from the clergy.[15] The appeal that such stories possess is undeniable, both for their qualities as imaginative and entertaining stories and for the attractive immediacy they can lend to one's own religious faith. The informant of Narrative 9 tells an incident of a seemingly miraculous nature as she experienced it with the Santo Niño de Plateros, in which a priest supported or encouraged such a belief. If we keep in mind that the attitude she attributes to the priest may be a product of her own invention or her own predisposition to that interpretation, the narrative will serve as a contrast to the above opinions of the Catholic priest with respect to La Virgen de Talpa.[16] Details of Narrative 9 will be discussed below.

[14] José Ernesto Ramos, *Voces de Talpa*, p. 89. The appendix, pp. 175–185, presents the formal petition for permission to publish this miracle in 1854. The same account and official documents may be consulted in Carrillo Dueñas, pp. 33–66.

[15] Compare the situation in Rael, tale no. 58, in which the priest would knowingly encourage belief in a pseudo-miraculous origin.

[16] Padre Feijóo treats this very matter in "Sobre la multitud de milagros," pp. 45–54. He points out and condemns the frequent propagation of pseudo-miracles on the part of the clergy: "¡Cuántos párrocos por interesarse en dar fama de milagros a alguna imagen de la iglesia, le atribuyen milagros que no ha habido!" (p. 47).

La Virgen del Rosario of Narrative 5 is another example of the holy image that resists being moved from the place of its choice. This one, however, rather than persistently returning as is said of La Virgen de Talpa, defies removal by becoming impossibly heavy to carry. The informant emphasizes the mysterious nature of the incident by telling of the ease with which the image was originally brought from Rosario to Pánuco, the place of its choice.

This type of phenomenon is discussed in an article by Loomis, wherein he cites many examples, including some found in India, in Persia, and in Greek mythology, and thus shows the tradition to be older than Christianity.[17] The classification of Peruvian legends by Morote Best lists this as Type 11, stating that "un prolongado conjunto de relatos aluden a las imágenes que se quedan en un lugar por razón de aumentar repentinamente de peso."[18]

The following account of just such an incident is found in the eighteenth-century work *El Lazarillo de ciegos caminantes*:

Todo este país, como el de Abancay, a excepción de algunos altos, es muy caliente y frondoso, y pasando por él me dijo el visitador, señalándome un elevado cerro, que a su falda estaba el memorable templo dedicado a la Santísima Virgen en su Soberana Imagen nombrada de Cocharcas, cuyo origen tenía de que pasando por allí un devoto peregrino con esta efigie, como tienen de costumbre muchos paisanos míos, se le hizo tan intolerable su peso que le agobió, y dando cuenta a los eclesiásticos y hacendados de la provincia se declaró por milagroso el excesivo peso, como que daba a entender el sagrado bulto que quería hacer allí su mansión. Desde luego que en aquella devota gente hizo una gran impresión el suceso, porque se labró en la planicie del primer descenso una magnífica iglesia, que fuera impropia en un desierto, para una simple devoción.[19]

In the work previously cited, George Foster refers to narratives about saints' images becoming too heavy to move, indicating will to remain in a specific place;[20] he also cites the example of San Blas, found near Puebla de Almenara, Spain, who could not be moved to Alme-

---

[17] C. G. Loomis, "The Miracle of Ponderosity," *CFQ*, 3(1944), 41–44.

[18] Morote Best, p. 89.

[19] Concolorcorvo, *El Lazarillo de ciegos caminantes . . . sacado de las memorias que hizo don Alonso Carrió de la Vandera . . . por don Calixto Bustamante Carlos Inca, alias Concolorcorvo* (1773), Capítulo XXI.

[20] Foster, pp. 161–162.

nara by a team of oxen, but was easily transported by a few burros to Almonacid.[21]

Frances Toor cites the example of Nuestro Señor de los Temblores, who was found floating off the shore of Callao and who could be moved only at the mention of the name of Cuzco, thus indicating his will to be taken to Cuzco rather than to Lima.[22]

Similar stories are told of La Virgen de la Soledad (Tzintzuntzan, Mexico) and of a Panamanian saint, El Jesús de la Atalaya (Atalaya, Panama). La Virgen de la Soledad, originally meant for Pátzcuaro, was mistakenly taken to Tzintzuntzan. When the townspeople discovered the mistake and attempted to move her, she could not be budged, although she was transported with ease in religious processions, and this was taken as an indication of her will to remain in Tzintzuntzan.[23] El Jesús de la Atalaya was to be the object of an exchange between a parish in Atalaya and one in Santiago, upon the orders of the vicar of the Santiago parish; thus the people of Atalaya reluctantly set out to carry him there. But after setting him down and resting at the halfway point, they were unable to pick him up again because he had become too heavy. Their feeling that this was an indication of his unwillingness to go to Santiago was substantiated when, having decided to take him back to Atalaya, they lifted him with ease.[24]

The style of delivery in Narrative 5 is typical of this informant in its somewhat rambling repetitive, and yet comfortably conversational flow. She lends a certain vividness and immediacy to the details, while also revealing how real they are to her, by referring to landmarks in her own West Los Angeles neighborhood to indicate how far the Virgin was carried before she became too heavy. The detail at the end, of bringing in her grandmother's expressed belief, is in keeping with the quality of skepticism that consistently marks this informant's comments. She herself describes the incident rather vividly, but avoids committing herself to an opinion about the miraculous nature of it.

<hr>

21 Ibid., pp. 209–210.
22 Frances Toor, *Three Worlds of Peru*, p. 120.
23 George Foster, *Empire's Children: The People of Tzintzuntzan*, pp. 192–193.
24 Ignacio de J. Valdés, *Cuentos panameños de la ciudad y del campo*, pp. 35–36.

She leaves it to her grandmother to call it a miracle and to interpret it as the Virgin's having thus indicated her preference for Pánuco.

The next three narratives of this section, numbers 6, 7, and 8, have to do with appeals made to three different holy images and the manner in which they were granted. Numbers 6 and 7 relate, in addition, the consequences of failure to comply with the wishes of the saint or virgin.

The incident recounted in Narrative 6 also incorporates a previously mentioned characteristic of attributing lifelike qualities to certain images. When the rancher fails to keep the promise made to the Santos Reyes in exchange for restoring him to health, they appear to him in the guise of three horsemen ("en figura de tres paisanos a caballo") [K1811] and retaliate by giving him a terrible beating, leaving him near death. Later, when he is miraculously relieved of his ailments, he is inspired to fulfill his promise and take his gift to the Santos Reyes.

The very common belief in the efficacy of appealing to the Virgin (or a saint) for more propitious weather conditions [V268] is seen in Narrative 7. The informant refers to two historical events, a drought and a flood in the city of Guadalajara, in which the favor of La Virgen de Zapopan was sought to remedy the situation. The opposite natures of these two weather crises make this narrative well suited for observing the accepted psychology of dependence on the patron saint. She does not necessarily act spontaneously in the interest of the people, but must be actively appealed to and her intervention actively sought out. Either the unfavorable conditions have to be called to her attention, as in the case of the drought, or they may actually be considered the result of having neglected an obligation to her, as was thought to be the cause of the flood [A1018]. The patron saints demand attention, so to speak, and, as in Narrative 6, there are consequences to be borne for defying, neglecting, or simply forgetting them.

Additional details of interest in this narrative are the comments that root it in history. The initial appeal to halt the progressive drying up of the land was to ex-president Lázaro Cárdenas, who as owner of a large portion of the state of Michoacán was thought to be diverting the water for his own use and to whom the advice to seek the aid of La

Virgen de Zapopan is attributed. The other example occurs in connection with the flood, when the informant suggests a possible explanation for the failure to bring the Virgin on the accustomed pilgrimage from Zapopan to Guadalajara as a "cambio de ideas o de arzobispo o de gobierno" (a change of ideas or of archbishop or of government). It would be interesting, more from a sociological or a historical perspective, to pursue the significance of the comment, and to seek to fill in the information gap it suggests. Had there been an explanation that lent itself to shedding more light on the punitive nature of the storm, a natural inclination would be to incorporate the explanation into the story.

The following narrative, number 8, has the structure of a well-defined local legend: the poor man kills his rich friend, repents, and implores the aid of the Santo Niño de Atocha (Holy Child of Atocha) in bringing him back to life [E63]; the miracle is granted [E121.4]; and the poor man fulfills his promise to carry the stone he used to kill his friend to the shrine of the Santo Niño de Plateros. The informant remarked at the end that the stone can still be seen there at the shrine with the account of the miracle engraved upon it.

The Santo Niño de Plateros is the object of devotion in Narrative 9. This narrative differs from those already discussed in that it represents a personal and intensely emotional account of an illness and a cure felt by the informant to have been a miracle granted her by the Santo Niño [V221]. This was not the only miracle of which she spoke during the interview. She told of several other miraculous cures of physical illnesses, diagnosed medically as incurable, and related all of them with a depth of feeling and a display of emotion that at times led to tears.

Of especial interest in this narrative are the details of the informant's actual visit to the shrine of the Santo Niño, her not finding the image in its niche, and the priest's comment that the Santo Niño was often out, but that she might await his return [D1620]. This latter point is an interesting example of the potentially significant role played by the clergy in the preservation, or propagation, of beliefs about the miraculous qualities of certain religious images; it should be noted how it stands in contrast to the opinions of the priest who commented on the beliefs about La Virgen de Talpa.

The popular idea about the Santo Niño's being "muy paseador" (fond of going about), in the words of the priest as recounted by the informant, is very common. In the words of a popular verse:

> El Niño de Atocha
> no se halla en Plateros,
> se halla en los caminos
> amparando arrieros.[25]

This type of legend is classified by Morote Best as Type 17, images believed to habitually travel about and return bearing traces of their travels.[26]

Another reference to the Santo Niño can be found in a collection of folk material from San Pedro Piedra Gorda, Zacatecas. Referred to as the Santo Niño de Atocha, he is said by the informant to display traces of mud on his sandals as evidence of his coming and going.[27] The fixing on the detail of his shoes is paralleled in Narrative 9 by the reference to his "guaraches rompidos de la punta" (torn sandals), also indicative of considerable traveling about. In a story called the "Holy Child of Chimayó," included in a collection of legendary material from the southwestern United States, another reference is found to this type of Santo Niño who often leaves his niche.[28] The idea that he is often out ministering to the needy seems to be a popular concept about the Holy Child.

It was then a most wonderful gift to receive from the priest one of the Santo Niño's tiny sandals, which the informant goes on to say she passed on to a sick friend who was also cured by a miracle granted her by the Holy Child.

The somewhat strange or incongruous quality of Narrative 9, which must inevitably strike the reader (or listener), can be clarified by look-

[25] Vicente T. Mendoza, *Lírica infantil de México*, p. 46.

[26] Morote Best, p. 98.

[27] Vicente T. Mendoza and Virginia R. Mendoza, *Folklore de San Pedro Piedra Gorda, Zacatecas*, p. 401.

[28] Nina Warren, *Old Spain in Our Southwest*, p. 149.

ing not only at the content but also at the style of delivery. The content is certainly in keeping with Roman Catholic tradition. It is the tone of the narrative, carried over in the style of delivery, which seems to indicate some additional influence. A very likely explanation can be devised on the basis of other information gathered during the interview. Among the miraculous incidents related by the informant were several that she had witnessed or heard about during the visit of a faith healer to the Pentecostal Church in Santa Paula. Brother Jenkins performed miraculous cures before large audiences for several days, inspiring numerous conversions; it was obvious that the informant was quite intrigued and moved by these performances, although they were not within the context of her particular religious faith. It seems almost certain that this contact suggested to her the style that she employs in narrating her own experiences.

Three basic elements, or stylistic devices, in the construction of this narrative can be pointed out as illustrative of what seems to speak specifically of the strong impact of Brother Jenkins' faith healing on this informant. The tone of the introduction, "Tengo otro milagro también que publicar" (I have another miracle to proclaim), is markedly evangelistic and obviously fancied as directed to an audience of some size. Although it was never suggested that the tape was to be used for that purpose, the informant chose to assume that attitude, indicating that she now sees her own earlier religious experiences as fitting naturally into a subsequently acquired framework. She goes on to present a detailed build-up, setting the scene as vividly and convincingly as possible, and exploiting the valuable element of suspense as she leads up first to the diagnosis of incurable illness and then to the miraculous recovery. It is a polished delivery, which is not to deny a deep sincerity that was very obvious, but which also suggests the purpose of persuasion characteristic of the evangelist. The third, and perhaps most blatant, example is in the manner in which the informant terminates the account:

Si ustedes tienen fe y creen en milagros pueden pedirles de todo corazón. No le hace que no estén con ellos; no le hace que no los conozcan. Pueden pedirle al uno o al otro, al Santo Niño de Plateros o a la Santísima Virgen de San Juan.

[If you have faith and believe in miracles you can appeal to them with confidence. It doesn't matter if you are not near them; it doesn't matter if you don't know them. You can appeal to either one, to the Holy Child of Plateros or to the Holy Virgin of San Juan.]

This comment was conceived of as a type of concluding appeal to the vacillating listener, although it does not terminate her comments, for she does go on to elaborate spontaneously on a previously mentioned detail. It does, however, function as a conclusion to the "planned" part of the narrative. The duality that characterizes the narrative as a whole is very nicely illustrated within this concluding remark, for one would instinctively be listening for the name of God as the one who will indeed hear such appeals and not a saint or the Virgin.

The curious combination of style and content that has been pointed out here makes for an interesting hybrid narrative, which further collecting could reveal to be a predictable product of the meeting of two divergent religious cultures.

Other Religious References, Nos. 26, 55–57, 68–70, 82

As stated at the beginning of this section, religious references can be found in narratives other than the traditional legendary ones about saints and virgins. The latter are a fixed type, of learned influence, whose very existence presupposes the purpose of glorifying the religious figure as well as edifying the individual, both directed at furtherance of the religion; the former can often be identified as popular expressions of conflicting feelings on the subject of religion. Any authority, especially one as powerful as that represented by the Church in the life of the Mexican, must inevitably provoke antagonistic sentiments of a strength equal to the degree of dependence felt. While the traditional saint and virgin legends are the vehicle for the expression of positive religious sentiments, the other narratives into which religious commentary is incorporated frequently reveal themselves as vehicles for expressing negative feelings.

These references are frequently hostile, and most often it is the clergy who are the objects of the hostility. By comparison, it is infrequent to find active hostility directed at God, the Virgin, or the saints. When negative feelings are expressed toward God, the Virgin, or the saints, they tend to be conceived of as justified reactions to an unjust, even an oppressive, state of affairs. They are rebukes for needs left unmet and are therefore characterized in part by an essential sadness, as opposed to the mischievous delight felt at any "victories" won over the priest.

A particularly good example of such delight in ridiculing the clergy is found in Narratives 55 and 56, two versions of an identical incident. A priest is called upon to exorcize evil spirits, in this case *duendes*, or goblins, and in the midst of his attempt to perform the ceremony there is a sound of knives being sharpened, and a voice is heard to say: "Estos cuchillos son para capar al padre" (these knives are for castrating the priest). The priest, of course, runs in terror.

In Narrative 26 there is a rather less aggressive expression of this same inclination to render the priest vulnerable and ineffectual. Instead of the specific threat of castration, he is simply shoved from behind, and he flees in terror from the presence of the evil spirits, since he is not able to dominate them, as is expected of a priest.

In fleeing, the priest of Narrative 26 refers not to evil spirits or to *duendes*, but specifically to the devil. This detail provides a connecting link with a type of story referred to by Alexander Krappe in his comments on local legends. The story is applicable to all three of the above-mentioned narratives. With regard to the propagation of such stories he comments: ". . . another type of devil stories was certainly *not* encouraged by the clergy, as will readily be seen. In one legend of considerable popularity the Devil haunts a certain house. The priest is called to drive him off, but without success. The Devil resists all his efforts and replies by pointing out the various little shortcomings of the holy man. The latter is as a rule completely abashed and thinks it wise to beat a prudent retreat."[29]

These narratives, then, very effectively offer the opportunity for expressing hostility toward the priest by rendering him psychologically impotent and threatening him with physical impotence, and for "getting by with it" by displacing such inclinations onto the *duendes* and the evil spirits. The attitude of the informant as he narrates will almost inevitably reveal evidence of the innate appeal of such stories.

[29] Krappe, p. 96.

The three who told the stories referred to here revealed their vicarious enjoyment of the spectacle in the tone of guilty, sheepish amusement with which they narrated the spectacle. The difficulty the informant of Narrative 56 had in finding an acceptable way to express the threat to the priest is obvious in the roundabout wording she chose. It reflects a great deal of discomfort on her part.

A contrast to the ineffectual priests of the above narratives is the priest of Narrative 57, who, when confronted with a similar situation, retains complete control and is successful in exorcising the evil spirits. As the informant affirms: "Pos ellos saben, ellos saben cómo tratarse en lo que se les debe, ¿verdad? Ellos saben sus oraciones y todo con que pueden acabar todo." [They know, they know how to do their job, you know? They know the prayers and everything with which to put an end to it all.]

These two conflicting anecdotal treatments of the priest really serve as expressions of the basically conflicting feelings felt about the priest. The folk tradition remains, however, readily available to be used as a vehicle for expressing basic human sentiments.

Turning to the traditional tale, several more examples of negative feelings about religious questions can be pointed out. A priest is once again the object of derision in Narrative 82, in which the well-known rascal Pedro de Ordimalas not only robs the priest of his money, but also arbitrarily plays the hostile trick of blackening his face with soot while he sleeps. The tale, in effect, proceeds to parade the priest about before a number of people, adding to the derision through the device of a play on words whereby the priest appears to be stupidly calling even greater attention to himself: "¿No me han visto Así?" (Haven't you seen Así? or, Haven't you seen me like this?) The delight of the informant at this part of the tale was openly expressed, as can be seen by the indications of his laughter included in the text. Here, as with the examples from legendary material, there is also a displacement of the hostility, although to a somewhat lesser degree. Pedro de Ordimalas is an acknowledgedly fictitious and, as his name indicates, malicious character. Nothing more is expected of him. The other people who enter into the action, however, being less fictionalized characters, do not enjoy the freedom of expression granted to Pedro. They are

more real, more nearly like the informant himself; and, functioning as
a type of group conscience, they offset the antagonism of Pedro and
ultimately respond helpfully to the priest.

The acknowledged fictitious nature of the tale, as opposed to legendary material, permits the personification of the figures of God and
the Virgin. As can be seen in Narratives 68–70, these figures are also
the object of negative sentiments, but there is a marked change in tone
from the active aggressions perpetrated upon the priest. As suggested
earlier, the feelings are more *reactive*, they are justified responses to
what is seen as deep injustice. The tone is serious, rather than delight-
fully malicious, for there is more at stake.

The narratives referred to here are three versions of the same tale,
in which a very poor man refuses to share his almost literally "once in a
lifetime" full meal with passersby who are later found to be God, the
Virgin, and the devil. The man feels completely justified in his action,
and, when God reveals His identity, he stands even more firmly on his
decision: "Pos menos le doy." (See Narrative 68.) In the second version the man not only points out the inequities sanctioned by God, but
also makes the further claim that certainly it is not he who ought to
be giving to God, but rather the reverse: "Tú eres el que me había de
dar para alimento de mis hijos." (See Narrative 69.) His answer to
the Virgin is similar; he would give to her only if she were to intercede
on his behalf, which she does not offer to do.

The reproach is outspoken. There are injustices difficult to reconcile
with religious faith, and God does not in fact care for man as He
ought to. The tale permits expression of an understandable complaint,
and it is not difficult to see a great deal of identification with the poor
man on the part of the informant who chooses to tell this tale.

Having refused God, the Virgin, and also the devil, the poor man
does consent to share with Death, for Death is fair and treats all men
equally. But it is certainly a hollow victory for the poor man, since he
could not really feel much enthusiasm over the figure of Death. The
praise with which he regales him can only be a device for indirectly
reproaching God, and, therefore, a negative satisfaction. Although the
first two versions stop at this point, the third completes the irony and
reveals the basic futility of the protest, for the choice is in reality non-

existent. In rejecting God, man cannot simply share with Death but, ironically, must become its victim. (See Narrative 70.)

1. El Señor del Encino

(Recorded by Alfonso Domínguez Franco on November 15, 1966, in Los Angeles, California)

A rancher from Zapote, Guadalajara, whose custom it was to make a weekly trip to town and to return home drunk became annoyed at a tree branch that always knocked off his hat as he would pass under it in his inebriated state. He asked permission from his boss to cut off the branch, and when he did so it oozed blood. Frightened by this phenomenon, he then requested and was granted permission to cut down the tree and examine what was inside of it. They found in the wood a statue of Christ, called El Señor del Encino.

En un rancho llamado Zapote fue aparecido un santo que se llama el Señor del Encino. Se le apareció a un borracho, que cada ocho días iba al pueblo y se emborrachaba y de regreso una rama del encino le tumbaba el sombrero. Y éste, enojado, le dijo . . . dijo un día: —Te he de tumbar, rama.

Y un día que venía él borracho se acordó y tumbó la rama. Y la rama vertió sangre. Donde él se asustó y corrió con el patrón. Y le dijo que si lo dejaba tumbar ese árbol. Y le explicó los motivos. Y el patrón lo dejó tumbarlo. Tumbando el árbol, llevaron unos carpinteros para que sacaran de allí a ver qué había dentro del árbol. Sacaron un santo . . . Cristo, llamado el Señor del Encino (1).

(1) V127. Images of deity in wood (stone).
  Morote Best, Type 2. [Statues made from wood of miraculous tree.]
  Sinninghe, no. 92, p. 128. Religious legends: a statue is found. The statue
    grows out of a tree.
  Robe, *Mexican Tales*, nos. 164–165.
  Yáñez, pp. 93–96.

2. La Virgen de San Vicente

(Recorded by Ismeria Garay on October 12, 1966, in Los Angeles, California)

The informant tells of having witnessed the appearance of the Virgin to a woman in San Vicente, Nayarit, about twenty-one years before.

While at a park with her daughter she was suddenly drawn to a great commotion at a nearby home, where a woman claimed that the image of the Virgin had miraculously appeared on her living room wall. The informant, however, expresses considerable doubt and suggests that the woman might very well have painted the image there herself. The room was subsequently converted into a chapel to the Virgin, who was named La Virgen de San Vicente, and the woman acquired considerable wealth.

En San Vicente también hubo una . . . de otra Virgen también. Ésa se apareció, allá estaba yo . . . en San Vicente. Ésta . . . fue una señora que estaba, tenía una casita allí, muy pobre la señora. Y un día en la tarde, todos los domingos íbamos nosotros a Tuxpan, Nayarit. Y yo tenía no más una niñita, esa que trabaja en el Seguro de San Luis, Sonora. Yo tenía una no más. Y me iba de . . . San Vicente, me iba a Tuxpan. Es no más pasar un río. De San Vicente pasa uno un . . . un, ¿cómo le nombran aquí? Allá le nombran ríos. . . . Arroyo. Pues, no más de San Vicente pasa uno a Tuxpan. Pues fuimos a Tuxpan. Me fui yo en la tarde, . . . así al kiosco y todo eso, . . . a pasearse uno. Aquí le dicen park. Pues ya nos fuimos allá y ahí ando con mi muchachita.

Bueno pues, que estábamos ahí cuando . . . un alboroto, que en la casa de la señora que una luz se había . . . metido en la casa de la señora. Un rayo así. Bueno, así que se había estampado una Virgen allí. Pues al alboroto . . . ahí voy. También con todo y muchacha. Pos mero me tumba la gente. Que la chamaca la llevaba de la, de la mano. Pues llegué y sí, un alboroto, y que la Virgen, y que la Virgen, y pues áhi, ya llegamos. Y luego luego, pues, me metí entre la bola de gente, con todo y criatura. Y ya fui a ver, pues, en dónde estaba la Virgen. Y efectivamente, estaba la Virgen en la pared (1). Pero yo no sé decirle, también . . . de mucha creencia, que la Virgen se haiga aparecido allí, porque la señora, por lo pobre que estaba, y por . . . puede haber pintado la Virgen allí. Sí. [Laughs, as if at true probability of it.] Sí. Mire, bueno, . . . se hizo rica la señora. Se hizo rica con la Virgen que se apareció allí. Yo sí la vi, la Virgen. La Virgen de San Vicente le pusieron. Pero mire, tan linda, . . . nuevecita pintada en la pared. Como ahora sí hay, no había ventana, ¿no? Así, mire, estaba la Virgen. [Indicates spot on wall.] Y la señora muy pobrecita.

La señora se llamaba Luisa. A mí se me grabó todo porque, pues, era señora conocida. ¿Luisa de qué? Eso sí, no me acuerdo. Pero Luisa se llamaba, porque a mí se me grabó por la tanta [emphasis] gente que se apeló. Así, mire, se amontonó la gente a ver. [Gestures.] A ver la Virgen. Que hasta yo fui. Y, pues, todavía vi eso hace muchos años y estoy en duda. Que yo pienso que la jeñora [i.e., señora] en la noche la pintó y en el día hizo su alboroto. Pero, ¿quién sabe? Muy linda la Virgen, linda. Después allí, . . . yo entonces me vine de allá, y después dicen que le hizo capilla ahí. Toda la sala donde se apareció la hizo capilla. Ya no fue sala, fue capilla. Dicen que está muy bien. Y hace muchos años que yo estuve allá. Hace . . . veintiún años. . . . Eso sí, lo vi, pero, ¿cómo le digo? . . . no lo creo. [Laughs.] Sí, porque yo fui a verles, y como a la semana, mire estaba . . . pero así de milagros, así [gestures], que le llevaban y todo. Pero eso fue. Que dice que una luz así se estampó allá. Y que, pos, quedó la Virgen. Y la jeñora se me grabó a mí. No sé si viva o no viva. Porque yo les escribí a varias personas de allá y no me contestaron nada. Yo de Mexicali les escribí, y no, no me contestaron nada. Yo no sé si viva o muere . . . no sé.

(1) V263. Portrait of the Virgin appears to devotee.

3. La Virgen de Talpa

(Recorded by Isaura Benicia on May 15, 1966,
in Los Angeles, California)

The Virgin of Talpa in Guadalajara is known as a sweating image. The informant tells of having seen the image, its face and dress bathed in perspiration; she then comments that the perspiration is more difficult to observe now since the Virgin has been placed higher up out of reach.

Y en Guadalajara existe una Virgen de Talpa también . . . que suda (1). ¿Usted sabe? Estaba en una . . . nicho, como ahí la mesa [indicates a table in her living room], muy bajito. Y entonces iba usted y se acercaba y, y tenía todo esto, toda la cara, bañada de sudor, así de gotitas de agua. Y toda, toda, toda ella, y su vestido incrustado en, en sudor. Eso, sí. Eso nosotros lo vimos. Eso yo lo vi. Estaba en San Fran-

cisco de Asís en Guadalajara. En el templo de San Francisco de Asís.
Allí existe esa imagen. Dicen . . . ahorita ya, ya está alta. Pero cuando
uno podía acercarse a verla así, muy cerquita, así se veía. Y es también
la Virgen de Talpa.

(1) D1620. Magic automata. Statues or images that act as if alive.
     Sinninghe, no. 142, p. 131. Saint legends. The statue perspires: warning
       from danger.
     Bourke, "La Virgen Suadanda [*sic*]," *Scribner's Magazine*, ca. 1894.
     ————, *JAF*, 7(1894), 129–130.

4. La Virgen de Talpa

(Recorded by Isaura Benicia on May 15, 1966, in Los Angeles, California)

The Virgin of Talpa protested against being moved to Mascota by
miraculously reappearing in her niche at the altar in Talpa each time
she was removed. The church bells would ring to announce her arrival,
and her footprints could be seen in the dust of the road. The blister the
image still bears on its cheek was caused by a nonbeliever who, desiring to disprove the notion that the Virgin had the qualities of a
living being, put his lighted cigar to her face. It is believed that the
Virgin's wish was to remain in Talpa, and she was not removed again.

La aparición de la Santísima Virgen de Talpa, es que se apareció en
Talpa. Despuésn, la recogían de Mascota, municipio de Talpa, para
que estuviera allá con ellos. Pero siempre . . . se regresaba. Se regresaba. Y estuvieron por espacio de algún tiempo llevándola y trayén-
dola de Talpa a Mascota y así, y ella regresándose sola (1, 2). Cuando
regresaba las campanas repicaban y . . . y todos después se juntaban
para ver qué, y ya iban al altar y ya encontraban a la . . . imagen allí.
Entonces cuando ya iban las autoridades a intervenir en eso, vieron
que la Santísima Virgen llegaba sola y que se veían, . . . las huellas de
ella pintadas por el . . . en la tierra.

Luego también de un capitán que dicen que no creía. Era un capitán incrédulo. Y entonces él dijo que quería ver si de veras era verdad
que era . . . viva. Porque dicen que es viva. Nosotros creemos que solamente la imagen y todo eso, ¿verdad? Y entonces él con el cigarro se
lo puso en la mejilla y le hizo la ampollita. Y esa ampollita la tiene to-

davía. Esa ampollita existe en la Virgen. La tiene todavía. Y ella se quedó en Talpa, porque ya . . . ya . . . ya quedó allí. Ella . . . era su voluntad que quedara allí.

> Christiansen 7070ff. Legends about churchbells and also other sacred objects protesting against removal.
>
> Morote Best, Type 17. "Las imágenes que salen de sus camarines, abandonan los templos y andan por calles y caminos casi de modo habitual"; and Type 12. "Imágenes que no se quieren quedar en un determinado sitio y que por eso se trasladan al que por razones incomprensibles han escogido."
>
> Sinninghe, no. 131, pp. 129–130. Saint legends: Statue cannot be transported to a different location. The statue returns (three times) to the place where it was found (or to the place where it once stood); no. 71, p. 127. Bell begins to ring by itself.
>
> (1) D1654.8.1. Sacred image impossible to remove from the spot.
> (2) D1620. Magic automata. Statues or images that act as if alive.
> Carrillo Dueñas, pp. 33–66, 68, 364–365.
> Foster, *Culture and Conquest*, p. 161.
> Ramos, pp. 89, 175–185.

5. La Virgen del Rosario

(Recorded by Ismeria Garay on October 12, 1966, in Los Angeles, California)

An attempt was made to move the Virgin of Rosario [Sinaloa] from Pánuco, where she had been for ten years, to Rosario, but the image suddenly became so heavy that it was impossible to move it. This was understood to indicate the Virgin's wish to remain in Pánuco, and she has not been moved since.

Pues, es una virgen que . . . de Rosario, Sinaloa. Cuando . . . se terminó el mineral de Pánuco y quedó completamente solo, entonces, pues hubo, . . . todas las gentes decían que mejor sacarla de ahí. Que llevarla a su lugar, al Rosario.

Caminaron una distancia, . . . pues no sé si de . . . como de aquí a la Sunset [street two blocks away from informant's home]. No lejos. De aquí a la Sunset. . . . Ya no la pudieron la Virgen . . . muy pesada (1, 2). Entonces decidieron regresarla otra vez al mineral, a su templo, y allí está todavía hasta la fecha allí. Porque seguramente el lugar le pertenece en Pánuco, no, no en Rosario. Y por eso se ha quedado allí. Ella tenía como diez años en Pánuco, cuando determinaron sacarla, y no . . . no pudieron. No pudo la gente sacarla. Y muchos hombres cargándola, y no la pudieron. La regresaron otra vez al templo, y allí está, hasta la fecha. Ya tiene, pues, como . . . como treinta y nueve años allí en Pánuco. Como para traerla de . . . de allá de Rosario a Pánuco, sí la pudieron traer. Cuando la quisieron regresar, no la regresaron. Porque hasta la fecha está allí.

Mi abuelita dice: —No, dice, —todo eso es puro milagro de ella, que dijo: "No quiero Rosario; quiero Pánuco." Y allí está.

> Christiansen 7070ff. Legends about churchbells and also other sacred ob-
> jects protesting against removal.
> Morote Best, Type 11. "Un prolongado conjunto de relatos aluden a las
> imágenes que se quedan en un lugar por razón de aumentar repentina-
> mente de peso."
> Sinninghe, no. 133, p. 130. Saint legends: statue cannot be transported to
> a different location: cannot be lifted up.
> (1) D1654.7. Statues that cannot be removed.
> (2) D1654.8.1. Sacred image impossible to remove from the spot.
> Foster, *Culture and Conquest*, pp. 161–162.
> Loomis, *CFQ*, 3(1944), 41–44.
> Olivares Figueroa, p. 66.
> Other holy images about which this type of story is told:
> La Santísima Virgen de Cocharcas: Concolorcorvo, Chapter 21.
> Nuestro Señor de los Temblores: Toor, *Three Worlds of Peru*, p. 120.
> La Virgen de la Soledad: Foster, *Empire's Children*, pp. 192–193.
> El Jesús de la Atalaya: Valdés, *Cuentos panameños*, pp. 33–36.
> San Blas: Foster, *Culture and Conquest*, pp. 209–210.
> Christ Image: Miles, *TFSP*, 27(1957), 171–179.
> San José: De Huff, pp. 89–93.
> La Virgen de Guadalupe: *Colorado: A Guide to the Highest State*, pp.
> 399–400.
> El Señor de la Misericordia: Robe, *Mexican Tales*, no. 164.

6. Los Santos Reyes

(Recorded by Alfonso Domínguez Franco on November 15, 1966, in Los Angeles, California)

Three saints called the Santos Reyes, who appeared in Cajititlán, Jalisco, were placed in a chapel in that town and became the object of great devotion on the part of the people. A rancher became very ill one day, and his wife appealed to the Santos Reyes, promising them a calf in return for restoring her husband to health. The husband was saved, but he refused to honor the vow. The Santos Reyes appeared to him in the guise of three horsemen, demanded fulfillment of the promise, and severely beat him when he again refused, leaving him near death. The next day, however, he awakened completely recovered with no trace of the beating and was thus inspired to believe and to take the promised gift to the Santos Reyes.

En un pueblito llamado Cajititlán que es pueblito de indios, se encuentran tres santos llamados Santos Reyes. Fueron aparecidos. Esos Santos Reyes, el sacerdote, de ver la . . . pues de ver que los indios adoraban mucho a los santos, se los quitó, se los escondió, y les puso otros de madera. Llegó el tiempo que el santo padre murió, y se apareció el sacristán diciendo que estaban sepultados los Santos Reyes en la sacristía y que los sacara y los pusiera. El sacristán los sacó y los puso, y los otros . . . los colocó en otra capilla.

Un día ocurrió con un señor ranchero que estaba muy grave. Y como eran muy milagrosos y son, la señora acudió a ellos a que aliviaran a su . . . su marido. Y lo aliviaron, prometiéndole una vaquilla . . . de regalo porque lo aliviaran. Y lo aliviaron (1). Y éste, después que lo aliviaron, se negó a pagar la prenda. Se le aparecieron los Santos Reyes en figura de tres paisanos a caballo (2) . . . diciéndole que les pagara lo prometido a los Santos Reyes. Y él se negó. Y uno de ellos le, lo apaleó con uno de sus . . . su espada. Lo dejó bañado en sangre, muy malo el hombre, muriéndose.

Pero al siguiente día amaneció bien aliviado, sano, sin ningún golpe ni una dolencia. Cuando creyó en ellos y fue y les llevó su prenda. Y son santos milagrosos que toda la gente, pos, los sigue mucho.

(1) V221. Miraculous healing by saints.
(2) K1811. Gods (saints) in disguise visit mortals.

7. La Virgen de Zapopan

(Recorded by Isaura Benicia on May 15, 1966, in Los Angeles, California)

When the Laguna de Chapala [Lake Chapala, on the border of Michoacán and Jalisco] began to dry up about eight years ago, the people went to ex-President Lázaro Cárdenas to request that he stop diverting so much water for use in the irrigation of his own lands. He replied that he could do nothing and that they should appeal to the Virgin of

Zapopan. Pilgrimages and petitions to her resulted in the long-awaited rainstorm, and the people in their gratitude presented the Virgin of Zapopan with a boat that is now in the temple at Zapopan. It was customary to bring the Virgin from Zapopan to Guadalajara, on a pilgrimage each year. One year, which the informant places at about twenty-two years ago, this practice was not done, and a violent storm ensued that did much damage to the city of Guadalajara and that was thought to be the result of having neglected to make the pilgrimage. Since that time the visit of the Virgin of Zapopan to Guadalajara has been strictly observed.

Fíjese que eso de la, de la Laguna de Chapala, . . . se empezó a secar y a secar, . . . porque usted, como no sabe a Guadalajara, no, no le puedo decir. Hay unos restauranes allí, bares para bailar y todo eso, . . . y están pegados al, a la orilla del lago. Entonces la laguna empezaba a secarse. . . . Ha de hacer, no sé exactamente el tiempo porque, . . . pero sí, hace de esto como unos ocho años más o menos. Entonces fíjese que el, que la, la laguna empezaba a secarse y empezaba a secarse.

Hay un ex-presidente que es . . . Lázaro . . . Cárdenas, que fue un ex-presidente. Y entonces él vive en, en el estado de . . . ¿cómo es? . . . lo tengo aquí. Michoacán. Él vive en el estado de Michoacán. Entonces decían que, que la laguna tenía unos canales para donde él estaba sacando el agua para regar . . . sus siembras. Porque él tiene . . . casi, todo el estado de Michoacán es parte de él. Entonces fueron a decirle, ¿verdad?, por una comisión de . . . posiblemente la Acción Católica. Y fue a decirle que, que les . . . devolviera el agua de la laguna, que tapara aquellos canales por donde estaba saliendo el agua. Entonces dicen que, que ese señor les contestó que, . . . que ese señor les contestó que por qué, que qué iban a pedirle a él, que él no podía hacer nada, que por qué no le pedían a su mono. . . . Que le pidieran a su mono [patron saint].

Entonces todos, peregrinaciones y cosas así por el estilo. Que le empezaron a pedir a la Santísima Virgen. Entonces hubo unos años que llovió mucho, exagerado, que hasta ríos se vinieron. Arrasaron pueblos. Pero todo el agua, . . . y ahorita está la laguna más llena que antes que empezara a secarse. Está más llena. Y a ella le prometieron llevarla, y sí la llevaron en peregrinación a, a la laguna. Y ya le digo. Así,

pues, como la llevaron antes de que la laguna estuviera . . . llena, y
después la llevaron en acción de gracias (1).

Su . . . su . . . que le regalaban a ella, es un barco. Es una lancha,
muy bonita. Ésa existe en el templo de . . . Zapopan. En Zapopan existe ésa. Es donde tiene ella todos sus retablos, porque es un templo en
donde tiene tantos retablos, como igual que en San Juan de los Lagos.
Dicen que igual también que en Talpa.

Y cuando la Santísima Virgen, hubo una temporada en que no la
trajeron, un año, . . . hace mucho de esto, unos veinti . . . tantos años,
unos veinte años, más o menos, o poquito más, unos veintidós años,
. . . que pasó una época que no la trajeron a ella a Guadalajara. Dijeron que no porque, bueno, cambio de ideas o de . . . arzobispo o
ideas, o de . . . gobierno. Posible, ¿verdad? No se sabe, no sé exactamente decirle de qué. Pero no la trajeron ese año. Pues . . . cayó una
tormenta tan fuerte que las . . . que la . . . se andaba inundando Guadalajara. Hay un barrio que decimos San Juan de Dios en la Calzada Independencia que puede ser . . . poco menos que el centro de la ciudad.
Está muy céntrica la Calzada Independencia. Es un río que está tapado.
Y ahorita es una calzada. Entonces se inundó todo aquello. Hay un
mercado allí, unos markets, como aquí. Ésos son unos mercados, y
afuera había puros puestos de madera. Entonces todos aquellos puestos
los arrasó, carros, y todo (2).

Pues entonces fueron por ella y la trajeron, y desde ese año vieron
que . . . es muy necesario que, . . . nosotros los católicos tenemos esta
creencia que . . . si no la traen, . . . pues un temporal muy, muy fuerte
y, y así no. Así pasan las aguas pacíficas y naturalmente, como no llue-
ve como aquí. Allá es un llover . . . mucho.

(1) V268. Miracles performed under protection of Virgin Mary.
(2) A1018. Flood as punishment.

8. El Santo Niño de Atocha

(Recorded by Praxedis Ramírez on October 31, 1966, in Los Angeles, California)

A poor man killed his rich friend while they were traveling together and then repented and appealed to the Santo Niño de Atocha

[Holy child of Atocha] to bring him back to life in exchange for a promise he vowed to fulfill. His friend appeared to him, alive, believing only that he had been deserted by the poor man while he slept. The murderer then fulfilled his vow to carry the rock with which he killed his friend to the shrine of the Santo Niño in Plateros [Zacatecas].

Es una historia de dos hermanos, de dos amigos . . . íntimos. Que uno era de dinero; otro era . . . pobre. Decidieron venir a los Estados Unidos los dos. Cuando el uno dormía el otro, el otro lo, lo cuidaba. Cuando el otro dormía el otro le cuidaba.

En una ocasión el rico se quedó dormido. El pobre, se le hizo fácil, cogió una piedra, se la tiró en la cabeza, lo mató, y allí siguió su camino. Al poco tiempo se arrepintió él de su, de su . . . error que él había cometido, y le pidió con todo su corazón al Santo Niño que le volviera la vida a su amigo (1, 2). Entonces él se regresaría y llevaría la piedra en su cabeza . . . hasta donde estaba el Santo Niño.

Cuando él menos pensó, su amigo lo alcanzó y le dice: —¿Qué has hecho conmigo? ¿Por qué me dejaste?

—No, dice, —no te dejé, dice. —Te maté.

—¿Cómo?, dice. —Si aquí vengo.

—No, dice. —Yo te maté, dice. —Vamos y te lo demuestro.

Entonces se regresó, cogió la piedra, y se fue hasta Plateros con su piedra en la cabeza, Y allí está . . . la prueba.

(1) E63. Resuscitation by prayer.
(2) E121.4. Resuscitation by saint.

9. El Santo Niño de Plateros

(Recorded by Josefina Márquez on May 7, 1966, in Santa Paula, California)

The informant tells of an attack of blindness that she suffered about thirty years before and how her appeal to the Santo Niño de Plateros brought about a miraculous recovery from the condition her doctor had diagnosed as permanent. When she went to fulfill her promise to visit the shrine of the Santo Niño, she was told by the priest that the saint was not in just then, but that she might wait for him. Having drifted off to sleep while seated there, she was awakened by the sound of tapping and was greeted by the sight of the Santo Niño back in his niche. Her enthusiasm and devotion were so great that her request for one of the Holy Child's tiny sandals was granted her by the priest. She later gave the sandal to a very sick friend of hers in Los Angeles, who in turn was miraculously cured of her illness and has worn the sandal on her person ever since.

Tengo otro milagro también que publicar. Que este milagro me lo hizo el Santo Niño de Plateros de Fresnillo, Zacatecas, en mil novecientos . . . treinta y nueve. En ese tiempo yo cosía mucho, de día y de noche. Y un día estando cosiendo en la noche . . . salí en la madrugada para fuera. Estaba haciendo brisa y yo voltié para el cielo. Cuando regresé para dentro quise seguir cosiendo. Cogí mi costura . . . y ya no veía nada. No veía la luz, no veía la costura, no veía nada. Dejé la costura a un lado y me acosté a descansar.

Y me quedé dormida otro día en la mañana. Estaba esperando yo que amaneciera, que diera la luz del día para poderme levantar, para ir a llevar a mi marido de desayunar a la prisión.

En eso entra mi cuñada hermana de mi marido, y me dice:—Josefina, ¿no te vas a levantar? Ya son las ocho. Ya entra el sol hasta media pieza.

Entonces le dije yo: —¿Tú estás jugando? Todavía no amanece. No se ve nada.

Me dijo ella: —No, dice, —ya son las ocho, y les voy a dar de comer a los pájaros. Levántate.

Entonces ella se fijó que me levanté ya . . . y que no veía. Me puse el vestido con lo de atrás para adelante. Porque no veía nada en verdad. No veía nada. Me cogió ella de la mano y me llevó afuera y yo no veía nada.

Inmediatamente me llevó ella con el médico. Y dijo el médico que si veía era por un milagro, pero que era una enfermedad que se llama "gota serena," que no vuelve a ver la gente nada.

Yo le pedí al Santo Niño de Plateros con todo mi corazón que si él me volvía mi vista yo iba a verle, a visitarle . . . de limosna. Fue una cosa que prometí yo porque yo tenía fe que él me sanara. Y como yo . . . me encontraba en esa tribulación no pensé en la vergüenza que yo iba a pasar al pedir la limosna. Fui casa por casa, cuando él me regresó mi vista a los tres meses de estarme dando tratamientos. . . . Que me quitaban las vendas, y entonces vi que me había hecho el milagro, que me regresó mi vista; porque miraba perfectamente bien. Todo . . . no me dolía mi vista para nada (1).

Desde allí empecé yo a colectar mis limosnas, a pedir mi limosna para ir a verlo, hasta darle su manda como le había prometido. En muchos hogares me avergonzaron porque no eran católicos. Me decían que ellos no creían en eso. En otros me ayudaron con tres centavos, con cinco centavos, como podía la gente. Porque mucha gente es muy pobre. Pero yo ajusté el pasaje para ir a verlo . . . que eran cinco pesos veinte y nueve centavos de ida y vuelta, que viene siendo . . . vuelta redonda.

Fui, pagué yo mi . . . mi manda. Fui a visitarlo, a publicar mi milagro allí en el santuario de él. Es un niñito muy pequeñito. No estaba allí cuando yo llegué. Tuve que esperarlo como tres horas porque él no estaba en su silla sentado. Le pregunté a un sacerdote de allí del templo . . . que dónde se encontraba el Santo Niño de Plateros. Entonces me dijo él: —Es muy paseador. No se encuentra en este momento aquí (2). Espéralo.

Yo estaba desesperada porque tenía que regresar a Zacatecas. Había ido sola y tenía que regresar. Y ya estaba cansada, pero no me salía de allí con esperanza de . . . de mirarlo que regresara. Me empecé a quedar dormida . . . y en el sueño oí . . . unos toquidos que sonaban [she taps four times] así, y desperté. Cuando voltié vi que el Santo Niño estaba sentado en su silla. Entonces le hablé al padre y le dije que si me permetía arrimarme a verlo. Me dijo él que sí. Entonces me arrimé yo, y . . . vi el Niño, con sus ojos que parecía que estaba sonriéndose . . . muy pequeñito, muy chiquito. Me daban ganas de cogerle la carita. Le pregunté al sacerdote que si me daba permiso de tocarlo. Y como me vieron a mí . . . que estaba encinta, . . . el padre me permitió que le tocara los piecitos. Cuando le toqué los pies le vi sus guaraches rompidos de la punta. Entonces le dije yo al sacerdote que si me regalaba un guarachito de él. Y me lo regaló. Pero en este momento no lo tengo porque yo le regalé más delante a una persona que le tenía mucha fe y no lo conocía. . . . Pero es muy milagroso el Santo Niño, mucho muy milagroso.

Si ustedes tienen fe y creen en milagros pueden pedirles de todo corazón. No le hace que no estén con ellos; no le hace que no los conozcan. Pueden pedirle al uno o al otro: al Santo Niño de Plateros o a la Santísima Virgen de San Juan. [The informant had previously told of a miracle granted her by the Virgen de San Juan.]

El guarachito que le digo que me regalaron del Santo Niño de Plateros, . . . tenía yo una amiguita en el hospital que se encontraba internada con tuberculosis, que viene siendo TB. Una vez que fui a verla yo, a visitarla, ella creía en el Santo Niño pero no lo conocía ni nunca le había hecho un milagro. Entonces le dije yo que le pidiera con todo su corazón, que era muy milagroso. Y me dijo que le regalara el guarachito . . . del Santo Niño. Con ese guarachito ella cogió mucha fe, y le pidió al Santo Niño de Plateros. Y cuando menos pensó ella, la llamaron que no le habían encontrado tuberculosis en sus pulmones. Salió libre del hospital sin tener que regresar para nada (1). Pero nunca me quiso regresarme el guarachito. Ella lo carga . . . en su seno como si fuera alguna reliquia o alguna medalla de algún Cristo, alguna cosa así. Ella lo cargo muy bien guardado en su seno todo el tiempo. Esa señora vive en Los Angeles, California en este tiempo. Su nombre de ella es Jesusita Paredes. Pero esa viejecita existe todavía, y tiene mucha fe porque sanó ella de la noche a la mañana.

(1) V221. Miraculous healing by saints.
    Morote Best, Type 17. "Las imágenes que salen de sus camarines, abandonan los templos y andan por calles y caminos, casi de modo habitual."
(2) D1620. Magic automata. Statues or images that act as if alive.
    Mendoza, *San Pedro Piedra Gorda*, p. 401.
    Pérez, *TFSP*, 24(1951), 103. (" El Niño Perdido.")
    Warren, p. 149. (Holy Child of Chimayó.)

Devil Narratives

The nine narratives included in this section are of a very disparate nature. They range from well-structured stories indicative of established local legends to anecdotes about personal encounters and fragmented commentaries functioning as expressions of beliefs rather than as stories.

C. W. von Sydow, in a work on the classification of various prose

traditions, has pointed out a basic difference between "actual folk beliefs and superstitious fictions,"[30] a distinction that may be useful in
considering the devil narratives presented here. The category of superstitious fiction applies to Narratives 10, 11, and 12; in accordance
with the further breakdown suggested by von Sydow, number 10 may
be classified as an aetiological legend, and numbers 11 and 12 as what
are described as anecdotes more in the nature of jokes rather than fac-
tual accounts.[31] These three devil narratives are the only ones having
the structure and the tone of established local legends.

The second category, legendary material very closely related to belief, would accurately describe the remaining narratives, numbers 13
through 18. These are less-structured narratives, often comprising a
single episode or incident, or relating a personal experience. The latter
may either stand alone or function as affirmations of popular beliefs.
This second category of legendary material is generally more static and
subjective, as opposed to the development and objectivity characteristic of the first. The informant who relates a legend of the type described as "superstitious fiction," regardless of whether he believes
the event described actually happened, enters into a mood best described as that of fiction.

Narrative 10 is an example of the aetiological legend—the phenomenon being explained is the twisted grating over a jailhouse window. There is also an underlying current of didacticism to the story,
for the man is in jail for drunkenness, and his soliciting the aid of the
devil [G303.6.1.2.] in escaping proves unsuccessful. When in great
consternation he utters the name of the Virgin, the devil of course flees
[V254.4], leaving the man stuck between the bars, which must then
be pulled apart in order to free him. The informant solemnly affirms
the truth of this story, which was told her by her parents, by telling
how the twisted bars remained as evidence for a long time.

Narratives 11 and 12, as previously mentioned, are structured as
anecdotes attributed to real people. They do, however, have a definite
aura of fiction to them in which the informant seems to participate.
Narrative 11, for example, is really a combination of personal recollec-

---

[30] C. W. von Sydow, "Kategorien der Prosa-Volksdichtung," pp. 60–88.
[31] Ibid.

tion and imaginative creation, and draws on the material of folk tradition. The informant himself, as a young boy, participated in the
search for the lost man, and to that extent he is drawing on a personal
experience; but from that point on, the lost person becomes a convenient figure to which to attach the popular tradition of the abducted
musician who plays for the devil's dance in Hell [G303.25.17.2].
Once again, as in the previous narrative, the opportunity is seized to
attach a moral to the story. The abducted man, once returned home,
thinks it well to speak of his experience in order that it may inspire
others to good behavior.

A curious detail in the story is the Devil's specific instruction to
leave the fiddle and to bring only the guitar. The man protests, for it is
his "arma principal," but the Devil insists, assuring him that he will
find it there when he returns. The indication that the musician is primarily a fiddler is in keeping with the popular tradition, since the fiddle is often considered "the devil's own instrument";[32] but the usual
conclusion of this theme, whereby the musician recognizes the devil
among the dancers and breaks his instrument never to play again, is
lacking in this narrative. The moral is of a slightly different nature, for
it is directed at a more generalized concept of evil rather than at the
specific instance of playing for dances. It is therefore obviously related,
although not identical, to Woods Lt. 116 (Fiddler playing for dance
sees devil among the dancers; breaks his instrument and never plays
again). There is a documented instance of the instrument being an ac-
cordion rather than a fiddle,[33] a parallel to the replacement of it by the
guitar in Narrative 11. The explicit rejection of the fiddle in this narrative remains something of a puzzle, but may perhaps be explainable
simply as a more meaningful choice in a culture where guitars pre-
dominate.

Krappe points out the frequency of stories in which the devil makes
a pact with a mortal who then cheats him of his reward through some
clever device [K210].[34] Narrative 12 is an example of this type of an-

<hr>

[32] Barbara Allen Woods, *The Devil in Dog Form: A Partial Type-Index of Devil
Legends*, p. 66.
[33] Ibid.
[34] Krappe, p. 96.

ecdotal legend which, as was true of the previous story, is also attributed to a real person. The specific person, the protagonist, is introduced by the informant through a device that is especially effective in structuring the story. He begins by saying: "En mil novecientos seis conocí un hombre. Se llamaba Isabel Ramírez." [In 1906 I met a man. His name was Isabel Ramírez.] The informant's acquaintance with Isabel Ramírez coincides with the introduction of him to the hearer of the story, with the result that, while the comment is ostensibly aimed at lending an air of truth to the narrative by identifying the man as a personal acquaintance, it has the paradoxical effect of endowing him with a special fictitious quality by delineating his existence purely within the context of the incident narrated. The story, then, seems best described as a legendary treatment of the same material that constitutes Mt. 1170–1199, having to do with a man's selling his soul to the devil and then saving it through deceit.[35] (In this case, the device of setting the time for fulfillment of the bargain as "mañana" [K231.12].)

Not only the introductory comment but also the closing one contribute significantly to the structuring of the story and serve to round out the fictional framework. The informant ends by saying: "Y ese mañana nunca se llegó y ni se llegará nunca" [and that tomorrow never came and never will], a closing that invests the incident with a timelessness peculiar to fiction. Isabel Ramírez is in essence an immortal figure, for only as such can his eternal victory over the devil be fully appreciated.

Legendary anecdotes about encounters with the devil that are similar in tone to the above can be found in a collection entitled "Spanish American Devil Lore in Southern Colorado."[36] They too are presented as the personal experiences of an acquaintance of the narrator; and the author concludes, as is also borne out by Narratives 10, 11, and 12, that the devil is "both feared and laughed at" and that he "seldom wins."[37]

The didactic note dominates in Narratives 13 and 14. The devil

<hr>

[35] Antti Aarne and Stith Thompson, *The Types of the Folktale.*
[36] William J. Wallrich, *WF,* 9 (1950), 50–55.
[37] Ibid., p. 50.

functions as a frightful apparition, and the moralistic intent of the story is to point out the evil nature of drinking, an evil that in turn has led to inappropriate flirtation. The informant of Narrative 13, in fact, calls her story an *ejemplo*: "Total, ello es un ejemplo, ¿verdad?"[38] Of the different types of devil stories in existence, Krappe suggests that such moralistic narratives would be the type encouraged by the clergy, as opposed to those which tell of the ridiculed priest: "The moralizing tone is evident in all these tales, and one may conjecture that the clergy not only did not discourage them, but may have helped to give them as wide a circulation as possible."[39]

As in Narratives 10 and 11, the devil in Narrative 13 is represented, quite typically, as a gentleman [G303.3.1.2] on horseback [G303.7.1]. He appears to a group of married men who are out drinking and flirting with other women [G303.6.2.5], and, when they flee in separate directions, he simultaneously pursues each one. Along with the devil's supernatural power to be in several places at once is the curious detail about his always maintaining with ease the same distance from the man he is pursuing. Each of the men reported that the devil kept up with him "sin verlo que se apurara" [without seeing him hurry]. This particular detail can be put in very significant perspective if considered in relation to the following comment: "Nowhere is the role of guilt in folk legends more evident than in those which tell of an evil spirit's appearance being occasioned by a person's wrong-doing."[40] The devil's relentless pursuit and the rigidly unvarying distance maintained suggest an essential oneness of the devil and each individual man. The psychological implication is that of a merged identity, the devil being in fact each man's conscience. The men are pursued by their own inescapable guilt.

The didacticism in Narrative 14 is carried a step further, for the lesson learned is specifically stated: "Pero él ya no volvía a andar en la

---

[38] The *exemplum* is a literary form of didactic intent popular in Spain during the Middle Ages, which has survived to the present in popular tradition. Important *exempla* collections from Spain are Juan Manuel's *El Conde Lucanor*; the *Libro de Calila y Dimna*, compiled under the direction of Alfonso el Sabio; and the *Libro de enxiemplos por a.b.c.*, arranged by Clemente Sánchez.

[39] Krappe, p. 95.

[40] Woods, p. 63.

noche. Se acordaba del diablo, y no más." [But he didn't go about at night anymore. He remembered the devil, and never again.] This anecdote, about the man who has been out drinking [G303.6.2] and on the way home pursues what appears to be a beautiful woman who turns out to be the devil [G303.3.1.12], is very common.

In anticipation of the section on the *llorona*, there exists a similarity between the story of Narrative 14 and a *llorona* narrative that appears in a collection of Mexican folk narratives from Texas. Both are of a didactic nature, for the beautiful woman turns out to be an evil apparition that gives the inebriated men a bad scare and presumably cures them of their bad habits, both the drinking and the chasing after women. Although it is the devil who appears in Narrative 14, the evil apparition of the second anecdote is the *llorona*, as is indicated in the title "The Weeping Woman."[41] Bacil Kirtley's reference to one of the roles of the *llorona* being that of a "frightful apparition"[42] is well illustrated in the comparison of these two narratives, in which, structurally, the devil and the *llorona* fulfill the same function.

Narratives 15 and 16 are best described as statements of beliefs, since, in contrast to the preceding narratives, there is no development and no story to tell. The common figure of the headless horseman [E422.1.3.1] is the topic of Narrative 15. Accompanied by a dog giving off sparks, the horseman made repeated rides through the informant's neighborhood in the early hours of the morning and was felt by many to be the devil [G303.7.1]. The frequency of stories about the devil in dog form indicates a confusion or blending of two common forms of incarnation of the devil. He is the horseman, but it is also clear that he is represented by the dog [G303.3.3.1.1]. The informant goes on to moralize about his appearances being due to the presence of so much evil in the town [G303.6.2.5]. She elaborates very emotionally on the shameless, immoral behavior indulged in by a certain segment of the population; to her, there is a very simple and logical correlation between sinful behavior and the presence of the devil. The devil, however, does not seem to be functioning here in a didactic role, an idea the informant specifically rejects, but rather as an

---

[41] Soledad Pérez, "Mexican Folklore from Austin, Texas," *TFSP*, 24 (1951), 76.
[42] Bacil F. Kirtley, " 'La llorona' and Related Themes," *WF*, 19 (1960), 156.

inevitable concomitant to such shameful goings-on. In Woods' work on devil lore, one of the categories established is described as characterized by the "basic assumption . . . that sin invites the devil's appearance";[43] such is certainly the conviction of this informant.

Narrative 16, the second of the two that constitute mainly statements of belief, illustrates a basic inclination to devise some satisfactory explanation for an otherwise unexplainable or unintelligible phenomenon. As the informant states, a rather "operatic" voice was quite often heard to come from the direction of the hills nearby, generally around midnight. Social custom then combines with folk belief to produce a likely explanation. No woman could possibly be going about at that hour, and, midnight being the traditional hour for supernatural manifestations [G303.6.1.1], it becomes easy to accept such an explanation as the devil.

There are documented descriptions of the quality of the devil's voice, such as G303.4.7 (Devil speaks with the voice of a he-goat); thus, by extension it is not surprising that almost any particular type of voice could be attributed to him, according to the demands of the situation. Together with the idea that the devil does appear at times as a beautiful woman, the conclusion reached by the people of this informant's hometown about the operatic voice heard from the hills is perhaps more understandable. What is very interestingly illustrated by this narrative is the ready availability of, and, therefore, easy recourse to, folk tradition for an explanation of seemingly mysterious phenomena.

In the classification system of C. W. von Sydow, the term *memorat* is applied to narratives based on personal experience, one of three subcategories of the larger classification—legendary material very closely related to belief.[44] Narratives 17 and 18, the last two dealing with the devil, are of this type. In both of these stories the underlying belief that the devil can be invoked, either unwittingly or intentionally, is expressed by the informant as she tells of two separate childhood experiences of encounters with the devil.

---

[43] Woods, p. 63.
[44] Von Sydow, pp. 60–88.

In Narrative 17 the informant and a group of playmates accidentally invoke the presence of the devil through a song they sing
[D1275] while at play, an incident of the type indicated in Motif C12
(Devil invoked: appears unexpectedly). The song, which is a children's rhyme, refers to a humpback, and after the first singing of the
song a real humpback appears and threatens to carry one of the children off. After the second singing, however, a more recognizable figure appears, with horns [G303.4.1.6.1] and extremely large ears.
The girls are then informed by a neighbor woman that they must not
sing that song; although it is not specifically stated, it is implied that
it summons up the devil.

The devil who appears in the informant's second experience, Narrative 18, is the more colorful as well as the very common depiction of
the giant figure dressed in red [G303.5.3], with enormous teeth and
eyes [G303.4.1.2.4], and fire in his mouth and hands [G303.4.8.
2.1]. A brief comment made by the informant in the course of this
story illustrates very well the close relationship of certain narratives to
folk belief. As the little girl reluctantly goes off on an errand, the
angry mother curses her to the devil [C12.5] for her disobedience.
The informant then describes her feelings in retrospect: "Pues ya me
fui, pos, creyendo que no había demonio, porque la hermana de ella
[de su mamá] me dijo que no había diablo." [So off I went, thinking
that there was no devil, because my aunt told me there was no devil.]
The story, then, not only expresses the belief, but in addition contributes to its preservation, for the incident functions as a testimony to its
validity.

The concluding episode in this story, in which the aid of a priest is
sought to break the devil's spell [D2176.3.2], reveals the informant's
very childlike, ingenuous religious sentiment:

Pues luego después el padrecito me dijo que tenía que hincarme en el
arroz. En el cemento puso arroz, y que me hincara en el arroz pa que me
doliera, y que le pidiera perdón a mi mamá y que otro día le hiciera yo
caso.

[Then the priest told me I had to kneel on the rice. He put rice on the ce-
ment floor and told me to kneel on the rice so that it would hurt and to ask
my mother's pardon and to obey her in the future.]

Even in retrospect, the informant does not show resentment of what was really a very cruel and degrading punishment dictated by the priest, and, furthermore, a very unfair one in view of her mother's excessively harsh treatment of her. On the contrary, she goes on referring to the priest with the affectionate diminutive "el padrecito."

In closing, it may be of interest to note the remarks made on the subject of the devil by another informant, a Roman Catholic priest (previously cited as an informant in the section on religious legends). His comments and his stories deal mainly with diabolical persecution, which he considers to be an indisputable fact, since it is spoken of in the Holy Scripture: "En concreto, la posesión diabólica es un hecho ya que el Santo Evangelio nos lo narra." He tells of an incident in which a bishop who was known as one of those singled out for persecution by the devil was attacked by him in the very familiar form of the black dog:[45]

Salió el Señor Obispo [el Obispo de Veracruz, Guízar y Valencia]. De pronto apareció un perro grande, negro, y le dio una mordida en la pierna al Señor Obispo, y lo . . . lo lanzó hacia un lado, sacudiéndolo fuertemente. El Señor Obispo cayó. El Padre Manuel Hernández le preguntó: —¿Qué pasa?

Y él dijo: —Tú sabes. Sabes quién es. Le ayudaron a incorporarse. El se quedó en la casa.

As previously stated by the informant, this particular bishop was generally regarded as one of those people especially chosen for persecution, and, in this rather terse account of the incident, he recognizes the dog immediately and unquestionably as his adversary, the devil.

This same bishop, on another occasion, experienced the persecution of the devil in the form of a sudden chaotic confusion and marching about of the sacerdotal garments and other religious objects just after he had finished saying mass and was praying in the sacristy. The informant relates as follows:

En cierta ocasión se manifestaba claramente la persecución del demonio sobre él. Quería impedir sus obras, especialmente cuando iba a predicar a alguna misión. En cierta ocasión estaba él dando gracias después de la Santa

---

[45] This type of incident is cited as G303.3.3.18.4. Devil in form of snarling dog threatens priest, in John E. Keller, *Motif-index of Mediaeval Spanish exempla.*

Misa, orando en la sacristía, y de pronto se abrieron los cajones de todas las cómodas y empezaban a salir los ornamentos y a marchar en torno a él, bailando, . . . se oía ruidos, voces, para perturbarlo en la oración. Llegó el sacristán, llamó al señor cura, lleno de espanto, y vieron que la salva, los amitos, todos los ornamentos andaban marchando y gritando en torno al obispo, como en procesión para perturbar en la oración. No hallaban el párroco ni el sacristán de qué se trataba. El señor cura le preguntó al señor obispo qué era. Dijo: —No hagas caso. Y luego ya: —Métanse. Acomódense. Y todos regresaron al lugar en donde estaban los ornamentos.

Once again the bishop knows immediately who is behind the malicious act, and here he seems very well in control of the situation, for his simple command suffices to return the objects to their places.

Before telling this story the informant had commented on a question pertinent to it: why there were so few cases of diabolical persecution these days, as compared to the relative frequency of it in biblical writings. His explanation was that God permits miraculous works (which indicate victory over the devil) in the evangelistic stages of the religion, when they are a valuable incentive to acceptance of the doctrine being preached: "Los que explican el Santo Evangelio cuando se van de misioneros a tierras salvajes, al principio de la misión Dios permite que los misioneros obren milagros para que . . . para poder impulsar a los habitantes de esa región a creer. Digamos en otras palabras, autorizando la doctrina con el poder de Dios, obrando milagros." Bishop Guízar y Valencia had the above experience while visiting at a mission; and, as was stated at the beginning, the devil liked especially to interfere with his work at the missions.

A third example of the persecution suffered by the Bishop of Veracruz at the hands of the devil is much more in the spirit of popular tradition than the previous two, although the style of narration and the vocabulary are, once again, learned. The informant relates as follows this third incident, involving a very painful attack of hordes of fleas upon the bishop's person:

En cierta ocasión también el Señor Obispo fue a la visita pastoral y decidió quedarse en la parroquia esa noche, como con frecuencia lo hacía. Se despidió del párroco y se dirigió el Señor Obispo a su cuarto para recogerse. De pronto se escucharon . . . golpes, tumbos, gritos, lamentos. Se dirigieron al cuarto del Señor Obispo. Por más que tocaron nadie les abrió, y adentro se escuchaban grandes ruidos y quejas y lamentos. Entonces tuvieron que romper la puerta. El Señor Obispo estaba en la mitad del cuarto, boca abajo, y todo el cuerpo cubierto con una capa espesa de pulgas, como de dos pulgadas, que nadie se puede explicar que en un lugar pueda haber tanto. . . insecto, tanta pulga. El Señor Obispo no hallaba qué era. Quería levantarlo y no podían levantarlo. El se quejaba atrozmente. Entonces recordando él que con frecuencia el Señor Obispo sufría persecución diabólica, trajo agua bendita y rezó el exorcismo, nada más para impedir el influjo de Satanás. Lo que sé es que puso agua bendita y rezó, y desaparecieron todas las pulgas. El señor quedó absolutamente agotado, prosternado, y toda la espalda convertida en una gran llaga. No se pudo explicar el hecho de ninguna otra forma. Sabemos de hecho que el demonio ejerce su persecución diabólica sobre almas muy escogidas.

The exorcism was successful, and the incident was to be understood as an act of diabolical persecution, for, as the informant concludes, we know for a fact that the devil directs his persecution at very carefully selected souls.

10. El diablo y el preso

(Recorded by Elvira Higuera on October 31, 1966, in Los Angeles, California)

A man from Capirato, Sinaloa, who had been thrown in jail for drunkenness appealed to the devil to help him escape. The latter appeared as a horseman dressed in black and told him to put his head through the bars and he would manage to escape. The prisoner followed this advice, but quickly got stuck. In his dismay he uttered the name of the Virgin, whereupon the devil disappeared, leaving the prisoner in his predicament. It was necessary to cut the bars in order to free him. The informant affirms the truth of the story because she saw the twisted bar.

Éste se trata de un . . . de un preso que por borrachera lo habían metido allí en la . . . cárcel. Y . . . una noche en la noche él, desesperado, le empezó a hablar al diablo. Y . . . llegó un señor (1), a caballo (2), vestido de negro (3), y luego le brindaba un . . . trago de licor. Y le dijo él que no quería licor ya, que lo que quería era que lo sacara de aquella prisión.

Le dijo: —Mete la cabeza por . . . por entre la reja y te vas a salir (4).

Entonces el preso metió la cabeza por entre las . . . metió la cabeza por entre las rejas y, y se quedó con, cuando ya tenía en el cuello la reja, dijo: —¡Ay, María Purísima! Esto no es cosa buena, porque salga yo por estas rejas tan chicas. Entonces al decir María Purísima, el diablo desapareció (5), y quedó el . . . el preso metido con la cabeza . . . solamente el cuello en las rejas. Y tuvieron que cortar las rejas después.

Esto sucedió en Capirato, Sinaloa, un pueblo . . . cerca de Pericos. Me lo contaron más bien mis papás ya hace mucho tiempo, y, y varias personas de allí de Capirato. Y eso fue verídico, porque allí se vio la reja, que quedó mucho tiempo así doblada.

> Woods 200. Person conjures the devil and he appears.
> (1) G303.6.1.2. Devil comes when called upon.
> (2) G303.7.1. Devil rides horse.
> (3) G303.5.1. Devil is dressed in black.
> (4) G303.22. Devil helps people.
> (5) G303.16.8. Devil leaves at mention of God's name. [Here it is the Virgin's name that sends him away.]

11. El diablo y el guitarrista

(Recorded by Inocente Rocha on November 17, 1966, in Oxnard, California)

Three musicians were traveling down the road together, when one of them, named Lucas, realized he had forgotten his violin bow. He returned to get it, but, before he was able to rejoin his companions, he was intercepted by a man on a black horse, the devil, who urged Lucas to accompany him to a very large dance hall and to play for a large group of people. He instructed him specifically to leave behind his violin and bring only the guitar. At the dance, Lucas recognized some of the people as personal acquaintances. When it was over, he was put on a horse and sent back to the spot where he first met the devil, but he remained lost for an entire week, during which time he was the object of an extensive search on the part of the townspeople. When he finally returned home and told his wife of his experience, he expressed the feeling that he ought to talk of it to others so that it might serve as an example to them. The informant places this incident in Purísima del Rincón, Guanajuato in the year 1905.

En mil . . . mil novecientos cinco, a mí me consta, iban unos músicos en el camino y . . . y cuando llegaron a unas paredes viejas, se le ocurrió al señor . . . Lucas, que era el . . . el principal de los músicos, se le había olvidado la vara. Porque llevaba dos instrumentos. Llevaba guitarra y llevaba violín. Pero al mismo tiempo se regresó.

Y cuando llegó a las paredes viejas de regreso, allí le . . . le salió un, un hombre de un caballo negro (1). Cuando él le dijo: —¿Para ónde vas, Lucas?

Dijo: —Pues, voy a alcanzar a mis compañeros, que van a tocar.

Dijo: —Deja áhi el violín, tráete no más la guitarra (2).

—Bueno, dice, —¿pero cómo quieres que lo deje, si es . . . mi arma principal?

Dijo:—Pos, sea lo que sea, déjalo. Y después, cuando vengamos de allá, lo mismo lo hallas. Te lo prometo.

Bueno. Entonces se fue. Y cuando llegó al . . . un salón muy grande, había muy bonito, había mucha gente, mucha concurrencia. Y al tiempo que . . . el mismo tiempo que llegaron, cuando soltaron la primer pieza, va viendo muchas de las personas que él conocía en vida. Y les . . . iba él a . . . a hablar, pero no, al mismo tiempo se arrepintió él de hablarles. Duró tocando . . . durante el . . . el tiempo que, que duró el baile. Cuando el baile ya terminó, entonces lo echaron arriba del, de un caballo, y vinieron hasta las paredes . . . que, que estaban abandonadas.

Duró ocho días este hombre . . . perdido. Y hasta la, a mí me consta que la autoridad . . . andaban buscándolo. Y no no más la, la autoridad, sino hasta los, los muchachos de la escuela dieron por andarlo buscando. Y no pudimos encontrarlo.

Y cuando regresó le dijo a la esposa, dijo: —Tú verás, dice, —allí las personas que estaban. . . . Allí mentó los nombres de las personas, pero que yo me acuerde de ellas . . . es imposible. Pero a mí . . . a mí me consta que no es mentira. Eso pasó en Purísima del Rincón, Guanajuato, México.

[The informant later went on to explain that the man who had ex-

perienced this felt it would be a good idea to talk about it, so that it
might serve as an example to others.]

> Woods 116. Fiddler playing for dance sees devil among the dancers;
> breaks his instrument and never plays again. [Narrative 11 is basically
> of this type, although with minor variation.]

(1) G303.7.1.1. Devil rides on black horse.
(2) G303.9.5.8. Devil takes violinist when he needs a good fiddler in hell.
    [Here, he takes guitarist.]
    Robe, *Mexican Tales*, no. 156.

12. El diablo e Isabel Ramírez

(Recorded by Inocente Rocha on November 21, 1966, in Oxnard, California)

A man who appeared to have extraordinary luck in everything he
undertook was asked by a friend what he attributed such good fortune to. He answered that he had solicited the aid of the devil, and he
described the procedure whereby one might contact the devil and make
a pact with him. He hoped thus to secure his own freedom by present-
ing the devil with another soul, since his own time was running out.
The friend followed his instructions, which were to go to a hilltop
and shout the devil's name three times. The devil appeared and a pact
was agreed upon in which the man was to receive great wealth in exchange for his soul, but the clever man escaped payment forever by
agreeing to fulfill his obligation "tomorrow." The informant places
this incident in San Francisco del Rincón, Guanajuato, in the year
1906.

En mil novecientos seis conocí un hombre. Se llamaba Isabel Ramírez. Era muy afortunado en todas . . . pleitos, jugadas, en todo lo que
sea. Y le dijo el compadre: —Compadre, ¿cómo te hicistes todas estas
. . . fortunas y todo? ¿Sabes por qué estás tan valiente?

Dice: —Ay, compadre, dice, —el diablo me ha ayudado en todo
(1). Yo te lo puedo . . . te lo puedo probar porque a mí me ha pasado.
Yo soy afortunado en todo, en juegos . . . de barajas, en juegos de todas clases.

Y, y luego se . . . uno de los compadres le dijo: —Oye, compadre,
¿cómo fue cuando te hicistes tú rico?

—Ir al cerro y le gritas al diablo, pero le gritas tres . . . tres veces
(2).

Al mismo tiempo, el compadre desesperado y tan pobre, cuando le dijo: —Diablo, . . . Diablo, . . . Satanás, dice. —Quiero que vengas a mí para que me des dinero, me hagas rico.

—¿Sí? Entonces le dijo: —¿Cuándo . . . cuándo lo vas a pagar? ¿Me vas a dar alguna cosa? ¿Me vas a dar tu alma?

—Sí, te la doy.

Entonces hicieron el contrato, de todo . . . el dinero y su alma, con lo que se . . . cumplió (3).

Ya se estaba cumpliendo cuando el otro compadre le dijo: —Ay, compadre, ¿cómo te hicistes tan rico?

—¿Yo?, dijo. —No más es animarse a irse. Te vas a la . . . a la falda de aquel cerro y le gritas al diablo. Tres veces que le gritas, ya te prometo que viene.

Y le gritó y le dijo: —¿Qué quieres, . . . buen hombre?

Dijo: —Quiero que me des dinero, riquezas, para darles a mis parientes, a mis familiares, para que se sostengan.

Al mismo tiempo el diablo anduvo con él, y . . . y les hizo ricos a todos (1). Y luego hicieron el contrato. Le dijo: —¿Cómo quieres el contrato?

—Mi contrato, dice, —yo lo quiero . . . que sea todo para pagar mañana.

Y ese mañana nunca se llegó, y ni se llegará nunca (4, 5).

Esta historia pasó en San Francisco del Rincón, Guanajuato, México.

Woods 200. Person conjures the devil and he appears.
Qvigstad, no. 29B, p. 42. The devil is cheated out of his bargain (when he tries to fetch the man who had promised himself to him).
(1) G303.22. Devil helps people.
(2) G303.6.1.2. Devil comes when called upon.
(3) M211.9. Person sells soul to devil in return for the granting of wishes.
(4) K210. Devil cheated of his promised soul.
(5) K231.12. Debt to be paid "tomorrow." Tomorrow never comes.

13. El diablo en San José del Carmen

(Recorded by Isaura Benicia on May 15, 1966, in Los Angeles, California)

The informant relates an incident that took place in San José del Carmen, Jalisco, in which the devil appeared to a group of married men who were out drinking and flirting with other women. He appeared in the form of a well-dressed gentleman, riding a very fine horse that breathed flames and gave off a flood of sparks from its eyes and its hoofs. As the men ran frightened to their homes, the devil simultaneously followed each of them.

Sucede eso de, de que estando esos señores allí, en San José del Carmen, . . . eran unos señores, y fíjese que todos jóvenes, casados, pero . . . ellos . . . tratando de andar de novios todavía, seguramente. Y se refiere uno que por eso, . . . total ello es un ejemplo, ¿verdad? . . . de que se les apareció eso para que ya volvieran a sus . . . a su lugar, a sus casas, sin andar de novios porque, . . . se refiere a eso, ¿verdad (1)? Y como le digo, en aquel tiempo todos creíamos todo, todas las cosas muy. . . .

Y, entonces, fíjese, que pasó eso, de que venía ese señor. Lo vieron que abrió la puerta, y que . . . creían conocer, conocerlo. Y cuando iba . . . a unos doscientos metros de ellos, vieron que no era persona conocida, que ni era persona. Que era . . . pues, para ellos, el diablo. Y todos vivían en diferentes calles, en diferentes rumbos. A todos los seguía el mismo . . . jinete.

Era un señor muy bien vestido. Muy bien vestido, . . . en traje elegante se puede decir (2). El caballo, un caballo, pues, muy distinguido, desde su modo de caminar y todo (3). Y, y dicen que . . . el señor se veía, pues, muy bien, ¿verdad? Que iba muy bien vestido, como ninguno de los que vestían allí. En este tiempo toda la gente vestía todavía con sarape. Y . . . echaba lumbre por el hocico y, y los ojos. Y, y al pisar, las pisadas en el, en las piedras, porque no es asfalto, es empedrado, . . . y al pisar . . . brincaba lumbre de las patas del caballo. Posiblemente las herraduras al, al pisar cualquier caballo sí, despiden lumbre, pero no como la que aquel caballo despedía ¿verdad? Pero fíjese que, . . . y . . . por el hocico del animal y por los ojos, sí, veían que . . . aventaba . . . que chisporroteaba lumbre, y lo mismo el. . . . Ya ve, que cuando está uno que hay neblina o que hay algo, siempre el aliento de uno cómo se ve la, . . . ¿verdad?, como, como un . . . humo. . . . Y así se veía aquello. En lugar de vapor, se veía que era como lumbre, que él iba respirando, que iba despidiendo esa lumbre en lugar de . . . su aliento (4).

Pues, es todo lo. . . . Y a todos los seguía, y a la misma distancia, la misma distancia, sin verlo . . . que se apurara. Y ellos corrían a todo lo que daban, según . . . sus pies, ¿verdad? Y a todos les viene. Y todos, después cuando se juntaron, decían: —Pues a mí también me seguía el mismo, y . . . y el mismo. Los seguía a todos y todos iban por diferentes caminos. Sí, digo, pues posiblemente son cosas . . . chistosas, pero que sí pasaron. Eso sí, pasaron, y fue una . . . realidad para ellos, como le digo, entonces. Y cree uno que son ejemplos en verdad que sí pasaban.

> Woods 110. The devil appears where people are carousing.
> Woods 118. Evil spirit appears to drunk.
> (1) G303.6.2.5. Devil appears to persons ready to abandon their integrity.
> (2) G303.3.1.2. The devil as a well-dressed gentleman.
> (3) G303.7.1. Devil rides horse.
> (4) G303.6.3.4. Devil appears in an intense light and with strong odor of sulphur.
> Robe, *WF*, 10(1951), 310–315. [Points out the frequent appearance of the devil in a physical form in the *exempla*.]

14. El diablo en forma de mujer

(Recorded by Juana Esquer on June 2, 1966, in Los Angeles, California)

An uncle of the informant, on his way home from a bar one evening in Alamos, Sonora, caught sight of what appeared to be a beautiful woman walking ahead of him, and he decided to follow her. When he finally caught up with her, she turned to him and revealed very large eyes and teeth; he became terrified, believing he had encountered the devil. The next day he told his mother of the incident, and she replied that it was a good punishment for running after women. The fright served to cure him of the habit.

Esto pasó en la . . . en la suidad de Alamos. Mi tío . . . se fue . . . fue a la cantina, y se echó sus copas. De vuelta, iba una trenzuda delante de él con el pelo suelto (1). Decía: —Hey, espérame. Me gustas, le decía, pues borrachito. —Ándale, espérame. Mira qué trenzuda tan bonita, le decía. Y caminaba mi tío detrás de ella, y aquel pasito de la . . . de la muchacha delante, . . . muy bonita. Y por más que se apuraba no le alcanzaba.

Caminaría como unos cinco blocks . . . cuadras, . . . cuando . . . se

le adelantó, y fue a dar a una casa vieja. —Aquí sí te agarro, dijo él,
pensó. Y él se acercó más a ella a tiempo de . . . de decirle: —¿Me esperas, chiquita? Cuando ella volteó y le peló tamaños ojos (2) y dien-
tes (3), ¿ve? Ya se asustó mi tío. Dice: —¡Ave María Purísima! Yo
creo que esto es malino, dice, —es el diablo.

Otro día en la mañana le platicó a mamá lo que le había sucedido.
—'Tá bueno, le dijo ella. —Por andar de . . . de enamorado. Muy bueno estuvo que te pasó eso. Es el diablo (4). ¡Ave María Purísima!, le
dijo mi mamá.

Pero él ya no volvía . . . a andar en la noche. Se acordaba del diablo
y no más. Es todo.

> Woods 118. Evil spirit appears to drunk.
> (1) G303.3.1.12. Devil in form of woman.
> (2) G303.4.1.2.4. Devil has saucer eyes.
> (3) G303.4.1.5. Devil's teeth. [Here, they are very large.]
> (4) G303.6.2.5. Devil appears to persons ready to abandon their integrity.

15. El jinete sin cabeza

(Recorded by Petra Franco on November 15, 1966, in Los Angeles, California)

The informant tells of a headless horseman who used to ride
through the town of Valle de Guadalupe, Jalisco, accompanied by a
dog giving off sparks. She is convinced that it was the devil and goes
on to attribute his presence to the existence of so much evil in the
town.

[Interviewer: —¿Podría usted contarme lo del hombre sin cabeza,
que andaba a caballo?]

Pues no más que pasaba por el pueblo. Eso se decía. Pasaba por el
pueblo en la noche. Y, y en la madrugada . . . pasaba por allá, por . . .
por la colonia que le digo [San Juan Bosco]. Era soldado. Pasaba . . .
como a las dos de la mañana. Pero no . . . no sin cabeza aquél. Pero ese
del pueblo [Valle de Guadalupe] sí; pero ése es el demonio (1). Muchas . . . fantasmas, no sé cómo le dicen . . . que, que, que veían. Yo
no, como no, a mí no, yo nunca salgo, salía, ni de noche, menos.

[Interviewer: —¿Qué contaban?]

Pos que lo vían sin cabeza (2). Y que . . . que vían también un . . .

un perro . . . un perro echando chispas de lumbre (3). Sí. Pero eso sucede yo digo, pues, porque andan muchos . . . en, . . . ¿cómo le dijiera?
. . . en la maldad en la calle, borrachos, haciendo maldades, ¿verdad?
Pues que muchas veces se llegaban a hallar . . . tambos que tenían . . .
en las, . . . fuera de las tiendas . . . rodadas en otra parte, y cosas que tenían allí . . . los puestos, hasta . . . los desbarataban y todo. Toda la
plebe, ¿verdad?
[Interviewer: —¿El diablo aparece para asustarlos?]

Pues, no. Es que ya de tanta maldad, pues ya también él. . . . A asustarlos, ¿por qué? Si yo creo que los que andan en eso ni se asustan.

(1) G303.7.1. Devil rides horse.
(2) E422.1.1.3.1. Headless ghost rides horse.
(3) G303.3.3.1.1. Devil in form of dog.
    Woods 110. The devil appears where people are carousing.

16. El diablo que cantaba

(Recorded by Elvira Higuera on October 31, 1966, in Los Angeles, California)

The people of Capirato, Sinaloa, used to hear around midnight the
"operatic voice" of a woman coming from the hills, and it was generally believed that this was the devil, for what woman could be going
about at that hour?

Allí platicaban también que en Capirato salía mucho el diablo . . .
en ese tiempo. Que salía, . . . que se oían, se oía cantar por los cerros
una voz como de ópera. Que se oía una voz muy bonita (1), iban a ver
y no, solamente, no, no encontraban nada. Hasta que ocurrió una vez
que era el diablo.
[Interviewer: —¿Por qué pensaban que era el diablo?]
Pues . . . ellos se imaginaban que era el diablo porque nadie podría
andar a esas horas, a las once, a las doce de la noche (2), cantando
aquella voz tan . . . bien que se oía. Y . . . y, ¿quién, qué mujer podría
haber allí? Cantaba en voz de mujer, ¿ve? Y no se podría estar allí. Por
eso descubrieron que era el diablo.

(1) G303.4. Devil's physical characteristics. [Here, he has the voice of a
    woman.]
(2) G303.6.1.1. Devil appears at midnight.

17. El diablo jorobado

(Recorded by Lola Cruz on May 23, 1966, in Los Angeles, California)

As a little girl in Zamora, Michoacán, the informant and a group of friends were playing out of doors one day, when they sang a children's song with which they unwittingly invoked the presence of the devil in the form of a humpback. The girls ran in fright to their mothers, who dismissed the incident as childish play, and so they returned to their games, only to find that the humpback had turned into "a person" with horns and very large ears, who was singing that same song. Once again they ran to their mothers with the story, and the entire neighborhood gathered at the spot. They were told by a woman who had lived there a long time that the "person" they had seen was the devil and that they must not sing that song again.

Pues un día me convidaron las muchachas de la vecindad que saliéramos a jugar . . . al patio. Y luego salíamos a jugar como . . . cosa de unas veinticinco o treinta muchachas. No me acuerdo porque yo era muy chiquita, era muy pequeña. [Interviewer: —¿Dónde pasó esto?] En Zamora. En esa misma suidad.

Pues, luego despuésn mi, mi mamá dijo: —Mucho cuidado. No te vayas a caer.

—Sí.

Pues cuando nos agarramos todas las muchachas a . . . a jugar, cantamos una canción que dice así: [recited]

> En la esquina de un palacio
> Miré un viejo jorobante,
> Que entre la joroba traiba
> Media arroba de picante
> Uijuyjuy, aijaijai.
> La que la abrace me la voy a llevar (1).

> [At the corner of a palace
> I saw an old humpback,
> Who carried in his hump
> Half an arroba* of pepper.
> Uijuyjuy, aijaijai.
> Whoever I grab I'll carry off.]

(*measurement of 25 pounds)

Pos luego despuésn estábamos todas . . . cuando se apareció un jorobado (2, 3). Y luego dijo pos . —Uijuyjuy, aijaijai. A la que abrace
me voy a llevar. Dijo el jorobado. Pos no nos dio mucho miedo, pero
se desbarató . . . toda la rosca, toda la mancorna que teníamos todas
agarradas, y fuimos a nuestras casas, que si nuestras mamases se habían levantado.

Dijo: —No estamos locas para ir a . . . a interrumpir las muchacha-
das.

Pos luego nos volvimos otra vuelta a salir . . . a jugar. Cuando ya no
era el jorobado. Y era . . . otra . . . persona, . . . con cuernos (4),
. . . y unas orejotas grandotas (3). Y empezó también a cantar . . .
la misma canción que estábamos cantando. Y entonces nos, nos ajusta-
mos [i.e., asustamos] y luego corrimos pa las casas. Y luego les dijimos . . . a nuestras mamás. Se juntó toda la vecindad fuera. Y luego
dijimos que . . . un hombre o mujer . . . que no sabíamos, porque no
había luces afuera en la calle. No más la luna.

Pues dijo . . . dijo una señora que vivía de mucho tiempo allí, dice:
—No, muchachas. Es el diablo. Que algún muerto se murió condena-
do. Y es el diablo que anda áhi con ustedes. Y ya no anden cantando,
porque esta canción está prohibida cantarla.

(1) D1275. Magic song.
(2) C12. Devil invoked: appears unexpectedly.
(3) G303.4. Devil's physical characteristics. [Here, the devil is first a hump-
    back and then has very large ears.]
(4) G303.4.1.6.1. Devil has two horns.

18. El diablo en la bodega

(Recorded by Lola Cruz on May 23, 1966, in Los Angeles, California)

When the informant was a young girl living in Mexico City, she
was asked by her mother to do an errand, which she tried to pass off
to her little brother. Her mother became annoyed, insisted that she go,
and uttered a curse to the effect that the devil would be her companion. When the girl arrived at her destination, she was in fact confronted, and then rendered immobile, by the sight of a gigantic man
with huge teeth and eyes, breathing fire from his mouth and holding
flames in his hands. Her little brother was sent to see what was taking

her so long, and he reported back that she was simply sitting motionless. The mother then sent for the priest who revived her by striking her with a switch and who then imposed a penance for disobedience to her mother.

Cuando nos fuimos para la Ciudad de México, que estaba mi mamá joven, . . . se casó ella. . . . Y luego mi mamá, cuando ella tuvo un niño, que se llamaba Carlitos, mi mamá me dijo a mí: —Ándale. . . . Lleva el . . . el boggie a la bodega.

Y yo le dije: —Yo, no. Que vaya José.

Y luego José dijo: —Yo, no. Que vaya Linda.

Entonces mi mamá dijo: —De . . . de modo es de que yo le mando al perro, el perro le manda al gato, y el gato a su compañero. Dice: —Ándale, demonio. Anda allí, me dijo a mí.

—Ándale demonio, y lleva ese boggie a la bodega. Y espera en Dios, que vas a ver el demonio tu compañero (1).

Pues ya me fui, pos, creyendo que no había demonio porque la hermana de ella me dijo que no había diablo. Pos cuando entré a la bodega con el boggie, entonces miré un señor tan grandote . . . desde la tapa de, de, de arriba hasta abajo (2), con una camisa colorada (3), con unas . . . ruedas blancas, un pantalón gris, lumbre en las manos (4), lumbre . . . en la boca, unos dientotes muy grandodototes (5), y luego los ojos muy grandototes (6) y colorados (7). Y yo me quedé mirándolo, mirándolo, mirándolo, y me senté pa acabarlo de mirar. Porque no tenía miedo. Pero luego después . . . quería mover mi, un brazo; no podía. Quería mover un . . . pie; no podía (8). Y allí me quedé sentada.

Cuando luego mi mamá le dijo a José que me fuera, . . . dijo: —Anda, José, a ver a Lola, a ver qué, qué tiene, por qué no viene.

Y luego José fue con mi mamá y le dijo: —No, mamá, está sentada y no se mueve. Ni me oye.

Pues luego mi mamá se levantó, así como había tenido el niño, y luego fue block y medio . . . a la iglesia a traer a . . . al padrecito. Y entonces el padrecito le dijo a mamá que qué tenía yo. Luego mi amá ya le dijo, y entonces el padrecito agarró una vara de membrillo y me pegó con la vara de membrillo hasta que ya . . . quedé, volví en . . . volví en sí [sic], yo pienso (9, 10, 11). Pues luego después el padrecito me dijo que tenía que hincarme en el arroz. En el cemento puso arroz, y que me hincara en el arroz pa que me doliera, y que le pidiera perdón a mi mamá y que otro día le hiciera yo caso. Que no . . . fuera desobediente, que fuera obediente con ella. Pues luego después ya . . . me confesé, y luego ya dijo mi mamá que no . . . que no tenía que desobedecerla cuando ella me decía una cosa. Pues luego ya después ya fui muy . . . muy obediente con ella, pero siempre ella estaba muy, muy dura conmigo. Me regañaba mucho.

Pues . . . la calle donde pasó esta . . . cosa . . . fue en la Ciudad de México en, . . . la calle se llamaba San Felipe Neri, número noventa y cinco. Allí fue donde sucedió esta cosa. Y el padrecito que vino, . . . se llamaba la iglesia . . . la Iglesia de . . . Jesús de Nazareno. Esa iglesita . . . estaba en la calle de San Felipe Neri.

Woods 205. Person curses self or others to the devil: he appears.
(1) C12.5. Devil's name used in curse. Appears.
(2) G303.3.1.1. The devil as a large, strong man.
(3) G303.5.3. The devil dressed in red.
(4) G303.4.8.2.1. Devil holds fire in his hands.
(5) G303.4.1.5. Devil's teeth. [Here, they are very large.]
(6) G303.4.1.2.4. Devil has saucer eyes.
(7) G303.4.1.2.2. Devil with glowing eyes.
Woods 54. Spook causes person to be transfixed on the spot for a certain length of time.
(8) D2070. Magic paralysis. (Person or thing rendered helpless.)
(9) D2176.3.2. Evil spirit exorcised by religious ceremony.
(10) G303.16.14. Devil exorcised.
(11) G303.16.14.1. Priest chases devil away.

The Return of the Dead

Tales of the return of the dead may be discussed in terms of the nature of the appearance and the mission involved (if any). With regard to the nature of the appearance, two very broad categories are easily discernible: the visible and the invisible dead. By also applying the second factor, the nature of the mission involved, a workable classification can be devised: (1) the *ánima*, or soul, which most often does not appear with the physical attributes of a living person and whose mission is generally to obtain the aid of a human being in fulfilling an obligation incurred but not met during the dead person's lifetime; (2)

espíritus, who may be considered rather generalized ghosts, whose role is predominantly antagonistic to humans, and who make their presence known by mysterious noises and annoying acts that may involve minor physical abuse; (3) the living corpse, a deceptively natural-looking apparition who interacts with the living in a perfectly normal way, disappears, generally in a mysterious manner, and is later discovered to have been a dead person; and whose mission is best explained as a vague compulsion to make periodic appearances at specific times or places, such as on an anniversary or at the site of an accident in which he was killed; and (4) the *llorona*, or wailing woman, who may incorporate various characteristics of the above-mentioned types, in her role as a siren, a grieving mother searching for the children she herself killed, or simply a frightful apparition; because of her specific identity, she will be discussed here as a separate type.

Ánimas, nos. 19–23

Of the five narratives presented here, three speak of actually seeing and identifying the *ánima* (19, 22, and 23); one refers to seeing, but not identifying, it enveloped in a cloud of smoke (20); and one makes reference only to touching and hearing it (21).

The nature of the appearance is interesting to observe. *Ánimas* may or may not be visible; in fact, a detectable pattern is that they are not so at the first encounter, but later become so (19 and 20). The important unifying characteristic is the nature of their mission. They are seeking to accomplish something left undone at the time of their death that is preventing them from entering heaven. The characteristic development is that a person becomes aware of being approached or pursued through mysterious phenomena, such as voices calling to him, objects thrown at him, or ghostly lights; the victim is encouraged by others to "talk to the ghost" using the formulaic address [E545.19.2] to determine what it wants and without which it cannot speak to human beings [E545.19.1]; the request is explained; and the person promises to fulfill it, in exchange for which he exhorts the *ánima* not to bother him again.

The formulaic question, "En parte de Dios te pido, ¿eres de este mundo o eres del otro?" is very common in ghost stories in general, and may be seen in Narratives 19, 20, and 21 of this collection as well as in various published collections.[46]

Narratives 19, 20, and 22 involve unfulfilled religious vows (*mandas*) [E451.3]; number 21 relates the repayment of a theft [E352]; and number 23 involves a penance that must be performed to atone for a sin committed during the person's lifetime [E402.0.2.1]. This last narrative differs from the rest in that the *ánima* does not approach a human being to carry out her mission; the nature of the mission in fact precludes this. The mother of the informant telling the story, whose personal experience it was to encounter this *ánima*, does, however, perform essentially the same function as those actually approached in the other narratives: she makes an unsolicited offer to pray for her and carry out the required penitential act, and assures her that God will pardon her.

Narrative 23 is unique in another respect, in that there are not the elements of hostility and fear that were either expressed or implicit in the other narratives. Otherwise, the person approached is generally fearful of the encounter, as is well illustrated by the man who needs to be fortified with tequila before he can face the *ánima* (19), and by the similar need for encouragement and support seen in Narratives 20 and 21. It is the *ánima* herself who says not to be afraid in Narrative 22. Numerous examples are to be found of persons who are rendered either physically or mentally ill [E265.1; E265.2] after such encounters, as is seen in Narrative 19. Seldom does an informant offer any reason for such fear; it is accepted that one fears ghosts and that they are indeed dangerous. It is very compelling to seek some more substantive explanation of this universal reaction to encounters with the dead; and, since it is applicable to all four categories dealt with here, some pertinent concepts will be mentioned in summation of the section, after all material has been presented.

Frequent elements of the *ánima* narrative not yet mentioned include the following: the *ánimas* always appear at the same hour at which they make their first appearances (20); also, they often reveal the location of hidden money that may be used to pay their debts and indicate

---

[46] See, for example, Jovita González, "Folklore of the Texas-Mexican Vaquero," *TFSP*, 6 (1927), 19.

that whatever is left over may be kept by the person who carries out their requests (19 and 20).

Many informants are skeptical about the existence of *ánimas*. While they express rational doubts, at the same time they seem emotionally committed to accepting the possibility that *ánimas* really do exist. The following comment by informant Ismeria Garay is typical of the ambivalent feelings that are often expressed:

Yo no sé. Yo cuando me muera si yo debo una manda y no he ido a pagarla, y cuando muera, si es cierto, voy a venir. Si es cierto. Sí, porque mi madre decía que el que se muere y no paga una manda, que él vuelve.

[I don't know. When I die, if I owe a *manda* and I haven't gone to pay it when I die, if it's true, I'm going to return. If it's true. Yes, because my mother used to say that one who dies and doesn't pay a *manda* will return.]

Espíritus, nos. 24–27

One informant, after relating an episode (the text is not presented here) in which her son was awakened by a mysterious sweeping going on in the house, only to find nobody there, was asked to what she attributed the incident—might it have been an *ánima*? Her reply was as follows:

Pos no, dicen que las ánimas no barren. Yo pienso que más bien es cosa de espíritus malinos. Eso es lo que pienso. Porque una ánima, pos, tiene otras cosas a que venir al mundo, si es que viene.

[Well no, they say that *ánimas* don't sweep. I think it's a question of evil spirits. That's what I think. Because an *ánima*, well, has other reasons for coming to the world, if it does come.]

The reply reveals a rather definite concept of the role of the *ánima* as distinguished from that of an evil spirit. The activities of the *ánima* are quite well delineated, as described in the previous section. Those of the spirit include a broader range. The *ánima* has a well-founded and rather narrowly defined mission to carry out, while the spirit seems to arbitrarily engage in mysterious, annoying, or threatening activities.

The term *espíritu* may sometimes be a type of catch-all term for anything that defies a more specific label; or it may occasionally appear in reference to other supernatural beings, such as the *duende*, or goblin. The four narratives presented here deal with *espíritus* felt to be traceable to human beings, normally referred to in English as ghosts, leaving *duendes* to be treated as a separate category.

The types of activities engaged in, however, quite often coincide. Narrative 26 is a good example of a tendency to see activities normally attributed to *duendes* as equally attributable to *espíritus*. The spirits causing the trouble here are, to the informant, quite clearly traceable to human beings who once lived in the house, experienced there a terrible disaster, and for that reason continue to haunt it [E275]. Among the abuses suffered, however, the dumping of great quantities of salt into the food is generally considered a favorite device of the *duende* [F473]. To top off the great blending of roles in this narrative, which is a phenomenon that accurately reflects the workings of popular tradition, the priest who is called upon to help does not mention either spirits or *duendes*, but flees from what he feels to be the presence of the devil.[47]

Narrative 24 might have been included in the previous section, as the informant does refer to *ánimas*. The nature of the incident, however, is closer to that of the ghost story, since it is without the element of the *manda*. The essence of the story is the hostility of the ghosts toward the human being who has intruded into their affairs and the manner in which the ghosts retaliate [E242]. They are not at all seeking the aid of a human being.

Narratives 25 and 27 (together with 26 as already discussed) represent the traditional haunted house type of story [E281]. The very amusing detail of being carried out of the house at night to awaken in the yard in the morning [E279.2], as described in 26 and 27, is quite frequent and is also often attributed to *duendes*.

Once again there is the fear of the power of the dead, as has been indicated with regard to the *ánima*. Methods of thwarting that power are presented in Narrative 24, in which a three-month-old child is used for protection against the ghosts (similar to G303.16.19.6), and in number 26, in which a priest is called upon to exert his influence, in

---

[47] See fn. 29.

the hope of exorcising the evil spirits. Both, however, ultimately fail. Encounters with evil spirits, just as with *ánimas,* may cause permanent illness or even death [E265.1; E265.2]. The girl who witnessed the activities of the ghosts (24) fell ill and died soon thereafter [E266].

It is interesting to note the frequency of the conviction described above, that death is directly relatable to such encounters. It has been mentioned, for example, that encounters with *ánimas* often leave one "never quite the same." Narrative 24 states that it was the specific intention of the *ánimas* to "carry off" the intruder. Even when this is not their intention, death may nonetheless result, as seen in Narrative 25, in which the victim of a frightful experience is seen to have almost literally "died of fright." In a narrative not presented here, the informant tells of an uncle's encounter with a skeleton and affirms, "y de eso fue su muerte que él tuvo. De ese susto." [And that was what caused his death. That fright.] This readiness to see death as caused by an encounter with the dead is related to the previously mentioned idea of the great fear the dead inspire. It is an extension of the belief in their power to inflict evil and an outgrowth of the conviction that they are innately hostile beings.

The Living Corpse, nos. 28–33

The living corpse differs from the two previous types, the *ánima* and the *espíritu,* in that, as the term indicates, it has the attributes of a living person. It "masquerades" as such, and it is only after a seemingly normal encounter or experience with it that one discovers its true ghostly nature.

Of the six narratives presented here, four (28–31) are of the vanishing-hitchhiker type [E332.3.3.1], one (32) relates a slightly different mysterious vanishing [E425.1.1], and one (33) tells of a headless horseman [E422.1.1.3.1]. The last tale does not fit perfectly into the above description, since the mysterious quality is immediately apparent; but the informant does see, hear, and identify the horseman, thus imparting a flesh-and-blood quality to him.

Narratives 28 and 29, about the girl in the dance hall, seem to refer to the same incident, as both informants named a Los Angeles newspaper article as the original source of the story. There is another documented instance of this type of material finding its way into the news, in a group of four published versions from Dallas, Texas. One of the informants states that "the legend is about three or four years old and has been discussed in Dallas papers and on the radio."[48]

Two other versions of this same type of incident, said by informants to have taken place in Los Angeles, are included among a collection of narratives published in the *California Folklore Quarterly* in 1942,[49] and in a collection of folk narratives from Arizona published in 1949.[50] In narrative 33 of the first collection, the informant relates an incident nearly identical to Narrative 28, likewise naming a Los Angeles newspaper article of approximately the same date as the source of his story. The Arizona version makes no mention of a newspaper story, but does place the incident in Los Angeles, California.

Narrative 30, a story said by the informant to have appeared in the same newspaper, is another of the vanishing-hitchhiker type; a unique element is the involvement of a cab driver. This detail makes possible the accretion of a theme not ordinarily associated with the vanishing-hitchhiker story. The cab driver, as a result of having accepted, and subsequently spent, the money of a dead woman, slowly wastes away and dies. Such a development, although apparently infrequent, is very much within the spirit of the story. Along with the incorporation of the already mentioned distaste for encounters with the dead, the popular acceptance of a forbidden quality about their possessions or their money advances the story a step further and makes it more esthetically complete than the usual vanishing-hitchhiker narrative. Such manipulation of popular elements, with an eye to completeness, is typical of this informant, who is one of the two best storytellers represented here.

Narrative 31 constitutes a rather standard type of vanishing-hitchhiker story: the sisters make repeated appearances to motorists at the exact location of an accident in which they were killed three years

---

[48] George Hendricks, "Four Southwestern Legends," *WF*, 27 (1968), 260.
[49] Rosalie Hankey, "California Ghosts," *CFQ*, 1(1942), 155–177.
[50] *Folktales from the Patagonia Area, Santa Cruz County, Arizona.* Collected by Patagonia Union High School, p. 23.

earlier. The pattern of threes (the motorists, the sisters, and the time period) seems to be a rather consciously symbolic device which enhances the quality of mystery in the story.

Narrative 32 has the very common detail of the mysterious, attractive girl at the dance hall. The narrative could be seen as a shortened, less fully developed version of essentially the same type of incident that occurs in Narratives 28 and 29. Once again the intense fear of ghostly encounters plays an important role in the narrative, for, as the informant relates, the public's reaction to the news of the incident was sufficiently strong to bring about the closing of the dance hall for lack of business.

Narrative 33 is an example of a rather common phenomenon in folk tradition, the headless horseman who appears at midnight. The informant relates that the consensus of opinion identified him as the former mail carrier riding his familiar route.

In summing up, the vanishing hitchhiker is a frequent and widely documented theme. It has even found its way into a popular song called "Strange Things Happen," the lyrics of which closely parallel the story told in Narratives 28 and 29:

> Last night at the dance I met Laurie,
> So lovely and warm, an angel of a girl.
> Last night I fell in love with Laurie.
> Strange things happen in this world.
>
> As I walked her home, she said it was her birthday.
> I pulled her close and said, "Will I see you any more?"
> Then suddenly she asked for my sweater
> And said that she was very, very cold.
>
> I kissed her good night at her door and started home,
> Then thought about my sweater and went right back instead.
> I knocked at her door, and a man appeared.
> I told him why I'd come. Then he said:
>
> "You're wrong son. You weren't with my daughter.
> How can you be so cruel to come to me this way?
> My darling left this world on her birthday.
> She died a year ago today."
>
> A strange force drew me to the graveyard.
> I stood in the dark. I saw the shadows wave,

> And then I looked and saw my sweater
> Lying there upon her grave.
>
> Strange things happen in this world.
>
> ("Strange Things Happen." Recorded by Dixie Lee. A Twentieth-
> Century Fox record: TCF 102–ZTSP 91656.)

La Llorona, nos. 34–42

Just under fifty years ago a writer of some prominence in Mexico expressed, with considerable satisfaction, the following conviction about the decline of belief in the *llorona* tradition: "La vieja tradición de La Llorona ha ido borrándose del recuerdo popular. Sólo queda memoria de ella en los fastos mitológicos de los aztecas, en las páginas de antiguas crónicas, en los pueblecillos lejanos o en los labios de las viejas abuelitas, que intentan asustar a sus inocentes nietezuelos, diciéndoles: —¡Ahí viene La Llorona! Pero La Llorona se va, porque los niños de hoy no se espantan con los fantasmas del pasado."[51] The *llorona* is not the forgotten figure suggested by González Obregón. Legendary material about her continues to be collected and reported. Among the informants contacted for this study it was unusual to find one who did not have either an explanation for the *llorona's* appearance or an anecdote about an encounter with her, either personal or otherwise. One such encounter, on the part of an informant's daughter, had taken place only one week prior to the interview.

Two published studies of *llorona* material taken from oral tradition have offered a classification of *llorona* types. Based on a study of forty-two narratives collected in Arizona, Betty Leddy suggests three general types: "the siren, the grieving woman, and the woman dangerous to children."[52] In a study of forty-eight versions from Mexico, Fernando Horcasitas Pimentel distinguishes the following three types: the woman condemned by God for killing her children; Malinche, the mistress and interpreter of Cortés; and the Matlacihuatl, seducer of men.[53] While the latter study does not propose a separate category

---

[51] Luis González Obregón, *Las calles de México*, p. 40.
[52] Betty Leddy, "La llorona in Southern Arizona," *WF*, 7 (1948), 277.
[53] Fernando Horcasitas Pimentel, "Textos modernos de 'La llorona,'" *Mesoamerican Notes*, 1950, no. 1, p. 34.

of "the woman dangerous to children," that role is nevertheless represented in one of the versions (see number 23). And, although the activity of Malinche is not specifically indicated in the Leddy classification, Narrative 6 casts her in the role of the grieving mother.

Another writer, however, portrays La Malinche as the siren, or seducer of men:

Legend has it that in a woodland that surrounds a very ancient church in
the village of Atzcapotzalco, about five miles from the city of Mexico,
where once stood the slave market of the early Chichimecas, there the restless spirit of Malinche, or Marina, still wanders along the stream which
flows through the forest of gigantic ahuehuete trees. Her remorse for her
betrayal of her land through her interpretations for Cortez and because she
loved this man not of her own race will not permit her to rest. Thus, to be
revenged, she walks at night midst the great trees beside the silvery stream,
using her wiles to lure men to destruction.[54]

Although traces of certain historical (i.e., Malinche) or mythological
(i.e., Matlacihuatl) personages can be readily detected in the *llorona*
material, the type of activity described is of greater value in classification than is a name, at least as far as the collection of oral material is
concerned. In other words, the informant does not necessarily distin-
guish consistently the different roles in conjunction with the three
names suggested.

The question of the ultimate origin of the *llorona* has not been satis-
factorily established. While she is felt by some to be of indigenous
origin, others see European connections. There are historical accounts
of a similar figure, which lend support to the former theory, in such
documents as the sixteenth-century manuscript *Histoire du Mechique*
and *Huaxtepec y sus reliquias arqueológicas.*[55] In an article entitled
"La Llorona," Virginia R. R. de Mendoza gives a survey of material
in Fray Bernardino Sahagún's *Historia general de las cosas de Nueva
España* (sixteenth century) that could be of significance to the *llorona*

---

[54] Bernice Goodspeed, *Mexican Tales*, pp. 202–203.
[55] *Histoire de Mechique*, Ms. del Siglo XVI citado por Ángel Ma. Garibay en
Épica Náhuatl, U.N.A. México, D.F., 1945; and *Huaxtepec y sus reliquias arqueológicas*, Enrique Juan Palacios, México, 1930. "Descripción de Guastepeque por el Al-
calde Mayor Juan Gutiérrez de Lievana, 24 de Diciembre de 1580."

legend.[56] More recent scholarship on the subject has been done by Bacil F. Kirtley and Robert A. Barakat, who have presented evidence, respectively, in support of the European versus the Aztec origins of the *llorona*.[57]

The nine *llorona* narratives presented here include references to the previously mentioned types: the siren (34), the grieving woman (35–42), and the woman dangerous to children (41). Only one, however, refers to the specific name of Malinche (37). Narrative 34 tells of the Xtabay, who is a siren and the counterpart of the Matlacihuatl. Narrative 37 illustrates the use of the name Malinche entirely out of the context of the relationship with Cortés and, in fact, places the incident in Spain. It has none of the element of the siren, as in the previous quotation from Goodspeed, but follows the more frequent pattern of the grieving woman, identifying her as one of three such women. Narrative 35 gives the name María la llorona, and numbers 37 and 38 speak of La Infeliz María. The rest do not name her any more specifically than *la llorona*.

To describe further the types of *llorona* narratives to be found in oral tradition, two basic approaches on the part of the informant may be indicated. The informant may provide an explanation of the *llorona's* history, or he may simply relate an encounter. Bacil Kirtley makes the following observation about this distinction in the two approaches: "The form of the Llorona legend which is primarily a biographical narration and which constitutes a relatively fixed type appears to have a history separate from the form which is fundamentally a documentation by individuals of their personal brushes with a phantom-species, and which, since it is fantasy prompted by tradition, is no more stable than the storyteller's imagination."[58]

I have found that the more readily acquired commentaries have to do with encounters rather than with biographical information about the *llorona*, and that the latter must often be specifically solicited from

<hr>

[56] Virginia R. R. Mendoza, "La Llorona," *Previsión y seguridad*, 14(1950), 225–228, 230, 232, 234.

[57] Kirtley, 155–168; and Robert A. Barakat, "Aztec Motifs in 'La Llorona,'" *SFQ*, 39 (1965), 228–296.

[58] Kirtley, p. 156.

the informant. Even when it is brought in, it seems to be a rare individual who can offer any information beyond the fact that the *llorona* was a woman who drowned (or killed) her children and was subsequently condemned by God to wander in search of them [Q211.4; Q503]. The rather detailed history presented in Narrative 37, and, to a lesser degree, the detail of the actual drowning site of each of the three children, as seen in Narrative 40, represent exceptions.

In those narratives which are not biographical in nature but which refer to encounters, Kirtley says the *llorona* represents an "image of supernatural danger."[59] Certainly, in relating encounters with her, fear is usually the dominant tone. It may be an undefined momentary fear, or a fear of dire consequences. For example, if one turns to look at La Infeliz María (37), who has the head of a horse, one's neck will stick in that position [C311.1.1]; an encounter can cause a serious fright (40) [E265.1], or it may work some mysterious incapacitating influence on the victim (42). The element of evil associated with such encounters substantiates the belief in the malicious intent of the dead.

An interesting detail occurs in Narrative 37, in which the second *llorona* type makes a pact with "un señor," subsequently referred to as "el espíritu malo," and agrees to kill her children in exchange for great beauty. She is "rewarded" with the face of a horse [Q233]. I have not found a similar detail of a pact with the devil in published *llorona* material, but, aside from the question of documenting such a motif, it does serve as a very nice example of the inclination to fill in what might seem to be gaps in the "logical" dramatic development. The natural desire to construct a meaningful interpretation of material can draw on a large body of folk themes to achieve it. In this narrative, a didactic theme of punishment for having succumbed to the temptation of the devil [Q233] in the interest of vanity functions as an explanation of the horse's face of La Infeliz María.

Reference has already been made to two very brief narratives that are essentially identical in structure and intent and that are climaxed by the appearance of the devil and the *llorona*, respectively. These two

---

[59] Ibid.

narratives illustrate the potential similarity of didactic function (in this case, admonishing drunken men) that both the devil and the *llorona* may be invested with by popular tradition.[60]

Of the nine narratives presented here, only one (40) gives a strictly historical explanation of the *llorona*; three (36, 39, and 42) relate encounters; and four (35, 37, 38, and 41) combine the two approaches. Narrative 42 simply explains the type of activity attributed to the Xtabay and is included mainly to serve as an example of a *llorona* type in the role of the siren.

The *llorona*, then, may be a siren, endlessly seeking to avenge her experience with an unfaithful lover; a grieving mother wandering about in search of the children she herself murdered (and it is generally in this context that she is seen as dangerous to children, as is specifically brought out in Narrative 41);[61] or a terror-inspiring apparition, potentially dangerous to all, not only to children, and essentially fused in function with other frightful or evil phenomena. In the latter role the details of her personal history or origin may be of little relevance.

An interesting detail brought out in Narrative 35, which I have not found expressed in published *llorona* material, is the assertion that only those having sufficient strength of mind and spirit are able to see and hear her and withstand the confrontation. This detail, if seen within the context of the *llorona*'s role as a frightful and potentially dangerous apparition, gives further support to fusing the role of the *llorona* with that of other evil apparitions. Special strength is needed to resist the devil, and special protection is often needed against ghosts.

Another detail of interest for its apparently inappropriate prosaic quality occurs in Narrative 40. Into a legend dominated by spectacular murders by stabbing or by drowning in a river or (more frequently) the sea, the informant injects a site that must be described as out of character—the toilet. The choice does not seem to be explainable

---

[60] The *llorona* also appears to drunks in Horcasitas Pimentel's collection of narratives, no. 47.

[61] The theme of danger to children is especially well developed in a story called "The Wailing Mother" in Calvin Claudel, "Tales from San Diego, *CFQ*, 2 (1943), 118. Here she is actually condemned by God to go about killing six-year-old children.

simply as an attempt to fill a memory gap, since it is the first of three sites mentioned by the informant and not a third choice resorted to after an obvious pause. Perhaps this narrative can be singled out as a good example of the modifications material may undergo as a result of the informant's attitude toward it. The *llorona* described here is a woman who killed her children in order to be able to pursue her own "sinful life" ["vida libre"]. She is not the tragic figure of the abandoned woman who commits a crime of passion, which somehow always inspires less repugnance. Her crime in this case is less dictated by emotion and, therefore, seems less "justified." As related by the informant, it is sordid, and the reference to the *excusado*, be it a faithful reporting of detail as heard or a spontaneous association of the moment, matches the mood. In fact, the choice has a quality suggestive of abortion and could have been originally introduced in response to that association on the part of the informant.[62]

The return of the dead and the expression of attitudes and ideas about the dead are certainly among the types of information most readily acquired from informants. Within the category of legendary material, which I have found more easily obtainable than traditional tales, references to the four types of narratives discussed here (*ánimas*, *espíritus*, the living corpse, and the *llorona*) are predictably very frequent. The basic and universal appeal they possess is not difficult to understand in view of man's essential preoccupation with death.

Preoccupation with death and fear of dying seem to be motivating forces in the propagation of this type of narrative. This fear of death, one of the constants in the twenty-four narratives presented here, becomes translated into a fear of the dead. In those stories dealing with encounters, the tension, the essential tone, of the narrative is the informant's endeavor to convey the fright of the experience. Such fear must rest not only on a belief in the power of the dead to inflict evil, but also on a conviction of their natural inclination to do so, their invariable hostility.

An excellent insight into this question may be gained from a reading of the section entitled "The Taboo upon the Dead" in Freud's

---

[62] An account of a *llorona* who did abort her unwanted children may be seen in Virginia R. R. de Mendoza, "La Llorona," p. 230.

Totem and Taboo.[63] Having pointed out the normal ambivalence of emotions in human beings, Freud illustrates how it is a "process of projection which turns a dead man into a malignant enemy."[64] It is not possible here to detail the development of this concept. Very broadly outlined, however, the conclusion arrived at is as follows: given the ambivalence of emotions attendant on any relationship, one tends to become very uncomfortably and painfully aware of hostility upon the occasion of the death of another, "in the form of satisfaction over the death." A psychic device for relieving this discomfort is to place the hostility upon the dead person himself, accomplished by a process of projection, as stated above. Freud concludes: "The survivor thus denies that he has ever harboured any hostile feelings against the dead loved one; the soul of the dead harbours them instead and seeks to put them into action."[65]

This insight adds a dimension to the narratives presented here and may fill a gap in the understanding of one of their most salient features, the fear of the return of the dead. It may also help to identify certain significant patterns of detail; for as Freud continues: "The taboo upon the dead arises . . . from the contrast between conscious pain and unconscious satisfaction over the death that has occurred. Since such is the origin of the ghost's resentment, it follows naturally that the survivors who have the most to fear will be those who were formerly its nearest and dearest."[66]

It is in the *ánima* narratives that the elements of threat and personal danger are most clearly expressed by the informants. One might think that the fear of *espíritus* would be greater, since, as is pointed out in the classification suggested at the beginning of this section, *ánimas* do not generally engage in physical abuse of human beings, while *espíritus* do. However, it seems clear from the tone of the informant's stories that the most upsetting and psychologically painful encounters are those with *ánimas*. The degree of personal involvement is greater with the *ánima*. The encounter threatens an all-enveloping influence,

<hr>

[63] Sigmund Freud, *Totem and Taboo,* in *The Standard Edition of the Complete Psychological Works of Sigmund Freud,* XIII (1913–1914), 1–161.

[64] Ibid., p. 63.

[65] Ibid., p. 61.

[66] Ibid.

to which its victims invariably respond with a plea to the *ánima* not to return.

In view of the intense fear inspired by the *ánima*, it may be significant that the soul is most frequently that of a relative or of a person with whom one had lived in close contact. It is not illogical that the *ánima* would approach a member of his own family with the request to carry out his wish; this assumption need not detract from the applicability of Freud's psychological observation. Furthermore, an understanding can be gained of the frequency with which the *ánima* is a mother or mother figure, since human experience teaches that the mother tends to be the object of the most intense ambivalent emotions. The *ánimas* in Narratives 19, 22, and 23 are, respectively, a grandmother, a mother-in-law, and a housekeeper, the latter's role being a type of mother substitute to an orphaned girl.

Insight may also be gained into another recurrent element that has been pointed out in the narratives presented or referred to here, the readily accepted idea that contact with a spirit can cause permanent illness or death and that people actually die of fright. (See Narratives 20, 25, and 30.) Conversely, this belief can be seen as an inclination to view death as always inflicted. As Freud suggests, "in the view of unconscious thinking, a man who has died a natural death is a murdered man; evil wishes have killed him."[67] This natural inclination finds a ready-made culprit in the dead and in evil spirits. Once the hostility has been attributed to the dead, it is but one step further to affix on them the ultimate responsibility for a death.

19. El ánima y la manda

(Recorded by Amalia Hernández on May 16, 1966,
in Los Angeles, California)

A man named Pedro Orozco from the rancho Los Guapos, Zacatecas, was passing by the cemetery on his way home one evening when he thought he saw someone motioning to him. Upon looking more closely that evening and the following one also, he saw nobody, although he

[67] Ibid., p. 62.

heard his name being called as he walked along. When he arrived home he fell unconscious, but he was soon revived by a group of friends who urged him to talk to the ghost and ask what it wanted. He refused. The next day the ghost appeared to him and he recognized it as his grandmother, but he refused to talk to her. His friends finally persuaded him one evening to address her with the formulaic question, "Are you of this world or of the other?" but once again he fell unconscious and was unable to hear the answer. The next evening the ghost appeared at the same hour, as is customary, and the man, having been fortified with tequila by his friends, asked what she wanted. He was told that he should go and find some money that she had hidden in her house, pay what she had promised to the church, pray for her, and then keep the remainder of the money. He agreed to do this and exhorted her not to bother him again.

Éste, éste pasó allí en el rancho de Los Guapos. Éste, era un señor que iba pasando cerca del panteón. Y él miraba que alguien le hacía señas. Y él volteó, y él creía que alguien estaba allí en el panteón, y no vio nada. Y otro día se fue a la casa. Esto era en la noche.

Y otro día volvió de vuelta a pasar por allí, a ver si otra vez le volvían a hacer señas. Y le volvió a salir otra vez, que él no más vía que le hacían señas, pero no vía nadien adentro del panteón. Entonces él, pues, ya le entró miedito, ¿ve?, que le hacían señas. Entonces fue a la casa. Y llegando a la casa, como ya estaba ya oscureciendo, dizque . . . tenían luz prendida. Y él . . . cayó. Que ya empezando a ir las gentes, que qué tenía, que qué tenía.

Ya le devolvieron en sí con alcohol y todo así, y ya les dijo él que . . . que andaba esa ánima. Porque eso era ánima. Y que él, . . . porque él oía que cuando iba caminando le decía: —Pedro, párate. Pedro, párate (1).

Y entonces él les dijo que él ya no quiso más. Y que luego le . . . dijieron esas gentes que por favor, que si era alguna ánima, pues, que a lo mejor era de su casa, que le hablara. Que hiciera la lucha de hablar.

Dijo: —No, dijo. —Yo no quiero verla, dice. —Yo no quiero nada.

Pero dizque . . . dizque el otro día entonces que la vía sentada allí, que dijo: —Ay, no, dijo. —Ella es conocida, dijo. —Es mi abuelita (2). Dizque, . . . y que él, que no quería verla. Que le decía que se fuera, que él no quería hablar con ella. Pero, ella ensistió y ensistió en hablarle.

Entonces una noche que todos, . . . porque tiene mucha gente allí, . . . le rodearon todos, y a animarlo que le hablara. Entonces lo pararon entre todos y le dijieron que por favor que le hablara a esa ánima, que no anduviera penando ya (3).

Entonces él, pues, lo que quiso es, es decirle que, . . . pues, que le dijo: —¿Eres de este mundo o eres del otro?, dice (4). Y se desmayó. Y no alcanzó a oir nada de lo que le dijo el ánima, sino que se desmayó.

Entonces otro día, . . . porque todavía a las mismas horas viene. Cada, cada, . . . en la misma hora que llegan un día, llegan otro día. Y que otra día, otra vez que estaba la gente allí animándolo, dándole tequila pa que agarrara el ánimo, ¿ve? Y entonces que ya lo tenían ya poco, un poquito entrado en tequila, . . . lo traían a él agarrado pa que le hablara al ánima. Entonces ya él le habló al ánima.

Entonces el ánima le contestó que, dijo:—No te asustes, dijo. —Yo soy tu abuelita, dijo. Dijo: —Lo que yo quiero es . . . a mí me, dice, —Dios no me deja entrar allá, dice, —porque yo tengo que tener, dice, —que tú me pagues una manda que debo. Dice: —Págame esa manda, dice, —en . . . tú vas a Tenostián. Dice: —Me pagas esa manda, dice, —y unos centavitos que tengo yo allí en la casa de Julano, en la casa donde ella vivía, dice, —pagas la manda, dice, —me rezas unos rosarios, dice, —y, es todo, dice. —Y lo que sobra, dice, —te quedas tú con ello. (5).

Y así lo hizo él, ¿eh? Entonces ya . . . pagó él. Le dijo que sí, que estaba bien, que él . . . se comprometía él a pagarle su manda. Dijo él, dijo: —Pero otra día ya no vuelvas, dijo, —más. Dijo: —No me vuelas [i.e., vuelvas] a molestar. . . . Eso es todo (6).

(1) E401. Voice of dead heard from graveyard.
(2) E421.1.1. Ghost visible to one person alone.
(3) E545.19.1. The dead cannot speak until spoken to.
(4) E545.19.2. Proper means of addressing ghosts.
(5) E351. Dead returns to repay money debt.
(6) E451.3. Ghost laid when vow is fulfilled.
   Qvigstad, no. 8, p. 40. Spook in church or graveyards; no. 11, p. 40. The dead go about and haunt.

20. El ánima y la señorita que se enfermó

(Recorded by Elisa Contreras on May 17, 1966,
in Los Angeles, California)

In 1964 a young woman named Chona Contreras from the rancho Los Guapos, Zacatecas, was being pursued by some sort of spirit. First it threw wet stones at her, and then it appeared to her as a wandering soul, as if enveloped in a cloud of smoke. It requested that she go and dig up some money that was buried at the nearby rancho Contreras, use it to fulfill a promise the *ánima* had made to the Santo Niño de Plateros [Holy Child of Plateros in Fresnillo, Zacatecas], and keep the remainder for herself. The woman invited a friend to accompany her, but the money that they were to uncover turned to charcoal, possibly, as the informant suggests, because of the unsolicited presence of the friend. She wasn't able to pay the debt to the Santo Niño, and so the ghost reappeared, this time revealing a very ugly face, and urged her once again to go and dig up the money, as it was meant for her. The woman's fear was too great, for she was never able to do so and was rendered permanently ill by the frightening experience. The money remains buried there.

Sabe que ésta . . . es una señorita. Tiene veintiún años de edad. Esto pasó en el rancho de Los Guapos, el año de mil novecientos . . . sesenta y cuatro. Esta muchacha, estaba ella en una casa con una cuñada. Sucede que allí le aventaban piedritas mojadas, que, que ella no sabía pues de ónde llegaran, porque no había medios de que alquien le aventara piedras (1). Entonces ellas se agarraron miedo y salieron de esa casa, y se fue con su papá. Allá apagaron la luz, porque a ella no le creyeron que, que pudiera . . . perseguirla algún asombro. Y apagaron ellos la luz y acostaron todos.

Entonces cuando ella se acostó allí, en junta con ellos porque tenía miedo, entonces miró como una, una . . . luz, como un humo que entró por la puerta (2). Entonces ella, pues, no creía que fuera . . . el asombro que se entrara allí. Ella siempre tenía sus ojos abiertos, cuando fue mirando que era una ánima. Y entonces ella le habló al papá luego luego, y le dijo que, que . . . allí estaba. Y nadien la miraba, hasta que luego luego que ella no más le decía: —Ahí está, ahí está. Ahí viene. Se me quiere arrimar (3, 4).

Entonces el papá le, la agarraron entre el papá y la mamá, y le dijeron: —Háblale, háblale, y dile que si es de este mundo o es del otro (5).

Y entonces ella se desmayó la primer vez. Y le dijo ella, no mas le decía: —Quilila quilota.

Pero luego después, al siguiente día la, la animaron. La volvieron a animar que si volvía el ánima a la misma hora estaban listos. Y que si volvía, que le dijiera ella si era de esta vida o era de la otra, y que le dijiera por qué andaba penando.

Entonces ella se agarró ánimo y le dijo . . . que si era de esta vida o era de la otra, y que le dijiera qué es lo que quería, porque ella se asustaba mucho y no quería que más volviera. Entonces él le dijo que quería que le pagara una manda al Santo Niño de Plateros, . . . que está en Fresnillo, Zacatecas (6). Y entonces el dinero que sobrara de la relación que le dejaba, que lo . . . era para ella. La relación estaba enterrada en el rancho de Contreras (7). Estaba en un cementerio, que es en una iglesia vieja, que estaba en el rancho de Contreras.

Y ésta invitó a un amigo, que fueran a sacar esa relación cuando, pues se, . . . no encontraron nada. Quizá que él tuvo envidia a la persona que llevaba ella, y se volvió carbón (8). No sacaron nada.

Entonces ella no fue a pagarle la manda. Y después, como no cumplió bien ella, volvió. Volvió el ánima otra vez. Y ella miraba bien que, que entró otra vez como un humo, y que era adentro ánima. Entonces le, ella vio que su, . . . pues era un rostro, pues feo, y era todo blanco pero menos la cara. Entonces ella vía que una mano de su pecho la levantaba pa hacerle la seña para un lado y para otro.

Él le decía: —Allí está la relación enterrada. Tú puedes irla a sacar. Encima tiene ropa, abajo esa . . . la relación. Tú no temas. Tú, anda, sácala. Es para ti.

Pero ella nunca pudo irla a sacar, porque ella todo el tiempo temía. Y ella está enferma hasta la fecha, todavía. 'Tá, . . . 'tá ella enferma de lo mismo (9, 10). Pero la relación allí quedó enterrada. Esto pasó en el rancho de Contreras, el año mil novecientos sesenta y cuatro. . . . Su nombre es Chona Contreras.

Qvigstad, no. 11, p. 40. The dead go about and haunt.
(1) F473.1. Poltergeist throws objects.

(2) E421.3. Luminous ghosts.
(3) E421.1.1. Ghost visible to one person alone.
(4) E545.19.1. The dead cannot speak until spoken to.
(5) E545.19.2. Proper means of addressing ghosts.
(6) E351. Dead returns to repay money debt.
(7) E371. Return from dead to reveal hidden treasures.
(8) N558. Raised treasure turns into charcoal (shavings).
(9) E265.1. Meeting ghost causes sickness.
(10) E265.2. Meeting ghost causes madness.
   Folktales from the Patagonia Area, p. 18. [Treasure turns to ashes.]
   Sonnichsen, *TFSP*, 13(1937), 122. [Treasure turns to coal when dug
   up.]

21. El ánima y los frijoles

(Recorded by Luis Cruz on May 19, 1966, in Los Angeles, California)

When the informant was a young boy he worked at farming on the
rancho del Saltillo near Guadalajara, Jalisco. One of his fellow workers
was a very poor man who needed food for his family, and the informant, in his sympathy for the man, helped him cover up the theft of
three fistfuls of beans from the farm. The man died that very same
night. The next night the boy was awakened by noises and the sensa-
tion that he was being pursued by someone in the room, but his parents
dismissed it as a dream. When his fear persisted, they became convinced it was something "from the other world," and they instructed
him to talk to the ghost and ask what it wanted. It turned out to be the
co-worker who had died with the theft of the beans on his conscience
and who wanted the boy to make amends for him and repay the debt in
order that he might be admitted to heaven. The boy agreed to do so and
exhorted him not to bother him again. The townspeople, when told of
the incident, did not believe it.

Pues sabe que, que este señor . . . era un señor muy pobrecito. Y
tenía su familia. Y no tenían qué comer porque su sueldo que le paga-
ban a él no le alcanzaba. Yo era sembrador de él. Y entonces, pues sabe
que . . . cuando nos llevaban el almuerzo, . . . andábamos como siete
yuntas, . . . y luego entonces, pues sabe que el señor . . . le daba vergüenza sentarse con todos nosotros allí a, a almorzar, como nos sentá-
bamos hechos rueda y los almuerzos de todos en medio de, de nosotros.
Pues, entonces el señor . . . le daba vergüenza traer su tortillita y hacer
su taquito de sal, porque no tenía qué . . . revolverle a la tortilla. En-

tonces . . . los demás hombres jueron y lo tomaron de la mano y lo trajieron y lo arrimaron allí a que comiera con todos nosotros. Tonces ya
empezó a comer el señor, muy avergonzado.

Pero en seguida pues . . . él . . . comió, y luego en la tarde me dijo él
que si . . . tomaba tres puños de frijol, que si no iba yo a decirle al patrón. Y entonces le dije yo que no, que tomara . . . el que . . . el que
quisiera. Entonces dijo . . . dijo el señor que le daba miedo. Tonces
le dije yo que no le diera miedo, que . . . tomara el frijol y, y desten-
diera su cobija y lo echara en la cobija y . . . lo envolviera en la cobija y
se lo pusiera debajo del brazo. Entonces como iban a, a soltar las . . .
yuntas de . . . de bueyes a la hacienda, entonces él iba atemorizado.
Porque él no . . . pos le daba miedo. Y entonces le dije yo que no le
diera miedo, que dejara su cobijita allí onde soltara sus . . . su yunta, y
entonces lo . . . levantara su cobija y se llevara, se llevara su frijolito.

Pues entonces ya . . . ya se jue para su casa. Y . . . ese día en la noche, pues, murió. Y entonces . . . otro día empezamos a . . . empezaron
a decir que, que no, que qué pasaría con Miguel, que todavía no venía.

Y entonces le dijieron, le dijieron a otro señor: —Anda, tú, a ver
qué . . . a ver qué pasa con Miguel.

Entonces el señor fue . . . y halló a la señora llorando . . . porque se
había muerto el señor. Había amanecido muerto. Entonces el señor que
jue a buscar a Miguel, entonces le dijo qué pasaba con Miguel. Entonces la señora le dijo que se había, que había amanecido muerto.

El señor le dijo: —Pues, ¿qué, qué, le pegó dolor, o qué, o qué tenía
o . . . estaba enfermo o qué?

—No, dice. —Se acostó a dormir y, y amaneció muerto.

Pues entonces ya el señor regresó a la hacienda y les dijo que Miguel
había amanecido muerto. Entonces . . . ya . . . al, al siguiente día, lo
sepultaron.

Y entonces . . . no, . . . como nosotros vivíamos allí junto a él, la
misma pader de la, de la finca, de la casa de él servía para la casa de
nosotros. Tonces mi apá y mi amá dormían en el cuarto de enfrente.
No había más que una . . . más que una puerta . . . para, para entrar.
Que en el cuarto de enfrente dormían mi apá y mi amá, y en el, en seguida del cuarto . . . que seguía, dormían mis hermanos, y en el otro
que seguía dormía yo.

Entonces en la noche, . . . ya como a las doce de la noche, . . . oyí pasos. Y mi apá tenía unas botellas de, de aguardiente colgadas en la pader. Y entonces oyí ruido en las botellas. Y como yo tenía mi cama despegada de la pader, donde cabía una persona, pues . . . oyí el ruido en las botellas, y estiré yo la mano . . . y le agarré las piernas. Como . . . él usaba los calzones . . . que traiba, la ropa que traiba . . . la usaba arriscada, porque . . . tenía su ropita . . . rompida. Pues, de modo es que le agarré el muslo, y se lo agarré frío, frío, frío (1). . . . Y entonces empecé yo a, a llorar, . . . asustado.

Y me dijo mi apá, me dice. —¿Qué tienes, qué tienes? Duérmete. Estás soñando.

—No, anda alguien aquí.

—Pero, ¿quién anda, hombre?, dice. —¿Por qué, por qué te asustas?, dice. —Yo creo que estás soñando, dice. —No, no la, . . . por la puerta de enfrente tenía que entrar alguien, dice, —porque las ventanas están altas. No puede . . . pasar una persona por la ventana. Tenían que pasar por el cuarto donde nosotros estamos.

—Pues, ¿quién sabe? Aquí está.

—Pero, ¿ónde está?

—Pos, aquí lo tengo agarrado.

—No, yo no veo nada (2).

Pues, entonces mi amá le dice a mi apá: —Tráetelo pa acá. Y me acostaron en medio de, de ellos. Y yo era así, y me dijieron: —Duérmete. No es nada.

Pos apagaron la luz, y luego que apagaron la luz, entonces . . . empecé yo a oyir pasos . . . de vuelta. Y entonces ya que encontré los, . . . que oyía los pasos yo, entonces me . . . me quedé . . . asustado, y decía yo, . . . yo gritaba: —Áhi viene, áhi viene, áhi viene.

—Pero, ¿quién viene? Nadien es. Duérmete.

Pos, no, luego entonces . . . me empezó a, a tentar de . . . de junto a los pies hasta el . . . hasta arriba de la, hasta el hombro. Y . . . sentía yo una cosa muy pesada, pesada en mi cuerpo, encima de mí. Y entonces me dice mi apá: —¿Qué tienes? Duérmete. No es nadien.

—Pos, que aquí está, aquí está.

—Pues, duérmete. Estás . . . estás soñando.

—No . . . aquí, aquí está él.

Y entonces dice mi amá, dice, pues: —Esto ya, ya no es cosa de . . . de este mundo. Ya es una cosa del otro mundo. Pues ya no se durmieron ni yo dormí tampoco.

Entonces . . . dijo . . . dijo mi apá . . . a mi amá, dijo: —Este muchacho está asustado. Alguna cosa vio en el día.

Otro día empecé yo a . . . a decirles que ya no me iba a dormir yo ya adentro . . . de la casa. Iba a dormir ajuera de la . . . de la cocina, porque la cocina estaba separada del . . . donde yo dormía. Y estaba ajuera.

Entonces mi apá me dice, dice: —Pero, hijo, dice, —¿te vas a acostar en la cocina? ¿Cómo vas a hacer eso? Allá . . . allá vas a tener más miedo.

—No, allá no me halla.

Entonces . . . jui y tendí mi tendido . . . allá en, onde se ponía . . . mi amá a moler. Y . . . y entonces mi apá mandó a mis hermanos que me acompañaran en la noche allí onde, onde, a la cocina.

Entonces mi apá me explicó cómo le dijiera o cómo le hablara a él (3). Que le dijiera: —En parte de Dios, te pido. ¿Eres de este mundo o eres del otro (4, 5)? Entonces él te va a contestar, pero no te asustes. Son cosas ya del otro mundo, dice. —La persona que ya Dios se la lleva de este mundo, ya, ya no hace nada. Ya ellas ya 'tán juzgadas de Dios. No les tengas miedo. Háblale.

Entonces ya les dijo a mis hermanos que estuvieran al pendiente de mí, y como la persona que me molestaba venía a las doce de la noche (6), y . . . entonces a mis hermanos les pegué con el, con mi brazo. No les hablé. Les pegué con mi brazo. Y entonces, ya le dije yo como me dijo, como me había explicado mi apá. Y entonces le dije: —En parte de Dios te pido. ¿Eres de este mundo o eres del otro?

Entonces ya me dice él, dice: —Soy del otro.

—¿Qué, qué, qué tienes? ¿Qué, por qué andas penando?

—Pues, ¿te recuerdas . . . el frijol que yo tomé . . . de la hacienda? Dice: —Quiero que lo pagues inmediatamente. Que es lo único que me falta para ir a gozar de Dios (7, 8).

—'Ta bueno. Voy a pagarlo. Pero no vuelvas más.

Entonces . . . luego me dijo mi apá que qué tenía, que qué tenía. —¿Qué te pasó?

Entonces . . . pues le dije yo que me había dicho que fuera . . . que debía un frijol que había tomado de la semilla que yo sembraba.

Y me dijo mi padre, dice: —¿Tú supiste cuánto?

—Sí, le dije. —Jueron tres puños . . . en dos manos. Y le dije yo que yo lo iba a pagar. Que no volviera más. Que lo iba a pagar inmediatamente otro día.

Entonces mi, mi apá me dijo que lo . . . juera y lo pagara inmediatamente. Pero que no le dijiera a nadien que contenía ese frijol, si alguien me vía que iba y lo echaba allí a la, a la hacienda. Entonces dijo: —Usted no más vaya y lo vacía allí, y no tiene que decirle a nadien . . . por qué va a echarlo allí o no.

Entonces yo jui y lo eché, y entonces . . . pues . . . yo le dije a él que, que lo iba a pagar inmediatamente y que no . . . volviera más, que se fuera a descansar, a gozar de Dios (9). Fue entonces.

Y la gente no lo creía . . . que las personas que se mueren que no vienen . . . a este mundo. Pero me decían que cómo, si Miguel ya se había muerto. Pero yo les dije que él venía a . . . a hablar conmigo.

—¿Y habló contigo?

—Sí, sí, habló conmigo.

Y mi padre después . . . les empezó a platicar allí a, a todos . . . los que vivían allí, pues les dijo que su muchacho, su hijo, había, había hablado con el difunto. Pero no le dijo . . . qué era lo que había . . . hablado conmigo, porque no quería que se, que el patrón se diera cuenta de lo, de lo que había pasado. No más únicamente que yo fui a pagar el . . . el . . . frijol por él.

Esto pasó en el . . . en el rancho del Saltillo, . . . que es, es un ladito de . . . de Guadalajara. . . . Y antes, pues, era Cañadas pero ahora es Villa Obregón. . . . Ocho años tenía yo . . . cuando pasó esto.

Qvigstad, no. 11, p. 40. The dead go about and haunt.
(1) E422.1.3. Revenant with ice cold hands. [Here the revenant's leg is ice cold to the touch.]
(2) E421.1.1. Ghost visible to one person alone.
(3) E545.19.1 The dead cannot speak until spoken to.
(4) E545.19.2. Proper means of addressing ghosts.
(5) E451.4.1. Ghost asked to identify itself in name of God.
(6) E587.5. Ghosts walk at midnight.
(7) E411. Dead cannot rest because of a sin.

(8) E352. Dead returns to restore stolen goods.
(9) E451.2. Ghost laid when penance is done.
     González, *TFSP*, 6(1927), 19; Sonnichsen, *TFSP*, 13(1937), 122. [Formula for addressing ghosts.]

22. El ánima y la manda

(Recorded by Juana Gómez on November 12, 1966, in Los Angeles, California)

A cousin of the informant, who lived in the rancho Gran China near Valle de Guadalupe, Jalisco, was visited by the ghost of her mother-in-law who had died twenty-seven years earlier and was requested to fulfill a vow made by her to the Sagrado Corazón de Jesús de Pegueros (Sacred Heart of Jesus in Pegueros).

Pos un . . . esposo de una prima un día, un día se fue el esposo a misa, un sábado de gloria. Y ella, como estaba en la cama de . . . de un niño, entonces ella se quedó. Le dijo: —¿Te quedas?

Dijo: —Sí. Ciérrame la puerta. Entonces se . . . se, se quedó ya dormida.

Y . . . al rato vio una luz. Y entonces ella abrió los ojos y vio . . . y vio una ánima . . . que era la mamá de su esposo (1). Y le dijo que pagara . . . una vela de a peso al Sagrado Corazón de Jesús de Pegueros . . . Pegueros, Jalisco (2). Y luego una entrada de rodillas al . . . allá al mismo santo de Pegueros. Y ya le dijo: —Soy tu suegra, y no me tengas miedo (3).

[Interviewer: —¿Había muerto hacía mucho tiempo?]

Había muerto hacía veintisiete años.

[Interviewer: —¿Dónde vivía ella?]

En el Valle de Guadalupe, en un ranchito del Valle de Guadalupe. Ahí cerquita. . . . El rancho se llamaba la Gran China. La Gran China, cerquita del Valle de Guadalupe.

Qvigstad, no. 11, p. 40. The dead go about and haunt.
(1) E421.3. Luminous ghosts.
(2) E351. Dead returns to repay money debt.
(3) E451.3. Ghost laid when vow is fulfilled.

23. El ánima y las sobras

(Recorded by Lola Cruz on May 20, 1966,
in Los Angeles, California)

The informant's mother, an orphan, was raised in the home of the Archbishop Ochoa in Zamora, Michoacán. She often helped in the kitchen there and would ask permission to give leftovers to beggars or to the animals, but the housekeeper was a very unkind person and always threw away all leftover food, refusing charity to anyone. Many years later, believing her dead, the girl encountered this woman on the street. She expressed her surprise and was told by the woman that it was true, that she had died, but had been sent back to eat all of the food she had thrown away in her lifetime before God would admit her to heaven. The girl took pity on her and promised to pray for her and attempt to make amends by giving the day's leftovers to the pigs. She told her to go in peace, and that God would surely pardon her.

Mi mamá me platicó una historia, . . . una cosa, mandado que ella vio. Una señora que mi mamá le ayudaba a lavar los trastes, porque mi mamá era huérfana, y se crió en casa de un Canónigo Ochoa, que era . . . arzobispo o canónigo. Y luego la señora, . . . mi mamá le decía que le diera comida para los puercos, y la señora dijo que no.

Y luego mi amá la iba a ayudar a la señora a lavar los trastes y le decía: —Mira, Pachita, no te lleves la comida. Dámela. Y luego la señora dicía que no, que mejor ella tiraba la comida que darla a la gente pobre.

Pues ya a la edad que mi amá se casó, mi mamá salió pa fuera, y veía aquella señora y le dice: —Oiga, señora, pos, ¿no me habían dicho que usted se había muerto?

—Sí, dice, —pero Dios Nuestro Señor me ha mandado a este mundo para que yo me coma toda esta comida, que viene siendo la comida que tú me traibas, desperdicios, y la comida que yo tiraba. Y hasta que yo no acabe de comer de toda esta comida, no me voy . . . para atrás. Porque tengo que venir todos los días hasta el fin (1, 2).

Le dijo: —No, señora. Vaya en paz y que Dios la perdone. Yo le prometo una comunión, y le prometo agarrar la comida que está en el caño y echárselo a los marranitos pa que los marranitos se la coman. Pa que usted vaya a descansar de Dios, y Dios la perdone, y no vuelvas más a penar (3).

Esto fue en México, . . . en el estado de Zamora, Michoacán.

(1) E411.0.2.1. Return from dead to do penance.
(2) E411. Dead cannot rest because of a sin.
(3) E451.2. Ghost laid when penance is done.

24. La muchacha que espiaba las ánimas

(Recorded by Lola Cruz on May 19, 1966,
in Los Angeles, California)

The informant tells of an incident described to her in a letter written by her aunt from León, Guanajuato, in 1922. A cousin of the informant used to enjoy watching from her window when the ghosts would emerge from the cemetery at eight o'clock in the evening for a prayer gathering. One of the ghosts realized they were being watched one evening, and two weeks later a group of them went to the girl's home to announce that they were going to carry her off in punishment for having observed their activity. The girl, in great fear, sought the advice of the priest and was told to find a three-month-old child to have with her when the ghosts came after her. She followed this advice and was not carried off immediately; but she soon fell quite ill and died about twenty-four days later. It was then, the informant states, that the ghosts took her away. The informant goes on to explain that a three-month-old child possesses the power of God and thus provides protection against the devil and against ghosts.

En mil novecientos veintidós recibí una carta de una tía mía, . . . de una prima. Vivían enfrente de un panteón. [In León, Guanajuato.] Y mi prima le gustaba todo el tiempo ver cuando las ánimas salían del, del panteón. A las ocho de la noche salían las ánimas . . . a hacer oración. Y ella, cuando supo que las ánimas salían, se sentaba en la reja de la ventana.

Cuando un día una de las ánimas se dio cuenta de que mi prima estaba mirándolas.

Y entonces ya pasaron como unos quince días, cuando luego después las ánimas vinieron a su casa de ella. Y le dijieron: —Pues, tú, por estar mirando . . . lo que estamos haciendo, te vamos a llevar (1).

Y entonces ella se metió temblando y le dijo a la mamá. Y entonces la mamá dijo: —Mañana vamos con el padre.

Fueron a, con el padre y el padre les dijo . . . que entonces tenía que conseguir un niño de tres meses (2). Y el padre tenía que estar allí con ellas tamién. Entonces el padre y mi tía se escondieron y le dejaron el niño de tres meses.

Entonces le dijo la . . . ánima principal: —¿Por qué trajistes este niño? Si tu alma es de nosotros.

Entonces dijo: —Porque no me pueden llevar ustedes.

Dice: —Sí. Para que otro día no te andes informando de lo que no debes.

Entonces el niño pegó tres lloridos. Que no quería estar con aquella muchacha porque las ánimas se la querían llevar. Pues luego ella se desmayó, y calló el niño.

Le pegó una fiebre tan dura, . . . que luego vino el doctor y le inyectó (3). No se murió ese día, pero como a los veinticuatro días, entonces falleció. Y, y fue cuando las ánimas se la llevaron (4).

[Interviewer: —¿Por qué tuvo que conseguir un niño de tres meses?]

Bueno. Esto del Niño Dios, . . .a la edad de tres meses, como es Dios él, él tiene el derecho, Dios le dio el derecho de hablar, porque no hay ningún niño que hable edad de tres meses, ni se siente ni nada. Cuando vino el soldado a buscar a la Virgen y al Niño Dios . . . para degollar el rey Herodes, entonces el Niño Jesús de edad de tres meses, . . . que le dijo, que le dijo el soldado que se fueran de allí porque los querían matar. Entonces dijo el Niño Dios: —Di más y serás conmigo en el Paraíso.

Cuando un . . . espíritu o un muerto viene a agarrar a alguna persona, que quiere llevársela aquel muerto, entonces no se lo puede llevar, porque está escrito en la palabra de Dios que un niño de tres meses . . . tiene . . . desfiende [i.e., defiende] del demonio y desfiende de cualquier muerto malo o bueno. Como a esta prima mía, que se la iba a llevar el muerto. Agarró mi prima un . . . niño de tres meses. Y

no se la llevó por cuestión de que tenía aquella criatura de tres meses.
Entonces el muerto dijo que nadien podía arrimarse a una criatura de
tres meses. Porque de tres meses tienen el mismo poder de Dios Nuestro Señor. Porque no tienen pecados . . . de ninguna clase (2).

Christiansen 4015. The Midnight Mass of the Dead.
(1) E242. Ghosts punish intruders into mass (procession) of ghosts.
   Vicuña Cifuentes, *Mitos y supersticiones*, no. 161. "La compañía de un
      niño inocente defiende de apariciones temerosas y de malos encuentros."
(2) G303.16.19.6. Man protected from devil by holding three-year-old child
      through the night. [The woman in this story is protected from ghosts
      rather than from the devil, but the incident reflects the importance at-
      tached to the number three.]
(3) E265.1. Meeting ghost causes sickness.
(4) E266. Dead carry off living.
   Qvigstad, no. 8, p. 40. Spook in church or graveyards; no. 11, p. 40. The
      dead go about and haunt.
   Folktales from the Patagonia Area, p. 25.
   Palma, "La procesión de ánimas de San Agustín," *Tradiciones peruanas*,
      p. 488. [A new-born child is held by woman in order to keep from
      being carried off by *ánimas*.]

25. Los espíritus en la casa

(Recorded by Isaura Benicia on May 15, 1966,
in Los Angeles, California)

The informant tells of ghostly noises, mysterious incidents, and mischievous deeds that she and her family experienced repeatedly in their
home in Guadalajara, Jalisco.

Pues sí, esto es curioso, porque en nuestra casa (1, 2) pues el primer
día que nos cambiamos allí al ir a encender la lumbre con carbón, al
prender la . . . el cerillo, la mecha, la apagaban. Una persona la apagaba. Así, de estarla encendiendo, . . . y la apagaba (3). Fue el primer,
primer día, . . . primera noche. . . . La casa estaba en Guadalajara, en
Belisario Domínguez y José Agustín Domínguez. Allí existe todavía
esta casa.

Entonces así pasó, cuando después estuvo una señorita de visita allí.
Habíamos muchas . . . muchachas en ese tiempo. Todas, ¿verdad?,
todas con novio. Y la casa tiene dos ventanas a la calle. . . . Y todas platicaban a ratos, unas por la ventana, otras por la puerta, y total de que
todas teníamos novio.

Entonces dice Berta, la amiga de nosotras: —¿Quien está platicando allí? Que voy a hacer una travesura. Y al entrar ella, porque ligerita la acabo de ver que entra, . . . y no era nadie. Era la . . . el ánima aquella que, que se aparecía, ¿verdad? Que ella la vio que entró. Vio que entró esa persona a la sala, pero al entrar ella a hacer una travesura no había nadie. Era solamente el ánima aquella que, . . . nosotros creemos que era una ánima.

Después, al poco tiempo, se cambió otra persona, que estaba paralítica. Tenía reumatismo en todo el cuerpo. Entonces ella ocupaba una pieza. Y cuando ella no podía moverse, tenía un banquito allí. Para . . . hacer sus necesidades usan unas, que les decimos . . . vasija. ¿Usted sabe lo que es esto? Aquí no existen, creo. Aquí no las usan, pero allá, sí, eso es muy usado. Y entonces . . . ella trató de coger el . . . el bacín, ¿verdad? Se agachó para cogerlo, y ¿sabe lo que cogió? Una calavera. . . . De aquí [indicates eye sockets]. De los ojos. Entonces ella la levanta, dice: —¡Ay!, dice. —Si no es esto lo que yo quiero. Era temprano, empezando a oscurecer. Y entonces ella lo ve a la luz, y al verlo así a la luz ve que es . . . una calavera. . . . Y ella le mete los dedos aquí. Entonces ella grita, ¿verdad?, asustada: —¡Ester, ven, porque mira! Y se le zafa aquello y rueda para abajo de la . . . de su cama de ella. Ella, posiblemente de ese susto su muerte fue más próxima, y al poco tiempo murió (4). Se llamaba Emilia Cardicho. Yo le digo, pasó ese caso en esa casa.

Después esos ruidos (5, 6). Que una hermana trabajaba de velada en una fábrica. Y ella, pues, tenía que dormir de día. Pues no la dejaban dormir (7). En cuanto se, se quedaba dormida, iban y la destapaban. Iban y la destapaban. Pues si quería dormir, quedarse dormida algún rato, tenía que estarse mi mamá sentada allí, para que ella pudiera dormir un rato. Porque en cuanto se quedaba sola iban y la destapaban en el día (8, 9).

Y eso que le platico de esos ruidos. Mi hermana se había acostado temprano. Entonces ella, que llegaba de trabajar, otra de mis hermanas que llegaba de trabajar, ya llegó allí. Y le dice mi mamá: —¿Vas a cenar?

—No, vamos a dormir.

Mi mamá se pasa a su pieza, y ella y yo nos quedamos en esa pieza que le digo que . . . la destapaban. Y nos empezamos a, . . . en cuanto nos sentamos se empezó a oir las sillas del, . . . era un corredor grande, un corredor grande. Y, y empezamos a oir las sillas que se movían, ¿verdad? Y se oyó, pues, se caían todos los trastes en la cocina, que era una alacena. Mmmm, pues, una casa muy antigua, ¿verdad? Era una alacena. Y entonces se oía que aquella alacena se caía, y se tiraban todos los . . . platos y vasos. Y se oía el ruido de aquello (6, 10).

Entonces mi mamá se levantó, . . . va a la cocina. Cuando ella va a la cocina, . . . el baño estaba pegado, pero tenía que dar vuelta así [indicates direction]. Era una pared. Era un corredor que tenía . . . unos arcos, esas casas antiguas, ¿verdad?, como le digo. Y tenía unos arcos así grandes. Entonces vivía en esta parte así, y dar vuelta así hasta coger para acá, para el lado del baño. Entonces ella va al baño porque oye que se están bañando. Y nada. Y así, diferentes ruidos se oían. Pues nunca dio con nada. Nunca dio con nada.

Cuando iban a salir para México, que se iban ellos, empezaba a oscurecer cuando se empezaban a oir silbidos en la calle. En la calle, pero que silbaban. Era la casa . . . muy cerca de la esquina. Más o menos esta posición [refers to location of her own apartment], la casa aquí, otra casa, y ya era la esquina. Entonces se oía que silbaban como aquí, y les contestaban allá. Silbidos largos, largos, ¿verdad? Como . . . de personas que se avisaran de una cosa o otra, así. Bueno. Era en el día, ¿no? Y en la calle. Como en la casa no había teléfono, ¿verdad?, entonces tuvieron que pedir un taxi desde en la noche, para que en la mañana viniera a recogerlos. No dormimos por eso que le digo, de que ella estaba preparando su viaje y todo eso. Se iban a ir muy temprano y . . . todo eso. Y entonces ellos estaban listos, cuando llegó el carro por ellos. Ya . . . se fueron. Y yo me quedé de más grande en la casa. Y . . . otra hermana enferma, y . . . y así, ¿verdad? Una prima que estaba con nosotros con sus niños en una pieza, nosotros estábamos . . . entonces, otras estaban en otra, otros en otra. Pero cuando ellos se fueron, los que se iban de viaje, nos juntamos en aquella pieza todas. Bueno.

Acabábamos de cerrar, la puerta era de ésas . . . puertas muy fuertes, ¿verdad?, muy gruesas. Unas llaves, aquí no han de existir. Allá son unas llaves de este tamaño, muy grandes [indicates size]. Y lleva una cosita por dentro. Es un fijador, como un pasador, como ése [indicates lock on her own door], pero grande. También así. Y luego, tienen una cosa que pasa y una cosita así. Se asegura completamente. Luego era la entrada así, la puerta muy grande. Y luego el cancel también. Era un espacio así, luego el cancel. Es un hall, y luego es una puerta de fierro, . . . grande también, al tamaño de la, de la entrada, que es de madera. Es una puerta de fierro, también con su llave, muy grande y muy seguro, ¿verdad?

Pues cerramos todo aquello muy bien encerrado, ¿verdad?, cuando llegan y tocan, pero muy fuerte, la puerta de la calle.. Aa, primero, el claxón de un carro que se, el ruido de un carro, que se para aquí afuera en la calle. Luego empieza a pitar. Les digo: —Saben de que allí está el señor que iba a venir por ellos. Posiblemente el que llegó no era el carro que los iba a llevar, y hasta ahorita llegó. Voy a levantarme para decirle que, que ya se fueron. Pero luego pensé: —Este señor ya vino y va a querer dinero porque . . . su viaje que echó, y está mejor que se vaya sin que le digamos nada.

Y se oye que . . . después de que deja de pitar, se sale, ¿verdad? Porque el portazo del carro, que se abre y se cierra. Y luego viene y con la mano así, en la puerta, pero muy fuerte, ¿verdad? Digo: —Pos sí, si es el señor del carro, que los iba a recoger. Y ellos ya se fueron. Entonces . . . como . . . nada, nosotros callados. Entonces se oye como que el señor se viene, ¿verdad?, con todo esfuerzo, y le golpea la puerta y la abre. Porque la puerta se . . . se oye que se abre de par en par, fíjese. Entonces luego el cancel al abrirse se arrastraba un poco en . . . el piso y rechinaba. Pos se oía que el cancel se abre. Imagínese. Y los silbidos aquellos que de aquí, allá contestaban. Luego cuando el carro no pitaba, se oía como que . . . una moto andaba en la banqueta, pero en ese trayecto solamente.

Y luego ya se oyeron pasos, adentro de la casa, que andaban. Y era una mesa en el comedor, una mesa grande, muy pesada. Y entonces ya se empezaba a oir que arrastraban las sillas, la mesa. Y luego en la siguiente recámara, . . . hay una recámara allí, . . . la otra está aquí, . . . y esa . . . no había puerta de madera, a la cocina. Y estaba la cama, una cama, muy cerca de la puerta. Entonces se oyó que la empezaron a, a aventarla así (10). Y rechinaba la cama al, al cogerla. Rechinaba, ¿verdad? Y nosotros todos en suspenso. Fueron como . . . dos horas y, y

posiblemente ha de haber sido como . . . las cuatro, de cuatro a cinco de
la mañana. Alrededor de las cinco se empiezan a llamar al alba . . .
para la misa. Se acabaron los ruidos (5).

Otro día nos levantamos, asustados todos, porque no dormimos.
Llorando todos, mis . . . la tía que estaba con nosotros, bien asustada
también con sus niños, todos los chiquillos. Porque como dije, yo era la
más grande. Todos los demás, la lloradera, porque . . . asustados. Y yo:
—Cállense, cállense. Que no vayan a ver que aquí estamos. Pues,
creíamos que eran personas las que había allí. Otro día nos levantamos
. . . nada. Todo en su lugar, perfecto, sin mover nada de su sitio. Fíjese.
Así. Y así duramos en esa casa doce años. Y continuamente esos ruidos. La casa existe todavía.

  (1) F473. Poltergeist. Invisible spirit (sometimes identified as ghost or witch)
        responsible for all sorts of mischief in and around household.
  (2) E281. Ghosts haunt house. (It is sometimes hard to tell whether haunt-
        ers are supposed to be ghosts or familiar spirits of some kind.)
  (3) F473.2.3. Spirit puts out lights.
  (4) N384. Death from fright.
  (5) E402. Mysterious ghostlike noises heard.
  (6) F473.5. Poltergeist makes noises.
  (7) F473.3. Poltergeist mistreats people.
  (8) F470.1. Spirits pull off sleeping person's bedclothes.
  (9) E279.2. Ghost disturbs sleeping person.
 (10) F473.1. Poltergeist throws objects.
        Qvigstad, no. 11, p. 40. The dead go about and haunt; no. 13, p. 41.
          Poltergeister (i.e., noisy ghosts).
        Sinninghe, no. 456, p. 79. The poltergeist in the house.
        Creighton, pp. 240–250; 250–252; 273–275.
        Folktales from the Patagonia Area, p. 22. [Covers jerked off and bed
          overturned in haunted house.]

26. Los espíritus maliciosos

(Recorded by Lola Cruz on May 20, 1966, in Los Angeles, California)

Around the year 1933 the informant and her family were living in a
house in San José, California, in which a variety of mysterious things
went on. Bedclothes would be removed from the beds, dishes taken
down from the shelf, pictures removed from the walls, and great quantities of salt dumped into the food. The inhabitants were even removed from their beds one night, to awaken in a shack in the back
yard. When they told the owner they wanted to move, they were

begged to stay there and, thus, it was hoped, rid the house of the spirits that had been haunting it ever since an incident had taken place thirty years earlier involving multiple murders within a single family. They called on a priest for help, but he sensed the presence of the devil and fled in terror.

En el . . . mil novecientos treinta y tres fuimos a Fresno, . . . y luego de Fresno nos regresamos a San José [California]. Allí en San José vivíamos en una nopalera, . . . que era . . . una casa que era muy barata. Nos costaba ocho cuartos de renta por . . . ocho pesos. Y luego después nos dijo el mismo dueño que nos fuéramos pa otra casa que estaba en seguida. Pero como eran casas que no tenían calles ni números, porque en este tiempo, pues, estaba un desierto allí.

Pues en esta casa (1, 2), cuando . . . nosotros estábamos en la cocina, se oían los pasos arriba de . . . de los cuartos de dormir (3). Y nos destendían las camas (4). Iba y tendía las camas, y luego me . . . se iban ellos al trabajo y yo me quedaba. Y todos los trastes me los bajaban del trastero. Y luego los subía, y luego me los, . . . mientras que estaba poniendo unas cosas en otra parte, las otras estaban deshaciendo. Y luego puse unos . . . cuadros que me habían dado en la pared, y me los bajaban.

Y, y todo el día trabajaba, y luego en la noche nos acostamos a dormir, y luego nos sacaron . . . en puras cobijas nos sacaron afuera de la yarda. Allá hay una casa de pájaros como una casa. Pos allí nos metieron adentro de esa casa de pájaros (5, 6). Porque no supimos ni quién ni supimos.

Y luego le dijimos a la dueña: —¿Por qué nos dio esta casa?

Dice: —O, porque esta casa, todo el que se duerme adentro lo sacan pa fuera. Y siempre, pos, teníamos miedo.

Y luego le dijimos a la dueña: —¿Por qué nos la renta? Nos queremos cambiar.

Y dijo la dueña: —No, mejor les pago porque vivan aquí en la casa. Porque quiero que viva gente para que se vayan los espíritus. Porque aquí, hace como unos treinta años, hubo un accidente. Que hijos, padres, y hermanos se mataron, y ésos son los que están haciendo las travesuras aquí en esta casa (7).

Y luego una vez fui y la, me . . . dijo la señora que estaba viviendo con nosotros: —Mira. Dejo a cocer . . . la comida y el caldo. Le pones la verdura y le pones la sal.

Pues . . . cuando fui a buscar la sal, no tenía ni una gota el bote. Era un bote grande. Pos, toda la sal la tenía el caldo. Porque todo me echaron a perder. Y entonces le dije a Tina: —Tú, que sabes hacer pasteles, haz unos pasteles. Pero yo no sé qué . . . qué le volteó, o le echarían a los pasteles, que nos hicieron daño (5).

Y luego oíamos unas carcajadas (3), que se reían y dicían: —Hora, sí, se van a reñir con nosotros porque ya les hicieron daño los pasteles.

Y luego le dije a la dueña, le dije: —No, señora. Ni dada me gusta esta casa.

Dice: —No, pues, a ver, . . . vive en ella, a ver qué pasa.

Entonces fuimos a una . . . iglesita que está ahí en San José. Y le dije yo al padrecito que, . . . ya sabía qué pasaba allí. Entonces dijo el padre: —Yo me voy a estar allí contigo cuando. . . . No te lo creo. Voy a estarme allí contigo cuando se vayan al trabajo.

Entonces se fueron todos al trabajo, y fui y lo traje al padre. Fui a la carrera y lo traje. Y luego cuando el padre iba entrando, lo pucharon pa dentro.

Entonces dijo el padre, dice: —¡Jesús, María y José! Aquí está el diablo. Ya me voy. Y no se quiso quedar el padre allí, sino que dijo: —No, vale más que se cambien. Y nos cambiamos de esa casa, porque en esa casa nos sacaron a empujones pa fuera.

(1) E281. Ghosts haunt house. (It is sometimes hard to tell whether haunt-
     ters are supposed to be ghosts or familiar spirits of some kind.)
(2) F473. Poltergeist. Invisible spirit (sometimes identified as ghost or witch)
     responsible for all sorts of mischief in and around household.
(3) F473.5. Poltergeist makes noises.
(4) F470.1. Spirits pull off person's bedclothes.
(5) F473.3. Poltergeist mistreats people.
(6) E279.2. Ghost disturbs sleeping person.
(7) E275. Ghost haunts place of great accident or misfortune.
     Qvigstad, no. 9, p. 40. Ghosts (spook) at scenes of murders; no. 11, p. 40.
       The dead go about and haunt.
     Sinninghe, no. 456, p. 79. The poltergeist in the house.
     Creighton, pp. 240–250; 250–252; 273–275.
     Folktales from the Patagonia Area, p. 22 [Covers jerked off and bed over-
       turned in haunted house.]
     Krappe, p. 96. [Reference to defeated priest.]
     Shoemaker, pp. 52–54. [Haunted room scene of previous tragedy.]

27. La casa de los espíritus

(Recorded by Luis Cruz on May 20, 1966, in Los Angeles, California)

The informant tells of a haunted house in West Los Angeles, California, that was promised by the owner as an outright gift to whoever succeeded in spending an entire night in the house without awakening outside in the yard the following morning. Many have tried, but without success. The house remains there near the corner of Santa Monica Boulevard and Bundy Drive.

Pos sabe que, que hay aquí en los límites de Santa Monica y Sawtelle, . . . West Los Angeles, está esa casa onde, onde . . . nos decían que, que salían unos . . . unos espíritus (1). Y luego entonces, la gente que vivía allí en esa casa se acostaban en la noche, y amanecían . . . ajuera. . . . Y . . . los sacaban para ajuera (2, 3). Y . . . y entonces, pues, ya, ya que pasaba eso, entonces ya la gente ya . . . ya no quería vivir allí. Ya se iba. Y luego pues, los que no sabían, allí iban a . . . a vivir la vuelta . . . otras . . . personas. Y, y . . . pasaba la misma, . . . se acostaban adentro y amanecían ajuera en la yarda. De modo es que . . . por eso es de que después, el señor de la casa prometía que la, la gente . . . que se acostara, que viviera allí, se acostara adentro y, y durara allí dentro, que no amaneciera ajuera, que les regalaba la propiedad. Y no hubo quién, quién se animara a, a hacerlo. Porque hacían el try de . . . de . . . vivir allí, pero nunca . . . los dejaban estar allí en la casa. Solo que . . . los sacaban. Se acostaban en la noche adentro y amanecían acostados ajuera en la yarda en la mañana.

[Interviewer: —¿El dueño es americano o mexicano?]

Es americano. Y todavía, todavía esa casa existe. Y se ve muy asombrosa . . . allí. Y . . . y yo me alegraría que . . . que la viera, que la viera un día. Y todavía está, porque hace . . . hace, hace siempre bastantito tiempo que no, que no he pasado yo por allí, . . . pero pueda ser que todavía exista, porque esa casa todo el tiempo ha estado allí, y se ve muy asombrosa.

(1) E281. Ghosts haunt house. (It is sometimes hard to tell whether haunters are supposed to be ghosts or familiar spirits of some kind.)
(2) F473.3. Poltergeist mistreats people.

(3) E279.2. Ghost disturbs sleeping person.
   Qvigstad, no. 11, p. 40. The dead go about and haunt.
   Sinninghe, no. 456, p. 79. The poltergeist in the house.
   Folktales from the Patagonia Area, p. 20. [People can have haunted house
   rent free if they manage to stay there a certain period of time.]

28. La muerta en el baile

(Recorded by Lola Cruz on May 20, 1966, in Los Angeles, California)

The informant tells of an incident said to have taken place at the Paladium Ballroom in Los Angeles, California, in 1939. A young man was attracted to a very pretty girl, he danced with her, and when he took her home she left her coat in his car and accidentally carried off his scarf. When he went to her home the next day to return her coat and pick up his scarf, he was told by the girl's mother that she had been dead for four years. They went to the cemetery and found his scarf there on her tombstone.

En mil novecientos treinta y nueve, en la ciudad de Los Angeles, se le apareció una difuntita a un muchacho que bailó con ella en un baile (1). [Next-door neighbor adds: —Paladium se llamaba el salón. El Paladium Ballroom.] El Paladium. Y luego el muchacho le dijo que si, quería llevarla a su casa . . . a la muchacha. Y luego esta muchacha dijo que sí. Pero primero tenía que llevarla a dar una vuelta allí, a un lugar que era cerca del cementerio. Pero después dijo él que era más mejor llevarla a la puerta de la casa.

Y luego se le olvidó a ella el sobretodo de ella en el carro. Y a él se le olvidó pedirle la bufanda, que traiba la bufanda ella en el pescuezo pa no agarrar frío en la noche.

Pues luego otro día él, luego que llegara él a su casa, se acordó del sobretodo y la bufanda, y fue otro día a la, a la misma parte donde él la dejó. Y tocó a la puerta y le preguntó que si ahí estaba la muchacha que . . . había dejado anoche. Y cuando abrió la señora la puerta, lo primero que vio fue el retrato . . . de ella. Y luego le dijo: —Ésta es la muchacha con que . . . yo salí a bailar, y aquí traigo el sobretodo.

Y entonces la señora dijo: —Sí, es . . . mi hija. El sobretodo de mi hija. Dice: —Y ahí está el retrato. Sí, ésta es mi hija, la del retrato.

Entonces dijo: —Quiero mi bufanda.

Dijo: —Su bufanda no está aquí. Porque ella tiene . . . cuatro años de muerta.

Y, y ese tiempo, fueron la señora y él al panteón. Y ahí en la lápida de ella, ahí estaba la bufanda del señor. En la lápida. Áhi era donde encontraron la bufanda.

Y entonces el señor, el muchacho, dijo: —¡Ay, caray! Hasta que bailé con una muerta.

Y . . . eso es todo.

[The informant named *La Opinión* as the newspaper in which the story appeared.]

(1) E332.3.3.1. Vanishing hitchhiker.
   Beardsley, *CFQ*, 1(1942), 303–335; *CFQ*, 2(1943), 13–25. [Several versions of this type.]
   Creighton, p. 198.
   Folktales from the Patagonia Area, p. 23. [Two narratives.]
   Furnier, *NMFR*, 5(1950–1951), 33–35.
   Hankey, *CFQ*, 1 (1942), nos. 33, 36, 37.
   Hawes, *WF*, 27(1968), 255–262.
   Jones, *CFQ*, 3(1944), 284–292; *Things That Go Bump in the Night*, pp. 161–184. [Several versions of this type.]
   Parochetti, *Keystone Folklore Quarterly*, 10(1965), 54–55.

29. La muerta en el baile

(Recorded by Elvira Higuera on October 31, 1966, in Los Angeles, California)

A woman went with her son to pay a sympathy call on a friend whose daughter had died four days earlier. The boy recognized a photograph of the girl and said she was the girl with whom he had gone dancing only two days earlier. When he had taken her home, he noticed that, instead of going into her house, she disappeared into the cemetery, and he later found the coat he had loaned her lying on a grave. The informant says the incident took place in Los Angeles, California, about ten years before and that it was told to her by her cousin who heard it from a friend who had read about it in a Los Angeles newspaper in Sinaloa, Mexico.

Bien, pues eran dos amigas que fueron, . . . fue a visitar una amiga a la otra porque había . . . fallecido la hija de ella. Y llevó a su hijo, a un hijo de ella a que fuera a visitar . . . la señora. Entonces el hijo vio una fotografía de la hija de la señora que había . . . ya había muerto, y se quedó sorprendido porque dos días antes le había tocado bailar ella con él (1). Entonces le preguntó a la mamá que quién era la . . . la muchacha que estaba viendo en la foto. Entonces ella le dice que era una . . . que era la hija de la señora que había muerto hacía cuatro días. Y él se quedó sorprendido porque dos días antes había ido a bailar él con ella, . . . y tanto que le quitó el . . . saco que llevaba porque llevaba frío, . . . la sweater. Y al tiempo . . . y entonces ella pidió que la fuera a dejar a su casa. Cuando la dejó en . . . para llevarla a su casa, entonces él, . . . cuando ya al bajarse ella, vio el muchacho que la muchacha no fue a llegar a su casa, y llegó al panteón. Y allí desapareció en una de las tumbas, quedando el saco encima de la, de la tumba. El muchacho entonces quedó sorprendido viendo que era la muerta, y preguntó, él preguntó el nombre de la muchacha. Y se dio cuenta que era con . . . la muerta que había bailado.

Me lo platicó una prima mía, hace como unos diez años, más o menos. Está en Sinaloa. Ahí está en Sinaloa. Sí, que a ella le había platicado otra señora también, que ella había leído el periódico de aquí de Los Angeles. Lo leyó el periódico en Sinaloa en español, . . . lo que había pasado aquí. Está curioso, ¿no?

See Narrative 28.

30. La muerta y el chofer de taxi

(Recorded by Lola Cruz on May 20, 1966,
in Los Angeles, California)

In the year 1940 a Santa Monica, California, cab driver was stopped by a woman dressed in black who asked him to take her to the cemetery. She paid her fare with a check for $100 and gave him the name of a store where he could cash the check. When he arrived at the store, he noticed that the check was for $1,000 rather than $100. The store owner recognized the signature on the check as that of his mother, who had been dead for twenty years, and agreed to give the cab driver the money, since that was his mother's wish. The cab driver, however, bothered by the idea of spending the money of a dead woman, became quite ill and died the following year.

En mil novecientos cuarenta [in Santa Monica, California] era un chofer, de esos de los . . . taxis. Entonces había una señora vestida de negro, tapada con un velo negro. Y luego paró el del taxi. Y luego le dijo al . . . señor que la llevara a su casa. Y entonces la casa era en el panteón (1). Y luego le dijo . . . le, le dijo la señora que le daba un cheque . . . para que cobrara en una tienda. Pero luego allí se, se desapareció la señora en el panteón. Y la, y era de cien dólares. Y cuando el . . . chofer llegó a su casa vio el cheque y no eran cien. Eran mil dólares. Y allí decía que era dinero . . . que tenía que pagarlo al contado.

Y luego despuésn . . . el, el señor cuando llegó a la tienda le dijo . . . al de la tienda que si conocía aquel cheque. Dijo: —Sí. Es de mi madre. ¿Quién se lo dio?

Dijo: —O, pos una señora vestida de negro que dejé en la esquina del, del cementerio.

Dice: —Pos, mire, señor, . . . mi madre tiene veinte años de muerta. Y . . . le voy a dar el dinero porque este dinero es de mi madre. Y le dio mil dólares.

Y el señor cada dólar que gastaba se acordaba . . . que era dinero de una difunta. Y se puso muy pálido, pálido, y en mil novecientos cuarenta y uno, él falleció.

(1) E332.3.3.1. Vanishing hitchhiker.
    Beardsley, *CFQ*, 1(1942), 303–335; *CFQ*, 2(1943), 13–25. [Several versions of this type.]
    Hankey, *CFQ*, 1(1942), 155–177. [None of these narratives is exactly the same situation, involving a cab driver and the element of payment, but the structure is basically the same.]
    Hendricks, *WF*, 27(1968), 255–262.
    Jones, *CFQ*, 3(1944), 284–292; *Things That Go Bump in the Night*, pp. 161–184. [Several versions of this type.]

31. Las tres muertas en el camino

(Recorded by Elvira Higuera on October 31, 1966,
in Los Angeles, California)

Three young men traveling by car from Culiacán to Mazatlán, Sinaloa, stopped to pick up three girls who were hitchhiking. They took them to their home and were invited to return a week later for a party, but when they did they found the house abandoned. A neighbor in-

formed them that the three girls who used to live there had been killed
three years earlier in an accident, which turned out to have occurred
at the same spot where the young men found them hitchhiking. He
added that they were not the first to whom the girls had mysteriously
appeared.

Iban tres muchachos de Culiacán, Sinaloa para . . . Mazatlán. Y
salieron tres . . . tres muchachas en el camino, pidiéndoles raide. Las
subieron . . . y, y que, y se fueron platicando con ellas tanto que se hicieron amigos. Y en el camino les dijeron que fueran a verlas el siguiente domingo. Que ellas vivían en . . . en un pueblo, en un ranchito
ahí cerca de Culiacán. Ahí tenían su casa. Quedaron los muchachos de
volver allí con ellas.

A los ocho días los muchachos vinieron a . . . a ver las muchachas.
Vinieron a la casa de ellas, esperando que estuviera la fiesta. Y resulta
que cuando llegaron . . . estaba la casa sola. Les tocaron la . . . puerta
y no salió nadie. Y les hablaron y tampoco. La casa estaba sola. Solamente habían allí los cigarros que . . . que habían tirado ellos, desde
que ellos se habían ido la . . . el día anterior [i.e., la semana anterior].
Y ya se dieron cuenta.

Hasta un señor que estaba cerca de la casa de ellas les pregunta,
dice: —¿A quién buscaban? Y entonces . . . le dicen los muchachos que
buscaban a la muchacha que, a las muchachas que vivían en aquella
casa. Y el señor les dice que no, no hay muchachas, porque tres muchachas que vivían allí, hacía tres años que habían muerto . . . en un accidente. Y . . . y en el mismo pedazo, en la misma parte en donde ellas
les . . . les hablaron a los muchachos. Y que no eran los primeros a los
que . . . les habían hablado, que ya a otros les había pasado igual (1).

(1) E332.3.3.1. Vanishing hitchhiker.
  Beardsley, *CFQ*, 1(1942), 303–335; *CFQ*, 2(1943), 13–25. [Several ver-
    sions of this type.]
  Creighton, p. 198.
  Folktales from the Patagonia Area, p. 23.
  Hankey, *CFQ*, 1(1942), nos. 28, 30, 32, 38.
  Hark, p. 61.
  Hendricks, *WF*, (1968), 255–262.
  Jones, *CFQ*, 3(1944), 284–292; *Things That Go Bump in the Night*, pp.
    161–184. [Several versions of this type.]

32. La muerta en el baile

(Recorded by Socorro Higuera on October 31, 1966, in Los Angeles, California)

At a dance hall in Los Mochis, Sinaloa, about five years earlier, a young man, a friend of the informant, was attracted to a very pretty girl and invited her to dance. When they went out onto the terrace afterward, the girl began to move slowly away, beckoning to the young man to follow her as she took on a very ghostlike appearance and finally disappeared into the hills. Word of the incident spread, and the club was forced to close because people were too frightened to go there.

Bueno, esto sucedió en Sinaloa. Le digo a mi amigo: —¿Por qué no me llevas a bailar a . . . al lugar aquel del cerrito que queda en, en Los Mochis?

—No, no, me dice, . . . —No, allí, allí en ese lugar no te puedo llevar. Porque en ese lugar sale una ánima.

Le digo: —¿Cómo? A ver, cuéntame, le digo.

Entonces dice: —Mira, dice, —íbamos mis amigos y mis amigas, ya sabes quiénes son. Bueno. Y luego me dice: —Se, se quedaron mis amigos en . . . en un lugar, como en la barra. Y luego llega una muchacha muy bonita.

Le dice: —¡Ay! Yo con esa muchacha voy a bailar. Luego se dirige a ella y la saca a bailar (1).

Al poco rato de estar bailando con ella le dice la muchacha: —¿Quiere usted bajar conmigo a la terraza?

Le dijo: —Sí, cómo no. Encantado.

Sale con ella, y al salir con ella le dice . . . la muchacha: —Venga, véngase para acá. Luego bajando ella poco a poquito, cuando ya ven ellos que están al plan del cerro, la muchacha únicamente se ve como una sombra blanca (2). Desaparece. Y el muchacho se queda ahí muerto de miedo.

Muchos hablaban de esa historia. Pero yo no la sabía. Únicamente que me dice mi amiga. . . . Han cerrado ese club. Precisamente hace como unos . . . cinco años que sucedió eso. Y lo cerraron por eso. Porque ya nadie quiere ir a bailar allí. Les da miedo. Les da terror.

[Interviewer: —¿Cómo se llamaba el club?]

O, no recuerdo.

(1) E422. The living corpse.
(2) E425.1.1. Revenant as lady in white.

33. El jinete sin cabeza

(Recorded by Juana Gómez on November 12, 1966, in Los Angeles, California)

The informant tells of a headless horseman who used to ride through the streets of Valle de Guadalupe, Jalisco, around midnight, and who was thought to be the mail carrier, Pancho Márquez, riding his route between Valle de Guadalupe and Jalostotitlán.

Había otro, otro que, pues . . . según dicen, era un correo que hubo allí en el pueblo de Valle de Guadalupe. Y . . . y se murió. Y después, seguro quedó el . . . sería el asombro del, del señor ese. Se llamaba Pancho Márquez . . . el señor. Y . . . y luego le . . . en las noches, como de las doce de la noche (1), pasaba uno, un hombre a caballo. Bajaba . . . de, de una calle. Y allí por . . . donde nosotros vivíamos, era la casa . . . del señor. Pasaba . . . allí el caballo, como . . . sus herraduras, un caballo como anda, ¿verdad?

Y luego . . . un día yo me asomé . . . a, a ver, a ver el, . . . y yo no, no, no vi nada. No vi nada. Y luego otra señora más abajo . . . también lo oyó. Y se asomaba y no lo vía. Y . . . figuran que era el señor ese que era el correo . . . de allí del pueblo, de Valle de Guadalupe. El correo, que era el que llevaba las cartas . . . del Valle de Guadalupe a . . . a Tepatitlán de Morelos. No, a, a . . . a Jalostotitlán era donde llevaba él . . . la correspondencia, ¿verdad? Y . . . seguido, seguido vían ese, ese, ese bulto.

[Daughter adds: —Jinete sin cabeza.]

Jinete sin cabeza (2). Sí, que una señora se asomó a la ventana y vio que era el caballo, y iba el jinete pero no tenía cabeza. No más el bulto del hombre menos la cabeza.

(1) E587.5. Ghosts walk at midnight.
(2) E422.1.1.3.1. Headless ghost rides horse.
     Creighton, pp. 173–175. [Several stories of headless horsemen.]
     Folktales from the Patagonia Area, pp. 10–11. [Several accounts of mys-
     terious (or headless) horsemen.]

34. La Xtabay

(Recorded by Hugo Massa on March 27, 1966, in Los Angeles, California)

The informant tells of a *llorona* type called the Xtabay who fre-
quents the forested areas of Yucatán, appears to men who are out very
late at night, seduces them, and then turns into a venomous serpent.

Según las viejas leyendas mayas, en los árboles de la tierra yucateca
acostumbra salir una mujer [la Xtabay] de pelo largo y túnica blanca
(1) con grandes ojos negros, muy bonita, la cual llama a todos los
hombres que . . . digamos . . . salen a altas horas de la noche. Esta mujer, en verdad muy atractiva, invita a estos hombres a hacerle el amor
(2). Estos hombres, por supuesto atraídos por la belleza, se acercan, le
hacen el amor, y de pronto esta mujer se vuelve una serpiente de las
más venenosas (3, 4).

(1) E425.1.1. Revenant as lady in white.
(2) E425.1.3. Revenant as seductive woman.
(3) F441.6.3. Sexual relations with wood-spirit fatal.
(4) D191. Transformation: man to serpent (snake). [Here it is a woman who
     is transformed.]
     Foster, *UCAAE*, 42(1945), 202, no. 11.
     Horcasitas Pimentel, nos. 4, 5, 32, 36, 40, 42, 46, 47, 48.
     Negrón Pérez, pp. 134–136.
     Pérez Serrano, *ASFM*, 5(1944), 37–40.
     Redfield, p. 34.
     Toor, *Treasurey*, pp. 531–532.

35. María la llorona

(Recorded by Josefina Márquez on May 7, 1966, in Santa Paula, California)

The informant tells of the *llorona*, or wailing woman, named María
la llorona, who used to appear near the home of the governor in Zaca-

tecas, Zacatecas, where the informant herself used to hear her. Her cry would grow louder and louder, and then at its peak one could see her. She had long hair and was dressed in a long robe, but her face was never visible. The informant was told that the *llorona* appeared because her children had been killed, and that not everyone was able to see or even hear her, but only those having sufficient strength of mind and spirit.

Esa llorona, María la llorona que le dicen, se aparecía cerca de onde es ahoy la casa del gobernador en Zacatecas, . . . en la ciudad de Zacatecas como a una cuadra o cuadra y media retirada de la casa del gobernador . . . que es ahora. No, no sé qué gobernador estará ahorita. Pero es la casa del gobernador. Es la casa de gobierno, que le dicen allí. Porque mi casa quedaba cerca de ahí.

La llorona a mí me, me llegó a tocar verla también. No se ve nada más unas veces. Se empieza a oir el llanto como de una mujer, un llanto muy ladino. Un llanto muy ladino, y va subiendo recio, recio, más fuerte (1), y cuando ya está llorando muy fuerte, entonces se ve. No . . . no se ve la cara, no se ve nada. Se ve el bulto, se ven los brazos, el vestido largo y el pelo largo. Se ve que se levanta y camina por el viento. A mí me contaron que era porque le habían matado sus hijos (2, 3).

Mi cuñada, hermana de mi esposo, . . . porque la primera vez que la vi yo, yo me asusté, y me dijo mi cuñada: —No te asustes, es la llorona. Porque yo nunca había oído eso. Dice: —No te asustes, es la llorona. Dice: —Se ve muy seguido aquí. Dice: —Pero no toda la gente la mira, ni toda la gente la oye. Dice: —La gente que la oye y la gente que la ve, dice, —es gente que tiene espíritu . . . y cerebro, que no se desmayan. No tienen, . . . dice, —que son fuertes. Dice: —Esa gente es la que la ve. Dice: —Y seguro que tú eres fuerte . . . de cerebro, dice, —porque tú la vistes, y la oístes. Yo nada más la oí, pero yo no la vi. Dice: —La vi en un tiempo. Dice: —Estaba yo muy joven. Dice: —Pero ahora ya no la veo. No más la oigo.

(1) E547. The dead wail.
(2) Q211.4. Murder of children punished.
(3) Q503. Wandering after death as punishment.

36. La llorona

(Recorded by Amalia Hernández on May 16, 1966, in Los Angeles, California)

The *llorona*, or wailing woman, used to be heard along a river bed near the home of the informant's grandmother in Zacatecas, and the grandmother tells of once when she came right up to the house and paced back and forth in the patio wailing very loudly.

Entonces la llorona, cuando mi abuelita estaba ella pero casi recién casada y mi abuelito viajaba, y ella se quedaba sola. Y se llevaba un niño de compañía nada más. Entonces dice ella que una noche . . . venía, bajó la llorona de, como del pie del cerro. Se oyó que venían los lloridos (1). Y ella solita. Dice que entonces ella lo que hizo fue que se atrancó la puerta. Y la llorona venía entre más, más, entre más, más, acercándose con unos lloridotes. Y llegó hasta onde . . . cerca de la casa de ella. Dizque allí se paró. Dizque echó unos lloridos largos. Y entonces dizque se metió allí. Pasó, porque había un, como un puentecito allí en el arroyo.

Entonces pasó por el puente, ¿ve? Y, y pasó al patio de mi abuelita. Al patio, dizque, porque allí no . . . había puros nopales. Allí es una casa muy, muy sombría. Y entonces pasó al patio la llorona. Y se quedó paseándose allí. Dizque a llora y llora ella. Entonces que mi abuelita estaba reza y reza y reza y reza, dizque más asustada ella. Entonces de allí salió la llorona y dizque otros lloridos largos. Se paraba como que lloraba muy afligida ella. Y luego se fue. Se jue por toda la orilla del arroyo. Y ya dizque fue a salir. No sé aónde iría. Pero eso, esa llorona siempre pasea allí. Paseaba. Eso me lo contó mi abuelita, ¿ve? Se llamaba María Viernes.

(1) E547. The dead wail.

37. La llorona, la Malinche, y la Infeliz María

(Recorded by Lola Cruz on May 20, 1966, in Los Angeles, California)

The informant relates the history of three *llorona* types that she des-

ignates as la *llorona*, la Malinche, and la Infeliz María, who were
linked together by a ring passed on from one to the other, which auto-
matically condemned the wearer to death. The first, la *llorona*, killed
her infant son and then herself after being abandoned by her lover,
and was condemned to wander in eternal suffering. La Malinche had
three sons by three lovers and systematically drowned each one. When
a mysterious voice told her that they had become a doctor, a priest, and
a lawyer, she set out to seek them along the rain-swollen rivers, endlessly calling to them. La Infeliz María succumbed to the temptation of
the devil and killed her three sons in exchange for a promise of great
beauty, whereupon her head turned into that of a horse and her feet
became those of a horse and a cock. Her wailing sounds like an ambu-
lance siren, and it is said that when it sounds close she is actually far
off, and when it is heard as if from a distance she is really quite near.
Those who turn to look at la Infeliz María have their necks stuck in
that position and must be cured by a *curandero*, or healer. The informant's stepfather had such an experience, and his neck remained twisted
for three years before he was cured by the application of an egg plaster.

Como en el año de mil ochocientos . . . había un, uno en España, un
español, que la española que se iba con un . . . español sin casar, no la
querían los familiares. Pues luego éste tenía tratos con una muchacha
que nunca se casó con ella. Y tenía una. . . un hijo que tuvo con ese
señor.

Y cuando el niño tenía cuatro años, que cumplió cuatro años el niño,
entonces él se iba a casar . . . con otra, con doña Ana. Entonces cuando
el padre dijo que quién impidía el matrimonio del español y doña
Ana, entonces salió la . . . la muchacha y dijo que impidía, porque ella
era la primera amante del español y tenía un hijo que tenía cuatro
años. Entonces no se . . . dijo el matrimonio. Se desbarató. Entonces él
calló. Ella se fue para su casa y llevó a su niño.

Y luego después, el . . . señor llegó a quererle quitar el hijo y se desa-
fió con un amigo de la mamá del muchachito. Y entonces mató el . . .
español al amigo del . . . de la señora, . . . que viene siendo la llorona.
Pues luego la, la señora, cuando vio que mató a su . . . el amigo, entonces ella se iba a matar también, porque no se iba a casar con el español.
Agarró a su hijo y le dio una puñalada. Y lo degolló, y lo mató (1). Le
. . . pegó en el corazoncito (2). Y luego entonces le agarró de los piecitos y le dijo a su amante: —Aquí está tu hijo. ¿Quieres agarrarlo?

Entonces él ya quebró la puerta para entrar a matarla, cuando ella se mató.

Pero la llorona era una historia, que traiban un anillo. Que la . . . el anillo aquel que traiban . . . esa persona se debía de matar (3, 4).

Entonces se dio una puñalada y salió por la ventana . . . del cuarto de dormir ella, el espíritu de ella en . . . vestida de blanco (5). Y empezó a dar un grito, como haciendo: —Aaaayyy (6). Y ese grito era que otra tenía que pagar otra . . . otra cosa de ésas.

Entonces después la, la criada le quitó el anillo a la señora cuando estaba en su cuerpo, pero su alma no estaba porque su alma tenía que penar por toda la vida. Y hasta esta fecha anda penando la . . . en nombre de la llorona.

Pues luego la criada se puso el anillo y se lo dio . . . a su hija. Que su hija viene siendo . . . la . . . [difficulty remembering name]. Entonces ésta era una niña que, que crió la señora esta del anillo. Y le regaló el anillo en prueba de, de cariño a la muchachita. Que después le decían la Malinche. Tuvo . . . tres hijos que, que fueron de, de tres amorcitos que tenía ella. Y cada hijo que tenía lo ahogaba . . . en el río, y lo tiraba. Volvió otra vuelta a tener otro hijo, y lo tiró . . . al agua, al río. Y luego volvió a tener otro, y lo tiró (7). Pos entonces oyó una voz que le dijieron que el primer niño era doctor, . . . el segundo niño era padrecito, . . . el tercer niño era un abogado. Y entonces la señora, cuando crecían los arroyos, que acabó de llover, gritaba buscando sus hijos, y dicía, ya muerta ella, dicía: —Aaayyy, mis hijos. ¿Dónde están (3, 4, 6)?

Y entonces ya cuando estaba ella que, que estaba allí muerta, que salió gritando su espíritu, entonces otra señora le robó el anillo, que fue la. . . la Infeliz María. Luego la, la Infeliz María . . . se arrimó donde estaba la Malinche. Entonces dijo: —Ya estás tú muerta. Ahora te voy a quitar el, tu anillo, a ver qué cosas . . . hago yo.

Entonces como esa señora no, no pensaba con buenos pensamientos, pensaba con pensamientos del demonio, . . . entonces le, se le apareció un señor y le dijo: —Anda. Si tú haces esto, yo te puedo hacer muy bonita. Y entonces ella le agarró el anillo a la Malinche, y se lo puso. Y tenía . . . tenía ella los tres hijos. Y los mató, y los echó por consejo del espíritu malo.

Entonces ella, se le hicieron la cabeza de . . . de caballo (8, 9).
Cuando . . . ella lloraba . . . como una . . . de estas ambulancias era el
chillido de ella, . . . y cuando ella lloraba retirado, era que estaba cerca. Y cuando ella lloraba cerquita, era que estaba lejos (6). Entonces
la . . . la cabeza de caballo. Entonces se volteaba una gente y la miraba
. . . y se quedaba torcida la persona para el lado que volteaba, y no se
componía hasta que un curandero las curaba (10). Pos que era aire
que agarraban. Los pies de ella, . . . un pie era de, de caballo y otro pie
era de gallo (11). Eran los pies de la . . . Infeliz María. Y los padres la
conjuraban y le pusieron . . . el nombre de la Infeliz María. Esto empezó desde mil ochocientos, . . . y todavía existe en territorio de México.

Esto me lo contó a mí . . . mis abuelos. Y luego mi padrastro. Mi
abuelita, mamá de mi papá, me contó de la . . . llorona, que es la primera. Y la segunda, me la contó mi mamá, . . . que era la Malinche. Y
la tercera me la contó mi padrastro. Pos que mi padrastro la miró, y se
le, . . . y él nos contó . . . que se le volteó, cuando volteó así pa tras. Y
duró como tres años con el pescuezo volteado. Hasta que no lo curaron,
se puso su pescuezo bien. Él se llamaba Rosendo González, . . . mi padrastro.

Le pusieron una plasta de . . . de huevo en el pescuezo porque tenía
la . . . el pescuezo volteado cuando miró la llorona. Y luego le pusieron
una venda alrededor, huevo batido. Pues luego tenía que durar con
esa . . . venda como cerca de seis o doce días, para que, podía mover el
pescuezo, porque le había quedado el pescuezo torcido.

(1) S113. Murder by beheading.
(2) S115. Murder by stabbing.
(3) Q211.4. Murder of children punished.
(4) Q503. Wandering after death as punishment.
(5) E425.1.1. Revenant as lady in white.
(6) E547. The dead wail.
(7) S131. Murder by drowning.
(8) Q233. Punishment for yielding to temptation by the devil.
(9) E425.2.2. Revenant as man with horse's head. [Here, a woman.]
(10) C311.1.1. Tabu: looking at ghosts.
(11) E422.1.6. Revenant with chicken feet. [One chicken foot, one horse's
 foot.]
 Goodspeed, pp. 202–203; Lizano, p. 107; Leddy, *WF*, 7(1948), 274. [La
 Malinche.]
 Horcasitas Pimentel, nos. 6, 16, 18, 19, 20.

Hiester, *TFSP*, 30(1961), 229; Lizano, p. 106; Pérez, *TFSP*, 24(1951), 76; 26(1954), 130. [*Llorona* with horse-face.]
Mendoza, Virginia, *Previsión y seguridad*, 14(1950), 230. [Reference to children's having been destined to be important: "obispo, cura, sacerdote, monja."]
Riva Palacio, pp. 37–51. [Literary version, in verse, is a parallel, showing the woman, rejected by lover, who murders children.]
Toor, *Treasury*, p. 532. [*La llorona*.]

38. La Infeliz María

(Recorded by Luis Cruz on May 20, 1966, in Los Angeles, California)

La Infeliz María used to appear at midnight along the river near the informant's home in the village of Saltillo, Jalisco. The informant's father would warn the children not to look at her and described her as having the head and the hoofs of a horse. From midnight to 3:00 A.M. she would wander along the river crying out for her children whom she had drowned.

Mi apá me dijo que . . . ésta se llamaba . . . la Infeliz María. Y, y en las noches cuando salía a las doce de la noche (1) empezaba a gritar (2). Y decía mi amá: —Oye, no más. ¡Ave María Purísima!

Y dice mi apá, dice: —No te fijes, dice, —es la Infeliz María.

Dice: —¿Y cómo es la Infeliz María?

—Y, pues, mira, dice, —tiene la cara de caballo . . . y . . . las pezuñas de caballo (4, 5) . . . y . . . el pescuezo largo, dice. —De modo es que, . . . y por eso es que le dicen la Infeliz María. Y ella anda por el río porque tiró sus, sus hijos (6, 7, 8,). Y los anda buscando. Y por eso dice:—Aaayyy, Dios, mis hijos. Y, y ahora pues ella, ella por eso anda por los ríos. Es su . . . sus habitaciones de todo, de toda la noche hasta las . . . las tres de la mañana. Y por eso es de que ella . . . ella anda, anda buscando sus hijos por todo el río. Y . . . y cuando está la luna, de la noche, dice, voltea . . . así de lado [indicates her movement], y se le ven los ojos brillantes, y las orejas de caballo.

[Interviewer: —¿Dónde fue que la vio su padre?]

En la . . . en el rancho del Saltillo. Porque el río estaba cerquita de la casa. Y . . . 'taba . . . no 'taba muy retirado de allí, de la casa, y por eso era que la oíamos en las noches cómo gritaba.

[Interviewer: —¿Tenía nombre el río?]

El Río de la Presa, . . . del Salto. Y por eso es de que . . . todas las, casi las más de las noches lloraba ella allí en el, en el río.

(1) E587.5. Ghosts walk at midnight.
(2) E547. The dead wail.
(3) C311.1.1. Tabu: looking at ghosts.
(4) E425.2.2. Revenant as man with horse's head. [Here, a woman.]
(5) E422.1.6. Revenant with chicken feet. [Here, horse's feet.]
(6) S131. Murder by drowning.
(7) Q211.4. Murder of children punished.
(8) Q503. Wandering after death as punishment.
Horcasitas Pimentel, nos. 16, 19.
Hiester, *TFSP*, 30(1961), 229; Lizano, p. 106; Pérez, *TFSP*, 24(1951), 76; 26(1954), 130. [*Llorona* with horse-face.]

39. La llorona y el susto

(Recorded by Teresa Sánchez on May 24, 1966,
in Los Angeles, California)

In Flagstaff, Arizona, in the year 1949, the informant's daughter and a friend were returning home from church one evening when they saw what appeared to be a sheet floating through the air and then heard a wailing cry that gave them a fright that lasted for quite some time. The mother, who was at home that evening, heard the cry also, but thought it had come from people mourning the death of a next-door neighbor. Upon inquiring in the morning, however, she learned that the neighbor had not died and that others had thought the same thing, but it was really the *llorona* they had heard. The girl was given sugar to counteract the fright.

Mi hija venía de la iglesia. Eran como las once de la noche. Venía de la iglesia . . . metodista, cuando . . . venían algunas otras muchachas. Y entonces al pasar un puente cercas [*sic*] de mi casa . . . vido ella un bulto como . . . una sábana que el viento levantaba. Y al caminar un poco ahí se . . . soltó un llanto, un llanto tan . . . fuerte (1) que ellas quedaron asustadas por mucho tiempo (2). Y cuando llegaron a la casa, ese llanto yo lo oyí. Pero en seguida . . . estaba un señor enfermo, que creía que se había muerto y los hijos lo estaban llorando. Y no, no le creí, que eso sería, sino que . . . siempre ella llegó asustada. Y . . . y le di . . . azúcar, que dicen que es bueno para el susto. Y la acosté. Y entonces otro día le pregunté a la señora, doña Paulita, que si su esposo, qué le había pasado. Y dice que no, que estaba bien. Le dije: —¿Qué, no oyó un llanto anoche?

Dice: —Sí. Un llanto que se oyó . . . oímos todos. Cuando oyeron ese llanto creían que mi esposo había muerto. Y . . . y no, es la llorona.

Pero yo me quedé en silencio, pensando que si era cierto si es la llorona. Y mi hija dice que sí es cierto. Ella, pues, era chica de edad y . . . y vio eso y . . . dos veces lo ha oído ese mismo llanto . . . muy fuerte, que es un llanto que corre. Pero nunca ha visto más . . . bultos, sino nada más el . . . el llanto tan fuerte que . . . que no, no se entiende lo que dice.

Esto pasó en Flagstaff, como en mil novecientos cuarenta y nueve.

(1) E547. The dead wail.
(2) E265.1. Meeting ghost causes sickness.

40. La llorona y sus tres hijos

(Recorded by Elvira Higuera on October 31, 1966, in Los Angeles, California)

The informant says the *llorona* was a woman who killed her three sons in order to be free to pursue her own wicked life. When she died, however, God demanded that she tell Him what she had done with her three sons. She replied that she had drowned them all: one in the toilet, one in the sea, and one in a river, whereupon God refused to pardon her until she could bring them to Him. She has been wandering in search of them ever since.

De la llorona solamente sé que era una señora que tuvo tres hijos. Y que . . . los mató para seguir ella su vida libre. Y cuando ella . . . ya se murió, que fue a dar las cuentas a Dios, entonces Él le dijo que solamente que le llevara sus hijos, que dijera qué había hecho con sus hijos (1). Ella le dijo que . . . uno echó al excusado, otro echó al mar, . . . y que el otro lo había echado en . . . en un río (2). Entonces Dios le dice que para . . . poderla . . . perdonar, que se fuera a buscar sus hijos (3). Y desde entonces la señora anda en busca de sus hijos. Y por eso dice con ese grito: "Ay, mis hijos" (4).

(1) Q211.4. Murder of children punished.
(2) S131. Murder by drowning.

(3) Q503. Wandering after death as punishment.
(4) E547. The dead wail.
  Mendoza, Virginia, *Previsión y seguridad,* 14(1950), 230. [*Llorona* who aborted her unwanted children.]

41. La llorona y sus seis hijos

(Recorded by Ismeria Garay on October 12, 1966 in Los Angeles, California)

The *llorona* was a woman who had six children, who drowned them all in the sea, and who was then heard going about crying for them. The informant is somewhat disbelieving and rather sarcastically questions why she did it in the first place if she was then going to regret it and go looking for them. She conjectures that she must have had some deep emotional problem. When the informant was a little girl in Pánuco, Sinaloa, her mother used to frighten her with stories of the *llorona*, and with threats that the *llorona* would come and carry her off if she did not behave. Once when the airplane was still quite new, her mother gave her a terrible fright by making her believe that the noise she heard as one approached was the *llorona* coming after her. The informant laughs at this now and says it was common practice for parents to attempt to discipline their children with threats of the *llorona*.

Pues, [la llorona] era una señora que tenía seis hijos. Y los echó al mar (1). Y después, mmm, dondequiera la oían gritar: "Ay, mis hijos." [Laughs.] Decía la señora así (2, 3, 4). Yo digo, pues, ¿para qué los echó al mar, ¿verdad?, si después andaba gritando que jus [i.e., sus] hijos? Algún problema grande debe haber tenido, ¿verdad?, la señora. Por eso los echó al mar. ¡Ay, qué feo!

[Interviewer: —¿Y fue su mamá quien le contó eso?]

Mi madre, . . . Emilia Garay. En Mazatlán . . . en Majatlán la . . . oía la . . . de la llorona esa. A nosotros cada segundo . . . yo era muy chica, yo me acuerdo que mi mamá me decía: —Áhi viene la llorona. ¡Ay, y Dios! Un día estábamos en una . . . en una piedra un hermano mío y yo, sentados en una piedra . . . cuando dijo: —Ahí viene la llorona. Y quedamos oyendo un . . . una así, una cosa como un llanto, ¿no? Pero era un canijo avión que iba por arriba. Fue el primer avión que oímos nosotros . . . que pasara. ¡Ay, pero qué susto nos dimos! [Laughs.]

[Interviewer: —¿En dónde fue eso?]

En Pánuco [Sinaloa]. . . . Porque fue el primer avión que pasó, cuando se empezaron a . . . se puede decir a usar los aviones.

Pero vierá qué susto nos dimos con ese avión mentado. Pensamos que era la llorona. Ella oyó el ruido, ¿no?, y ella sabía que era el avión, y a nosotros dijo que era la llorona. Cállese la boca, nos tiramos a matar. [Laughs.]

[Interviewer: —Entonces les decía eso para asustarlos.]

Sí, para asustarnos, porque . . . pues no, no hacíamos caso según entendíamos. Y para asustarnos nos dijo: —Ahí viene la llorona. Ella oyó el ruido del avión, ¿no? Pues, . . . usted cree . . . nunca se oía eso. Oyó el ruido y dijo: —Ahí viene la llorona. ¡Ay, madre mía! Corrimos nosotros, . . . no hallamos en dónde meternos. Porque oíamos eso, y era el avión. No era nada llorona, era el avión. [Laughs.]

[Interviewer: —¿Otra gente de la vecindad hablaba de la llorona?]

Sí [emphatic]. Si a la llorona le tenían mucho miedo. Mucha gente le tenía miedo a la llorona y mucha, toda la gente asustaba a los niños con la llorona mentada. Nosotros creíamos de chiquitos, así, pues yo de pequeña, creía que la llorona iba a venir y nos iba a llevar a nosotros para echarnos al mar también. Sí, como así decía mi madre, ¿no?, que había echado los hijos al mar, también nosotros creíamos que nos iba a echar también (5). Sí. Ya de más grande, ya fue cuando yo me hice incrédula. Porque yo no vi nada verídico. Por eso.

(1) S131. Murder by drowning.
(2) Q211.4. Murder of children punished.
(3) Q503. Wandering after death as punishment.
(4) E547. The dead wail.
(5) E266. Dead carry off living. [The narrative reflects this belief.]
     Horcasitas Pimentel, nos. 23, 41. [*Llorona* will hurt children.]
     Leddy, *WF*, 7(1948), 274 (reference to manuscript versions not presented); González Obregón, *Calles*, p. 40 [*Llorona* used to threaten children.]

42. La llorona y el caballo

(Recorded by Tecla Rocha on November 21, 1966,
in Oxnard, California)

The informant's brother was out riding along a river one day on the hacienda Jalpa de Cánovas, Guanajuato, when he saw the *llorona*. His

horse became terrified and refused to move. He decided to seize the
opportunity to kill her, but his gun fell from his hand into the river.
Although quite frightened, he turned to have a look at her and saw a
woman with long hair, who seemed to be draped in a sheet, but he was
unable to see her face. The informant chuckles as she imitates the wail
of the *llorona.*

Un hermano mío vio la llorona. Iba pasando un río . . . y el caballo,
luego que la vio, se paraba de manos y no quería caminar (1). Porque le daba miedo. Y . . . y luego la, la siguió mi hermano. Sacó la pistola y . . . él dijo: —Hora la voy a matar. Y cuando pensó hacerlo se le
cayó la pistola en el río . . . de la mano.

Fue en una hacienda que se llama Jalpa . . . de Cánovas [Guanajua-
to]. Allí fue. Hacienda de Jalpa, . . . Cánovas, de Cánovas era. Eran
los dueños. Se apellidaban Cánovas.

[Interviewer: —¿Cómo se llamaba su hermano?]

Esteban Espinosa. El se murió ya. Y . . . y luego, dice que . . . cuando
ya salió del río que . . . el, el caballo bufaba y bufaba y . . . y luego, . . .
él no quería voltear, y volteó una vez así para atrás [imitates the move-
ment], y se veía una mujer con . . . el pelo largo, y como, como una sábana . . . cubierta (2). Pero no le vio la cara. No más el, . . . y hacía:
—Aaayyy. [Chuckles.]

(1) B733. Animals are spirit-sighted. Scent danger.
(2) E425.1.1. Revenant as lady in white.
     Horcasitas Pimentel, no. 42.

Buried Treasures

The classification suggested by von Sydow for working with legendary material, which was referred to in the preceding section on devil
lore, may also be applied to the treasure stories presented here. Only
the first of these eight narratives (43) has the structure of a fairly well
developed story and could therefore be described as functioning more
as a superstitious fiction or an anecdote attributed to a real person
rather than as an expression or affirmation of folk belief.

The next six narratives (44–49) are in the nature of personal experiences, either of the informant himself or of a neighbor or a rela-

tive; they contrast with Narrative 43 in that their veracity is affirmed with absolute conviction. They belong to the other category suggested by von Sydow, stories very closely related to folk belief, some of which are told with the overt intention of proving the truth of the very belief on which the story is based. They are of a less complex structure, often dealing with a single incident, and are not characterized by the careful build-up or development of the superstitious fiction.

The last narrative (50) is different in perspective from the previous ones in that it relates a belief tied up with a type of popular local history, with only vague references to actual individual experiences. It is a question of reverse emphasis: the information is given within the context of "they say . . . ," rather than as a personal experience intended to corroborate a generally held belief.

Stith Thompson has made the observation that "some [legendary material] assumes such definitive narrative form that it differs little from the complex folktale."[68] Narrative 43 has something of the quality that Thompson is referring to. While the treasure is specifically located near Colotlán, Jalisco, the story attached to it, about the man and the preparations he is to make and the tasks he is to accomplish in order to disenchant both the maiden and the treasure, has a development and complexity normally characteristic of traditional tale material. The informant's choice of opening phrase lends additional support to the atmosphere of fiction: "Era un viejito y una viejita. . . ."

In her work *The Devil in Dog Form*, Barbara Allen Woods has incorporated a section on treasure legends, inspired mainly by the frequency of the motif of the dog as guardian of hidden treasures in Germanic folklore. Lt. 1008 of this work is described as the following type of story: " To release an enchanted lady and obtain treasure, man must hit the black dog (whether transformation of lady or merely guardian of treasure not specified)."[69] Although there is no black dog in Narrative 43, there is an obvious parallel to it in the snake, which, likewise, the man must strike in order to gain access to the treasure.

The comments the author makes concerning Lt. 1008 are applicable

---

[68] Stith Thompson, *The Folktale*, p. 271.
[69] Woods, p. 127.

to Narrative 43, and may shed light on some of the seemingly poorly integrated details of the story:

Legend-type 1008 includes texts that are only remotely connected with the basic story of the Schlangenjungfrau. In these tales there is no transformation of the lady and there is no kiss of disenchantment. The only vestige of the original story is the motif of disenchantment by striking; the rescuer must hit the dog guarding the treasure in order to release the lady. The dog is not the lady in enchanted form, however; and there is little reason for the striking motif at all except possibly as a fear test. On the whole, the striking of the dog here looks to be a disenchantment motif that is no longer understood. Legends in this type form a kind of transition between tales of the Schlangenjungfrau and other tales of the lady in white.[70]

In Narrative 43, instead of striking a dog, the treasure seeker is to crush the head of a snake, for no apparent reason other than the "fear test" mentioned above. The snake is not a transformation of the lady. When the treasure seeker fails to fulfill the condition and steps on the body of the snake rather than the head, he does not get the key to the treasure vault but has to dig for it instead.

There is a striking similarity between this situation and that of Woods' Lt. 1000. Here, too, the snake is the obstacle to obtaining the key, for the man must remove the key with his own mouth from the mouth of the snake. As pointed out by the author, this act is clearly linked to the kiss of disenchantment, although the original erotic content is lost.[71]

In short, as the story of the Schlangenjungfrau has developed in oral tradition there has been a shift in emphasis from the disenchantment of the lady to the obtaining of the treasure, with a corresponding modification of the motifs involved.[72] Although the informant refers to both the lady [N572] and the treasure as enchanted, the emphasis of the story is on attaining the treasure; there is no activity overtly concerned with disenchanting the lady. If the latter is to be considered an additional objective, it would have to be inferred on the basis of the belief that unearthing a buried treasure will free its ghostly guardian [E451.5]; even so, the concept of disenchantment in popular legendry

70 Ibid., pp. 125–126.
71 Ibid., p. 124.
72 Ibid., pp. 124–125.

seems to have undergone a metamorphosis, resulting in a concept more closely akin to that of laying a ghost. As stated by Woods: "If the idea of disenchantment has any import for the folk, it seems to be in the release of a restless soul from pain."[73]

The treasure seeker in Narrative 43 fails, first, because he does not obtain the key and, second, because he has brought nothing in which to carry off the treasure. Thus, the treasure remains in the cave [N512], and the ghost continues to appear year after year. Concerning the very common outcome, the failure to secure the treasure, and the causes to which the failure is attributed, Woods makes an interesting psychological observation: "The taboo on speaking, as well as the others [i.e., taboos] . . . , although obviously "pre-Christian" in concept, [has] probably persisted because of the psychological need of unsuccessful treasure seekers to rationalize their failures."[74] The preservation of a detailed ritual that is no longer very well understood may perhaps be seen in the same way. Failure to comply with the ritual, for instance, by stepping on the body of the snake rather than on the head, accounts for the failure to obtain the magic key, and thus the task is more difficult from the start. The ultimate reason for failure to acquire the treasure is, however, somewhat less mysterious. It has nothing to do with failure to comply with a ritual and is, therefore, rather anticlimactic: the treasure seeker, having finally located the treasure, has brought nothing in which to carry it off.

Other details of Narrative 43 have to do with the preparations that must be made before setting out on the search: the man is to get drunk and eat a large quantity of bread. The informant explains the former as a device for avoiding the ill effects of the gas ["pa que aguantes tú el gas"]. The idea that buried treasure sometimes causes gases that may be lethal is mentioned in three published narratives collected in New Mexico and California; in the first two, the treasure seeker is actually killed by the poisonous gas.[75] In another story, called "Treasure at the Hacienda de los Albarcones," collected in Texas, the narrator

<hr>

[73] Ibid., p. 124.
[74] Ibid., p. 124.
[75] Ruth B. Tolman, "Treasure Tales of the Caballos," *WF*, 20 (1961), 153–174, nos. 13, 14, and 15.

states that "where money is buried, there is usually a fetid and poisonous gas that can kill a person."[76] Whatever scientific confirmation
there may be for the existence of such atmospheric conditions in caves,
popular belief tends to connect the poisonous gas with the presence of
buried money, making it one more obstacle to attaining the treasure as
well as expressing the feeling that there is a definite evil quality about
buried treasures.

The second detail, the eating of a large quantity of bread, is not
explained by the informant, nor does it seem to be a motif common to
treasure stories. Following the theme further into the story, it turns out
that after the man has eaten the bread he is requested by the enchanted
lady to return it to her; and, although he complains that it is impossible for him to do this, since he has already eaten it, he follows her instructions, finds it, and returns it to her. It seems possible that this
rather poorly integrated theme (or poorly expressed by the informant)
represents what was originally a task assigned the treasure seeker, possibly in the nature of H1071. Task: eat bread but bring it back whole.
The connection is pure conjecture, however, for in this story the man
does not regard the task as such and does not devise any scheme for
fulfilling it (i.e., "Center of loaf eaten," as in H1071); in fact, he is
more a pawn than an active participant in the matter of the recovery.
The rather unsatisfactory incorporation of this theme into the narrative may be attributable to the faulty memory or style of the informant
or to something inherent in the story; however, the theme of eating the
bread and the subsequent recovery of it does not seem to function
originally as one of the numerous obstacles, tests, or tasks commonly
placed before the treasure seeker.

The treasure is revealed to be very large and very valuable through
reference to the forty mules used to transport it to its hiding place.
The formulistic number forty [Z71.12] seems to be a popular choice
when dealing with treasure stories, undoubtedly because of the ready
association of Ali Baba and the hidden treasure cave of the Forty
Thieves. In a collection of treasure stories already referred to, a story

---

[76] Soledad **Pérez**, p. 97.

from New Mexico has this same detail of the "forty mule loads" of treasure hidden by bandits.[77]

The next three narratives, 44, 45, and 46, are examples of the tendency to regard mysterious phenomena as indications of the presence of buried treasure. In number 44 the recurrent appearance of a mysterious man sitting silently on a rock [N511.6] by the side of the road leads the informant's father to suggest to his parents that they dig for what must surely be a treasure buried there. No specific identity is given this mysterious guardian of the treasure [E291.2.1], but he is by inference a somewhat sinister character, for the children are instinctively frightened. The description of him as "muy curro, muy guapo" [very elegant, very handsome] could imply wealth and position, and thus make him the ghost of the owner of the treasure [N576.3] who no longer appears after the money has presumedly been uncovered [E451.5], as does happen in the story. The frequent personification of the devil as a well-dressed gentleman [G303.3.1.2], however, would also permit one to interpret the guardian of the treasure as the devil [N571]. The very brief and fragmentary nature of the narrative leaves openings for various interpretations, but it serves well as an illustration of the belief in ghostly or supernatural guardians of treasures.

Also evident in the narrative is the strong inclination or predisposition to belief in a veritable proliferation of buried treasures, for almost any seemingly mysterious phenomenon may be taken as a clue to the existence of such a treasure. Perhaps it is not difficult to understand the persisting strong appeal of the possibility and the ready credence lent it in such a country as Mexico. Two realistic factors have undoubtedly added to an already established folk tradition. Historical events, especially the revolution, have involved the Mexican in a period of chaos during which, undoubtedly, the ground seemed the only reliable place for the safekeeping of valuables, and it is true that some secreting of funds by rival factions took place. Furthermore, for the lower-class Mexican, economic survival has been exceedingly difficult,

<hr>

[77] Tolman, no. 18.

and the only way to achieve the desired security has been regarded as the fortuitous discovery of a treasure. Steady application and effort have so often proved futile.

Narrative 45 also interprets a seemingly unexplainable phenomenon as an indication of buried treasure. An unknown horseman repeatedly rides into a house, feeds his horse there, and then leaves. Although no treasure was actually found on the spot, nor does the informant mention that anyone even attempted to dig there, she does feel that such was the significance of the repeated visits of the horseman.

Several similar stories about mysterious or headless horsemen can be found in a collection of tales from Arizona. In one of these narratives, a treasure is actually found, and the horseman is felt to be connected with it, as in Narrative 45.[78]

The informant also comments that many people say that money is buried with "azoros" [frightful things] and that he who digs it up will have to reckon with them. She mentions specifically snakes, a traditional embodiment of evil and therefore appropriate in view of the already mentioned aura of evil surrounding buried treasures. The following is one popular explanation of the origin of these snakes: "En Michoacán rodean los tesoros escondidos con zurumuta enrollada, y cuando se descubren, ésta se convierte in víboras." [In Michoacán they wind rope around hidden treasures, and when they are found, the rope turns into snakes.][79]

Another type of *azoro* alluded to in the comment "o matan algún cristiano" [or they kill someone] is the skeleton. Narrative 47 has an example of such an encounter. It also bears out the informant's belief that *azoros* have to be dealt with, for here the successful treasure seeker is pursued by the skeleton to her ultimate death. There is, of course, some basis in reality for expecting to encounter skeletons buried with treasure. A very efficient manner of ensuring the secrecy of the treasure site is (and undoubtedly was) to kill any witnesses, who may have even been the diggers of the hole, and bury them on the spot.

Narrative 46, also centering around the theme of horses, is the third example of a mysterious incident taken to be an indication of treas-

---

[78] *Folk Tales from the Patagonia Area, Santa Cruz County, Arizona*, pp. 10–11.
[79] Mendoza and Mendoza, p. 405, fn. 1.

ure. The disappearance from the stable of the body of a dead horse, the death of which was a very mysterious matter, leads the people to dig at that spot, and they find a horsehide full of money. Money buried in a horse's hide is a frequent motif in treasure stories, as in Boggs 311*A, in which a man is told to kill a horse, make a sack of its skin, and fill it with gold. Once again, the people feel they are being mysteriously instructed to dig for a buried treasure. Naturally, stories about the accuracy of such indications play a big role in preserving the belief.

Narratives 47 and 48 further illustrate a theme introduced in Narrative 45, the element of danger connected with digging up buried treasures. Two motifs developed in this story, which is told as a personal experience of the informant's aunt, are the cursed treasure [N591] and condemnation of greed on the part of the treasure finders; the latter seems to be related, although not actually identical, to the idea that treasure finders must not take all the money [N553.3]. The difference between what is suggested in this story and the situation described in N553.3 is that here it is a question of sharing with another person, not of leaving some money behind. The informant's grandfather says that if they had shared the money with his daughter, who was the one who really found the treasure site in the first place, they would not have had the bad luck that befell them.

The motif of bones uncovered along with a treasure, already discussed in connection with Narrative 45, receives a rather fanciful development in this story, for the bones actually resume the form of a skeleton and pursue the woman to her death. The husband is then convinced that he will be the skeleton's next victim, and an attempt is made to find out what remedy there might be by sending the little girl to "speak to the hole" and ask what "it" wants. But this is to no avail; the deed is done, and the greed of the treasure finders is punished, for it is implied that the husband will not escape the revenge of the skeleton either. As the informant concludes, "tienen [*sic*] que tener mucho de misterio el dinero que se sepulta." [Buried money is always a very mysterious matter.]

Other elements in the narrative include belief in the special power, or perhaps it is more a question of rights, of the original finder of the treasure site and the talking to the hole to ask its will in the matter. When trouble happens, the finders go to the little girl in the belief that she will be able to set things right. These ideas seem to be related to the belief that a treasure is intended for some specific person [N543]. There does not seem to be a motif for the practice of "talking to the hole"; perhaps it may be considered a variation of N554: "Ceremonies and prayers used at unearthing of treasure." Or, in accordance with the belief that treasures are often guarded by ghosts, it may really be a matter of talking with the ghostly guardian, expressed here as "the hole" [E291].

Narrative 48 also deals with the misfortune one may bring upon oneself as a result of finding a buried treasure. The man who digs up the old coins falls ill, gradually wastes away, and dies soon thereafter. Once again, there is a curse on the treasure [N591]. The wife of the informant, who was the narrator of the preceding story, gave the following explanation of this mysterious phenomenon:

Cuando una persona se halla un dinero enterrado, ese dinero, como el dinero que dice mi esposo que la ardillita sacó y se la halló el señor, él murió porque ese dinero tiene como una especie de un veneno. Y se llama azogue en español. Cuando una persona agarra ese dinero entonces se hacen pálidos. O el miedo, sea el miedo que sea, que tienen de aquel dinero, pues creen que sea dinero de muertos. Ése es el que se lleva pronto a la gente que agarra dinero . . . hallado, que un muerto lo entierra.

[When someone finds buried money, that money, like the money my husband says the squirrel found, and the man took it, he died because that money has a sort of poison. And it's called quicksilver (*azogue*) in Spanish. When someone takes that money then he becomes pale. Or fear, maybe it's the fear they have of that money, because they think it's the money of a dead person. That's what very quickly finishes off people who take the money they find, buried by a dead person.][80]

It is clear that an important part of the danger associated with buried treasure has to do with a fear of the dead and of the consequences of meddling in their affairs or with their possessions. Attitudes toward the dead, and the terrible fear of their return, have been

---

[80] George M. Foster refers to this belief about "deadly quicksilver fumes" in "Treasure Tales, and the Image of the Static Economy in a Mexican Peasant Community," (*JAF*, 77[1964], 39).

discussed in the section "The Return of the Dead"; these stories of buried treasure further illuminate those attitudes. A very frequent and predictable outcome of treasure stories is the death of the one who takes the treasure. This outcome has been stated in a summing up of the general characteristics of treasure legends from Normandie: "Le trésor a été découvert, mais ceux qui l'ont enlevé de sa cachette sont morts misérablement avant l'anée révolue!"[81] [The treasure was found, but those who took it from its hiding place died a miserable death before the year was out.]

The other important theme in Narrative 48 is that of the ghostly apparition that used to appear on the premises where the money was buried [E291] and that no longer appeared after the treasure was dug up. Although the connection is not very well developed in the story, it is obviously related to the belief about laying a ghost by unearthing a treasure [E451.5]. The informant does express the felling that the ghost had something to do with the buried money, since it no longer appeared after the money was discovered: "Tal vez era el entierro que estaba áhi, porque no más ese señor sacó el entierro, que era el dinero, y se acabó todo." The explanation is not clear to him, but his attempt to connect the ghost and the treasure conforms to Krappe's observation that "ghosts as guardians of treasure are very common throughout Europe, and the tale will attempt to explain the connection of treasure and ghost."[82]

In Narrative 49 the informant tells of an experience she had as a little girl, in which she and some friends set about to find a treasure they were sure was buried in a certain room of an old abandoned house [N517.1]; they were confronted with a variety of ghostly noises and incidents that they felt were connected with the presence of the buried treasure. The main interest of the story is in the mysterious things they saw and heard while digging for the money, all of which are commonly experienced by the treasure seeker. One writer comments as follows: "Wherever a treasure is buried there is sure to be a ghost or a number of ghosts watching over it. They make their pres-

---

[81] Amélie Bosquet, *La Normandie romanesque et merveilleuse: Traditions, légendes et superstitions populaires de cette province*, p. 145.
[82] Krappe, p. 224.

ence known by apparitions, moans, groans, clanking of chains, and clashing of swords."[83]

The girls were sure that a ghost was guarding the treasure [E291] and so they carried along a "virgencita" for protection [G303.16.1]. They also heard mysterious noises, such as the sound of horses' hoofbeats bearing down on them ["un tropel que parecía que, pos, que iban a llegar con nosotros"]. This sound is commonly "heard" by treasure seekers, as documented in a collection entitled "Spanish American Superstitions";[84] it is often sufficiently intimidating to put an end to the search.[85] The "tropel" first heard, that of horses' hoofbeats, is followed by the sound of loud snorts; then a second type of "tropel" is heard, as if a tumultuous group of children were approaching. Another story told by this same informant (not included with texts) included the same type of incident. An aunt of hers, sitting in vigil over her dead child, heard the sound of the approach of a large, noisy group of people, which turned out to be nonexistent.

Entonces ella dizque oyó que mucha gente venía, plática y plática y plática por toda la orilla del arroyo. Que dice: —Ah, pues, que vienen a visitarme a mí. Pues, no, dice que esa platicadera llegó hasta contra la casa, hasta la esquina, y dizque allí se acabó la platicadera. Y ella estaba fuera ya esperando a que llegaran. Y dice que lo único que hicieron fue que . . . agarrar como un puño de cadenas, y que lo aventaron y que cayó en medio de un troncón de un mesquite que está ahí al medio patio onde nosotros vivíanos [i.e., vivíamos]. Y que allí cayó no más. Eso fue todo. Dizque se acabó la platicadera. Y dice ella que entonces ella salió, pues, a ver, y que . . . ya no vio nada, que le dio miedo y se metió pa dentro.

The informant's comment about these incidents is that they are simply noises and nothing more: "Es puro ruido, ¿ve?, que se oye. Y no es nada."

Another illustration of the mysterious noises often heard where there is a buried treasure can be seen in Narrative 50. Once again, there are the clinking sounds already mentioned in connection with the preceding narrative [E291], described here by the informant as "espuelas, así muy claritas, como es decir, plata que suena" [spurs,

----

83 Jovita González, p. 14.
84 Wesley R. Hurt, "Spanish American Superstitions," *El Palacio*, 47 (1940), 200.
85 Soledad Pérez, p. 99.

very clear, or rather like clinking silver]. This narrative, which simply describes a belief held rather than an anecdote, reflects the common tradition of the robbers and the treasure cave of the Ali Baba story. Here there are not only mysterious noises but also wild animals to be feared, and the danger of losing one's way in the depths of the cave. All these obstacles account for no one's having ever succeeded in finding the treasure.

Referring by name to this same cave, the Cueva de la Fábrica, another informant from the same area corroborated the belief:

Se cree que alguna cosa que . . . como digamos como . . . Francisco Villa, que fue el más afamado, o de más atrás, se da pues a comprender que, que alguna cosa tiene. Pero es que nadien lo puede trabajar. Se han encontrado papeles, documentación, y escrito, lo que dice y todo, a la hora que la pueden ir a, a destapar, pues a abrir la puerta—la otra, porque pasa uno y entra y luego vuelve uno a destapar otra puerta. Y es la que no han podido abrir. Porque ya tienen miedo por tanta fiera y víbora, y mucha cosa peligrosa que hay. Por eso no han podido.

[It is believed that . . . let's say someone like . . . Francisco Villa, who was the most famous, or even earlier, it is thought that there is something there (in the cave). But the fact is that no one can get to it. They've found papers, documents, notes indicating at what time they can go to get it, to open the door—the second door, because you have to pass through two doors. And it's the second one that they haven't been able to open. Because they are afraid of the wild animals and snakes, and all the other dangerous things there. That's why they haven't been successful.]

A number of treasure stories from the same area (the State of Zacatecas) are published in the collection *Folklore de San Pedro Piedra Gorda, Zacatecas* and incorporate some of these same motifs.[86]

The informant makes a very brief reference to a belief about the existence of still another treasure close by in the same mountain range [N512]. This fragment shows the already mentioned inclination to regard mysterious phenomena as indications of buried treasure. Mysterious bells are said to be heard to ring [E533] every year on Holy Thursday at the hour of eight, and the popular assumption is that there is a treasure buried there, related in some way to the Church ("cosas de la Iglesia").

---

[86] Mendoza and Mendoza, pp. 403–407.

In conclusion, two general observations can be made about treasure stories. First of all, they are extremely popular in comparison with other types of narratives. The number included here is not intended to reflect this disproportion, but based on my own collecting experience in the Los Angeles area, and judging from the large number of published treasure story collections, it seems that the story of the hidden treasure represents a very strong and persistent tradition and is therefore one of the most easily acquired types of narratives.

Possible explanations for such popularity have been proposed by various scholars.[87] Alexander Krappe touches on the historical basis for this type of narrative:

Among the legends that may be said to have a general historical foundation one must count two more classes, namely, treasure stories and tales about outlaws. Stories of buried treasure-trove are found all over the Old World. They can be said to be as popular with the modern peasants as they were with the Arabs at the time when the Nights were first put into shape. The general truth underneath this type is no doubt the fact that before the rise of commercialism Mother Earth was found to be the safest bank, and accordingly people did not hesitate, in time of trouble, to bury their currency and their valuables. Often enough it then happened that these were dug up by a late comer, the rightful owners having been massacred or died a natural death before they had a chance to return to the spot.[88]

This historical explanation undoubtedly receives additional support, as has already been discussed in connection with Narrative 44, from historical events in such countries as Mexico, with its recurrent periods of revolutionary activity and accompanying banditry.

Not only the fact that people have buried money for safekeeping but also the extreme economic hardships in a country like Mexico probably act to perpetuate the appeal of the treasure story. There is an economically based psychological attraction to such an idea, for the hope of finding a large amount of money or an amount of money simply adequate for one's needs is more satisfying to indulge than is the idea of working against what have often proven to be insurmountable obstacles to the accumulation of it.

One informant, an extremely poor woman, made a comment that

[87] See Foster, "Treasure Tales," *JAF*, 77 (1964), 35–44.
[88] Krappe, p. 83.

revealed the importance of the fantasy of the existence of great riches and treasure. Referring to the already mentioned treasure in the Cueva de la Fábrica, she lamented what she described as Mexico's extreme backwardness in exploiting the great riches that supposedly lie buried under its soil.

No sé por qué Mexico está tan torpe en eso. Que esa cueva algo indica. . . . Es una cosa [el tesoro] que le voy a decir, efectivamente; no más que el mexicano, . . . pues digamos, como no hay mucha, pos digamos mucha civilización en eso de los tesoros. Pero es una cosa muy rica la que está allí. Es un tesoro muy grande.

[I don't know why Mexico is so backward in these matters. Because that cave is indicative. . . . It's something (the treasure) that I tell you is absolutely true; it's just that the Mexican, . . . well shall we say, they aren't very . . . very advanced in this business of buried treasures. But there is a great deal of wealth there. It is a very valuable treasure.]

That is the belief—not only of this informant, but also of many of the people in the area. The treasure is there, but neither the government nor any individual has known how to exploit this great source of wealth. The explanations given by the informant, along with the reference to the "backwardness" of the country, include the usual obstacles found in treasure stories: "No han podido trabajarla porque le tienen miedo, porque hay muchas fieras. Y ánimas pero ya se han agregado animales." [They haven't been able to extract it because they are afraid, because there are a lot of wild animals. Ghosts, too, but now there are also wild animals.]

The second general observation about treasure stories is that they are characterized by a fairly predictable pattern in structure and detail. The existence and often the location of the treasure are frequently indicated by some mysterious phenomenon, such as a stranger sitting by the side of the road (44), a mysterious horseman (45), the disappearance of a horse's carcass (46), invisible tolling bells (50), and so on. There does not seem to be a specific *type* of occurrence, but simply an otherwise unexplainable one. Also, there is often an element of danger, a risk incurred in actually unearthing a treasure, as for example in Narratives 45, 47, 48, and 50.

Any seemingly mysterious phenomenon may quite understandably be seized upon by people who find themselves in a struggle for economic survival. The obstacles, the fear, and the danger associated with acquiring a buried treasure may be part of what Barbara Woods calls the "psychological need of unsuccessful treasure seekers to rationalize their failures." (See fn. 72.) To go one step further, it might be asked if the element of failure is not a self-imposed, inherent psychological dictate, in view of the vast array of obstacles, including taboos, put in the way of the treasure seeker. The successful treasure seeker so often pays with his life for his success. In the treasure classics, such as *Treasure Island* and numerous other stories of pirates in search of treasure, the penalty often paid for the activity is the loss of an eye, a leg, or less frequently, an arm; that is to say, a token sacrifice is made, in place of death. The psychological implications of suffering injury or death are, it seems quite likely, punishment for wanting to take the treasure; it has already been mentioned how this situation may be related to fear of the dead and punishment for meddling with their possessions.

Psychological interpretations of the treasure story have been offered by a number of scholars. These interpretations offer intriguing insights into certain aspects of the treasure story and contribute immensely to the appreciation of the constant elements in the composition of the stories. The contribution of these scholars is in connecting the treasure story with certain characteristics or qualities found both in the "infancy" of the race and in that of the individual.

On the connection between the treasure story and the "history of the race," the following idea was put forward by Freud (paraphrased by Marie Bonaparte): "One hardly dares venture it, lest it seem too far-fetched, but there must be, in the unconscious, a connection between tales of seeking or finding treasure and some other fact or situation in the history of the race; something that belongs to a time when sacrifice was common and human sacrifice at that. The 'buried treasure' in such cases, would be the finding of an embryo or foetus in the abdomen of the victim."[89]

Selma Fraiberg has subsequently extended this thought to apply it

---

[89] Marie Bonaparte, "A Tale of the Earth: 'The Gold Bug,'" in *The Life and Works of Edgar Allan Poe: A Psychoanalytic Interpretation*, p. 363.

to the psychosocial development of the child, that is to say, to the infancy of the individual rather than that of the race, in an article entitled "Tales of the Discovery of the Secret Treasure." The article presents a very compelling discussion, illustrated with case study material, of the associations between treasure, babies, sexual curiosity, and oedipal conflicts.

What comes out most clearly in the psychological interpretations is a very believable explanation of the inevitable factor of risk, sometimes resulting in death, which accompanies so many endeavors to seize buried treasure. To conclude, a good example of this type of analysis of a treasure tale is Marie Bonaparte's discussion of Edgar Allan Poe's treasure story, "The Gold Bug."[90]

43. El tesoro encantado

(Recorded by Alicia Salinas on May 26, 1966,
in Los Angeles, California)

A man was told by a ghost that an enchanted treasure was meant for him and that the preparations he was to make in order to find it and disenchant it included getting drunk and eating a large quantity of bread; uncovering a key, a padlock, and a horseshoe; and crushing the head of a snake that was to be thrown at him by an enchanted maiden. He succeeded in all but the last, managing only to step on the body of the snake, and therefore had to dig for the treasure rather than have the door magically open to him. He uncovered the treasure but had brought nothing in which to carry it off, and so the treasure remains there in the cave near Colotlán, Jalisco, and the ghost continues to appear every year.

Era un . . . viejito y una viejita [chuckles], y se querían, bueno, digamos mucho, ¿ve? Nunca se habían separado. Y este . . . el señor . . . una vez le . . . fueron y le tocaron en la puerta. Y . . . él, como quería mucho a su esposa, se encelaba mucho porque le iban a tocar la puerta.

Y era una ánima. Lo seguía más bien a él.

Y ella le dijo: —Mira, le dice, —mira, dice, —sabes de que nos tocan mucho la puerta, dice, —y no sé quién sea.

90 Ibid., pp. 353–369.

Dice: —Yo tengo celos, porque se me figura que es un hombre que a ti te quiere.

Dice: —Ándale, dice. —No, dice. —Mira, es una ánima, y es que esa ánima, dice, —yo ya la vi. Dice: —Te quiere dar dinero.

Dice:—¿Por qué? ¿Que ya hablastes con ella?

Dice: —A ti te habla.

—Bueno, dice, —pues voy a ir, dice, pos, el día que se le apareció y le tocaron la puerta, ¿ve? Y él se enfrentó con el . . . ánima. Que le dijo: —Pos, ánima, dice, —¿por qué andas penando?, dice.

Dice: —Mira, dice, —es que te vengo a decir que en tal parte está un . . . un dinero, dice, —un tesoro, dice. —Yo quiero que lo vayas a sacar . . . tú, dice, —porque es para ti (1).

Pos él se puso medio triste, y ya no quería ir porque . . . pos tenía un, . . . le dolía en el corazón dejar a su hijita. Entonces ya le dijo: —Pos sabes de que mañana me voy, dice. —Ya el ánima me dijo que me fuera. Dice: —Porque . . . pero me dice que me voy a ir al cerro, dice. Cercas de Colotlán, Jalisco está ese cerrito, mas no recuerdo el nombre . . . del cerro (2).

Dice: —Mira, dice. —Áhi, dice, —cuando tú vayas a sacar el dinero, dice, —necesitas de un día antes ponerte una borrachera buena, dice, —pa que aguantes tú el gas. Pos que sí.

Entonces . . . le dijo: —Y otro día, dice, —vas a comer mucho pan, dice. —Porque ese tesoro, dice, —está encantado.

Dijo: —Sí, dijo. —Pues no le hace, dijo. —Voy.

Pero ya el viejito pues, ya . . . a última hora se . . . pues tomó mucho valor, porque no quería. Entonces ya le dijo: —Mira, dice, . . . dice, —yo lo voy a ir a sacar, dice, —pero tengo mucho miedo, dice.

—Anda. Adiós. Se dio la despedida con la viejita y se fue.

Entonces le dice, . . . ya le dio su beso, pues, creyendo que ya no iba a volver. Entonces le dijo: —Mira, dice, —arréglame, dice, —todo, dice. —Tú, arregla todo en mi casa, dice, —que ya no nos volvemos a ver, dice.

—Pos tú, aquí me buscas.

Ya se fue . . . el señor. Y ya . . . se emborrachó y . . . luego así comió otro día el pan y le dijo: —Mira, dice, —en aquel . . . encino . . . roble, dice, —ahí, dice, —me esperas.

Pos que ya llegó el ánima y le dijo: —Mira, dice, —no más que te voy a decir una cosa, dice. —Allí, dice, —tienes que encontrar por primera vez, dice, —una llave, dice, —un candado, y una herradura, dice. —¿Sabes lo que indica eso?

Dijo: —No.

Dice: —Mira, es un tesoro muy grande, dice. —Es que . . . fueron, dice, —en aquellos tiempos, dice, —los guerrilleros (3), dice. —Echaron cuarenta viajes, dice, —con cuarenta mulas (4), dice. —Y allí está, dice, —en esa cueva, dice, —muy grande. Dice: —Y tú lo vas a sacar, dice, —porque yo prefiero que tú lo saques, dice. —Es para ti ese tesoro.

Pos se fue el viejito y ya pues él no quería. Dice: —Pero está encantado, dice, —pero tú lo vas a poder desencantar, dice, —porque tú te vas a comer el pan, dice. —Si te lo comes todo.

Dice: —Sí, sí, me lo como, dijo. —Pues ya la suerte me . . . me traerá ese, ese tesoro, dice. —Será en la suerte para mí.

Pos que ya se comió el pan, y fue y . . . y empezó a, . . . ah, luego le dijo: —Mira, está una señorita, dice, —que es más o menos como de dieciocho años de edad, dice, —y está encantada (5), dice. —Pero ella te va a hablar, dice. —Si ves . . . que te tira un cabresto. . . . Y ese cabresto tenía que mirarse, si la señorita esa encantada o dueña del tesoro que estaba ahí, si le aventaba el, el . . . el cabresto, . . . pa fuera. Pero él iba mirando una serpiente. Le dijo: —Te vas a asustar, dijo, —pero no te asustes. Tú la pises. Pos que ya le . . . le, él le daba la pisada, pero . . . dijo ahí: —Cuando pises tú, dice, —la serpiente aquella, dice, —te vas a asustar, dice. —Pero tú te subes al árbol, dice, —y entonces va a aparecer, dice, —el llavero, dice, —pa que tú vayas y abras, dice (6, 7).—Pero mira una . . . una llave, . . . y está con una figura, dice. —La llave es muy grande, dice. —Bueno, está grande, dice. —Tú, . . . trae, trae la figura del candado, dice, —la herradura, dice, —pero tú lo vas a sacar.

Pos quiso que no quiso él se fue. Y siempre, ya, se bajó del árbol y se comió todo el pan. Y cuando se acercó, pues, pisó la serpiente, ¿ve? Y esa serpiente, si le pisaba la cabeza, pos claro que . . . se abría la puerta. Y si no se la . . . pisaba, que le pisara otro lado, pos entonces no se iba a abrir la puerta. El tenía que escarbar pa abrirla. Y así fue.

Entonces él, pos, no pudo pisarle la cabeza. Entonces le pisó a la mitad, y le tocó escarbar.

Y ya que estaba escarbando, que le dijo, . . . apareció la muchacha encantada y le dijo: —Mira, dice, ¿ya te comistes el pan?

Dijo: —Sí.

—Pos ahora me vas a traer el pan.

Dijo: —¿Pero cómo? Si yo iba a sacar un tesoro, dijo, —que está aquí.

Dijo: —Pues, no le hace, dijo. Dijo: —Ahora, dijo, —tú vas a . . . a traerme el pan que te comiste..

Dijo: —¿Pero cómo? Si ya me lo comí. Si me es imposible regresarlo para atrás, dijo. —Si ya me lo comí.

Dijo: —No. Entonces fue y dijo: —Mira, allí debajo del encino, dijo, —donde tú te subistes para defenderte de la serpiente, dijo, —allí está el pan. Dijo: —Ve a traerlo. Entonces fue y agarró la bolsita muy desconsolado. Pero era cierto. Es de, de, de . . . ellos platican, pues, a mí me llegó a platicar la señora . . . Angelita, o sea suegra de . . . de la señora esa, la viejita . . . de las familias Díaz. Entonces me dijo . . . pos él ya se fue y le abrió pues. Le llevó el pan. Y sabe que ya le dijo . . . dijo: —Pos ahora, sí, puedes abrir. Puedes escarbar.

Pues ya escarbó y todo, y que va viendo el tesoro.

Entonces dijo: —Pues no traigo en qué llevarlo.

Dice: —Pues ahora, dijo, —mira, dijo, —este tesoro es para ti. Dijo ella.

Y todavía existe ese tesoro. Es una cueva muy grande. Está en un cerrito cerca de Colotlán, Jalisco. No me acuerdo cómo se llama el cerro pero . . . la cueva tiene nombre. Está escrita . . . en una piedra ahí. Y año por año se aparece el ánima.

(1) E371. Return from dead to reveal hidden treasure.
(2) N512. Treasure in underground chamber (cavern).
(3) N511.1. Treasure buried by men.
(4) Z71.12. Formulistic number: forty.
(5) N572. Woman as guardian of treasure.
(6) N554. Ceremonies and prayers used at unearthing of treasure.
(7) N591. Treasure from striking animal or person and disenchanting him.
     Christiansen 8010ff. Hidden Treasures.
     Qvigstad, no. 74, p. 47. Legends of (lost) treasure of various types.
     Sinninghe, no. 301, p. 68. The "woman in white" guards (and indicates) a treasure.

Woods 1008. To release enchanted lady and obtain treasure, man must hit
the black dog. [Here, the man must strike a snake.]
Folktales from the Patagonia Area, p. 32. [Reference to poisonous gas.]
Foster, *JAF*, 77(1964), 39. [Reference to deadly fumes.]
Mendoza, *San Pedro Piedra Gorda*, pp. 403–407. [A number of treasure
narratives here incorporate some of the themes of Narrative 43.]
Pérez, *TFSP*, 24(1951), 96. [Reference to poisonous gas.]
Tolman, *WF*, 20(1961), nos. 13, 14, 15, and 18. [References to the forty
mule loads and the poisonous gas where treasures are buried.]

44. El tesoro desaparecido

(Recorded by Ana María Romero on December 3, 1966, in Oxnard, California)

The informant's father, as a little boy in San Pablo Meoqui, Chihuahua, used to go out to play with a group of friends in the evening. One
night the children were frightened by the sight of a man seated on a
rock by the side of the road. After seeing him there several nights in a
row, the boy suggested to his parents that they go and dig at that spot
because there must be money buried there. The parents, however, were
too frightened to do so. Later the boy found the stone moved and a
hole dug at that spot, and the man never again appeared.

Me platicaba mi papá que allá por las orillas en San Pablo Meoqui,
pueblito de Chihuahua, jugaban muchos muchachos con él en la noche.
Y una noche venían, venían para la casa. Era ya noche y la luna estaba
muy hermosa, alumbraba mucho, muy bien. Y había una piedra al dar
vuelta el camino (1). Y en la piedra estaba sentado un hombre muy
curro, muy guapo (2). Y no . . . no habló nada, sino no más que todos
se asustaron y corrieron a sus casas. Y así sucedió por varias, varias noches, porque se les olvidaba que ese hombre estaba allí, y se quedaban
de noche a jugar. Pero siempre . . . regresaron.

Y un día mi padre le dijo a sus padres que fueran a escarbar allí porque había dinero. Ellos tuvieron miedo, mis abuelos, y no fueron. Pero
después mi padre siguió yendo a jugar, y ya con sorpresa de él, halló
que la piedra había sido movida y estaba un hoyo no más . . . onde estaba la piedra (3). Y ya no volvió el curro más a verse (4). Y eso es todo lo que sé de mi . . . historia.

(1) N511.6. Treasure under stone.
(2) E291.2.1. Ghost in human form guards treasure.

(3) N563. Treasure seekers find hole from which treasure has recently been moved.
(4) E451.5. Ghost laid when treasure is unearthed.
Christiansen 8010 ff. Hidden Treasures.
Qvigstad, no. 74, p. 47. Legends of (lost) treasure of various types.

45. El jinete y el tesoro

(Recorded by Petra Franco on November 15, 1966, in Los Angeles, California)

A mysterious horseman used to appear every day at a particular house near the Cerro de Ramblás, Jalisco. He would ride his horse into the house, feed it, and then leave. The informant feels that this recurrent incident indicated the location of a buried treasure. She goes on to mention the types of frightful things that are said to be buried with treasures, and that must be reckoned with by those who uncover them.

Estaba una señora viviendo en una casa . . . de los patrones. Ellos se bajaron de . . . allá por la Revolución. Y, y luego todos los días vían que entraba un . . . un hombre a caballo . . . allá al corredor, en un caballo blanco. Y luego el señor llegaba y le echaba maíz . . . a su caballo. Y el caballo comía y todo. Luego que comía luego se . . . sacaba el caballo y se iba.

[Interviewer: —¿Esto pasaba dentro de la casa?]

Adentro de la casa. Adentro de la casa. Y que, pues, . . . dinero enterrado, o dinero que . . . que allí (1). . . . Allá sí se dice, yo no sé, . . . que cuando entierran dinero que lo entierran con azoros. Y cuando se lo hallan, . . . el que lo saca, salen aquellos azoros. Como por ejemplo víboras . . . que, que les echan sogas, o matan algún cristiano, no sé. Y cuando se lo hallan todo eso tiene que verse. Y así esa, esa señora vía ese, ese señor que llegaba . . . en la noche . . . y sacaba maíz, lo echaba a su caballo, y comía el caballo y . . . y luego que comía se iba (2).

[Interviewer: —¿Dónde vivía ella?]

En . . . ese cerro de Ramblás.

(1) N517.2. Treasure hidden within wall (under floor) of house.
(2) E432.1.3.5. Actions of ghostly horse.
Christiansen 8010ff. Hidden Treasures.
Qvigstad, no. 74, p. 47. Legends of (lost) treasure of various types.

Folktales from the Patagonia Area, pp. 10–11. [Several stories involving mysterious horseman and treasure.]
González, *TFSP*, 6(1927), 14.
Mendoza, *San Pedro Piedra Gorda*, p. 405.[Rope around buried treasure turns into snakes.]

46. El tesoro en la cupina de un caballo

(Recorded by Juana Gómez on November 12, 1966, in Los Angeles, California)

An uncle of the informant from the rancho El Coscusillo, in Jalisco, was out riding with his sons one day. In their absence his wife went to the stable and discovered that one of their horses was dead. She asked them about it upon their return, and they answered that the horse could not possibly be dead, for they had just returned from riding it. When they went to the stable to check, the horse was gone. They decided to dig at the spot where the wife had seen the dead horse, and they uncovered a horse hide full of money.

En un rancho que, que se llamaba el Coscusillo, cerca de la Capilla de Guadalupe, vivía un tío mío. Se llamaba Mateo Díaz. Y tenía dos hijos . . . y su esposa y dos hijas en su companía [*sic*]. Y, y un día ellos paseaban un caballo de su patrón administrado en el rancho. Y paseaban ese . . . los caballos del patrón. Y . . . y en uno, era el más consentido del patrón ese, lo paseaban con más, con más anhelo.

Entonces se fueron y la señora fue después a la caballeriza donde dormía el caballo y, y lo vio muerto. Y ella, pues, le agarró mucha apuración. Dijo: —Sabe qué le pasaría al caballo. Y cuando vino su esposo y sus hijos les dijo: —¿Qué le pasó al caballo de doña Concha? Dice: —Está muerto allí en la caballeriza.

—No, mamá, dice. —Si lo traemos. Andábamos en él.

—Pero si yo acabo de verlo muerto en la caballeriza.

Y fueron y no había nada de caballo. Y entonces ellos escarbaron derecho donde estaba, . . . ella vio el caballo muerto. Y estaba una cupina de un caballo llena de pesos (1). Y lo sacaron . . . lo sacaron, y ya le hablaron al patrón, al dueño de la finca . . . que era el patrón de ellos. Y él fue y les dio la mitad. La mitad le, le dio a . . . a mi tío y la otra mitad se llevó el . . . el dueño de la casa.

[Interviewer: —¿Cómo sabían que había que escarbar?]

Pos ellos se imaginaron, porque . . . porque el . . . se les hizo misterioso que . . . el caballo lo habían visto ellos, lo traían ellos, y ella les dijo que estaba muerto. Y entonces fueron a ver qué era lo que había visto ella y no hallaron nada. Sino que luego se pusieron a escarbar y allí estaba el dinero, en la cupina del caballo.

(1) N511. Treasure in ground. [Here, it is found wrapped in a horse's hide.]
Boggs 311*A has treasure in horse's hide motif, but this is the only similarity.
Christiansen 8010ff. Hidden Treasures.
Qvigstad, no. 74, p. 47. Legends of (lost) treasure of various types.

47. El tesoro y el esqueleto

(Recorded by Lola Cruz on November 8, 1966, in Los Angeles, California)

The informant's aunt, as a very young girl in Mexico City, accidentally stumbled across the site of a buried treasure one day and was immediately enticed away from the scene by a woman who had observed her discovery. As the woman was uncovering the treasure she discarded some bones that she found buried with it, and they in turn took the form of a skeleton, which subsequently pursued her to her ultimate death. Her husband was advised to have the little girl who first saw the treasure go to the hole and inquire what "it" wanted. She did this, but received no answer. The husband, who feared that the money was cursed [had quicksilver] and would eventually cause his death also, was told that had they been willing to share the money with the little girl such evil might not have resulted. The informant adds that buried treasure is always a very mysterious matter.

Mi tía Matiana, cuando ella tenía como unos seis años, o cuatro años, no sé cuántos años tendría, ella me platicó que ella andaba jugando, que la mandaron a jugar a un desiertito, como un . . . lote . . . un . . . baldío. Esto fue para allá para el estado de México. Ella andaba jugando por allá, cuando luego en eso ella vio . . . unas cositas allí, flores, o sabe que vería (1).

Entonces una señora la vio y le dijo: —Mira, Tita. Porque mi tía se llamaba Matiana Feliciana, Tita o Tana. —Toma, toma, Tita, estos diez centavos. Anda . . . compra, a la tienda. Y como la tienda quedaba retirada de allí de, del . . . lugarcito ese, del lote baldío, entonces . . . la señora fue la que sacó primero unos güesos . . . de allí. Y aquellos huesos cuando los sacaba, ella los estuvo sacando, pero los huesos estuvieron reformando . . . en un esqueleto. Pero la señora no se dio cuenta. Porque aquella señora no le importaba los huesos, no le importaba el miedo, le importaba el dinero (2).

Entonces fue a la casa y le dijo al señor que mi tía se había hallado . . . aquellas monedas de oro, pero que. . . . Le dijo: —¿Cuánto le distes a la niña?

—Pos, nada. No más le di diez centavos.

Dice: —No seas mala. Está bueno que le des centavos (3).

—O, no, dice. —Al cabo, es una criatura y, ¿qué va a saber?

Pues todos los días aquel esqueleto iba y molestaba a la señora (4). Todos los días iba y molestaba a la señora, porque quería una cosa. Pero no sabía qué cosa, porque la señora no le daba tiempo al esqueleto. Pues la señora se asustó de las [*sic*] bilis y se enfermó y se murió (5). Y quedó el señor.

Y entonces el . . . el señor le, le dijieron que le dijiera a la que había visto primero el dinero, que fuera a hablarle. Entonces le dijieron a mi tía: —Anda, niña. Anda, Tina, a ver al, aquella cosa, a ver aquel hoyo. Háblale al hoyo y dile que qué quiere. Y luego mi tía fue y le habló al hoyo. Y el hoyo no le respondió nada (6).

Entonces luego el señor se asustó y fue y le dijo . . . al papá de . . . de mi tía, a mi abuelito . . . que ónde estaba la niña.

Le dijo: —No, pues, ya la niña ya no está aquí. Ya la niña ya se fue para otro lugar.

Dice: —Válgame Dios, porque ella no va, yo también me voy a morir, dice, —porque este dinero está . . . tiene . . . azogue. Y que . . . y este dinero me va a llevar a mí también a la sepultura, dice. —Ya se llevó a mi esposa, y ahora también a mí me va a llevar.

Dice: —Bueno, pues a ver. Haga usted como, como pueda, dice. —¿Por qué no le dieron parte también a mi hija? Si le hubieran dado parte a mi hija, pueda ser de que esa . . . ese espíritu, esos huesos, ese esqueleto hayan sido alguna cosa buena (7).

Porque cuando un dinero se entierra, pueda ser algún padrecito, pueda ser alguna madrecita, pueda ser algún bandido, pueda ser algún asesino malo, algún dinero robado, y tienen [*sic*], y tienen que tener mucho de misterio el dinero que se sepulta . . . en la tierra de aquellos años. Ahora no lo sepultan porque ahora lo ponen en el banco. Pero en aquel tiempo todo . . . toda la gente enterraba su dinero en el suelo.

(1) N534. Treasure discovered by accident.
(2) N511. Treasure in ground.
(3) N553.3. Treasure finders must not take all of money.
(4) N591. Curse on treasure. Finder or owner to have bad luck.
(5) N384. Death from fright.
(6) N554. Ceremonies and prayers used at unearthing of treasure.
(7) E291. Ghosts protect hidden treasure.
   Qvigstad, no. 74, p. 47. Legends of (lost) treasure of various types.
   González, *TFSP*, 6(1927), 14.
   Mendoza, *San Pedro Piedra Gorda*, p. 405. [Treasures buried with *azoros*.]
   Pérez, *TFSP*, 24(1951), 96.
   Tolman, *WF*, 20(1961), nos. 13, 14, and 15.

48. El ánima y el tesoro

(Recorded by Luis Cruz on November 8, 1966, in Los Angeles, California)

When the informant was four years old (1909), his family lived across the street from the largest store in the town of San Julián, Jalisco. One day the owners of this store disappeared, suddenly and mysteriously, leaving the store completely stocked and unattended for a period of about a year. During that time the building and the property gradually fell into a shambles, and the people took to looting the merchandise of the store. Meanwhile, people began to talk of seeing a mysterious, ghostlike figure dressed as a woman that would walk about the property and then disappear. Although many people, including the informant's brother, attempted to follow her and discover her identity, no one was ever successful. One day a man who was hunting squirrels on the property shot and killed a squirrel that he found holding an old square coin in its mouth. Guessing correctly that the squirrel's nest was located on the site of a buried treasure, he went to it and dug up three boxes of the same old-fashioned square coins. But the man became ill soon afterward, gradually wasted away, and died. The informant speculates that the mysterious ghostlike figure was connected with the buried money.

Tenía yo la edad de cuatro años. Era cuando vivíamos en San Julián, Jalisco, en donde yo nací, en la Calle del Jónuco. Y enfrente de la casa de nosotros estaban los dueños de una tienda, y la tienda estaba enfrente de la Calle Real. Le decían la Calle Real porque la calle que pasa por medio pueblo es Camino Real. Ese camino va para León de los Aldamas. Y nosotros vivíamos cerquitas de la Calle Real, que venían siendo una casa que era la de Don Encarnación Olivares, y en seguida áhi vivíamos nosotros.

Y las casas del Jónuco estaban enfrente de las de nosotros. Y esas gentes tenían esa tienda que tenía un corral muy grande, casi media cuadra de corral circulado de una tapia alta de adobe. Y entonces esas gentes de la noche a la mañana desaparecieron, que eran los dueños de la tienda por mucho tiempo. Que yo figuro, que desaparecieron como por un año. Y dejaron la tienda cerrada y no volvieron más. La tienda quedó bien surtida. De todo vendían áhi. Tenía ropa, tenía azúcar, tenía frijol, tenía jabón, tenía dulce, arroz, tenía garbanzo, tenían cigarros. Todo tenían. Era la tienda más grande de áhi del pueblo. Pero las gentes dueños de esa tienda desaparecieron de la noche a la mañana y nunca volvieron más.

Entonces al año que no se vían los dueños, de estar la tienda cerrada, las puertas de la tienda se empezaron a caer a pedazos ya de podridas que estaban tanto de estar sola. Y nadie reclamaba estas gentes que habían desaparecido por tanto tiempo y a nadie dejaron de encargados. Sólo dejaron cerrado. Pues luego que las puertas estaban todas rotas, muchachos y gentes grandes empezaron a sacar todo poco a poco. Los muchachos el azúcar, el dulce. Hasta yo también. Pero ya todo estaba meado de ratones. Pero así nos lo comíamos. Y gentes grandes sacaban ropa pero ya podrida, y cigarros y arroz apolillado de tanto estar la tienda cerrada. Y las gentes ya no volvieron y no hubo quién reclamara a las gentes ni la propiedad. Así es que se fue destruyendo todo, hasta cayéndose la finca.

Y luego en las paredes del corral todas ya con hoyos de los animales, que eran zorras. Entonces estaba un señor que él iba a cazar zorras [the informant identified the *zorras* as squirrels] con un rifle. Entonces después de desaparecer las gentes que eran los dueños de allí, entonces gentes veían una cosa como una gente vestida de negro, en forma de una mujer. Pero no daba la cara. No más se le veía el cuerpo. Pero no le veían cara. Y seguían al bulto pero no lo podían alcanzar. Y llegando a la esquina onde terminaba el corral, que era la orilla de la propiedad, allí se perdía. Y eso salía todas las noches y toda la gente la veía, y nunca supieron quién fuera ni nunca se pudieron desengañar por qué el bulto se desaparecía (1).

Y luego mi hermano Refugio lo llegó a seguir, y nunca se pudo desengañar qué era. Porque nosotros vivíamos enfrentito, y llegábamos a ver el bulto pasearse todas las noches. La gente, que lo veía a cualesquier hora, pero a las ocho de la noche empezaba a salir. Pero lo seguían y no lo alcanzaban y se desaparecía. Se volvía nada. Y se paseaba no más hasta donde llegaba la orilla de la propiedad. Áhi se perdía el bulto. La gente que lo veía lo vían que salía de la tienda y se paseaba hasta fin de la propiedad.

Así es que el señor que iba a cazar zorras, él vio una zorra que salió del pie del fondo, del cimiento, y traía una cosa agarrada con los dientitos. Que salió del agujero y se paró con las manitas para arriba. Y luego traía la cosa en la boca la zorrita. Y luego el señor le tiró y la mató. Y fue y la levantó. Y la zorrita, cuando le dio el tiro, soltó lo que traía, y era un peso cuadrado de los que habían antes. Que la zorrita lo había sacado de donde estaba el entierro, porque el entierro áhi estaba onde tenía su casita la zorrita.

Y luego este hombre que cazó a la zorrita se puso a escarbar derecho a la casita donde tenía el hoyo la zorrita por dentro del corral de la propiedad, donde salía el bulto vestido de mujer. Y el señor sacó el entierro. Tres cajones de puros pesos cuadrados (2). Pero el señor después se fue enflacando diatiro hasta que se vía él puro hueso, hasta que se murió (3).

Pero nadie de los que veían al bulto, nadie se desengañó qué era. Pero tal vez era el entierro que estaba áhi, porque no más ese señor sacó el entierro, que era el dinero, y se acabó todo (4). Pero la zorrita fue la que dijo dónde estaba el dinero, porque la zorrita salió de su hoyito con un peso en la boquita, y fue cuando el señor la mató y él sacó el dinero. Pero él murió y la zorrita tambien murió. Así que se acabó todo, el señor que sacó el dinero y la zorrita también.

Esto pasó en la fecha de 1909. Tenía yo cuatro años.

(1) E291. Ghosts protect hidden treasure.
(2) N511. Treasure in ground.
(3) N591. Curse on treasure. Finder or owner to have bad luck.
(4) E451.5. Ghost laid when treasure is unearthed.
 Christiansen 8010ff. Hidden Treasures.
 Qvigstad, no. 74, p. 47. Legends of (lost) treasure of various types.
 Foster, *JAF*, 77(1964), 39. [Reference to the deadly fumes encountered with buried treasure.]

49. El tesoro guardado por una ánima

(Recorded by Amalia Hernández on May 16, 1966,
in Los Angeles, California)

When the informant and her sisters were young girls, in the town of Sánchez Román, Zacatecas, rancho Los Guapos, they went to look for a treasure that they believed to be buried in a particular room of an abandoned house. In order to protect themselves from the devil or from ghosts they carried with them a statue of the Virgin. Their candle was mysteriously put out several times, and they heard mysterious ghostly noises. After digging a large hole and finding nothing, they abandoned the task because of the late hour. The informant affirms her belief that the treasure was guarded by a ghost.

Esto es, es un . . . el pueblo este, Sánchez Román. El rancho donde vivo yo es Los Guapos. Y . . . bueno, sabe que estábanos [i.e., estábamos] todas chamacas. Nosotros estábanos chamacos, y éranos [i.e., éramos], . . . mi mamá se casó de vuelta, ¿verdad? Éranos tres hermanas mías y tres la otra, . . . de mi padrastro. Y vivíamos juntos. Ese ranchito era . . . pues, muy solo de allí, cuando vivía mi padrastro. Entonces esa casa estaba sola y nadien la dejaba ver que, . . . que el señor no, no quería que nadien viviera allí.

Entonces nosotras estábanos chicas. Y dijimos: —Bueno. ¿Por qué este señor no quiere . . . dejar vivir a nadie? Porque allá hay dinero en un cuarto, y ese cuarto lo tiene encerrado (1). Entonces nosotras estábanos como de unos doce años.

Entonces le dije yo a la, la otra, dije, que era casi de mi edad, le dije: —Bueno, pues, vamos entrando.

Dijo: —Sí, dijo. —Pero si está el diablo ahí, dice, —y nos va a agarrar (2).

—No, le dije. —Sabes que vamos entrando con una virgencita (3).

Entramos allí. Agarramos una virgencita y unas velitas, y entramos adentro del cuarto, oscuro, oscuro. Entonces anduvimos midiendo los pasos. Dijimos: —A ver. Dicen que es que onde está hueco hay dinero. Andamos pisando recios y que: —Aquí mero está, ¿no?

Entonces ya empezamos. Ahí llevábamos hacha y pala, y empezamos a escarbar. Una escarbaba y la otra sacaba la tierra. Y a otra . . . muchacha, la teníanos [i.e., teníamos] con la vela y, . . . entonces nos apagaron la vela una vez. La vela, ¿ve? Porque era una velita, y la apagaron la vela (4). Y no llevábamos cerillos. Tuvimos que salir pa fuera. Todas . . . ajustadas [i.e., asustadas]. Entonces ya cuando entramos, ya entramos a prevenidas. Entonces ya empezamos a escarbar, y no. Le volvían a apagar la vela. Y la otra estaba lista con la mecha, . . . a prender. Entonces ya seguimos escarbando. Entonces oímos un, un ruido, un tropel por toda la, . . . lo que es la pader, ¿verdad?, del cuarto. Un tropel que parecía que, pos, que iban a llegar con nosotros. No más estábanos mirando, yo y mis compañeras y . . . que ni ellas se asustaban ni yo tampoco.

Entonces ya . . . volvíamos a seguir. Y se acabó ese ruido. Entonces oímos unos bujidos [i.e., bufidos] . . . fuertes. Y nosotras no más . . . no más mirábamos nosotras. Parábamos de escarbar y nos mirábamos. Y luego despuésn, oímos un . . . casi un tropelito de chiquitos, ¿ve?, que , que llegó de la esquina así, a no más a donde estábanos escarbando (5). Era yo creo dinero. Pos, pa mí, que era. Entonces escarbamos mucho nosotras. Ya casi yo me sentaba arriba, ¿ve? Que ya me . . . los pies quedaban colgándose abajo. Y, y sentadas nosotras ya, casi en el hoyo, ¿ve? Pero ya, de mucho, ya estaba queriendo oscurecer. Y como mi amá me había dicho que . . . llegara pronto, entonces de allí nos, nos regresamos. Porque a mí me agarró mucho sueño, ¿ve? Y ya nos, nos fuimos y paramos allí. Pero oímos esos ruidos. Los oímos nosotros, sí. Es ánima (6).

(1) N517.1. Treasure hidden in secret room in house.
(2) N571. Devil as guardian of treasure.
(3) G303.16.1. By the help of the Virgin Mary the devil may be escaped.

(4) F473.2.3. Spirit puts out lights.
(5) E402. Mysterious ghostlike noises heard.
(6) E291. Ghosts protect hidden treasure.
     Christiansen 8010ff. Hidden Treasures.
     Qvigstad, no. 74, p. 47. Legends of (lost) treasure of various types.
     Sinninghe, no. 949, p. 109. Devil guards treasure: holds back treasure
       hunters.
     González, *TFSP*, 6(1927), 14. [Ghosts guard treasure; mysterious noises.]
     Hurt, *El Palacio*, 47(1940), 200. [Mysterious noises; sound of horse's
       hoofs.]
     Pérez, *TFSP*, 24(1951), 99.

50. El tesoro de la Cueva de la Fábrica,
y el tesoro y las campanas

(Recorded by Elisa Contreras on May 17, 1966
in Los Angeles, California)

The informant tells of a treasure believed to have been hidden in a
cave near the rancho La Majada in Zacatecas at the time of the Revolution and that is inaccessible, because those who enter become lost and
are unable to find their way out. Ghostly noises are heard, including
the sound of clinking spurs or money, but no one is able to get to the
treasure.

In the same mountain range there is believed to be another treasure,
attested to by the ringing of mysterious bells at the same hour on
Thursday of Holy Week every year.

En el rancho de La Majada [Zacatecas], . . . está en la sierra, está
cerca de la sierra, . . . está una cueva muy grande que se llama la Cueva de la Fábrica. Y allí dicen que permanecían mucha, muchos ladrones cuando la . . . Revolución pasada (1). Entonces allí, es, . . .
abajo dicen que es un soterráneo muy hondo, y allí hay mucha plata
(2). Pero no puede entrar nadien, porque dicen que el que entre no
sale porque no encuentra la puerta. Y por eso es que nadien puede
entrar. Entran hasta donde la luz es, . . . pues, les dan abasto, pero
más pa dentro, no, no entran. Pues, tienen, tienen temor que haiga
animales o algo (3). Se oyen muchos estragos. Dicen que se oyen
muchos ruidos, espuelas, así muy claritas como, es decir, plata que
suena (4). Y la gente trata de entrar, porque dicen que allí está un
tesoro muy grande. Pero no hay quien tenga valor de sacarlo. Es todo.

En el rancho de La Majada, en la misma sierra donde está ese
. . . la Cueva de la Fábrica, allí se encuentra otro tesoro, relacionado
a cosas de la Iglesia. Porque cada jueves santo a las ocho en punto
repican las campanas muy clarito (5). Así que pueda ser que, pues,
haiga algún tesoro ahí en ese mismo lugar. La gente mayor es la que
comenta eso, que hace muchos años que . . . que están oyendo esas
campanas repicar allí.

(1) N511.1. Treasure buried by men.
(2) N512. Treasure in underground chamber (cavern).
(3) E291. Ghost protects hidden treasure.
(4) E402. Mysterious ghostlike noises heard.
(5) E533. Ghostly bell.
     Christiansen 8010ff. Hidden Treasures.
     Qvigstad, no. 74, p. 47. Legends of (lost) treasures of various types.
     Sinninghe, no. 24, p. 125. Sound (ringing) of bells (from below the
       ground).
     Hurt, *El Palacio*, 47(1940), 200. [Clinking sounds while digging.]
     Mendoza, *San Pedro Piedra Gorda*, pp. 403–407. [Several treasure stories
       incorporating some of these same themes; and from the same area as
       Narrative 50.]
     Pérez, *TFSP*, 24(1951), 99.

Duendes

As pointed out in the section "The Return of the Dead," there
is often an overlapping of the activities engaged in by *ánimas*, *espíritus*, and *duendes*. The mysterious throwing about of objects, for example, is attributable to all of them: the *ánima* of Narrative 20
throws wet stones at its victim; the *espíritus* of Narrative 25 throw
things around in the kitchen; and the *duendes* of Narratives 51, 52,
and 57 throw bricks or stones. Generally bothersome or mischievous
acts, especially involving the kitchen and the preparation of meals,
are thought to be the work of *espíritus* in Narratives 25 and 26, and
of *duendes* in Narratives 52, 53, 54, 55, 56, and 57. In another favorite spot for pranks, the bedroom, the *espíritus* of Narratives 25,
26, and 27 pull off bedclothes or actually dump people out of their
beds and even carry them off physically into the yard. This same type
of mischievous prank is attributed to *duendes* in Narratives 52 and 53.

The frequency of these motifs indicates that popular opinion attributes such incidents to the work of supernatural beings, if "supernatural beings" may be used as a heading under which to group *ánimas*, *espíritus*, and *duendes*. Conversely, it can be concluded that, once one is convinced of the presence of such supernatural beings, the tendency or inclination is to expect these types of pranks and to feel oneself the victim of them.

Some concepts that may offer partial explanation of, or at least insight into, attitudes toward *duendes* have been discussed in the concluding remarks on the section "The Return of the Dead." The three —*ánimas*, *espíritus*, and *duendes*— can be conveniently discussed together, and, as has been indicated above, patterns can be seen in characterizing them. On the other hand, *duendes* can be discussed as a separate category on the basis of the differences in identity and function that folk tradition attributes to them. Unlike the *ánimas* and the *espíritus* of these narratives, the *duendes* are not felt by the informant to be traceable to once-living human beings. In addition, the acts engaged in by *duendes* are often similar to those committed by *ánimas* and *espíritus*, but the purpose is different. While the *ánima* may throw things, it is inevitably with the purpose of attracting the attention of a human being in order to solicit his aid in accomplishing a task or paying a debt (the *manda*) required of it before it can be at rest. The *espíritu* is not seeking aid when it engages in mischievous or annoying acts, but is simply carrying out its generally accepted role of being antagonistic to the living. The *duende* is not seeking human aid either, and his mischievousness and antagonism often seem to be purely arbitrary; but, in contrast to the *espíritu*, the *duende* may also be helpful (as in Narratives 53 and 54).

Alexander Krappe, in dealing with the question of the identity of the Teutonic dwarfs and the Celtic elves and fairies, makes comments that are relevant to the *duende* as well; for one story told about those creatures, which he cites, is in essence that of Narrative 54. Krappe comments on three different theories about the existence of these dwarfs, elves, and fairies:

According to one, they are the dead; according to another, they are elementary spirits; and according to a third they are due to reminiscences of former inhabitants, crowded out by the newcomers and compelled to retire into the mountains or near the sea-shore. Let us say at once that a good many stories are in accord with the first theory, in fact, probably a majority, that certain features are better explained by the second, and that there is no solid basis of fact behind the third.[91]

Krappe is speaking here of Teutonic dwarfs and Celtic elves and fairies; he does not purport to be dealing with the *duende* as a phenomenon in contemporary Hispanic folklore. Therefore, more research into the nature of the relationship would be necessary in order to be able to comment on the question of whether the *duende* in Hispanic folk tradition is really a manifestation of a dead ancestor, as Krappe suggests. It is certainly a convincing explanation for such stories as Narrative 54, in which the *duendes* are somehow tied to a specific house or family; it seems significant to state, however, that none of the informants represented here offered that explanation of the identity of *duendes*. The presentation, then, of *duendes* as a category separate from those manifestations of once-living beings (The Return of the Dead) is based not on theoretical origins, devised by folklorists for *duendes*, but rather on the informant's working concept of *duendes*.

Narrative 51 is not structured as a story, but rather as a statement of two types of belief commonly held in the informant's home town. The first belief is that *duendes* were responsible for the common occurrence of stones flying through the air [F473.1] and breaking the water jugs [F482.5.5] when the women went to a nearby spring for water. It is an extremely common notion that *duendes* throw stones, as may be inferred from the frequency of the motif in the narratives presented here and also from numerous published documentations of it.[92]

The second belief is that of the efficacy of burning a holy palm in order to counteract the power of the *duendes*. The informant's mother, believing that the *duendes* had carried off the boy's spirit when he lost consciousness one day, performed this ceremony in order to get them to restore it to him. This is probably best identified as motif F382: Exorcising fairies. (Fairies disappear when some name or cere-

---

[91] Krappe, pp. 87–88.
[92] See, for example, Mendoza and Mendoza, *San Pedro Piedra Gorda, Zacatecas*, p. 87.

mony of the Christian Church is used.) Once again, the question arises of equating the fairy and the *duende*; in view of this, a second motif could also be considered—D2176.3.2: Evil spirit exorcised by religious ceremony.

Burning a holy palm is considered efficacious for a variety of purposes. Among the Spanish-speaking people of New Mexico, it is documented as a means of warding off the danger of thunder and lightning.[93]

The same belief in *duendes* who throw stones and, here, bricks as well [F473.1] is found in Narrative 52, with an interesting modern touch in the informant's likening of the sight of the flying bricks to that of an approaching airplane. In this household the *duendes* would also shake the tree branches, make strange noises [F473.5], and choke the children in their beds at night [F482.5.5]. To put an end to the trouble, a priest was called upon to perform an exorcism, and the noises and strange incidents stopped immediately [F382; D2176.3.2]. This story can be compared with one found in the collection *Folklore de San Pedro Piedra Gorda, Zacatecas*, in which a family is bothered by the same phenomenon of flying bricks filling up the house and, attributing it likewise to the presence of *duendes*, resorts not to an exorcism performed by a priest, but to a policeman.[94]

The *duendes* of Narrative 53 engage in a wide variety of mischievous acts, but they are also helpful on occasion [F482.5.4]. Among their mischievous pranks are the common ones of pulling off the bedclothes at night [F470.1] and dumping people out of their beds [F482.5.5]. As has been mentioned, these bedroom pranks are also attributed to ghosts or *espíritus* on occasion. Examples may be found in Narratives 25, 26, and 27 and also in a collection of folk narratives from Arizona, which contains a story about a haunted house in which covers are jerked off and beds overturned.[95] Their pranks in the kitchen and interference at meals, by throwing feces in the food[96]

---

93 Benjamin S. Moya, "Superstitions and Beliefs Among the Spanish-Speaking People of New Mexico," p. 44.

94 Mendoza and Mendoza, p. 387.

95 *Folk Tales from the Patagonia Area, Santa Cruz County*, p. 22.

96 Freud expressed an interest in the belief in this type of abuse, the throwing of feces into one's food, and also the pulling off of bedclothes during the night, and

and knocking over glasses of milk at the table, are like the "maldades en la cocina" [pranks in the kitchen] told of in another of the folk narratives from San Pedro Piedra Gorda, Zacatecas.[97]

Two additional ideas about *duendes* are introduced in Narrative 53, one of them having to do with their appearance: "me platicaron que eran unos niños chiquitos, vestidos de verde" [they told me they were small children dressed in green] (F482.2.1). Furthermore, the family knew there were about eight or ten of them who would appear there, although they did not know where they came from. These comments raise the question of whether the description is based simply on a traditional concept of the *duende* or whether it is a product of the woman's conviction that she really saw them. They are invisible to guests, but the occupant of the house describes them as if she had seen them.

The other point introduced in Narrative 53 has to do with precisely this great familiarity between the occupants of the house and the *duendes*, which is not shared by outsiders. It seems to offer support for Krappe's idea that this type of creature is a representation of dead ancestors, those who actually occupied the same residence. The wife here comments that they have learned to live with the *duendes* and their sometimes helpful, sometimes annoying, presence; but, whenever outsiders or guests are around, the *duendes* cause the family a great deal of embarrassment ["nos hacen pasar muchas vergüenzas"]. This is a rather accurate expression of a true-to-life situation: the *duendes* are in a sense like members of the family, particularly the elderly members. One learns to live with them, adapts to their annoying quirks and habits, and yet feels affection for them; but these same

---

suggested a psychological interpretation of it in a letter written in 1897. His comment is as follows: "There is a class of people who to this very day tell stories like those of the witches and of my patients; they find no belief, though their own belief in them is not to be shaken. As you have guessed, I mean the paranoics, whose complaints that people put faeces in their food, ill-treat them at night in the most abominable ways, sexually, etc., are pure content of the memory. (*The Standard Edition of the Complete Psychological Works of Sigmund Freud*, vol. 1 [1886–1899], Letter 57, p. 244). These are, as can be seen, the very same acts which folk tradition attributes to the *duende*.

[97] Mendoza and Mendoza, p. 387.

people, in the presence of outsiders, can be the source of much embarrassment.

The next narrative, number 54, is almost ideally representative of the type of story cited by Krappe in support of the above-mentioned theory that identifies the Teutonic dwarf and the Celtic elf and fairy as representations of dead ancestors. A portion of Krappe's description is as follows:

They are attached to definite localities, often even to definite houses and definite families, with which they are supposed to be mysteriously connected and in which they take an interest, facts best explained by the assumption that they were themselves inmates of the houses in question and belonged to those very families, which simply means that they are dead ancestors. More, like those very ancestors they are the objects of a regular cult; for they expect to receive food, and if it is refused to them they demand it and take their revenge.[98]

The man in Narrative 54 feeds the *duendes* in order to keep them happy, and they help him with his work [F482.5.4]. But when he gets tired of their presence and tries to escape from them by moving, he discovers they cannot be left behind.

This particular story, which reflects the above statement of Krappe, is structured as a humorous anecdote. These *duendes* are tied obviously more to the family than to the house, and the main interest of the narrative lies in the final episode in which the couple, thinking they have succeeded in leaving the *duendes* behind, are humorously confronted with their inescapable presence.

The story is documented in a number of works. It is cited as Type 7020—Vain Attempt to Escape from the Nisse—in Christiansen's *The Migratory Legends*;[99] and as motif F482.3.1.1—Brownies move with farmer—in the Thompson *Index*. The same story appears in the *Cuentos populares de Castilla* as number 54[100] and also among the *duende* narratives in *Folklore de San Pedro Piedra Gorda, Zacatecas*.[101]

---

98 Krappe, p. 88.
99 Reidar Th. Christiansen, *The Migratory Legends*.
100 Aurelio M. Espinosa, hijo, *Cuentos populares de Castilla*, p. 149.
101 Mendoza and Mendoza, p. 387.

Narrative 55 has as its last part the same episode referred to above in Narrative 54 [F482.3.1.1]. In both these stories, the husband and wife realize they have forgotten the broom and are about to start back for it when the *duendes* are heard to say not to worry, for they are bringing it. This second presentation of the theme illustrates its migratory nature, for it is tacked on to the end of a story that constitutes a complete and separate narrative and that does in fact stand alone in Narrative 56.

These two narratives, 55 and 56, introduce the theme of hostility to the clergy: a priest is called upon to exorcise the *duendes* and is so intimidated by them that he is forced to flee. The two informants, who are related, are referring to the same incident, for they both identify the town as Tepozanes, Jalisco. This very common type of story, expressive of a great deal of hostility to the clergy, and these two narratives specifically are discussed in a previous section on the religious sentiments that find their way into folk narratives.

Narrative 57 tells a similar story, about a family bothered by the presence of *duendes* in its home; but in this case the exorcism performed by the priest is successful [F382; D2176.3.2]. The most interesting element in this narrative is the informant's attitude toward *duendes*. She expresses real shock and indignation that such a thing could happen to an upright Catholic family ["una familia . . . católica, honrada"] and is convinced that it is the work of the devil: "y es cosa de . . . del demonio, ¿verdad? Yo creo que es cosa de enemigo." Her faith in the ability of the priest to prevail over this evil, however, is absolute, for, as she says, "ellos saben sus oraciones y todo . . . con que pueden . . . acabar todo." [They know the prayers and everything with which to put an end to it.]

In summary, these seven narratives present many activities attributed to *duendes*, as well as a number of different attitudes toward them. The *duende* is known to throw bricks, stones, and other objects (51, 52, 57); shake tree branches (52, 57); make mysterious and sometimes frightening noises (52, 55); engage in bedroom pranks, such as pulling off bedclothes, dumping people out of bed, or otherwise physically abusing them (52, 53); interfere in the kitchen and with food preparation (52, 53, 54, 55, 56, 57); and threaten severe physical abuse, directed here at the clergy (55, 56). In addition to these annoying practices, however, the *duende* may also be helpful (53, 54).

There is a variety of attitudes toward *duendes*. Some see them simply as mischievous and annoying, but essentially harmless, creatures (51, 53, 54); others as somewhat more powerful and threatening beings (51, 52, 55, 56); and still others as outright manifestations of the work of the devil (57). They often inspire humor, which, although it may not be inherent in the story itself, is clearly a reaction of the informant as he relates it. While this may not always be evident from the printed narrative, it was in fact true, in varying degrees, of all the informants represented here except the last one. The amusement of the first five informants contrasts sharply with the indignation of the last.

There were attitudes expressed by two other informants not represented in these seven narratives that constitute individual evaluations and rejections of the belief itself. One informant felt that belief in *duendes* was simply a concomitant to a not very civilized way of life, and that with time and progress the belief has inevitably begun to disappear:

Esos duendes, . . . yo no sé cómo sean los duendes. Mi madre decía. —Mmm, áhi viene un duende. Que en la noche que se oyen ruiditos, que: —Áhi viene un duende. Yo nunca oía ruidos. Mi mamá sí creía. Decía: —Áhi viene un duende; hoy se oyeron los duendes. Porque se oía un ruidito y ella decía que era un duende. Tenía mucha creencia la gente de antes, ¿no? Mucha creencia en eso, en los duendes, en los que asustaban, en todo. Ahora la gente . . . ya no tiene creencia, porque . . . hay mucha civilización. Y antes, no. Más antes la gente . . . creían en cualquier cosita.

[These *duendes*, . . . I don't know what they could be like. My mother used to say. "Mmm, here comes a *duende*." Then at night when you hear noises: "Here comes a *duende*." I never heard noises. But my mother believed it. She would say: "Here comes a *duende*; today we heard the *duendes*." People used to believe a lot, you know? They believed in that, in *duendes*, in spooks, in everything. Now people . . . don't believe any more, because . . . things are more civilized. And before, that wasn't true. Before, people . . . were ready to believe in anything.]

A more dramatic comment came from another informant who delivered a scathing denunciation of those he considered to be the perpetrators of such beliefs. He became infuriated at the thought that people are actually so deceived by those who use the belief for their own evil purposes. He affirmed that so-called *duendes* are nothing more than "rateros, ladrones que roban las cobijas, los metates, y otras cosas" [thieves, robbers who steal blankets, *metates*, and other things], and that they encourage such beliefs in order to get away with their thievery.[102]

51. Los duendes que tiraban piedras

(Recorded by Rafael Gudiño on May 3, 1966, in Los Angeles, California)

Women from the Barrio Alto neighborhood in Mazamitla, Jalisco, used to go for water to a nearby spring called el Pasote; there, as they would stoop to pick up their water jugs, it was a common occurrence for stones to come flying from somewhere and break them. It was generally believed that these were the pranks of *duendes*. When the informant, as a small boy, fell unconscious once, his mother was convinced that the *duendes* had carried off his spirit, and she set about to counteract their power by burning a holy palm.

Bueno, ese pueblo está en la sierra . . . que le dicen la Sierra del Tigre. Mazamitla, Jalisco, es como se llama ese pueblo, ¿verdad? Y allí pues, cuando yo tuve entendimiento, allí vivía mi madre conmigo. Vivíamos en una parte que le nombraban el Barrio Alto. No tenían pedrado las calles ni tenía nada. Eran las casas de adobe pero tapadas con

---

[102] The informant was a man in his sixties from San Juan, Jalisco, who originally studied for the priesthood and then became an elementary schoolteacher in Aguascalientes. He was a volatile individual whose strong opinions were not limited to the subject of *duendes*. He would not discuss religious legends with me since he did not know my religious convictions; and he stated categorically that he was against any form of tale-telling because of its supposed unhealthy influence, which he referred to as "auto-sugestionamiento," or self-delusion. He saw a clear danger in one's becoming so immersed in fantasy as to lose one's grasp on reality; for example, in his own words, anyone at all could come to regard himself as "un Sancho Panza," which is presumably his way of expressing his disapproval of Sancho's participation in the fantasies of Don Quixote.

zacate. Y de allí nos cogía el ojo de agua que le nombraban el Pasote, como a una milla de distancia o poco menos. Y las mujeres se acostumbraban a ir allí a coger su cántaro de agua. Y entonces, cuando venían o cuando se iban a . . . agachar a coger su cántaro entonces de alguna parte surgía una piedra que no se sabía ni de dónde, y le rompía el cántaro. Pero la gente decía que . . . que eran los duendes (1, 2).

Inclusive, . . . mi mamá, como era poco creyente de . . . de esas cosas, . . . una vez que yo perdí el conocimiento ella pensó que a mí me habían llevado el espíritu los duendes, y ya me estaba gritando en los oídos y . . . y quemando una palma bendita y . . . esas cosas. Y . . . era lo que hacía para, según ella, para que volviera, . . . para que los duendes me devolvieran el espíritu (3, 4). Ésa es . . . la única cosa que . . . yo recuerdo, o que haiga sucedido en ese pueblo Mazamitla, Jalisco.

(1) F482.5.5. Malicious or troublesome actions of brownies.
(2) F473.1. Poltergeist throws objects.
(3) F382. Exorcising fairies. (Fairies disappear when some name or ceremony of the Christian Church is used.)
(4) D2176.3.2. Evil spirit exorcised by religious ceremony.
Dorson, *WF*, 11(1952), 12. [Stone-throwing brownies.]
Mendoza, *San Pedro Piedra Gorda*, p. 387. [*Duendes* throw stones.]

52. Los duendes maliciosos

(Recorded by Elvira Higuera on October 31, 1966, in Los Angeles, California)

A brother of the informant was living in a house in Culiacán, Sinaloa, in which a variety of mysterious phenomena were thought to be the work of *duendes*. Bricks and stones would fly through the air into the house, tree branches would mysteriously shake, and the children would sometimes feel they were being choked in their beds at night. It was only after a priest came and performed an exorcism that the mysterious incidents stopped.

Pasó una historia muy bien, la que contó tu tío. ¿Te acuerdas? [Directed to her daughter.] Es algo, . . . dicen como algo así que no, no creo yo estas cosas tampoco. Pero él lo vio y no era embustero. Y así dice que . . . en esa caso no, no saben qué es lo que haya tenido . . .

porque, porque se empezaban a tirar piedras (1). Se oía que tiraban
piedras y oían que . . . que . . . ruidos (2). Se oían ruidos de . . . de
tazas, de loza en la cocina, y que tiraban piedras. Amanecía la casa llena de piedras. Pero no sabían por dónde entraban esas piedras. Y
luego, se veían volar los ladrillos, se veían volar las piedras, en pleno
día, y no sabían qué era lo que había allí.

Hasta que un día llamaron al padre, que fuera a ver qué es lo que
pasaba allí. Entonces fue con . . . agua bendita, hizo rezos y todo, y
desapareció [*sic*] aquellos ruidos, aquellas . . . cosas que se oían allí
(3, 4).

[Interviewer: —¿A quién le pasó esto?]

A una señora que vivía cerca de Culiacán. Mi hermano vivía allí
con ellos, y él nos platicó que era cierto eso, que . . . se oían esos ruidos. Les tiraban piedras, querían ahorcar los chamacos, sentían que
se ahogaban en la noche . . . dormidos (5). Y amanecía, . . . y era
cierto, porque amanecían las piedras adentro de la casa, en las esqui-
nas de la casa más bien. Y luego . . . les caía piedra a las, a la loza que
tenían allí en la cocina, a los platos, a las tazas. Y no había nada, no
se miraba ninguna piedra allí. Y no los quebraban tampoco. Luego
que volaban los ladrillos. Se venían, se miraban como quien divisa un
avión, y al llegar allí sólo miraban que el ladrillo se caía, y no se par-
tía. Estaba una mata de . . . de . . . guayabo allí y en la noche se, se
movía el guayabo y se sacudía como si estuviera un, un . . . fuerte
viento. Y no, no era nada tampoco. Desde que fue el padre a . . .
hacer sus oraciones allí, se terminaron todos los ruidos. ¿Qué sería
(6)?

(1) F473.1. Poltergeist throws objects.
(2) F473.5. Poltergeist makes noises.
(3) F382. Exorcising fairies.
(4) D2176.3.2. Evil spirit exorcised by religious ceremony.
(5) F473.3. Poltergeist mistreats people.
(6) F482.5.5. Malicious or troublesome actions of brownies.
    Sinninghe, no. 258, p. 68. Tormenting spirit is banished (exorcised) by
       minister (or priest); no. 456, p. 79. The poltergeist in the house.
    Qvigstad, no. 13, p. 41. Poltergeister (i.e., noisy ghosts).
    Dorson, *WF*, 11(1952), 12. [Stone-throwing brownies.]
    Folktales from the Patagonia Area, p. 20. [Rocks fall on house.]
    Mendoza, *San Pedro Piedra Gorda*, p. 387. [*Duendes* throw stones.]

53. Los duendes en el rancho

(Recorded by Josefina Márquez on May 7, 1966,
in Santa Paula, California)

The informant tells of an experience she and her family had when
she was a little girl living in the state of Durango. On a journey to the
town of El Palmito they stopped to spend the night at a farmhouse that
turned out to be inhabited by *duendes* who subjected them to mischie-
vious pranks during the night. When they spoke to the owners about
it in the morning, they were told about the *duendes* and the variety of
activities they engaged in. Although they sometimes helped with
household chores, they would also pull off bedclothes during the night,
throw feces into the guests' food, knock over glasses of milk at the
table, and spin the baby's cradle causing the baby to fall out. When the
owners were first married and on their honeymoon, the *duendes* used
to dump them out of their bed at night. They soon lost their fear of
them, but were quite often exasperated and embarrassed at the rude
treatment given their guests. The wife described the *duendes* as small
children dressed in green.

En México en algunas partes hay duendes. En muchas partes hay. A
nosotros nos tocó parar en un rancho una vez. Andábamos viajando,
cuando andábamos con mi papá. Íbamos de una parte para otra. Y
como esta vez íbamos a caballo, y el burro, . . . nos tocó quedarnos en
un rancho cuando se nos oscureció. Era en el estado de Durango. No
recuerdo cómo se llamaba el rancho, pero sí recuerdo que era en el
estado de Durango. Nosotros íbamos para aún el estado de Durango,
pero íbamos para otro, otra parte, que se llamaba El Palmito, Durango.
Íbamos para allá nosotros. Y nos quedamos esa noche allí.

Y eran como las once o once y media cuando empezaron a llorar mis
hermanas. Que mi hermanos les habían quitado las cobijas. Se levantó
mi mamá y fue y les . . . las cobijó otra vez. Las cobijas estaban en la
puerta. Fue mi mamá y las, las acostó otra vez. Las cobijó. Apenas se
había acostado mi mamá, le quitaron la almohada. Le quitaron la almohada a mi mamá. Mi mamá se levantó otra vez y recogió la almohada. Pero mi mamá pensaba que eran mis hermanos. Un hermano que
mataron en el servicio era muy travieso. Le gustaba mucho . . . joking

around. Y ella pensó que él era. No se enojó ni se asustó ella. Se levantó otra vez y fue y recogió la almohada de la puerta. Se volvió a acostar.

Como a las dos de la mañana oíamos que andaban barriendo. Estaban moliendo en el metate, estaban haciendo ruido en el cazo para hacer el atole. Y fuimos a asomarnos nosotros a la cocina. Miramos el metate, el cazo y todo en la cocina puesto como que estaba alguna mujer trabajando, moliendo, haciendo todo. Pero nosotros no vimos a nadien.

Cuando se levantaron los dueños de la casa, dijeron que eran duendes. Eran los duendes que no les dejaban visitas allí. Que nadie quería visitarlos porque les quitaban las cobijas, les quitaban las almohadas (1), y les hacían travesuras (2, 3). Que por esto nadien los visitaba que porque tenían miedo. Dice: —Ellos vienen y muelen y hacen el atole, barren el patio, riegan, dice, —pero nosotros no les tenemos miedo (4). Dice: —Estamos acostumbrados a ellos.

Y entonces, pues, yo era muy curiosa. Yo tenía catorce años. Le pregunté que cómo eran los duendes. Entonces me dijeron, sería cierto o no, los mirarían ellos de veras o no, me platicaron que eran unos niños chiquitos, vestidos de verde (5), que eran muy, muy traviesos (6). Dice: —Son muchos. Dice: —Son como ocho o diez los que vienen aquí, que salen aquí. Dice: —No sabemos de dónde. Dice: —Pero ellos resultan aquí. Dice: —Nos ayudan a darles a las gallinas. Dice: —Nos ayudan a darles agua a los marranos. Dice: —Pero aquí cuando nos ayudan al quehacer a veces nos hacen muchas travesuras. Dice: —A veces tenemos visitas comiendo, de gente que va pasando en automóviles, del extranjero o algunas partes. Están sentados comiendo en la mesa. Dice: —Les ponemos manteles limpios, les servimos los platos de la comida y todo. Dice: —Cuando están comiendo ellos muy a gusto, dice, —vienen y les echan estiércol . . . en los platos. Dice: —Les echan estiércol en la comida, o les voltean los vasos de la leche (7). Dice: —Nos hacen pasar muchas vergüenzas. Dice: —Mucha gente cree en los duendes, y mucha gente no cree en eso.

Pues lo que ella vio, yo no lo vi. Ni lo conozco tampoco. Pero ella me platicó. Era una joven como de dieciocho años. Su marido tenía como veinte años. Tenían tres niños. Y nada más en esta casita vivían ellos dos, el esposo, la esposa, y los tres niños. Y los duendes que estaban ahí.

Me platicó ella, la muchacha de dieciocho años, que cuando se casó ella de quince años, la primer noche, que estaban en su . . . luna de miel, les tumbaron la cama los duendes (7). La muchacha se llamaba María Elena, María Elena . . . no recuerdo el último nombre. Y el muchacho se llamaba José Manuel. José Manuel Padilla. Y los niños, una se llamaba María Esperanza. La otra se llamaba María Elena. Y el niño se llamaba José Antonio.

Los duendes mecían la cuna del niño José Antonio. Y cuando no se quería dormir, decía la señora que cuando no se quería dormir el niño los duendes le torcían la cuna hasta el techo. Y luego la dejaban caer. Y se caía el niño de la cuna. Cuando estaba . . . destorciéndose la cuna se caía el niño de la cuna (7, 8). Dice: —Me hacen a veces muchas travesuras. Me da coraje, dice. —Pero, ¿qué hago? dice. —Los corro y no más se ríen.

Se reían, sí, decía ella. Ella decía que ella así los veía. Dice, . . . por eso era me explicó cómo eran. Dice: —Fue cuando empecé a perder el miedo, dice. —Porque yo al principio tenía mucho miedo, dice, —cuando me tumbaban de la cama. Dice: —Luego a veces cacheteaban a mi marido (7), y él volteaba y pensaba que era yo. Dice: —Volteaba enojado conmigo. Dice: —Hasta que nos desengañamos que eran los duendes, y que . . . los vimos. Dice: —Ahora no les tenemos miedo.

(1) F470.1. Spirits pull off person's bedclothes.
(2) F482.5.5. Malicious or troublesome actions of brownies.
(3) F473. Poltergeist. Invisible spirit (sometimes identified as ghost or witch) responsible for all sorts of mischief in or around household.
(4) F482.5.4. Helpful deeds of brownie or other household spirit.
(5) F482.2.1. Brownies dressed in green.
(6) F482.5.3. Brownies tease.
(7) F473.3. Poltergeist mistreats people.
(8) F473.2.1. Chair rocked by invisible spirit. [Here, the *duendes* spin the cradle.]
Chapiseau, I, 249. [Helpful deeds of elves.]
Sinninghe, no. 63, p. 55. The helpful dwarfs work during the night for the humans in exchange for food (tobacco; money); no. 456, p. 79. The poltergeist in the house.
Folktales from the Patagonia Area, p. 22. [Covers pulled off, bed overturned in haunted house.]

Mendoza, *San Pedro Piedra Gorda*, p. 387. [*Duendes* play pranks in kitchen.]

54. Los duendes que se mudaron con la familia

(Recorded by Rafael Gudiño on May 3, 1966, in Los Angeles, California)

Once there was a man who had *duendes* living in his house. They were helpful to him in his work, and in fact the excellence of his work was generally attributed to them. In order to keep them happy, the man always fed them first by throwing food over his shoulder before he himself ate. He soon tired of their presence, however, and one day he informed his wife that they were going to move. They had packed up their belongings and were starting down the road, when the wife suddenly remarked that they had forgotten the broom, to which a small voice answered, "Don't worry, we have it here."

Se cuentan historias de que . . . una vez un señor tenía . . . pues, esos duendes en su casa porque le ayudaban a trabajar, ¿verdad (1)? Ésa era la idea, que él era un trabajador muy bueno y que los duendes eran los que hacían el trabajo. Y todos los compañeros pues, . . . le tenían miedo porque decían que él estaba enduendado.

Pero al mismo tiempo él, cuando iba a comer, a todas horas del día, la costumbre para tenerlos a ellos contentos era de que . . . el primer bocado, en lugar de comérselo, lo tenía que tirar para atrás. Ése era para los duendes.

Pero un día, enfadado él de tener esos duendes en su casa, le dijo a su esposa que arreglaran todas las cosas, que los dos se iban a ir a otra ciudad para que, . . . para dejar allí a los duendes, porque él ya estaba enfadado de tener esos duendes. Entonces la señora arregló todo. Cargaron sus cosas en unas bestias y salieron de la casa y se fueron caminando.

Tenían unas dos horas caminando, cuando dice la señora: —¡Ay, Sebastián, se me olvidó la escoba!

Y entonces respondieron los duendes: —Acá la traemos. No se apuren (2).

Christiansen 7020. Vain attempt to escape from the Nisse.
(1) F482.5.4. Helpful deeds of brownie or other household spirit.

(2) F482.3.1.1. Farmer so bothered by brownie that he decides he must move
    to get rid of annoyance.
    Chapiseau, I, 249. [Helpful deeds of elves.]
    Dalyell, 530. A portion of food was set apart in houses for brownie.
    Sinninghe, no. 63, p. 55. The helpful dwarfs work during the night for the
    humans in exchange for food (tobacco; money); no. 69, p. 56. Dwarfs
    demand tribute; no. 456, p. 79. The poltergeist in the house.
    Espinosa, *Castilla*, p. 149, no. 54.
    Krappe, p. 88.
    Mendoza, *San Pedro Piedra Gorda*, p. 387, b.
    Robe, *Mexican Tales*, no. 193.

55. Los duendes y el padre

(Recorded by Guadalupe Gómez on November 10, 1966, in Los Angeles, California)

A family from Tepozanes, Jalisco, had *duendes* in their home, and
the wife was frightened by the mysterious things that went on there.
The husband was unable to intimidate them, and so they decided to
call on the priest to come and perform an exorcism. But when he was
in the midst of the ceremony he noticed some knives being sharpened
by invisible hands, and a voice was heard to say, "These knives are to
castrate the priest," whereupon he fled in terror. The frightened couple
decided to move from the house. They had packed their belongings and
gone only a short way down the road when the wife called to the
daughters to go back for the broom, which they had left behind; the
duendes answered, "We are bringing it."

El señor tenía un . . . se vino para acá, y estaba asustado. La familia
estaba pero asustada, porque el . . . porque los . . . los duendes los
asustaban. Que oían asombros en la noche. Y luego una noche . . .
una noche le . . . que oía espantos y quejas, ¿verdad? Entonces él . . .
cuando él fue le dijo ella: —¡Ay! . . . se llama Alisteo, . . . —¡ay, Alisteo!, hay, dice, —hay en la noche, sabe, asombros, y sacan las vasijas
para afuera, y. . . . Y había asombros (1).

Entonces él dijo: —Aa, a ver si pueden conmigo. Y se sentó en el
metate. Sí. [Laughs.] Me da risa. Entonces, . . . y cuando se acordó lo
traían . . . arriba, caminando, así sentado en el metate él. Él sentado
en el metate, sobre el metate. Él sentado en el metate, y lo traían caminando.

Después cuando, cuando fue, . . . llevaron al padre, a que conjurara,

¿verdad?, la casa. Entonces que el padrecito andaba queriendo bendecir la casa con . . . espantando los, los, . . . ¿qué son?, ¿qué decía yo?
. . . los duendes (2). Entonces él se . . . miraba . . . miró unos cuchillos, nada más miró los cuchillos que estaban afilando, y una voz que
oyó que dijo: —Estos cuchillos son para capar al padre. Entonces el
padre corrió. Pos se fue, ¿verdad? Se asustó y se fue. [Laughs.] Y no
pudo, no lo pudo bendecir.

Entonces después salieron de la casa ellos, asustados. Porque iban a
dejar . . . esa casa. Porque la iban a dejar. Cuando iban ya caminando
la señora dijo: —Hijas, tráiganse la escoba. Porque se les iba olvidando
la escoba.

Y dijo el, oían . . . oían los dos que dijeron: —Acá llevamos la
escoba (3). [Laughs.]

[Interviewer: —¿Dónde pasó esto?]

En . . . pues en un rancho en . . . en un municipio en Valle de Guadalupe. En un ranchito . . . Tepozanes.

(1) F482.5.5. Malicious or troublesome actions of brownies.
(2) F382. Exorcising fairies.
(3) F482.3.1.1. Farmer so bothered by brownie that he decides he must move
       to get rid of annoyance.
       Sinninghe, no. 456, p. 79. The poltergeist in the house.
       Blake, *JAF*, 27(1914), 238. [*Duendes* threaten to decapitate priest.]
       Krappe, pp. 88, 96.
       See documentation with Narrative 54, for Christiansen, Espinosa, Men-
       doza, and Robe.

56. Los duendes y el padre

(Recorded by Juana Gómez on November 12, 1966, in Los Angeles, California)

The informant relates an incident that took place in Tepozanes, Jalisco, around the year 1924. There was a house believed to be inhabited
by *duendes*, for mysterious things went on, such as food disappearing
from the table and objects being removed from their places. A priest
was called upon to say a mass there in an attempt to exorcise the evil
spirits, but during his visit a knife was observed being sharpened by invisible hands, and a voice was heard to utter a threat to castrate the
priest. The latter became frightened and left immediately.

En un rancho de, en el rancho de Tepozanes, había una casa que decían que había . . . duendes. Y pues, las personas se ponían a comer . . . a comer, y, y les desparecían . . . las, las tortillas o la comida. Se les desparecían de . . . sin, sin poder ellos ver nada (1).

Entonces un día llevaron un sacerdote que dijiera una misa, para que espantara los espíritus malinos, que les nombraban ellos (2). Así les nombramos. Y . . . y luego, pues, el padre, le iban a dar de cenar, y . . . y tenían allí su molcajete que . . . donde iban a hacer chile. Y, y cuando acordaban ya no estaba nada de molcajete. Y al rato el, el metate que tenían allí, pos estaba, estaba un cuchillo, afilándose solo. Y dicía . . . y oían una voz que dicía para mocharle al padre lo que lo . . . lo hacía . . . hombre. Y el padre ya no quiso estar, sino que se fue para . . . para su pueblo a dormir porque tuvo miedo.

Y luego en seguida, el metate lo sacaron, y estaba a medio patio, y a muele y muele la mano sola. Y no había mujer, no más el, la pura mano ya sale y sale. Pos, la gente asustada. Y ya se acabó. Yo no más esto sé.

[Interviewer: —¿Cuándo pasó esto?]

Pues como el año veinte . . . como el año veinticuatro, venticinco.

(1) F482.5.5. Malicious or troublesome actions of brownies.
(2) F382. Exorcising fairies.
   Sinninghe, no. 456, p. 79. The poltergeist in the house.
   Blake, *JAF*, 27(1914), 238. [*Duendes* threaten to decapitate priest.]
   Krappe, p. 96.
   Mendoza, *San Pedro Piedra Gorda*, p. 387, a. [*Duendes* play pranks in the
      kitchen.]

57. Los duendes en el rancho

(Recorded by Petra Franco on November 15, 1966, in Los Angeles, California)

In the year 1939 in Ramblás, Jalisco, a house was suddenly invaded by *duendes* who proceeded to commit all manner of mischievous acts, much to the discomfort of those living there. A priest was called upon to exorcise them and was successful. A similar situation occurred at another house in that same area. The *duendes* would throw stones and violently shake the branches of a tree in the patio. The exorcism was successful here, too. The informant is confident that priests know exactly what to do in such cases. She feels the presence of *duendes* is the work of the devil and considers it rather shocking and, indeed, puzzling that such indignities should be suffered by upright Catholic families.

En el rancho de . . . de Ramblás, Jalisco. . . . [Her son says to tell the date.] Pos eso sí, no sé. [Son: —Era en mil novecientos . . . mil novecientos treinta y nueve. Después de la Revolución fue.] Sí. Cayeron unos, . . . ¿qué modo digo? . . . unos, unos duendes en una casa de una familia . . . católica, honrada. Y les hacían muchas cosas. Sufrieron mucho con ellos. Cosas, pues . . . travesuras. Cosas de que les . . . echaban sal y todas las . . . a la comida que ponían. Todo les tiraban. El . . . hasta el metate les tiraban, y les quebraban todo. No les dejaron trastes que no les quebraron. Y . . . y ande, que no . . . no soportaban ellos. Pos ni, ni les dejaban sus trapos donde estaban, su ropa (1).

Y . . . y le hablaron al . . . al señor cura, y el señor cura mandó al padre capellán. Y fue a decir misa . . . allá. Y llevó el exorcismo chico. Y . . . y no, pues, pues unos ratos se quitaron y no los vieron. Pero volvieron. Y después le hablaron al señor cura. Y él fue. El fue y 'tuvo, pos, cómo andaría, subiendo y bajando, los saltos, y todo, y rezando y . . . y chicoteándolos con . . . una cuerda y todo, ¿verdad? Sí. Sabe cómo se llamará. Y . . . y con eso hubo de retirarlos (2, 3). Iba mucha gente de dondequiera, de ver lo que se platicaba de qué hacía. Iba mucha gente. Yo estaba cerca de ahí pero no, yo no, yo no fui. Pero decían . . . decían muchas cosas. Mis gentes, unas fueron y venían asustadas. Y con eso se . . . se desterraron . . . con el señor, cuando el señor cura fue y los . . . desterró. Pos ellos saben, ellos saben cómo . . . tratarse en lo que se les debe, ¿verdad? Y ya, pues, . . . pero las pobres gentes, eso ya le digo, sufrieron mucho. Fue . . . después de la Revolución.

[Interviewer: —¿Recuerda cómo se llamaba la familia?]

Sí. Candelario, . . . Candelario y Viviano de la Torre. Sí. Y la esposa era . . . Aristea Casillas . . . Barba, ¿o qué? Barba. Aristea era la mujer de . . . Candelario. Y . . . tenía su familia, sus hijas, grandes.

[Interviewer: —¿Y vivían cerca del Valle de Guadalupe?]

Sí, cerca, sí. No cerca, cerquita, de a tiro. No más que . . . le nombraban el Cerro del Ramblás, ¿verdad?, como era . . . era cerro.

[Interviewer: —¿Quiere contar la otra historia de duendes que el cura le platicó?]

Que . . . que cuando él estuvo por allá, como cuando están de padres los ponen . . . en, en ciertas partes, ¿verdad?, donde hay necesidad de sacerdote. Y . . . y él . . . no me acuerdo cómo era el punto donde él estaba. Y lo, lo llamaron a una casa porque no aguantaban ya . . . los, los duendes. Y que mientras que él estaba allí . . . silencio todo. Y cuando se iba estaban . . . que no aguantaban.

Bueno, pues, que en una de ésas . . . todavía no se iba el señor cura cuando empezó el árbol. Estaba en el patio de la casa ese árbol, un árbol grande. Empezaron todas las ramas a bullirse. Y que le dijo la señora: —Mire, venga. Y que luego que salieron, luego, luego estaba piedra y piedra y piedra . . . con ellos . . . con los de la casa. Y tuvieron que hacerlos encerrar. Se encerraron porque ya les andaban con las pedradas (4).

Eso nos platicaba . . . el señor cura. Dice . . . y nos dijo, . . . y después, dice, hasta que . . . hasta que se acabaron (5, 6). Se acabaron allí. Pos ellos . . . ellos saben sus oraciones y todo . . . con que pueden . . . acabar todo. Y él nos platicaba. Pues . . . pues, ellos con sus oraciones (7) y su . . . agua bendita (8), velas benditas. Pues ellos . . . ellos tienen sus . . . con qué. Pero pos, ¿qué será eso? Pues, ¿qué será? Yo no sé. Y es cosa de . . . del demonio, ¿verdad? Yo creo que es cosa de enemigo.

(1) F482.5.5. Malicious or troublesome actions of brownies.
(2) F382. Exorcising fairies.
(3) D1766.7.1.1. Evil spirits conjured away in name of deity.
(4) F473.1. Poltergeist throws objects.
(5) G303.16.14. Devil exorcised.
(6) G303.16.14.1. Priest chases devil away.
(7) G303.16.14.2. Devil's power over one avoided by prayer.
(8) G303.16.7. Devil is chased by holy water.
    Sinninghe, no. 248, p. 68. Tormenting spirit is banished (exorcised by minister or priest); no. 456, p. 79. The poltergeist in the house.
    Dorson, *WF*, 11(1952), 12. [Stone-throwing brownies.]
    Mendoza, *San Pedro Piedra Gorda*, p. 387, *a* and *c*. [*Duendes* play pranks in the kitchen; throw stones and bricks.]

Miscellaneous Legendary Narratives

El nahual

In Narrative 58 the informant tells of an incident involving what she herself refers to as a *nahual* [D141]. The story is about a man who, with the aid of a sheet, disguised himself as a dog and went into homes at midnight when the occupants were asleep to steal things, such as chickens, pigs, or money, or simply to frighten the young girls. One night they actually caught a *nahual* at this activity and gave him a severe beating, leaving traces of blood on the door. The next day they suspected a man who was seen going about with bruises and scratches on his face, and this was taken as an indication of the true identity of the *nahual* with whom they had had the encounter.

In view of the different types of phenomena commonly included under the heading of *nagualism*, it is important to put this particular narrative in proper perspective, in the light of research that has been done on the subject. An extremely valuable contribution toward the identification and clarification of these phenomena is George Foster's article "Nagualism in Mexico and Guatemala."[103] Looking to history for some possible sources of the general confusion, Foster comments as follows:

Few aspects of Mexican and Guatemalan witchcraft have been more discussed and often misunderstood than that assortment of beliefs which has come to be known as *nagualism*. Much of this misunderstanding goes back to Spanish missionaries who early learned the Aztec term *naualli* and applied it as a convenient handle to a wide variety of unrelated rites and practices. Some of their reports describe individuals called *naguals* who assumed the form of animals or objects for nefarious purposes. Others apply the term *nagualism* to the belief in a guardian or companion animal spirit so intimately linked to the fate of the human that should either die the other would follow. Further confusion has resulted from the disappearance of some of the early traits described as *nagualistic* and the substitution and spread of new concepts. Thus, a problem initially poorly defined becomes more complex because of temporal and spatial factors.[104]

The phenomenon of the "guardian or companion animal spirit" is

103 *Acta americana*, 2 (1944), 85–103.
104 Ibid., p. 85.

quite separate from that of the transforming witch; the suggestion
Foster makes for avoiding this terminological confusion is the use of
the word *tonal* (also Aztec in origin) for the former and *nagual* for
the latter.[105] Thus, one of the concepts commonly referred to as nagualism, that of the guardian animal, is by no means to be inferred
from the informant's use of the term *nahual* in Narrative 58.

The *nahual* described by the informant here is obviously in the nature of the "individual who assumed the form of animals or objects
for nefarious purposes," in the words of Foster. This particular incident, however, as described by the informant, contains an additional
element that should be considered. The so-called transformation here
is clearly nothing more than a disguise and is acknowledged as such
by the informant herself. Although her initial comment that he
changed into dog form ["se convertía en forma de perro"] admits
the interpretation of an authentic transformation, the further elaboration that he used a sheet and tied the corners in such a way as to simulate paws ["utilizaba una sábana, con la cual hacía las, amarraba las
puntas como pezuñas"] indicates that the informant is admittedly
speaking of a disguise and not a transformation.

Obviously the story itself is based on a belief in such power of
transformation, although this particular case may not be considered
authentic. But the curious question, if this narrative can be considered
representative, is whether the term *nahual* has come to be functionally
descriptive of the imitation, so to speak, as well as of the real thing.
That is to say, does it apply to the ruse—the individual who capital-
izes on such a belief—as well as to the person thought to truly possess
the power of transformation. Possibly this is what Foster is alluding to
in the previous quotation when he speaks of "the substitution and
spread of new concepts" about nagualism. The informant, however,
does not say that the man pretended to be a *nahual*, but that he was
one.

Among a collection of Texas-Mexican narratives is one entitled "El
Nagual y la Segua" in which a so-called *nahual* is thought to be a man
disguised as such in order to steal the attentions of the girls.[106] Here,

105 Ibid., p. 103.
106 Miriam W. Hiester, "Tales of the Paisanos," *TFSP*, 30(1961), 229.

too, then, is the belief in the *nahual* as an authentic phenomenon; but, in contrast to Narrative 58, the man is branded an imposter.

This type of *nahualism*, the thief in disguise, is one of those mentioned by Virginia R. R. de Mendoza. Among the various treatments of *nahualism* is one which deals with it ". . . simplemente como hombres que mediante un disfraz asustan a las gentes ingenuas que se recluyen en sus casas, mientras ellos se apoderan del maíz, tortillas, semillas y cuanto les viene en gana."[107] [. . . simply as men who through a disguise frighten innocent people who shut themselves up in their homes, while they go about stealing tortillas, seeds and whatever else they like.]

There are people, then, who take advantage of a real belief in the *nahual* and disguise themselves as such in order to carry on their thievery under the protective buffer of their victims' great fear of the *nahual*. An informant whose angry, emotional response to the widespread belief in *duendes* has already been cited may be quoted again here, for he lumped *duendes* and *nahuales* together as nothing more than hoaxes perpetrated upon the people by those who find the belief convenient. They commit crimes of robbery and go unapprehended because the theft is so readily attributed to a *duende* or a *nahual*. Once again, in the words of this informant, they are nothing more than "rateros, ladrones que roban las cobijas, los metates, y otras cosas, y hacen que crean eso [thieves who steal blankets, *metates*, and other things, and who make people believe all that (i.e., attribute it to a *duende* or a *nahual*)].

The activities engaged in by the *nahual* of Narrative 58, as has been mentioned, include the stealing of chickens, pigs, corn, and sometimes even money, and the practice of frightening girls. The former are included among those acts listed by Mendoza as commonly practiced by the *nahual*: "roba las gallinas" [he steals chickens] and "roba el nixtamal, las tortillas y otros objetos [he steals the *nixtamal*, tortillas, and other objects]."[108] These acts, together with the practice of frightening people, are cited as frequent components of *nahual* stories

---

107 "El nahual en el folklore de México," *ASFM*, 7 (1951), 123.
108 Ibid., p. 131.

in a geographical chart set up by the author to illustrate the distribution of motifs.[109]

Another element of Narrative 58, discovering the true identity of the *nahual* the next day through the traces he bears of a beating, is common in *nahual* stories, as well as in many witch stories. [110]

Before concluding the discussion of the *nahual*, it may be of interest to quote the following opinion, expressed by a Mexican writer toward the end of the last century, concerning the waning strength of the *nahual* tradition and his rather fanciful expression of the forces responsible for its demise:

Por fortuna tales supersticiones se han ido borrando para siempre. De los llamados *nahuales* apenas queda una idea remota en algún rincón de la República, en algún pequeño villorio o en algún humildísimo rancho. Parece que la majestuosa locomotora, como evocándolos por un conjuro, los ha hecho huir con su poderoso silbato, como una parvada de maléficos espíritus.[111]

[Fortunately, such supersitions are disappearing for good. As for the so-called *nahuales* there scarcely remains a notion of them in some remote corner of the Republic, some small village, or some poor hamlet. It seems that the majestic locomotive, as if evoking them by incantation, has made them flee with its powerful whistle, like a gang of evil spirits.]

It is, of course, transparent that it is his wish that such evidence of backwardness and lack of civilization disappear; his very similar comment about the *llorona* has already been cited.

Una bruja [A witch]

Narrative 59 tells of a witch who appeared first in the form of an owl (*tecolote*) [D153.2] and then as a sow (*puerca*) [D136]; after being chased off, she retaliated by returning during the night to blacken the informant's whole body with soot [G269]. The concept of the witch in animal form is quite common, and in terms of Hispanic tradition one of the most frequent manifestations is the *tecolote*. As

---

[109] "El Nahual: Cuadro geográfico de versiones impresas, orales, modos de transformación, acciones que ejecuta, y modo de capturarlos." (Ibid., opposite p. 134).

[110] See, for example, William J. Wallrich, "Five *bruja* Tales from the San Luis Valley," *WF*, 9 (1950), 359–362.

[111] Luis González Obregón, *México viejo*, p. 206.

stated by Aurelio M. Espinosa, "the *tecolote* is the animal whose form witches prefer to take."[112]

There is some question about the correct motif number to assign to the phenomenon of transformation into a *tecolote*, a word most often translated in English as "owl." Virginia R. R. de Mendoza gives a Spanish translation of a portion of Chapter D ("Magic") of Thompson's *Motif-Index*, in which she translates D152.1. Transformation: man to hawk, as "Transformación de hombre en tecolote."[113] Thus is explained the discrepancy between the original motif cited above—D153.2. Transformation: man to owl—and Mendoza's preference in translation for D152.1. Transformation: man to hawk.

Additional documentation of stories about witches in animal form, specifically as owls, can be found in Humberto Garza, "Owl Bewitchment in the Lower Río Grande Valley," and in another article by Virginia R. R. de Mendoza, "Las brujas en el folklore de México." The latter constitutes a summarizing of one hundred narratives; based on this number of accounts, the author has found statistical support for the idea that male witches (*brujos*) are often connected with the *nahual*. George Foster also comments in support of such a connection: "In short, we must assume that originally the term *nagual* was applied to the transforming witch."[114]

The witch in Narrative 58 seems to share some characteristics with the *nahual*. In the already cited geographical chart devised by Mendoza (see fn. 109) to indicate the distribution of motifs in *nahual* narratives, many examples of the type of successive transformations seen in Narrative 59 are cited. Another point of similarity, which has already been mentioned, is that the human identity of witches, like that of the nahual in Narrative 58, is often discovered through traces of beatings they received while in animal form.

La mala hija [The Bad Daughter]

Narrative 60 belongs to the very widespread legendary type of *El mal hijo* ["the bad son"], although in this case it is a story of a *mala*

<hr>

112 "New Mexican Spanish Folklore," *JAF*, 23 (1910), 396.
113 Mendoza, "El nahual," p. 134.
114 Foster, "Nagualism," p. 89.

hija ["bad daughter"]. As told by the informant, the girl defied her parents' instructions that she not attend a dance; she went and became involved with the devil in the form of a well-dressed gentleman [G303.3.1.2] who tempted her [G303.9.4.7] with the reward of great riches if she would kill her parents; she carried out the evil deed, treacherously stabbing them to death [K2214.1]; her father's dying words were a curse that she be swallowed up by the earth [M411.1; M448] in punishment for her crime [Q552.2.3]; the curse was fulfilled, and no amount of effort could save the girl as she slowly sank into the earth.

Among a collection of *mal hijo* narratives there is one reference to a *mal[a] hija*.[115] Parallels between it and Narrative 60 include the disobedience, being out late and speaking with the devil, and the mother's scolding. The outcome differs, however, for the girl's punishment is paralysis rather than being swallowed up by the earth. None of these versions is identical to the one told by the informant of Narrative 60, and frequently the bad son or daughter is only partially swallowed and then retrieved.

A similar story about the earth swallowing up a person as punishment is found in a group of Mexican *exempla* about the devil.[116] As in Narrative 60, the bad son who has killed his mother in an attack of anger is swallowed up by the earth, and all attempts to help him prove futile. An interesting contrast in the devil's function can be pointed out in these two stories: in Narrative 60 the devil goads the girl into the crime of patricide, whereas in the *exemplum* referred to the devil's role or presence is equated with being swallowed up by the earth ("the Devil took him").

The informant placed the incident in El Paso, Texas, in the year 1920, and said that a *corrido* was subsequently composed to tell the story. Perhaps this is the explanation for the rhymed form of the curse pronounced by the father: "Tres pasos de la casa vas a dar, y la tierra te va a tragar." [You shall take three steps from the house and be swallowed up by the earth.]

115 T. M. Pearce, "The Bad Son (*el mal hijo*) in Southwestern Spanish Folklore," *WF*, 9 (1950), 301.
116 Stanley L. Robe, "Four Mexican *exempla* about the Devil." *WF*, 10 (1951), 312.

El anillo de la rica [The Rich Woman's Ring]

Narrative 61, which tells the story of a proud, rich woman reduced to poverty, is a migratory legend classified by Christiansen as type 7050. Ring Thrown into Water and Recovered in a Fish.[117] The rich woman refuses aid to a beggar woman, who then tells her that one day she too will be poor; whereupon the rich woman removes her ring from her finger and casts it into the sea, proclaiming that she will be poor only when that ring finds its way back to her finger. Some time later, the maid buys a fresh fish from a vendor, and, when she cuts it open to prepare it for the meal, the ring is found inside. Within a year's time the woman is reduced to poverty. This motif is also found in the Thompson *Index* as L412.1.

William Jones comments on the frequency of legends that incorporate the theme of the ring found in the fish. He cites such examples as a legend told in Jocelin's *Life of St. Kentigern*; an Italian legend about the fall of the Venetian republic; and a "popular ballad of old," the "Cruel Knight or the Fortunate Farmer's Daughter."[118] None of the above legends parallels Narrative 61, the only similarity being the motif of the ring recovered in the fish. However, Jones cites another source that does parallel Narrative 61 very closely and that appeared as a news item in an eighteenth-century journal:

In the "Gentleman's Magazine" (January 1765), is the account of a Mrs. Todd, of Deptford, who, in going in a boat to Whitstable, endeavored to prove that no person need be poor who was willing to be otherwise; and being excited with her argument, took off her gold ring, and, throwing it out into the sea, said "it was as much possible for any person to be poor who had an inclination to be otherwise, as for her ever to see that ring again." The second day after this, and when she had landed, she bought some mackerel, which the servant commenced to dress for dinner, whereupon there was found a gold ring in one. The servant ran to show it to her mistress, and the ring proved to be that which she had thrown away.[119]

The account is remarkably similar. An important contrast, how-

---

[117] Christiansen, *The Migratory Legends.*
[118] William Jones, *Finger-Ring Lore*, pp. 98–100.
[119] Ibid., pp. 440–441.

ever, is the elaboration of the legendary version, which introduces a moralistic note and makes the story an illustration of the punishment of pride. While the Mrs. Todd of the journalistic account was simply proven wrong, the rich woman of the legend was quite dramatically punished, and ironically so, in that it was in a sense her own doing.

El viejo que quería novia [The Old Man Who Wanted a Sweetheart]

Narrative 62, told by the informant in the spirit of a joke, is a variation on motif J2212.1.1. Priest to have maid at least fifty years old: gets one aged 20 and one aged 30. This narrative is not about a priest, but about a widower who suggests to his son that, if he can't find a woman of thirty, he might bring him two fifteen-year-olds. The story obviously loses some of its subtle humor when the figure of the priest is eliminated. By replacing him with an "ordinary" man, some of the surprise element, based on an obvious impropriety when told of the priest, is lost.

58. El nahual

(Recorded by Raquel Rodríguez on November 7, 1966, in Los Angeles, California)

When the informant was a little girl, in the town of San Martín Texmelucan, Puebla, her mother used to tell her about an animal called the *nahual,* which was thought to be a man who periodically turned into the form of a wild dog and went about frightening people and stealing money as well as animals for his own sustenance. Some people said he would use a sheet and tie the corners in such a way as to simulate paws, in order to facilitate a disguise. She relates an incident told her by her husband in which his family was attacked by a *nahual* one night; they managed to defend themselves, however, and found traces of blood on their door the next morning as proof of the incident. After such occurrences, people were inclined to suspect any individual who was seen to be bruised and scratched the following day.

Cuando yo era chiquilla mi mamá nos . . . platicaba acerca de un animal que se llamaba el nahual. El nahual no era un animal, sino una persona que se convertía en forma de perro (1). Según dicen que . . . utilizaba una sábana, con la cual hacía las, amarraba las puntas como pezuñas. Y entraba a las casas a la medianoche, que la gente estaba dormida allá en los pueblitos donde a veces ni luz había. Entraba y robaba gallinas, . . . o ya sea puerco, puercos, o dinero que la gente a veces tenía, o para espantar a las muchachas simplemente. Y sabían que era . . . existía el nahual.

Pero hubo cierto día que lo descubrieron. Agarraron unas personas, según dicen, que unas trancas, y lo apalearon. Ensangrentaron la puerta. Y a otro día dicen que comenzaron a sospechar de cierta persona, que otra día lo encontraban con la cara toda morada, raspada. Y él no trabajaba ni nada, así es que él se dedicaba por las noches en disfrazarse de, de, de nahual, nahual del pueblo. Pero lo hacía para robar y de ahí . . . de eso vivía. Pero no era cierto animal, sino hombre . . . que se disfrazaba en forma de animal.

Según mi esposo nos platicaba del nahual, que sí existe en los pueblos. Es un hombre que se disfraza por las noches . . . en forma de perro. Se mete a las casas para robarse el maíz . . . o las gallinas. Pero cierto día, dice mi esposo que estaba de pie su papá y su mamá. Agarraron un . . . unos palos, unos leños y le, le golpeaban. Pero el animal estaba muy . . . muy ¿cómo se dice? . . . pues trataba de echárseles encima, ¿no? Pero ellos se defendían. El caso es que lograron . . . sacarle sangre. Y él brincó por una ventana. El caso es que se escapó. A otro día vieron que había amanecido la puerta con sangre. Y según . . . cuentan . . . de que el nahual sí existe, pero no es . . . animal, sino es una persona . . . que se disfraza como . . . nahual.

[Interviewer: —¿En qué pueblo fue que pasó esto?]

En San Martín Texmelucan, Puebla, Estado de Puebla.

(1) D141. Transformation: man to dog.
    Loorits, no. 176, pp. 65–66. A werewolf is wounded or shot to death: the person involved (i.e., who is the werewolf) is later recognized from the wound.
    Sinninghe, no. 822, p. 104. Werewolf is shot (or beaten), then takes on human shape again (and is redeemed or dies).
    González Obregón, *México viejo*, p. 206.
    Hiester, *TFSP*, 30(1961), 229. [Man posing as *nahual*.]
    Mendoza, *ASFM*, 7(1951), 123–138.

59. Una bruja

(Recorded by Rosa Flores on May 31, 1966, in Los Angeles, California)

The informant relates an incident that took place when she was a young girl living with her family in the village of Contreras near Tlaltenango, Zacatecas. Her mother had quarreled with a man who was grazing his oxen on her land and had chased him off. Very soon afterward an owl began to appear there every day, and it later turned into a pig, both assumed to be the metamorphosed forms of a witch. The informant's mother and brother succeeded in chasing off the pig one day, but that very same night, as if in retribution, the informant had her whole body blackened with soot. She expresses puzzlement at this having happened to her rather than to her mother.

Mi mamá y otro señor que se llamaba Gerardo . . . andaban . . . cuidando él una yuntita de bueyes . . . en la propiedad de mi mamá. Y allí se comió la labor. Mi mamá le dijo que no cuidara allí su yunta de . . . de bueyes porque le comía su labor. Y él dijo que no era de él, que eran otras. Y . . . mi mamá le espió y lo agarró con la yunta de bueyes comiéndose la labor. En seguida se enojaron muncho. Se pelearon.

Y de allí, empezó a venir una . . . un tecolote todos los días (1, 2). Y se vomitaba diario, diario, diario. Y ella juntaba muchas piedras y hicieron unas hondas . . . mi mamá y un hermanito que tenía yo chiquito, . . . añejito. Y salían a correrlo a pedradas.

Y cuando ya después de mucho tiempo, que ya había caña, . . . se volvió puerca, un [sic] puerca granda (1, 3). Y ya . . . hasta habíamos comido cañas allá, pues, había mucho garbanzo allí. Nos acostamos. Y en la noche, a deshora de noche, llegó aquel animal, como un puerco grande, y comiendo garbanzos.

Entonces se levantó mi mamá, y mi hermano, y le dijo a mi hermano: —Ándale, que ya tía Sarapia se volvió cochina. Y se levantaron, y ya no había nada en el patio. Se hicieron al oscuro de un mesquite y de un zapote, en la oscuridad, y la empezaron a buscar. Y la hallaron en lo oscuro. Y allí en lo oscuro, entonces la agarraron a pedradas, y corrió aquel animal. A la siguiente noche volvió, y me tiznaron todo el cuerpo (4). Pero no a mi mamá, sólo a mí.

Esto pasó en el rancho Contreras, Tlaltenango, Zacatecas.

(1) G211. Witch in animal form.
(2) D153.2. Transformation: man to owl. [Here, the witch is a woman.]
(3) D136. Transformation: man to swine. [Here, woman to swine.]
(4) G269. Evil deeds of witches.
  Espinosa, *JAF*, 23(1910), 396. [*Tecolote* is preferred form for witches to take.]
  Garza, *TFSP*, 30(1961), 218–225; Mendoza, *ASFM*, 6(1945), 477. [Witch as owl.]

60. La Condenada

(Recorded by Lola Cruz, on May 23, 1966, in Los Angeles, California)

The informant narrates an incident that took place in El Paso, Texas, in 1920. A young girl disobeyed her parents and went to a dance that they had forbidden her to attend. When she had not returned home by three o'clock in the morning her mother went to look for her and found her in a bar in the company of a very elegant gentleman. The latter, believed to be the devil, encouraged the girl to kill her mother with a dagger that he himself gave to her, promising her great wealth and happiness as a result of the deed. The girl followed his advice and then went home to kill her father, also. The father's dying curse was that within three steps from the house the earth would swallow her up, slowly, over a period of six days, and no amount of effort would save her. The curse was realized. The authorities, unable to help, blocked off the area, and the girl slowly sank into the earth.

Esto era una cosa que pasó en El Paso, Texas con una . . . señora y un señor. Tenían una hija. El señor le dijo a su hija que no fuera al baile, y ella dijo que sí iba. Y la mamá también le dijo que no fuera al baile. Y entonces ella dijo que sí iba a ir.

Pues ya eran las dos, tres de la mañana, cuando la hija no venía a la casa. Pues luego después el señor, como estaba tullido en una sillita, que no se podía levantar, le dijo a la señora, . . . y la señora también estaba viejita, . . . y le dijo a la señora:—Anda, vieja, trae a . . . a la muchacha de donde está en el baile.

Pero ya en el baile ya habían cerrado. Onde la encontró fue en una cantina que, que entran mujeres . . . a tomar. Y entonces vino a la carrera y le dijo al señor, dice: —No, está en la cantina. ¿Cómo voy a ir yo . . . allá a meterme?

Y entonces estaba ella con un señor, . . . la muchacha. Con un señor muy elegante, de . . . levita, . . . un vestido muy especial, de esos de baile, y un sombrero de esos altos (1). Entonces le dijo: —Mira, toma. . . . Ahora que te anda buscando tu mamá. Y si tú quieres gozar, toma esta daguita. Y con esta daguita, cuando venga tu mamá a llevarte, entiérrasela pa qui pa tras (2).

Bueno, pos, luego la mamá vino, enojada porque, pos era una gente muy honrada, muy buena. Y tenía mucha vergüenza. Entró y le dijo a la hija: —Vámonos para la casa.

Dijo: —Yo no me voy. Dijo: —Ándale, dijo. —No me hagas enojar, porque con esta daguita te voy a matar, . . . dijo la muchacha a la mamá.

Y entonces . . . cuando la mamá volteó pa tras, que ya se iba, le enterró la daga a la mamá por detrás la muchacha. Y cayó la . . . señora . . . muerta (3).

Y entonces le dijo el diablo, porque era el diablo que estaba con la muchacha, . . . le dijo el diablo: —Mmm, si tú quieres . . . gozar y divertirte y gastar todo el dinero que te voy a dar, anda, acaba con el que queda en tu casa (2).

Entonces llegó a la casa a . . . a matar al papá, cuando le dijo . . . la muchacha: —Ya les he dicho que no me anden buscando.

Dijo: —Pero si mira no más ónde estabas. ¿Y tu mamá?

—O, ya mi mamá no va a volver. Ya mi mamá está . . . pasada de este mundo. Entonces le dijo: —Y vine a acabar contigo.

Y cuando la muchacha le pegó al papá a matarlo, le pegó, le enterró la daga, entonces el papá dijo . . . cuatro palabras: —Anda, hija maldecida, condenada. Tres pasos de la casa vas a dar, y la tierra te va a tragar. Pero no te tragará luego luego, sino que poco a poquito. Durarás como seis días . . . hundiéndote . . . pa debajo (4, 5).

Bueno, pos que ella . . . dijo: —No le creo sus palabras de usted. Yo soy dueña de mi persona.

Y entonces el papá murió . . . matado por ella . . . también. Cuando ella salió tres pasos de, de, fuera de su casa de ella, entonces . . . se fue hundiendo. Pero no luego luego. Estaba, como dijo el papá, dos o tres días . . . o cuatro.

Pos luego pusieron un barrandal . . . allí, el mismo gobierno puso un barrandal, porque la muchacha no podían sacarla porque se estaba hundiendo. La tierra se la estaba tragando. Y así duró la muchacha día y noche . . . allí, hasta que la tierra se la . . . se la llevó pa abajo (6, 7).

Pues luego hicieron, . . . dijieron que lo querían poner en un libro. Y dijo, dijo allí una señora que, . . . y un señor que creo eran los que mandaban allí a todo El Paso, . . . y dijo que no, que mejor iban a poner un corrido. Y el corrido se iba a llamar . . . "La Condenada." Y eso pasó en mil novecientos veinte. Y en El Paso pueda ser de que encuentren alguna copia de ese, de ese verso en la librería. Mil novecientos veinte. Se llama La Condenada.

[Interviewer: —¿Cómo se llamaba la muchacha?]

No sé cómo se llamaba.

(1) G303.3.1.2. Devil as well-dressed gentleman.
(2) G303.9.4.7. Devil tempts girl.
(3) K2214.1. Treacherous daughter.
(4) M411.1. Curse by parent.
(5) M448. Curse: to sink into the earth.
(6) Q552.2.3. Earth swallowings as punishment.
(7) F942.1. Ground opens and swallows up person.
Num. 16: Dathan and Abiram.
Pearce, *WF*, 9(1950), 295–301.
Robe, *WF*, 10(1951), 312, no. 2; *Mexican Tales*, no. 155.

61. La historia del anillo

(Recorded by Ana María Romero on December 3, 1966, in Oxnard, California)

The informant tells a story told her by her father, who in turn heard it from his great-grandfather. A very rich woman was approached one day by an old woman asking for charity. When the rich woman refused to give her anything, the beggar woman replied that one day she would find herself very poor. The rich woman's reply was to remove a ring from her finger and throw it into the sea, boasting that she would be poor the day that ring found its way back to her finger. Some time later her cook bought a fish from a street vendor and brought it home to prepare for a meal. When she opened it up she found inside of it the ring that had been thrown into the sea. Within a year's time the rich woman was reduced to poverty.

Esta historia me la platicó mi padre, contada por su bisabuelo. Se llama "La historia del anillo." Era, . . . éste es el principio: Era una mujer muy rica. Demasiado rica. Un día llegó cerca de su . . . casa, o su palacio, una anciana a pedirle una limosna. Ella la negó. Dijo que no.

Y la anciana le dijo: —Tú no me das una limosna, pero un día serás pobre.

Y sacando un anillo de su dedo, lo arrojó al mar, y le dijo a la anciana: —Cuando este anillo vuelva a mi dedo, entonces seré yo pobre.

Vino un día en que un hombre . . . pasaba vendiendo pescado. Era día que no se comía carne. Y le dijo a su criada que fuera a comprar pescado. La criada compró un hermoso pescado que trajo a la casa. Y abriéndolo para cocinarlo, salió el anillo de la señora. Viendo que era de ella, fue y se lo entregó. Cuando ella lo recibió, ella se pegó en su frente.

Pero de todas maneras ella, poco a poco, quedó tan pobre que al siguiente año no se conocía en su pobreza (1). Y es todo.

Christiansen 7050. Ring Thrown into Water and Recovered in a Fish.
(1) L412.1. Woman casts ring into sea boasting that it is as impossible for her to become poor as for the ring to be found. Ring is found in fish: she becomes poor.
Gentleman's Magazine, January 1765.
Jones, *Finger-Ring Lore*, pp. 440–441.

62. El papá que quería novia

(Recorded by Francisco Flores on June 2, 1966, in Los Angeles, California)

A young man asked his father why he was so sad, and the father replied that life had been difficult since the death of his wife. The son offered to find him a girl-friend and asked what age woman he prefered. The father, delighted at the idea, said to find him a woman of about thirty; but, as soon as the son had gone out the door, he called him back and suggested that if he couldn't find a thirty-year-old he might bring him two fifteen-year-olds.

Éste era un señor . . . que se encontraba solo en su situación. Hacía
bastantes años que había quedado viudo. Y tenía un solo hijo nada
más. El hijo salía a trabajar y por la tarde regresaba a su casa. Y hallaba al papá muy triste. Y le decía: —¿Qué te pasa, papá? ¿Por qué
estás tan triste?

—No hijo, no es que esté triste. Pero siempre tú sabes que desde
que falleció tu mamá no he podido ser yo bueno. Sólo he estado pensando en la muerte de tu mamá y en la situación que nos encontramos
tú y yo.

—Así que, papá, no tengas cuidado. Si tú quieres, papá, yo te consigo una novia.

El papá sintió tanto gusto con lo que le dijo el hijo. —Bueno, hijo,
pues toma tus alimentos y en seguida vas.

—Está bien, papá. El joven terminó de . . . de tomar sus alimentos
y le dijo: —Papá, ya voy a salir; voy a buscarte la novia.

—Está bien, hijo. De lo que tengo yo bastante gusto.

Se jue el hijo. Y cuando iba a una distancia, como de unos . . .
treinta o cuarenta metros de retirado del papá, el papá le habló, . . .
porque el hijo le preguntó, dice: —Papá, ¿de qué edad te consigo la
novia?

El papá contestó, dijo: —Mira, hijo me la consigues de la edad de
treinta años. Y cuando el hijo se retiró, entonces el papá se paró como
él pudo y le dijo: —Mira, hijo, ven acá.

Se regresó el hijo y le dice: —¿Qué deseabas, papá?

—Mira, hijo, si no hallas una de treinta años entonces me traes dos
de a quince (1). Esto es todo, alright?

(1) J2212.1.1. Priest to have maid at least 50 years old: gets one aged 20 and
     one aged 30.

 II. Traditional Tales

Characteristics of the Traditional Tales in This Collection

I found in my fieldwork among the Mexican population of the Los Angeles area that it was much easier to collect legendary narratives than traditional tales. While twenty-five informants recorded legendary material, only five recorded tales. Of the twenty tales presented here, seventeen were told me by two informants: eleven by Candelario Gallardo and six by Lola Cruz. In effect, these two people were the only real tale-tellers among the forty informants I worked with. While I am sure there are many more such people in the Los Angeles area, I think the ratio indicated here would not change in an even larger, more comprehensive study.

Both these informants were excellent tale-tellers, and they both expressed delight at the rare opportunity of having an audience. They told me they had not actively engaged in telling tales for quite some time; in fact, they said they were reminded of the tales they knew, began to think about them again and to review the ones they could remember, only as a result of my interest.

Lola Cruz said that she had told some of the tales to her husband many years before but had already forgotten many. She did, however, have a fairly large number of legendary narratives to relate and did not speak of difficulty in remembering them. I think this reflects the greater immediacy, and therefore more ready availability, of legendary material. The tale, if not told with some frequency, is gradually forgotten.

In the case of Candelario Gallardo, the other principal contributor to this collection of tales, I was surprised to find that his family was totally unaware of his excellent ability as a tale-teller. When they listened in one day, they were surprised to learn what I had been recording with him, and they were amazed to hear how well he told his stories.

These brief comments illustrate what seems to be the decline, and very probably the gradual disappearance, of tale-telling activity among the Mexican people in Los Angeles. Both these informants did an interesting thing, which may be tied up with an awareness of this gradual disappearance, or, perhaps, with their awareness of the loss of an audience. They told several fairly long tales, composed of multiple tale types (see, for example, nos. 72, 80, 81, and 82); I wondered at the time if they might have been motivated by a desire to gather up whatever tale material they could remember and, wherever possible, incorporate it into a unit, less likely to be forgotten.

Lola Cruz, who was the source of seventeen of the narratives in this collection, is the bearer of an enormous amount of folk tradition. At each Christmas season she puts up a large *nacimiento* [nativity scene] that occupies almost an entire room in her house. She related to me an incident that suggested an interesting concept of time reference with regard to tales. The children in the neighborhood were accustomed to bringing her gifts for her *nacimiento*, and one little boy's gift had been a small china figurine of Snow White. She was telling me one day about the different objects in the *nacimiento*, and I asked her about the Snow White. She replied that, while she had of course accepted the boy's gift, she could not refrain from commenting to him, "pero, mijito, Snow White no debe figurar en el nacimiento; no estaba en el tiempo del Niño Dios." [But, my son, Snow White shouldn't appear in the *nacimiento*; she wasn't there in the time of the Christ Child.]

Both these informants had a very entertaining narrative style. They put themselves wholeheartedly into the telling of the tale and seemed to regard the activity as a true performance, which they themselves, as well as the listener, enjoyed immensely. They used movements and gestures, facial expressions, voice imitations in dialogues, and spontaneous emotional reactions, such as laughter, at the humor in their own stories. Unfortunately, it is impossible to reproduce the impact of these stylistic devices as detailed as the descriptions and notations may be. The distance between the personal encounter and the written page is tremendous. One becomes acutely aware of this as the informant's material passes through the mechanics of the tape recorder and the typewriter, taking on a different character with each stage.

Some of the stylistic characteristics identifiable in the structure of these narratives include the use of several types of formulistic expressions. The following are examples:

Introductory phrases
>   Éste eran dos ratoncitos . . .
>   Áhi va el cuento que se titula . . .
>   Este cuento que voy a contarles es de . . .
>   Vamos a contar un cuento de . . .

Question-answer exchanges
>   —¿Qué andas haciendo, buen hombre?
>   —¿Qué he de estar haciendo, buen pescado?
>   —¿Qué deseas?
>   —Pos, ¿qué voy a desear?
>   —¿Adónde vas, buen niño?
>   —¿Adónde he de ir, buen señor?

Cumulative expressions
>   rebuzna y rebuzna
>   fue anda y anda
>   y ponle y ponle y ponle
>   'taban pelea y pelea y pelea
>   y a llora y llora y llora
>   a busca y busca y busca y busca y busca y busca
>   préstame y préstame dinero
>   se fue rueda y rueda y rueda y rueda y rueda
>   áhi está a dale y dale y dale
>   y échele y échele agua y échele y échele agua y échele y échele
>   agua

Proverbs/sayings
>   Pena de la vida o cinco balazos.
>   Lo más encargado, lo más olvidado.
>   A la tierra que fueres, haz lo que vieres.
>   De modo es de que yo le mando al perro, el perro le manda al
>   gato, y el gato a su compañero.

Formulistic addresses

—¿Quién manda abrir mis puertas? Que no se las abriré mas que sean órdenes del rey.

—Ábrete sésamo.

—Niña, de parte de Dios te pido, ¿de cuál mundo eres? ¿Eres de éste o eres del otro?

—Varita, varita de virtud, por la virtud que Dios te ha dado . . .

Closing phrases

Y aquí se acaba el cuentecito.

Así es de que aquí termina la historia.

Y todavía están viviendo . . . casados.

Y vuelo por un camino, vuelo por otro, cuéntenme ustedes otro.

Y así jue la historia que pasó del . . .

Y hasta aquí se acaba el cuento.

Aquí termina el cuentecito.

Y ahí termina este cuento.

The structure of each tale is outlined and parallel versions are cited at the end of each individual tale.

Animal Tales

63. El Ratoncito Pérez

(Recorded by Lola Cruz on December 8, 1966, in Los Angeles, California)

A mouse named Ratoncito Pérez lives a rather comfortable life in a city store and has only to watch out for a cat named El Rey. One day he runs into a poor country mouse and invites him to visit his store and enjoy a real feast. The country mouse is delighted but is very soon frightened by El Rey and decides to return to his poor, but secure, home in the country. Shortly thereafter, however, the harvest takes place, and the mouse's humble home is destroyed by machines. In desperation he returns to the store in the city, and in his excitement over such an abundance of food he knocks something over and awakens the cat, who then eats up both of the mice.

Éste eran dos ratoncitos. Uno se llamaba el Ratoncito Pérez, porque era rico. Y era el Señor Ratón, porque tenía una tienda. Y no más se cuidaba de El Rey. El Rey era el gato. Así tenía nombre . . . de El Rey. Pos luego después el . . . cuando el gato dormía, el ratoncito comía chocolate, pan, azúcar, dulce, todo lo que podía comer en la tienda.

Bueno, en un día de ésos, sale el Ratoncito Pérez a dar un paseyito, y se encuentra con otro ratoncito del campo. Y ese otro ratoncito comía zanahorias, papas, lechugas, apio, repollo, era todo lo que comía el ratoncito ese otro. Era un ratoncito pobre. Y luego le dice: —¿Cómo te va, Ratoncito Pérez?

—Muy bien, ¿Y a ti?

—¡Uy, cómo estás tú gordo!

—O, pues, con el chocolatito que como, y mi panecito. Y tú, ¿qué comes?

—Mmm, pues no más cuando hay tiempo de comer, como lechuguita, zanahorias, papas, repollos, lo que me gusta. Pero yo ya tengo ganas de comer otras cosas.

—Dice: —¿Cómo no me das una visitadita a mi tienda? Y allá comes lo que tú puedas.

—Bueno. Con tu permiso, entonces, voy allá a verte, a visitarte.

Luego jue el ratoncito pobrecito a visitar al otro ratoncito. Y luego le dice: —¿Cómo estás, Ratoncito Pérez?

—Muy bien, ratoncito. Pásate.

Dice: —Voy a comer chocolate.

—Espérate, espérate, porque El Rey ha de estar dispierto. El Rey está dispierto, y luego después si te ve te come. Dice: —Mira, cuando El Rey tenga los ojos cerrados está dormido.

Y luego después el ratoncito . . . estaba muy, muy triste, triste, porque no hallaba cómo comer, y el . . . gatito no se dormía. Y luego empezó el gato: —Miau, miau. [The informant imitates cat.]

Y luego después el ratón se asustó. Y dice: —Ya me voy . . . otra vuelta para . . . para mi campo.

Cuando luego en eso andan tumbando toda la verdura, y pasa la máquina y tumba toda la verdura. Y luego el ratoncito estaba muriendo de hambre. Dice: —Ay, ¿qué hago? Y después si voy a la tienda me come El Rey. Y, luego ¿qué voy a hacer? Pues estaba muy triste el ratoncito porque habían tumbado, habían tumbado todas las verduras, y habían hecho hoyo y le rompieron su casita onde tenía él todo metido. Verduras y flores y todo se metió allí.

Cuando llegó una noche, y tocó en la puerta . . . de la tienda. Y le dice: —Pues, ¿que vinistes? ¿No ves que tú, tú eres muy agarrón, y luego El Rey te va a comer? Tú no te esperas.

—Ay, dame siquiera, tú, tráeme la comida.

—Tá bueno. Tú no te muevas de aquí, y yo voy a traerte lo que tú quieras comer.

Pos, cuando en eso que el ratoncito estaba . . . agarrando la comida, el otro ratoncito pobre era muy travieso. Siempre se, se fue, y tumbó una cosita de la tienda, y hizo ruido. Y cayó encima del, del . . . de El Rey. Y luego El Rey dispertó. Y luego hizo: —Miau, miau. [Imitates.] Y luego después . . . le dio olor al, al ratón. Y luego se comió a los dos ratoncitos, al ratoncito rico y al ratoncito . . . pobrecito. Y es todo (1).

[Interviewer: —¿Quién le contó el cuento?]

Este cuento me lo contó mi esposo.

Aarne-Thompson 112. Country Mouse Visits Town Mouse.
Boggs 112.
(1) Thompson J211.2. Town mouse and country mouse.
Jacobs, *Aesop* I, 7.
Libro de los gatos, no. 11.
Ruiz, Juan, *Libro de Buen Amor*, 1370–1385.
    United States: Rael, nos. 407, 408, 409.

64. Un bien con un mal se paga

(Recorded by Candelario Gallardo on November 25, 1966, in Oxnard, California)

A man frees a snake from under a rock, whereupon the snake threatens to bite him, asserting that a good deed is always repaid with evil. The man objects, and they decide to accept the judgment of three witnesses. An ox and a donkey agree with the snake because their own personal experience was that good was indeed repaid with evil. The third witness, a coyote, tricks the snake into reassuming his original position under the rock and then leaves him there, thus deciding the case.

Voy a contar un cuentecito . . . de un señor que venía por un camino. Este señor iba por un camino . . . ya muy . . . muy cansado. Y luego iba bajando . . . una vereda, cuando . . . estaba una culebrita enroscadita, y tenía una piedra encima. Dice el señor: —Ay, pobrecita culebrita, dice. —Mira no más cómo tienes esta piedra encima. Te voy a quitar la, la, la piedra de, de encima, culebrita.

Dice la culebrita: —'Tá bien, dice. —Hazme ese favor.

Entonces agarra la piedra y se la quitó. . . . Pero, qué culebrita. Luego que le quitó la . . . la piedra, entonces trató de, de morderlo . . . de picarle.

Le dice el señor: —No, culebrita, no seas mala conmigo. Después de que te quité, te salvé, pues ahora ya me quieres picar. No, no está bien, culebrita.

—Mmm, le dice la culebrita, —¿qué no sabes tú que un bien con un mal se paga?

—Hombre, no, dice. —Pos yo . . . pos no me lo sé.

—No, dice, —pues así es, que un bien con un mal se paga. Así es de que te voy a picar.

—Bueno. Pa que me puedas tú picar, culebrita, pues necesita . . . necesitamos unos testigos, . . . para si es justo que tú me piques.

—Pues, está bien.

—Entonces vamos a conseguir los, los testigos.

Entonces se fueron . . . los dos caminando. Y estaba una ciéniga [sic] . . . una ciéniga, que estaba un . . . un buey . . . atascado en un lodazal. Y dice: —Mira, dice, —áhi está un bueycito, dice. —Está atascado en el atascadero aquel. Ése va a servir para testigo. Llegaron donde estaba el bueycito. —Oye, bueycito, dice, —¿sabes qué?, dice. —Esta culebrita me quiere picar.

—¿Por qué razón?, dice el buey.

Dice: —Sabes que estaba enroscadita y tenía una piedra encima, y yo se la quité. Y luego ella me quiere picar. Así es de que le digo que no sea injusta, que yo le salvé la vida, y ahora me quiere, pues, picar. Y ella me dice que un bien con un mal se paga. Y yo le digo que . . . que vamos a los hechos, que busquemos unos testigos. Así es de que tú, si nos vas a hacer el favor, tú vas a ser un testigo.

Dice: —Es muy cierto lo que te dice la culebrita. Mira. Yo, cuando estaba nuevo, mmm, dice, —me tenían mis patrones con . . . con rastrojito y maicito, y . . . y estaba muy gordo, gordo, gordo, dice. —Y ahora que estoy flaco, me echaron a la ciéniga, y mírame en qué situación estoy. Estoy que no puedo salir aquí entre este apalladero. Así es de que soy testigo que fácilmente te pica la culebrita.

—Está bien, dice. —Vámonos adelante, culebrita. Son tres testigos que vamos a conseguir.

Se fueron anda y anda. —Allá más delante, dice. Estaba un burro viejo . . . ya con la cabeza cáida, ya muy flaco, flaco. Ya llegaron. —¿Quihubo, burrito?

—¿Quihubo? Apenas hablaba el burrito de flaco.

—Home [*sic*], dice, —nos vamos consiguiendo unos testigos.

—A ver, dice. —¿De qué . . . de qué testigos quieren?

—Sabes que esta culebrita me quiere picar, hombre. Tenía una piedra encima, dice, —y yo se la quité. Y ahora, pues, me quiere picar, luego que ya se salvó, que yo le salvé la vida. Y ahora me quiere picar. Le digo que no sea injusta, . . . que consigamos unos, . . . que no me pique. Solamente que . . . haiga unos testigos que aclaren que si es justo que me pique. Entonces yo lo doy por hecho.

—Home, dice, —pos sí, es cierto lo que te dice la culebrita. Sabes que cuando yo estaba nuevo, mmm, me traían con una silla nuevecita, y yo iba rebuzna y rebuzna con el patrón arriba. Y . . . y me traían, pues, me daban mi maicito, mi pajita, y estaba pero . . . bien gordo. Y ahora que estoy . . . ya que me hice viejo, dice, —aquí me tiene en esta situación. Dice: —Ay, dice, —a veces ni puedo rebuznar ya. Así es de que es muy cierto lo que te dice la . . . la culebrita.

—Está bien. Ya son dos testigos. Fácilmente me va a morder la culebrita. Me falta uno. A ver si aquél me salva la vida.

Estaba un coyote . . . aulle: —cacauuuuuu, cacauuuuuu [gives imitation of coyote]. Dice: —Home, éste es un coyotito, hombre. Vamos con el coyotito. Entonces áhi van con el coyotito que estaba aullando allí.

—Oye, coyotito, dice, —sabes que tú vas a ser un testigo. Es el último testigo pa mi . . . salvación.

Dice: —A ver, ¿de qué se trata?, dice el coyote.

—Sabes que esta culebrita, dice, —me . . . me quiere picar. Ella estaba . . . estaba con una piedra encima, y yo, pues, de condolido, se la quité . . . de encima. Y luego que se la quité me quiere picar. Y así es de que yo le dije que no juera injusta, que yo le había salvado la vida, y que no me picara. Pero andamos consiguiendo unos testigos. Y andamos consiguiendo los testigos. Y sabes que encontramos un buey, y dice que sí es cierto. Que estaba un, . . . que cuando él estaba nuevo que . . . lo tenían muy gordo, y que le daban mucho rastorjito [sic] verde y maicito, y estaba muy gordo. Y ahora que se hizo viejo, allí lo hallamos allá, . . . tascado [sic] en . . . en una ciéniga allí. Así es de que . . . pos él declara que sí me pique la culebrita. Y hallamos un burrito tamién . . . que tamién declara que me pique, porque estaba viejo ya, y que el patrón lo echó a la ciénega a que se muriera. De modo es que . . . no más nos falta uno. Tú, coyotito, ¿qué es tu opinión tuya?

Dice: —Mi opinión es de que . . . pos, vamos a onde estaba la culebrita, . . . en el lugar donde estaba la culebrita. A ver, culebrita, vamos.

Y áhi van . . . de donde estaba aquel hoyo, onde estaba. Dice: —Mira, dice, —aquí en este hoyo estaba la culebrita.

Dice: —A ver, dice, —culebrita, enróscate en el hoyo. Y ya la culebrita se empezaba a enroscar como estaba antes. Y luego llega el coyote, y se le echó encima. Dice: —Yo soy testigo [laughs], dice, —que . . . pa que no, no anden cobrándose ni uno ni otro. Dice: —Áhi te quedas, culebrita, como tú estabas, y no le picas aquí al . . . aquí al caminante. . . . Y . . . aquí se acaba el cuentecito (1).

Aarne-Thompson 155. The Ungrateful Serpent Returned to Captivity.
Boggs 155.
Hansen 155. The Ungrateful Serpent Returned to Captivity.
(1) Thompson J1172.3. Ungrateful animal returned to captivity.
Thompson, *Folktale*, p. 226.
Fábulas de Esopo, I, 10; Extravagantes 4, 8.
Hilka, *Disciplina clericalis*, no. 7.
Jacobs, *Aesop* I, 28, 235, 253.
Juan Manuel, *Libro de los enxemplos*, no. 2.
McKenzie, *Modern Philology*, 1(1903–1904), 497–525.
Ruiz, *Libro de Buen Amor*, 1348–1353.
Samaniego, II, 7.
Mexico: Aiken, *TFSP*, 12(1935), 4, no. 2; Boas, *JAF*, 25(1912), 209–

210, 247; González Casanova, pp. 111–115; Guerra, *TFSP*, 18
(1943), 191; Paredes, no. 25; Pauer, *JAF*, 31(1918), 552–553 (la-
garto/leñador); Radin, *JAF*, 28(1915), 392–393; Radin, *El folklore de Oaxaca*, 86; Radin-Espinosa, *JAF*, 28(1915), 392, no. 2;
Reid, *JAF*, 48(1935),121–124, no. 7; Robe, *Mexican Tales*, no. 14;
Storm, *TFSP*, 14(1938), 24; Wagner, *JAF*, 40(1927),139–140, no.
6 (lagarto/burro); Wheeler, nos. 195, 196 (sailor/alligator), 197
(rabbit/serpent), 198 (woodcutter/giant).
United States: Espinosa, *JAF*, 27(1914), 139, no. 19; Garnica Ornelas, no. 25; Rael, nos. 386, 387.
Argentina: *AFAA*, pp. 82–83; *AFAP*, p. 78; Álvarez, p. 81; Aram-
buru, *El folklore de los niños*, p. 169; Avila, pp. 168–169; Burgos,
pp. 33–36; Canal Feijóo, pp. 76–79; Cano, pp. 213–218; Cañete de
Rivas, pp. 55–58; Chertudi, 1st series, no. 6, 2nd series, no. 2; Co-
luccio, *Folklore de las Américas*, p. 45; "Cuentos de animales,"
BATF, pp. 226–227; Franco, pp. 147–149; Morales, *Azul*, pp. 6–7.
Chile: Laval, *Carahue*, II, no. 18; Montenegro, p. 111; Pino Saavedra,
no. 239; *RCHG*, vol 62, pp. 227–229.
Cuba: Guirao, pp. 63–66.
Dominican Republic: Andrade, nos. 245–259.
Peru: Jiménez Borja, no. 13.
Puerto Rico: Mason-Espinosa, *JAF*, 40(1927), 345, no. 32; 364, no.
56; 377, no. 75.
Spain: Ampudia, nos. 50, 171; Espinosa, *Castilla*, 68; Espinosa,
Cuentos, no. 264; *Folklore andaluz*, p. 319.
Uruguay: Pereda Valdés, pp. 131–132.
Venezuela: Olivares Figueroa, *Folklore*, pp. 48–49; idem,*Onza, Tigre
y León*, pp. 10–11, no. 97; Sojo, *AVF* (1953–1954), pp. 176–178;
idem, *BIF*, 2(1955), 80–81.

Tales of Magic

65. La sierpe de siete cabezas

(Recorded by Candelario Gallardo on July 16, 1967, in Oxnard, California)

Two children are abandoned in the forest by their father because he
is unable to support his large family. The sister picks three roses,
which subsequently turn into three marvelous dogs named Revientacadenas, Quiebrapuertas, and Mundo [Chainbreaker, Doorsmasher,
and World]. The children and the dogs arrive at the cottage of an old
woman, who tells them that the city is terrorized by a seven-headed
dragon and that the daughter of the king has just been voted the sacri-

ficial victim for that day. The two children tell her that they will save the princess and kill the seven-headed dragon with the help of their three marvelous dogs. They are successful, and the brother cuts out the tongues from the seven heads as proof of the deed, for the king has decreed that whoever slays the dragon shall marry his daughter. A woodcutter, however, happens upon the dead dragon, and, thinking it a golden opportunity to marry the princess and become very rich, he cuts off the seven heads to offer as evidence that *he* is the dragon slayer. When the wedding is about to take place, the boy challenges the woodcutter's evidence, telling the king to check and see if the heads have tongues. He is thus identified as the real hero, he marries the princess, and the woodcutter pays with his life for his dishonesty. Soon afterward, a giant who falls in love with the boy's sister is imprisoned by the brother, who does not like him; but the giant gets the sister to free him and instructs her how to kill her brother with a poisonous thorn placed in his pillow. The murder is accomplished, and the brother is buried, but the three marvelous dogs dig him up. The king then orders him thrown into the depths of the sea, but once again the dogs retrieve his body. Mundo removes the thorn from his head, thus resuscitating him, and the three marvelous dogs turn into angels and go off to heaven.

Señores y señoras, les voy a contar la historia de La Sierpe de Siete Cabezas. Espero que les guste, pues para que se diviertan, ¿verdad? Así es de que eso es lo que les voy a contar. La historia de La Sierpe de Siete Cabezas.

Empieza así. Éste era un . . . un hombre que tenía mucha familia. Y este hombre no podía soportar a, a mucha familia. Y la señora, pues, tamién, pues ella, pos no los podía atender. Y entonces, de ver todas esas batallas, le, le dice el esposo un día, le dice: —Hombre, dice, —ya no podemos soportar esta familia. Dice: —No sé qué hacer.

Y entonces se pusieron de acuerdo ellos y acordaron, dice: —Cómo no hacer una cosa. Llévate por allá a los, a los niños, dice, —pa que se nos aliviane, pos, la carga.

Pues el esposo acectó [*sic*]. Dice: —Pos sí, está bien. Dice: —Entonces, dice, —yo voy a, a llevarlos por allá, a perderlos por allá al . . . en un lugar, que ya no vuelvan para atrás.

Y así les hizo. El, el papá les dice a sus hijitos, los más chicos de edad: —Hijos, dice, —vamos, dice. —Vamos, dice, —tengo un, un lugar donde ustedes se van a devertir. Es muy bonito lugar y para que ustedes lo conozcan, y . . . ooo, dice, —y ustedes tengan ese recuerdo de ese lugar.

—Ay, papá, dice, —sí. Pos sí está bien, dice. —Llévanos.

Entonces ya los llevó. Se los llevó a una selva y por allá muy boscosa. Y este hombre, por allá, pos luego que ya, se escondió verdaderamente de ellos. Y se vino para su casa y los dejó en el bosque perdidos (1).

Entonces los niños, pos, lloraban y lloraban por su papá que, tal vez que se lo había comido alguna fiera porque el bosque estaba muy, muy boscoso. Y . . . pues ellos, ¿qué hacían? Pues no había más que llorar, ¿verdad?

Pero éstos vieron un, un prado muy bonito, que había muchas rosas. Y entonces la niña y el niño se fueron a ese prado a devertirse con las rosas. Y, y había unas tres, tres rosas. Pero . . . eran rosas de Castilla. Muy hermosas. Entonces la niña los cortó, las flores. Y las puso en una, en una canastita. Entonces se fueron. Se fueron, pues . . . por todo el bosque. Y las tapó, las tapó con un pañuelo las rosas.

Entonces . . . entonces ya no eran rosas. Cuando vieron ya no eran rosas. Eran tres perritos (2). Pero la cosa más hermosa. Y ya ellos dijeron: —Mira no más, dice. —Las rosas de Castilla ya se volvieron perritos, dice. —Mira, qué bonitos perritos.

Entonces en el transcurso del tiempo se pusieron muy grandes los perros y muy hermosos. Y todo lo que les mandaban, todo obedecían (3).

Bueno, pos que llegaron a una población . . . muy bonita. Y andaba una viejecita barriendo su, su, enfrente de su casa. Y ya le saludan:

—Buenos días, señora.

—Buenos días. Dice la viejita, dice: —¿Qué, qué andan haciendo, niños, ustedes aquí, dice, —con estos perritos? Mira no más qué perros tan grandotes. ¿No son bravos?

Dice: —No, señora. Estos perros no son bravos. Dice: —Son muy educados estos perritos. Dice: —Nada más, dice, —que no tenemos nosotros hogar, dice, —para, para existir. Si usted pudiera, dice,

—darnos un lugarcito, dice, —áhi, dice, —para dormir, para existir.

—Ay, dice la viejita, —cómo no, dice. —Si yo ni familia tengo. Dice: —Y a ustedes los voy a ver como mis hijos. Pasen para mi casa.

Entonces ya pasaron, ¿verdad?, y les dio pues la habitación y una cama muy bonita y, y el lugar para los perros y todo eso. Bueno. Pues entonces se pusieron a platicar con la viejecita.

Dijo: —Señora, dice, —¿y qué nuevas tiene aquí en esta ciudad? Figuro yo que es muy bonito, dice, —porque se ve muy bonito.

—Ooo, dice, —los [*sic*] nuevas que hay, niños, es de que . . . aquí hay una sierpe de siete cabezas (4). Y esta sierpe, dice, —mmm, todos los días le llevan una persona a que se la coma. Y no quieren que baje al pueblo porque devora mucha gente. Y hay una votación, . . . por el rey hay una votación que el que le toque no tiene más que ir a que se le coma la serpiente (5, 6). Y ahora, dice, —está de luto el pueblo, porque le ha tocado a la hija del rey. De modo es que se la va a comer la sierpe de siete cabezas.

—Bueno, dice, —y, y ¿en qué lugar puede estar la, la, la niña?

—Oo, dice, —si hày un lugar, dice, —en la selva. Si allá hay un árbol muy grande, y allí, pues atan a la . . . a la, a la niña, dice. —Luego viene la sierpe y se la come. Y luego se va muy satisfecha la, la sierpe.

—Bueno, dice. —Nosotros podemos salvar a la hija del rey . . . con nuestros perros. Estos perros, dice, —son virtuosos. Estos perros devoran la, la, la sierpe. Así es de que nosotros vamos a ir a salvar a la niña.

—Ooo, dice, —tanto gusto me dará, y cuánto gusto recibirá la ciudad, que ustedes, dice, —los perritos, pues, devoren a la sierpe.

—Pos así lo vamos a hacer.

Entonces ya . . . ya los perritos tenían nombre. Uno, uno se llamaba Revientacadenas. Otro se llamaba Puertas. [Later referred to by the informant as Quiebrapuertas.] Y, y el otro se llamaba Mundo.

Pues, que áhi van. . . . Se fueron con sus perritos. Pues ya hallaron la niña allí, pues, atada de pies y brazos para que no. . . no se moviera, pa que la sierpe se la comiera. Entonces ya llegan los niños y la saludan.

—Niña, dice, —¿se la va a comer la sierpe?

—Sí, dice. —Me tocó la votación y no tengo más que . . . pues, me va a comer la sierpe.

Dice: —Pues nosotros vamos a, vamos a salvarla. Aquí traemos nosotros estos perritos . . . virtuosos. Y aseguro, dice, —que van a matar la sierpe.

—Ay, dice, —¡cuánto gusto me dará!

—Bueno, dice, —señorita, dice, —¿y qué se siente cuando viene esa sierpe?

—Pos dicen que. . . que, los que ven o los que les ha sucedido esto, que se siente un aire muy frío, y un aironazo cuando viene. Que se siente un aironazo muy helado. Y, y es la seña . . . para cuando va a venir la sierpe.

Ya dice: —Pos entonces vamos a esperar.

No, pos que de repente se soltó un aironazo helado, muy frío, frío, frío. Y la niña empezó a temblar. —¡Ya viene la sierpe, niños!

Entonces los niños . . . ya les dijeron: —¡Aprevénganse, mis perritos! Ya viene la sierpe. Le van uno a la cola y otro en medio y otra a la cabeza, y devoren la, la sierpe.

No, pues los perritos, luego luego que vieron, se pusieron al pendiente, y que llega la sierpe. Y que se le van. Uno de la cola y otro de en medio y otro de la cabeza, y ¡tira!, la hicieron así. Pues la mordieron pues, toda. Y la mataron (7). Entonces ya, pues, ya desataron la, la niña. Y ya se la llevaron allá a la ciudad (8).

Y ya se venían con sus perritos, a la misma habitación donde estaba la, la viejecita. Y a la viejecita ya le empezaron a platicar. Dice: —¿Ya mataron la sierpe?

Dice: —Ya la matamos, señora. De modo es que ya no hay pendiente que baje la sierpe o que se coma la gente, dice. —Ya está muerta.

—Ooo, pues, que tanto gusto.

Bueno, pues que . . . cuando un leñador, su profesión de él era de ir a la leña a cortar árboles secos, porque ese leñador hacía carbón y traía sus burros y cargaba la leña y, y hacía el carbón para vender. Esa era su vida del carbonero. ¡Donde, que había encontrado la sierpe muerta!

Dice: —Ay, dice. —Aquí está mi suerte. Dice: —El rey ha dado órdenes que el que mate la, la sierpe de siete cabezas se casa con su hija (9). Y le da una fortuna. Así es de que . . . pos Dios me socorrió. Yo le voy a . . . les [*sic*] voy a mochar las cabezas y voy a probarle al rey que yo maté la sierpe (10).

Pos así lo hizo. Con el hacha les mochó las cabezas y en el lazo las hizo un rosario, y áhi las lleva con el rey. Y luego ya fue con el rey. Ya dice: —Aquí le traigo las, las cabezas de la sierpe (11). Yo la maté (12).

—Ay, dice, —pos, lo hablado hablado. Tú te vas a casar con mi hija, dice. —Te voy a dar una fortuna pa que te quites de pobre, dice, —porque así lo ordené yo (13). Así es de que tú vas a ser el esposo de mi hija. Y vas a ser inmensamente rico.

Pos que, al leñador le dio mucho gusto. Pues que ya dice el rey: —Pues, a celebrar la boda. A hacer la boda, dice.

Así es que ya llamó la niña, dice: —Mira, éste . . . éste va a ser tu esposo.

—Pos, 'ta bien, papá.

Pues que . . . ya estaban, . . . pues el padre los casó y, como es costumbre que cuando ya se casan van a desayunar, y estaban celebrando el desayuno. Y todo el pueblo, toda la ciudad ya conocían, pues, que el muchacho aquel se iba a casar con la, con la hija del rey.

Entonces el muchacho . . . supo bien que ya el leñador se iba a casar con la hija del rey. Entonces . . . el rey, pues él dijo en su balcón, públicamente, que se iba a casar aquel leñador con su hija. Entonces el muchacho, que traía las lenguas, que las había mochado de la sierpe, y las había amarrado en su paño, y le dijo a . . . a un perrito que las guardara él. Entonces el perrito ya las traía amarradas en el cuello, . . . las lenguas. Entonces ya fue el . . . el muchacho.

—Señor, dice. —Así es de que el leñador prueba con las cabezas. Pero las cabezas no tienen lengua (14). Así es de que usted, examine las cabezas y las va a ver que no tienen lengua. El no mató la, la sierpe. Las [*sic*] que mataron la sierpe, dice, —fueron mis perritos. Y así, dice, —aquí trae el perro que se llama Mundo, áhi en ese pañuelo que trae en el cuello, áhi trae las lenguas. O, pues, luego luego fueron a ver y desataron el, el paño al perro, y ahí traía las siete lenguas (15).

—Ooo, así es de que, ¿así pasó?

—Sí, así pasó. Dice: —Mis perros mataron a la sierpe. Entonces el, el rey se saca al leñador y le dice: —Oyes. ¿Qué sentencia dieras tú a la persona que te traicionara tu boda?

Dice el leñador: —Ooo, dice, —yo . . . lo amarraría, la amarraría con una cadena y lo pondría yo en un tiro de caballos que lo arrastraran y lo hicieran pedazos. Ésa es la sentencia que yo daría el que me traicionara mi boda.

—Bueno, dice, —pos entonces tú . . . ¿esa sentencia das?

—Sí. Esa sentencia.

—Pos tú la vas a cumplir. Porque tú no matastes la sierpe. El que mató la sierpe jueron los perritos de este joven. Así es de que te van a preparar la sentencia que has dado tú.

No, pues, ya estaba el tiro de caballos allí. Lo amarraron con las cadenas al leñador, y luego chicotearon a los caballos y lo arrastraron, y pedacitos lo hicieron (16, 17).

Bueno. Entonces ya el muchacho se hizo inmensamente rico. Se casó con la hija del rey. Y la niña, hermanita del niño, pues ella les servía como criada. Les hacía el quehacer y, y allí la, la mandaban ellos a, a que ella hiciera el quehacer.

Pero había, había un gigante que, que lo visitaba mucho al muchacho. Y vido la muchacha que estaba muy bonita, la hermanita del, del muchacho. Era muy bonita la niña. Y luego la empezó a enamorar . . . el gigante. Y, y se enamoraron. Tamién ella se enamoró del gigante. Pero luego que supo el muchacho que el gigante había enamorado, estaba enamorando a la hermana, le dio mucho coraje.

Entonces fue a buscarlo a su casa. Y, y lo halló muy dormido al gigante. Y luego llevaba un rifle para matarlo. Entonces no quiso matarlo dormido, sino que le habló. Y luego dispertó el gigante.

Dice: —Te voy a matar con este rifle.

Dice: —¿Por qué me vas a matar?

Dice: —Porque, dice, —porque tú andas enamorando a mi hermana, dice, —y no te quiero, dice. —Y así es de que vas a morir.

Dice el gigante muy asustado: —No me mates, muchacho, dice.

—Yo, dice, —mira, mejor . . . tengo yo un cuarto de puritito fierro, dice. —Secuéstrame allí, dice, —que me muera de hambre. Pero no me mates así. Dice: —Ten las llaves, dice, —y abre el cuarto, y secuéstrame en el cuarto.

Pos así lo hizo. Abrió aquel cuarto, pero . . . de puritito fierro y lo echó en el cuarto al, al gigante. Y le cerró las puertas.

Pero el cuarto siempre tenía respiración, o un enverjado de, de fierro, para que agarrara oxígeno el, el gigante. Entonces la niña, la hermanita del muchacho, estaba muy apurada. Ya ella ya sabía lo que le, lo que le había pasado. Y le buscó el modo de ir a visitarlo. No, pues, ya halló, . . . habló por el enverjado.

Y ya el gigante dice: —Pues aquí me tiene tu hermano, dice. —Así es de que yo aquí voy a morir de hambre y de sed. Pero si tú le buscas las llaves y me puedes abrir. . . . Búscale las llaves dónde las tenga, dice, —y, y húrtaselas, y luego vienes y me abres la puerta.

No, pues, la muchacha le buscó las llaves y . . . luego fue a abrirla, la, la puerta al gigante. Luego que le abrió la puerta, pues, dice: —Así es de que, ya te abrí yo la puerta, dice. —Cuando sepa mi hermano, dice, —a mí me va a matar.

—Bueno, dice, —de que te mate a ti, y que él muera, ¿cómo crees? Que muera mejor él, ¿verdad?

—Pos sí, dice.

—Bueno, dice, —yo tengo una manera de que tú lo mates.

Dice: —¿De qué manera?

Dice: —Yo, yo tengo un . . . tengo un, un espolón. Ese espolón es ponzoñoso. Y muy fino. Así es de que ese, ese espolón se lo colocas tú en la almohada de, de él. Y cuando él se acueste el espolón se le mete en el cerebro y inmediatamente, ni se dan cuenta de qué murió. El se muere luego luego.

—Pos que sí, lo hago (18).

Ya le dio el espolón, ¿verdad? Así grande, como una navaja de esas de rayo que les amarran a las patas a los gallos. Y se lo colocó en la almohada. Y cuando el muchacho, el hermano, vino, se dio el recargón en la almohada, y que se lo mete en el cerebro. Inmediatamente murió (19).

Bueno, pos que, pos no sabía toda la gente de qué había muerto. Lo examinaban por ondequiera, qué fue que le había pasado, y no, ni rastros. El espolón se le fue al cerebro.

Entonces el rey dice: —Bueno, dice, —pos éste ya murió, dice. —Vayan a enterrarlo.

Entonces fueron a enterrarlo allí al panteón. Y los perritos, luego que ya se fue toda la gente, áhi 'tan con las manitas, y lo sacaron al muchacho.

Otra vez lo volvieron a enterrar y los perros lo volvían a sacar.

Entonces dice, dice el rey, dice: —No, dice. —Éste, vayan a aventarlo al mar, para que naiden lo saque. Entonces hicieron una caja, y se fueron y lo aventaron en el fondo del mar.

Pero los perritos, qué listos. Luego luego se fueron nadando y se echaron un clavado y que lo sacan. Y lo sacaron. Y entonces, como eran, los perros eran virtuosos, Mundito era el más vivo. Entonces luego que ya lo sacaron, entonces Mundito le sacó el espolón del cerebro y vivió el muchacho (20, 21). Y luego que ya . . . pos, los perritos empezaron, pues a decirle lo que le había pasado, que él se había muerto y que con ese espolón lo había matado el gigante y todo eso.

Y entonces ellos . . . ya dijeron: —Hasta aquí te vamos a acompañar. Y vamos haciendo una oración. Y, y ellos se hincaron, los tres perritos se hincaron, y él también, se alzaron los ojos al cielo. Y ya no eran perritos, sino que eran tres ángeles. Y volaron. Se fueron al cielo.

Así es de que aquí termina el . . . la historia de La Sierpe de Siete Cabezas. Así es de que espero que les haiga gustado.

The story is structured as follows: S321. Destitute parents abandon children + 300 Ic (boy) bde (transformation from flowers) IIab IIIb IVf Vab VIIac VIcd + (Hansen) VII*F.

Aarne-Thompson 300. The Dragon-Slayer.
Boggs 300.
Hansen 300. The Dragon-Slayer.
(1) S321. Destitute parents abandon children.
(2) B319. Helpful animal otherwise acquired. [Here, the dogs are transformed from roses.]
(3) B421. Helpful dog.
(4) B11.2.3.1. Seven-headed dragon.
(5) B11.10. Sacrifice of human being to dragon.
(6) S262. Periodic sacrifices to a monster.
(7) B524.1.1. Dogs kill attacking cannibal (dragon).

 (8) R111.1.3. Rescue of princess (maiden) from dragon.
 (9) T68.1. Princess offered as prize to rescuer.
(10) K2262. Treacherous charcoal-burner.
(11) H83. Rescue tokens.
(12) K1932. Imposters claim reward (prize) earned by hero.
(13) M203. King's promise irrevocable.
(14) H105.1.1. False dragon-head proof.
(15) H105.1. Dragon-tongue proof.
(16) Q262. Impostor punished.
(17) Q416.2. Punishment: dragging to death by a horse.
(18) K2212.0.2. Treacherous sister as mistress of robber (giant) plots against
     brother.
(19) K2212.0.1. Treacherous sister attempts to poison brother.
(20) A524.1.1. Culture hero has marvelous dogs.
(21) B515. Resuscitation by animals.
     Grimm, no. 60.
     Krappe, *Folklore*, 34(1923), 141 (under Type 511).

       Mexico: Paredes, no. 43; Robe, *Mexican Tales*, nos. 37, 109; Wheel-
         er, nos. 57, 92, 103, 114, 121.
       United States: Espinosa, *SFNM*, nos. 22, 23, 24; Rael, nos. 246,
         247, 338, 339.
       Argentina: Chertudi, 1st series, no. 39, 2nd series, nos. 31, 38, 55;
         Draghi Lucero, pp. 195–234.
       Chile: *AUC*, vol. 92, pp. 31–39; Kössler-Ilg, no. 68; Laval, *Cara-
         hue*, no. 5 (and pp. 116–117); Laval, *Cuentos populares*, I, no.
         18 (and p. 286); Lenz, *Estudios*, pp. 242–249 (and pp. 326–
         337); Montenegro, p. 189; Pino Saavedra, nos. 1, 11, 12.
       Colombia: Pineda Giraldo, *RF*, p. 117.
       Dominican Republic: Andrade, nos. 95, 96, 97, 98, 99, 260.
       Puerto Rico: Mason-Espinosa, *JAF*, 38(1925), 529, no. 3a; 532, no.
         3b; 534, no. 3c; 536, no. 3d; 538, no. 3e; 600, no. 10h; 39
         (1926), 231, no. 15b; 299, no. 21ee.
       Spain: Caballero, *Cuentos, oraciones*, p. 11 = *Spanish Fairy Tales*,
         p. 29; Curiel Merchán, pp. 34–36, 172–177, 279–281; Espinosa,
         Castilla, no. 43; Espinosa, *Cuentos*, nos. 139, 157; *FA*, p. 357;
         Hernández de Soto, *BTPE*, X, pp. 249, 258 = Eells, p. 117.

66. Juan del Oso

(Recorded by Candelario Gallardo on December 2, 1966, in Oxnard, California)

A bear carries a woman off to live with him in his den, and from
their union two sons are born. When the boys are somewhat grown,
they and their mother manage to escape from the bear's den by
moving the rock that blocks the entrance. One of the sons, however,
is drowned in a river they must cross in their escape from the forest.
The mother is unable to care for the other son, and so she gives him
over to a priest to be educated; but he causes too much trouble at

school, and the priest decides to send him off to make his own way in
the world. He grants the boy's parting request, which is that he be
given a club for his journey—one so heavy that he alone is able to lift
it. In his wanderings the boy, now called Juan del Oso, acquires
three extraordinary companions, Arrancapinos, Redumbacerros, and
Buen Tirador [Pinetwister, Cliffbreaker, and Good Marksman]. The
four companions come across a house in the woods and decide to take
some of the marvelous assortment of foods they find there; but one by
one they are beaten off by the owner, a Negro, who catches them in the
act of stealing. Juan del Oso, however, is not beaten, and he cuts off
the Negro's ear and keeps it as a magic object with which he can call
the Negro to his presence and have his requests fulfilled. They follow
the trail of blood left by the Negro and find that it leads to a cave.
One by one they are repulsed in their attempt to penetrate the cave;
but once again Juan del Oso is successful.

He finds three princesses, in the form of birds, held captive by the
Negro, and disenchants them by removing thorns from their heads.
But he is then abandoned by his companions, who make off with the
princesses with the intention of claiming them as their wives. He finally escapes from the cave by using the magic ear and goes to a nearby
city disguised as a leper. Using the magic ear once again, he outfits
himself as a bullfighter and becomes a hero at two successive bull-
fights, which are attended by the princesses he had rescued; but he
escapes immediately afterward and remains unidentified. When the
wedding of the three companions and the princesses is about to take
place, Juan del Oso appears before the king with the three crowns of
the princesses as proof that he was their rescuer, the three imposters
are condemned to life imprisonment, and Juan del Oso chooses the
youngest princess for his wife.

Beuno. Áhi va el cuento que se titula Juan del Oso. Este Juan del
Oso . . . que habitaba en, en una selva. Este oso allí se mantenía . . .
allí, en una cueva. Era su habitación del oso. Y, y una viejita . . . una
viejita, también iba allá a la selva, pos a traer leña, a vendérsela. Era
. . . era su mantención de esta viejita, trayendo leña y vendiendo. Y
en un día el oso por allí se la halló. Y éste no le dijo nada, nada más
que cargársela, como . . . pues no hablaba. Pero . . . se la llevó a la
. . . a su habitación . . . que era la cueva. Allá existía el oso, y allí se
la llevó a la vieja, a la señora.

Pues allí . . . a la señora no le faltaba nada. Le tenía carne lo suficiente. Le tenía toditito. No le faltaba nada a la señora, porque el oso toda le acarreaba. Todito le . . . le llevaba. Bueno, como ustedes . . . pos . . . ya lo saben, . . . el oso y, y la señora . . . pues se casaron. Se casaron el oso con la, con la, con la señora . . . así vocalmente nada más. Y, y entre esto hubo dos . . . dos niños, de . . . de, del oso y la señora (1, 2).

Aquellos niños se crecieron y le decían a su mamá: —Oiga, mamá, dice, —¿pues, quién es . . . quién es nuestro papá?

—O, niños, dice, —pues, su papá es el oso.

—¿Cómo que el oso?

—Ese, ese animal que entra aquí y te trae carne, les trae carne de comer, dijo, —es tu papá. Es su papá.

Dice: —Mamá, dice, —pues vamos, vamos de aquí de esta cueva.

—No, dice, —pues no podemos salir, hijos. Nos pone de puerta una piedra enorme, muy pesada. Sólo él la puede mover. Así es que no podemos irnos (3).

—No, mamá, dice, —nosotros . . . podemos quitar esa piedra. Entonces los niños se arriscaron sus manitas, y le dieron un empujón a la piedra y la tumbaron.

Entonces la viejita, pues, . . . no, no viejita ya, pues señora . . . de buena edad, entonces agarró sus dos hijos y se jue rumbo a la ciudad. Pero para llegar a la ciudad, se atravesaba un río, un río que llevaba muchísima agua. Entonces agarró . . . sus hijos y como pudo se los echó al hombro, uno, uno en cada brazo, y atravesó el río. Pero atravesando el río, pues no, no . . . no soportó a los, a los dos niños. Uno se le cayó al agua. Se lo llevó. Se ahogó y se llevó . . . un niño.

Y ya llegó allá, a la ciudad, y . . . dice: —Pos yo voy a bautizar a mi niño. Y jue con el señor cura. —Señor cura, sabe que vengo a bautizar . . . este niño.

Dice: —Pero este niño, dice, —tiene trazas de animal. 'Tá muy peludo.

—Pos sí, señor cura, dice. Ya le contó lo que le había pasado.

Dijo el señor cura: —Bueno, dijo, —en realidad que hay que bautizarlo. Entonces lo bautizó y él jue el padrino, el señor cura, . . . del niño.

Entonces la señora le dice: —Pos, señor cura, usted lo va a educar, dice. —Áhi se lo dejo . . . a usted. Lo pone en la escuela, Yo soy muy pobre. Yo no puedo . . . sostenerlo, soportarlo. Para que . . . lo eduque usted, aquí se lo dejo.

—Pos está bien. Si es mi ahijado.

Entonces ya . . . ya lo echó en la escuela. Lo puso en la escuela. Y, y luego el muchachito, pos, era . . . muy malo (4). Mmm, se enojaba con los demás niños, y no más les daba un aventón, y ¡por dónde se iban a dar (5)! Y golpeaba a los niños. 'Taba muy fuerte. Era muy pelionero, muy perverso el . . . muchacho. Así es de que quejas y quejas y quejas, que el . . . Juan del Oso, pues, golpeaba a los niños.

Y luego el señor cura dice: —Home, dice, —ya no se aguanta este niño. Y él le avisó a la . . . señora. Dice: —Home, ya no aguanto a Juan . . . a Juanito, dice. —Tiene todos los muchachos allí, pues, golpeados. A cada ratito tienen quejas de él, que . . . pues, que golpea a los niños. Así es de que, échale un, un bastimiento para que se vaya (6).

Entonces la señora le . . . le, le compuso un bastimento, y ya le dijo: —Juanito, dice, —pos el señor cura ya no te quiere. Yo estoy muy pobre, dice, —pa poderte sostener. Así es de que te vas . . . a buscar tu vida. Al cabo, ya estás regular, dice, —para que trabajes por áhi.

—Bueno. Está bien. Entonces yo quisiera que mi padrino, que es el señor cura, me concediera un favor.

—¿Qué favor quieres?

—Yo quiero . . . yo quiero . . . un garrotito. Le dice al señora cura: —Yo quiero un garrote pa hacer mi camino.

—¿Y qué tan pesado lo quieres?

Dice: —Bueno, a palo, pesadito, dice, —pa poderlo mover. Yo lo quiero de . . . de tres arrobas de acero, tres arrobas de fierro, . . . bueno, como de seis arrobas de pesado.

—Pos, 'tá bien, dice. —Te lo mando hacer.

Lo mandó hacer, el garrote . . . a, a, a Juan del Oso. Cuando vido venir mucha gente por el camino, por la calle, y dice: —Padrino, dice, —pos tanta gente que viene áhi, dice. —¿Qué pasa?

Dice: —Es tu garrotito, hombre, que te traen (7).

—Pero, pos, tanta gente pa ese garrotito. Pos corrió luego luego a ver. Y el garrotito lo agarraba y lo alzaba pa arriba. Con una mano lo movía.

—¡Hombre, qué fuerzas tiene este . . . muchacho! Quedaron admirados todos.

—Bueno, pues, áhi 'tá tu garrote.

—Pos, muchas gracias, padrino. Mañana salgo.

Se fue por toda la orilla de un río. Ya se cansaba, y se tiró debajo de un . . . sabino, una sombra de un árbol . . . a . . . descansar, su garrotito por un lado.

Y luego vido venir otro, otro joven. Y ya le saluda: —¿Qué está haciendo usted allá, mi amigo? ¿Está descansando?

—Sí, yo estoy descansando aquí. ¿Y usted, para dónde va?

Dice: —Home, también voy sin rumbo. Yo también voy a descansar aquí en este árbol.

Tonces ya estaban descansando los dos. Y ya se estaban platicando, . . . qué rumbo tenían, y que qué porfisión [*sic*]. Le pregunta . . . Juan del Oso: —Bueno, y usted, dice, —¿qué sabe hacer?

—O, dice, —yo soy muy fuerte.

—¿Qué?

Dice: —Yo puedo arrancar este pino aquí, dice, —con una mano, y lo saco (8, 9).

—Hombre, dice, —a ver, a ver, arráncale.

—O, dice, —pos ¿qué me dura este árbol? Lo agarró con la mano y lo sacó con todo y raíz.

Dice: —¡Hombre, dice, —qué fuerzudo está usted!

—¿Y usted?

—No, dice, —yo no tengo tanta fuerza así, dice. —Pero aquí traigo este garrotito. Este garrotito lo muevo yo con una mano. A ver si usted puede moverlo. Entonces no pudo mover el garrote . . . el Arrancapinos. Entonces Juan agarró su garrotito y lo meneó por todos lados.

—¡Hombre, dice, —qué fuerzudo está usted también! Nos, . . . ¿quiere que seamos compañeros?

—Sí, cómo no.

—Pos entonces, vamos a hacer camino.

Y áhi van por todo el río. Volvieron a descansar. Cuando vieron venir otro, otro, otro joven. Ya se saludaron allí. Y . . . ya le pregunta Juan, . . . el otro, Juan del Oso: —¿Usted, qué sabe hacer, amigo?

—O, dice, —yo . . . yo redumbo [*sic*] los cerros (10).

—¿Cómo que redumba usted los cerros?

—Sí, dice, —los redumbo.

Dice: —A ver, túmbame ese muro que está áhi, de piedra y cemento. A ver, dice.

—Aaa, dice —¿qué me dura? No más lo agarró y . . . lo tumbó.

—¡Hombre, dice, —qué bueno está eso! Pos usted va a ser nuestro compañero tamién. Yo soy Juan del Oso y yo muevo este garrotito, y este compañero saca los pinos, y usted redumba los cerros. Pos, ¡qué buenos compañeros!

Y áhi van de camino. A más delante se hallaron otro . . . otro señor, cargado con una carabina terciada. Y ya se saludaron: —Y usted, ¿qué sabe hacer?

Dice: —Yo, dice, —soy muy buen tirador. Uy, dice, —volando los pájaros, los tumbo. Con el que se cuenta conmigo, no padece. Hay bastante carne y todo. No le hace. Soy muy buen tirador (11).

—Ay, dice, —pues vámonos de camino. Se jueron.

Ya les andaba de hambre . . . a los, a los cuatro. Porque Juan del Oso, y . . . Arrancapinos, y, y el Redumbacerros, y el Tirador, eran cuatro. Ya les andaba de hambre cuando . . . dice, dice Juan del Oso, dice: —Oyes, tú, Tirador, anda tráenos un animalito por áhi, a ver qué, . . . si lo cocinamos. Tú que eres buen tirador.

Se fue sin rumbo. Y halló una casa con mucha comida. Era la habitación de un negro. Ooo, él hacía muchas comidas. Todo había allí. —¡Ay, dice, —qué bueno está esto! Entonces se metió el Tirador. Pos, comió guajolote y gallina y todo lo que halló allí. Y luego quería traerles a los compañeros. Y que va viniendo el negro, mira.

—¿Qué anda haciendo usted aquí comiendo mi comida? Y agarra un chirrión, que cada chirrionazo, . . . lo tumbaba, lo botó al suelo. Y aquél, mientras quería preparar la carabina, no . . . el chirrión, . . . le daba de chirrionazos que no más le escurrió la sangre. Le dio una chirrioniza [*sic*], pero buena (12). Entonces se fue.

—¿Y qué, qué pasó?, dice Juan del Oso.

—Hombre, dice, —les iba a traer comida. En tal parte hay mucha

comida, pero si salió un negro allí, que cada chirrionaza me reventaba
en el cuerpo.

—Y, . . . ¿qué fue la . . . carabina?

—Pos, si no me daba tiempo. [Laughs.] No me daba tiempo el
negro.

Le dice Juan del Oso: —Pos anda a tumbar la casa, tú que . . . re-
dumbas los cerros, home.

Dijo: —Yo voy.

Pos, que áhi va. Sí, la comida distinta. Y, y comió, y estaba preparando para llevarles a los compañeros, cuando viene el negrito, home.
—Amigo, dice, —mira no más. Ayer te di una buena, y otra vez
vinistes. Y ahorita te pongo otra. Y . . . ¡Cuega! Le da unos chirrionazos, pero no, aquél, ni que qué quería redumbar la finca, pos si no
le daba tiempo de tanto chirrionazo que le daba. Lo bañó en sangre. Y
áhi va.

—¿Qué pasó, hombre? Mira cómo vienes.

—Hombre, dice, —sale ese negro que no le da tiempo a uno pa
nada. Mira no más cómo vengo.

—Tú, Arrancapinos, hombre, anda tú a ver qué . . . sabes hacer tú.

—Pues yo voy, ¡qué caray! Y áhi va.

Llega tamién. Muy distinta la comida. Y luego ya estaba preparando . . . también comida pa llevarles cuando llega el negro. —¡Ay, qué
amigo!, dice. —¡Qué terco es usted! Dice: —Le he dado unas chi-
rrionizas buenas y todavía viene usted aquí. Y, . . . ¡tópele! Otra vez.
Y ponle y ponle y ponle, chirrionazo y chirrionazo. Lo bañó en sangre.
No, pues, áhi va.

—¿Qué pasó, Arrancapinos, hombre?

—¡Uy, qué negro tan malo! ¡Híjole!

—Bueno, dice Juan, —ahora voy yo . . . a ver qué sabe hacer ese
negrito conmigo.

Y áhi va. Comió de toditita la comida. Y que va viniendo el negrito. —Ay, mi amiguito, dice. —Ah, cómo lo he volteado, y todavía
terco ya viene aquí a comerse mi comida. Y que quiso desenvolver el
chirrión, y que le atraviesa un garrotazo, y le mochó una oreja. Y luego le atraviesa otro, y lo tumbó.

Dice: —No te mato, dice, —porque yo soy zaino. Pero esta orejita que te tumbé, . . . ésta me la voy a echar a mi chaleco. Quería fusilarlo.

Dice el negrito: —No me mates. Dice: —Mire, esta orejita mía, . . . no más la muerdes y dices, ¿qué mercedes pido? . . . lo que tú quieras. Yo te salvo de donde tú quieras.

—'Tá bien.

Entonces . . . les llevó comida de la mejor que había allí, y comieron. Dice: —No, yo le gané al, al negro. Le moché una oreja, ¿ve? Aquí traigo la prueba. Entonces: —Vamos a seguirlo a ver dónde se mete ese negro, . . . por la sangre. Tiene que ir dejando la huella de la sangre.

Y áhi fueron, siguiendo la huella (13). Se metió a una cueva, muy fea la cueva (14). Entonces ya llegaron allí, y que tantean. —¿Le entramos a la cueva?

—Sí, le entramos, cómo no.

—Bueno, dice. —¿Quién, quién primero?

—Pos, tú, Tirador, home, éntrale primero. Ya sabes que si hay algo, pues, les, les echas balazos. Dios te ayuda.

Dice: —Pero cuando yo les mueva la reata, es que no puedo pasar. Entonces me sacan para arriba (15).

Y áhi va el Tirador. Y por allá . . . se halla un, una . . . abejas, que le picaban. Le picaban y todo. Picotearon y, ¡uy, enjambres de abejas! Y no pudo pasar. Bulló la reata y lo, lo subieron pa arriba.

—¿Qué pasó, hombre?

—Ay, dice, —no pude pasar. Tanta, tanta colmena, tanta abeja que . . . me picaron todas, y no pude pasar.

—Bueno, pos, ahora . . . hora que vaya . . . el Redumbacerros. No más, no vas a tumbar la cueva. [Laughs.]

Pos que áhi va. Y pasó el colmenero ese, y pasó pa . . . el colmenero, y luego allá más adentro, que muchos zopilotes, y . . . muchos animales bravos que ya lo hacían ciego. Bulló la reata, y áhi va pa arriba.

Para no alargarles mucho, los tres no pudieron pasar. Y luego le dice . . . Juan del Oso: —Hora yo voy. Y entre más les bulla la reata, . . . más me dejan ir. Y luego ya los, . . . pos lo lazaron, y áhi va Juan del Oso hasta la cueva.

Y les bulló la reata, y más la dejaban ir. Llegó a . . . llegó a . . . a un

Lola Cruz, informant who knew many traditional tales

Luis Cruz

Tecla Rocha

Isaura Benicia

Hugo Massa

...alia Hernández and Elisa Contreras

Inocente Rocha

Rafael Gudiño

Alicia Salinas

Candelario Gallardo also told traditional tales

patio (16). Sale una . . . una niña (17), dice: —¿Qué anda haciendo usted aquí, niño? Que va a venir el . . . el puerco espino, y . . . que es el diablo (18). Y se lo va a comer.

—Mm, dice, —en buscas de él vengo.

No, pos, que a poquito viene el puerco con tantos chicos colmillos, y . . . queriendo pelear. Dice: —Ya te conozco. Si te tumbé una oreja, te tumbo los colmillos. ¿Quieres pelear?

Ya lo conocía. Dice: —No, hombre, no vas a . . . no me vas a pegar. Ya te conozco. Áhi traes mi orejita. ¿Qué mercedes pides?

Saca la orejita y la muerde. No, pos luego, luego se le presentó un negro. —¿Qué . . . qué quieres que me, . . . qué mercedes . . . ?

—La merced que pido, dice, —que, ¿dónde están las reinas? ¿Dónde están las tres niñas que tienes tú encantadas aquí?

Dice: —Mira, dice, —áhi 'tán en el pasadizo. No me vas a matar. Llegas áhi . . . y no más las desencantas. Son niñas que tengo aquí encantadas. Pos luego llegó onde estaban unas . . . jaulas. Y luego luego, era la niña más grande. Jue y la destapó, y . . . tenían una espina en el, en la cabecita, . . . los pájaros. Y el negro le dice: —No más le sacas la espina, y luego luego, . . . luego luego la desencantas. Agarró el pájaro y le sacó la espina. Y ahí estuvo una niña hermosísima (19).

Dice: —Adelante, dice, —niño, dice. —Áhi 'tán mis hermanas también. Y las desencantó a las tres. Y luego la primer, la primer niña, la primera . . . grande, la lazó, y luego bulló la reata, porque ya les había dicho que bullendo la reata después de tiempo, entonces era el desencanto. La lazó y, y . . . áhi va pa arriba la, la niña.

Oooo, pos que va llegando . . . para arriba. Dice: —¡Ay, qué niña tan bonita! Ésta es mi esposa, dijo uno.

—Bueno, 'tá bien.

Y luego la otra, áhi va pa arriba. —¡Ay, dice, —pos ésta es la mía!

—Bueno, 'tá bien. Yo voy a esperar a ver . . . si viene otra.

No, pos eran tres aquéllos y tres niñas (20). —¡Ay!, dice. —Aquí nos habilitamos con nuestras esposas (21). Vamos amarrándole una piedra a . . . a Juan, pa matarlo (22). Entonces amarraron una piedra enorme, y la dejaron ir. Dice: —Cuando . . . a media cueva, reventamos la reata, pa que se muera Juan (23, 24). Si, pos, así lo hicieron.

Pero como Juan traía el negrito, . . . mordió la, la orejita y le dijo que qué le iba a pasar. Dice: —No vas a salirte, dice, —porque a media cueva te van a matar. No, pues, ya no, no salió pa arriba.

Pero como él tenía poder, no más mordió la orejita, dice: —Quiero que me saques de aquí para arriba, dice, —de esta cueva. No, pues ya se fue (25). No, pues, nada de aquéllos. Ya se habían ido con las tres niñas.

Y ya llegaron allá con el rey, platicándole que ellos las habían desencantado. Y que se iban a casar con ellas (26). —O, pos, sí, dice el rey, —cómo no, dice. —Hicieron . . . muy buen trabajo, dice, —y ustedes son sus esposos de mis hijas, dice (27).

—Pos, que está bien.

Entonces ya estaban haciendo los, los preparativos para la boda, . . . cuando Juan del Oso muerde la orejita. Dice: —¿Qué mercedes pides?

—Quiero que me hagas un hombre leproso (28), lleno de granos. Y, y voy a pedir posada por allá, a ver quién me da posada, dice. —Porque . . . yo sé que las niñas van a ir a la plaza, una plaza de toros. Y a ver de qué manera, dice, —yo traigo manera de torear esos toros bravos que dicen que, que van a torear.

Mordió la orejita, y le dice el negrito: —¿Qué mercedes pides?

—Yo quiero que me vuelvas un . . . un hombre leproso, lleno de granos. Oooo, pues, luego luego se volvió. Se fue a la ciudad.

Y luego ya se fue y pidió posada con un, con un señor allí. El señor casi, . . . estaba solo, y . . . no más con su, pos solo, pues. Tenía un departamento . . . solo tamién. Y le dio posada en aquel departamento al leproso.

Y, y luego el señor: —Señor, señor, ¿que usted no va a la plaza de toros?

—No, señor, dice, —yo no voy. Mire cómo soy de graniento, dice, —todo leproso. Yo no puedo ir a la plaza de toros.

Dice: —Pues yo sí, voy a ir. Van a ir las, las reinas desencantadas, dice, —a la plaza de toros, y que va a torear un, un señor muy bueno. Así es de que. . . .

—Está bien. Yo aquí le cuido la casa.

Y áhi va el señor a la plaza de toros. Y luego ya muerde la orejita. Dice: —¿Qué mercedes pides?

—La merced que pido que me pongas aquí un caballo fino, . . . y un vestido bonito, . . . y voy a torear a caballo. Que no más le levante las riendas al caballo y al otro lado voy, a la plaza de toros. Y quiero torear yo . . . a caballo. Pos así lo hizo. Un caballote pero fino. Y no más le levantó las riendas al caballo, . . . áhi va . . a la plaza de toros a torear a caballo.

Oooo, pues, que las niñas, y que ¿quién será ese joven muy bien parecido? ¿Quién será ese joven? Mira no más, toreando a caballo y tan simpático. ¿Quién será y quién será? Nadien pudo conocerlo. Cuando ya, . . . como allá iba gobierno, ¿verdad? . . . ordenaron las niñas que agarraran aquel . . . joven, para . . . decir que quién era. No, que querían agarrar, el gobierno, . . . no, no más le levantó las riendas al caballo y se despareció (29). Fue a dar allá a la habitación. Le dijo a la orejita que lo volviera otra vez leproso, y lo volvió.

Y áhi está en la habitación solito. Llega el hombre. —Ay, señor, dice, —viera no más. . . . Un, un joven, dice, —tan bonito que jue a torear allá a la plaza de toros, pero, ¡qué bien quedó, home! Las niñas quisieron agarrar, . . . echaron la, el gobierno a agarrarlo, dice. —Imposible de agarrarlo. No más le levantó las, las riendas al caballo y se despareció.

—¡Ay, dice, —qué suerte!, dice, —que yo no haiga podido ir. Dice: —Yo estaba aquí enfermo.

Bueno, pos que, pos era la temporada de la . . . corrida de toros. Al siguiente domingo fiesta grandísima. Y otra mordida a la orejita. Que le . . . se presentara otro caballo, . . . y distinto, y distinto vestido. Pos que quisieron agarrarlo otra vez. No, no, no pudieron. Imposible de agarrarlo.

Bueno. Ya, ya se iban a casar . . . los tres endividuos [*sic*] con las reinas. Y iban a hacer los preparativos. Ah, pero ya este Juan del Oso, al tiempo de, de sacarlas para arriba, les quitaba las coronas, . . . porque una reina trae corona, ¿verdad? . . . las coronas . . . de oro. Y Juan del Oso las tenía. Y luego ya se iban a casar, . . . cuando pidieron las niñas que les mandara hacer . . . las coronas igualitas como las que ellas traían. Pos áhi andaban con los plateros, que las coronas, y que las querían igualitas, y, y estaba un trabajo del diseño que tenían las coronas. No podían hacerlas. Hasta . . . habían aplazado el plazo y no podían hacer las coronas. Pos que, . . . no iguales las coronas.

Pero luego en eso, este Juanito . . . Juan del Oso fue y . . . se, le dijo al rey, le dijo al rey que esos endividuos . . . no eran los que la habían, las habían salvado. Que él las había salvado. Y que no era necesario . . . mandar hacer coronas para el casamento. Que él las tenía.

Dice: —A ver. Prueba. Tonces saca las coronas (30), y luego las niñas ven . . . a Juan del Oso.

Dice: —Mira, papá, este joven fue el que nos salvó. Y las coronas áhi las tiene. Dice: —Mira, igualitas.

—De modo es que estos otros, que estaban mintiendo.

—Pos, sí, mentían, dice. —Mira no más.

Así es de que si no se ha presentado este joven, yo hubiera casado a mis hijas con otros, con estos otros que no, . . . estaban mintiendo. Así es de que, como rey, yo, pos, les voy a dar un castigo de una cárcel, cárcel perpetua, a estos tres individuos (31, 32). Y usted, Juan del Oso, usted se casa con la que guste. ¿Cuál le gusta?

Dice: —Pues a mí me gusta la más chiquita (33).

Y con ésa se casó. Y todavía están viviendo . . . casados.

Y aquí se termina el cuento de Juan del Oso. Si les parece, . . . pos bien, lo pueden oir. Áhi queda.

The story is structured as follows: 301 Iah IIa (three) bc IIIab IVa (using Negro's magic ear) b Vab VIbf (crowns).

Aarne-Thompson 301B. The Three Stolen Princesses.
Boggs 301B.
Hansen 301A, 301B. The Three Stolen Princesses.
(1) F611.1.1. Strong man son of bear who has stolen his mother.
(2) B635.1. The Bear's Son.
(3) R45.3.1. Bear keeps human wife captive in cave with stone at entrance.
(4) L114.3. Unruly hero.
(5) F610. Remarkably strong man.
(6) F612.2. Strong hero kills (overcomes) playmates: sent from home.
(7) F835.2.1. Iron club so heavy that five men can hardly lift it.
(8) F601. Extraordinary companions.
(9) F611.3.1. Strong hero practices uprooting trees.
(10) F626. Strong man pulls down mountains.
(11) F661. Skillful marksman.
(12) G475.1. Ogre attacks intruders in house in woods.

(13) F102.1. Hero shoots monster (or animal) and follows it into lower
world.
(14) F92. Pit entrance to lower world.
(15) F96. Rope to lower world.
(16) N773.1. Adventure from following ogre to cave.
(17) R11.1. Princess (maiden) abducted by monster (ogre).
(18) G303.3.3. The devil in animal form. [Porcupine.]
(19) D765.1.2. Disenchantment by removal of enchanting pin (thorn).
(20) R111.2.1. Princess(es) rescued from lower world.
(21) K1935. Impostors steal rescued princess.
(22) F601.3. Extraordinary companions betray hero.
(23) K1931.2. Impostors abandon hero in lower world.
(24) K963. Rope cut and victim dropped.
(25) D2135.2. Magic air journey from biting an ear.
(26) K1932. Impostors claim reward (prize) earned by hero.
(27) T68.1. Princess offered as prize to rescuer.
(28) K1818.1. Disguise as leper.
(29) R222. Unknown knight.
(30) H83. Rescue tokens.
(31) Q262. Impostor punished.
(32) Q433.4. Imprisonment for imposture.
(33) L161. Lowly hero marries princess.

Grimm, nos. 91, 166.

Mexico: Aiken, *TFSP*, 12(1935), 77, no. 24; Barakat, *JAF*, 78
(1965), 330–336; Colgrave, *JAF*, 64(1951), 411 (reprint of
Dobie version, with analysis); Dobie, *Tongues of the Monte*, pp.
201–230; Foster, *UCAAE*, 42(1945), no. 38; Hudson, *SFQ*,
15(1951), 152–158 (study of Dobie version); Mason, *JAF*,
27(1914), 176, no. 14; Radin, *Tlalocán*, I, 22–30, no. 2; Radin-
Espinosa, *El folk-lore de Oaxaca*, nos. 109, 110; Robe, *Mexican
Tales*, nos . 33, 34; Suddeth, pp. 81–96 (adapted from Dobie version); Wheeler, nos. 94, 95, 96.

United States: Boas, *JAF*, 35(1922), 92, no. 6; Espinosa, *JAF*,
24(1911), nos. 3, 12; Espinosa, *SFNM*, nos. 17, 18, 19, 20, 21;
Goodwyn, *JAF*, 66(1953), 143–154; Paredes, no. 29; Rael, nos.
170, 171, 172, 173, 174, 175, 236; Warren, p. 173 (a different
development of story called "Juan Osito").

Chile: Guzmán Maturana, *AUC*, vol. 92, pp. 67–73, no. 14; Laval,
Carahue, II, 12; Laval, *Cuentos populares*, I, nos. 1, 8; Pino Saavedra, nos. 2, 3 (301A), 4, 243 (301B).

Ecuador: Carvalho Neto, nos. 2, 3.

Puerto Rico: Arellano, nos. 73, 88; Mason-Espinosa, *JAF*, 27
(1914), 249, no. 1a; 254, no. 1c; 256, no. 1e; 261, no. 1h; 284,
no. 21o; 39(1926), 356, no. 50.

Spain: Ampudia, *Del folklore asturiano*, pp. 19, 21; Busk, p. 148;
Caballero, *Cuentos y poesías populares andaluces*, pp. 51–58;
idem, *Spanish Fairy Tales*, p. 88; Cortes Vázquez, nos. 42, 43; Curiel Merchán, pp. 155–160, 324–327; Durán, *Romancero general*
1263–1264; Espinosa, *Cuentos*, nos. 133, 134, 135; Sebillot, p. 33
(French translation from Busk).

Canary Islands: Cuscoy, no. 2.

66a. El oso que se robó a una señora
(Recorded by Ana María Romero on December 3, 1966, in Oxnard, California)

The informant relates an incident, told to her by her husband, that took place in Chihuahua. A bear carried off a woman to live with him in the forest where he held her captive for some time. From this union the woman bore twin sons, half bear and half human. A group of men who were passing through the forest one day heard her cries for help and were able to remove the rock from the entrance to the cave and free her. They then killed the bear and also the sons, in order to spare people such a frightening sight.

Mi esposo me platicó que en Chihuahua, un oso . . . se robó a una señora y la llevó al monte, muy lejos de la ciudad. Y la puso en una cueva. Y la puerta la tapó con una . . . piedra muy pesada. Allí la . . . tuvo prisionera, por mucho tiempo (1). Ella no podía escapar del animal. Y así fue . . . como esa mujer . . . tuvo dos, tuvo dos hijos gemelos . . . del animal, con la mitad de gente y la mitad de . . animal, de oso (2).

Y fue libertada al fin por unos hombres que andaban . . . vagando por áhi, por el monte. Y al oir que hablaban, se . . . pudieron dar cuenta de que era una gente la que estaba hablando y pedía auxilio. Y fueron entre los dos, movieron la piedra, y salvaron a la mujer. Pero a los hijos los mataron, para que la demás gente no se fuera a asustar. Y . . . el oso, también lo mataron. Y . . . el animal, para sostener a la mujer mientras la tuvo con él, venía cerca de las orillas de la suidad, y robaba de las casas . . . ropa y comida. Y es todo.

(1) R45.3.1. Bear keeps human wife captive in cave with stone at entrance.
(2) B635.1. The Bear's Son.
This narrative and the one following (66b) are examples of what could represent a migration of tale material to legendry. See Narrative 66.

66b. Juan el Oso
(Recorded by Lola Cruz on December 8, 1966, in Los Angeles, California)

When the informant was a little girl her father used to take her to the circus quite often. She remembers attending the Escalante Circus near Albuquerque, New Mexico, at about the age of three, and being frightened by a boy, half bear and half human, who appeared in one of the acts. Her father explained to her that she need not be afraid, for he was simply a person whose misfortune it was that his mother had married a bear. He said his name was Juan del Oso and that he appeared with the circus because everyone really ought to work and that was his job.

Cuando yo estaba muy pequeña, como de la edad de . . . unos . . . tres años, entonces mi papá todo el tiempo me, me llevaba al circo. Y luego entraba a los circos, y entraba a dondequiera, porque él era el único que me llevaba a pasear.

Y luego una vez, al circo que fuimos, como el Circo Escalante, traiban allí un oso, y traiban una señora, y un . . . muchacho, que era mitad de oso y mitad de gente. Y me dijo mi papá: —Mira, hija, no te vayas a asustar. Ese muchacho, . . . su mamá es . . . una señora, y su papá es un oso. Pero lo traen en el circo porque debe de trabajar. Y él se llama Juan, y le dicen Juan el Oso (1).

Pos luego después empezaron a trabajar y todo. Y luego . . . yo no me le quería arrimar, y el oso se me arrimaba . . . para agarrarme los cabellos. Yo no sé qué, qué quedría con mis cabellos. El caso es que él se me arrimaba, y yo siempre lo sacaba, le tenía miedo. Y luego que dijo mi papá: —No te asustes, hija. Es una persona igual como tú, mas que la suerte que tuvo, que la señora se casó con el oso. Y por eso es de que él es Juan Oso, y es mitad y mitad.

[Interviewer: ¿Dónde pasó esto?]

O, esto fue pues, cuando yo tenía tres años. Sería como en mil novecientos trece.

[Interviewer: ¿Dónde?]

Fue en un lado de . . . un ladito acá, pa acá para, . . . ¿cómo se llama el lugar? [Informant's husband: —Albuquerque.] Sí, por allá, sí. Como en Albuquerque. Porque mi papá andaba en un carro andulante [*sic*], pintando estaciones, que le nombran depots. Y vivíamos en un carro, y dondequiera andábamos nosotros. Y el circo se llamaba el Circo Escalante.

(1) B635.1. The Bear's Son.
This narrative and the previous one (66a) are examples of what could represent a migration of tale material to legendry. See Narrative 66.

67. El buen pescador

(Recorded by Lola Cruz on December 8, 1966, in Los Angeles, California)

A fish promises great wealth to a fisherman in exchange for the first thing that greets him upon his arrival home. The fisherman agrees, thinking that as usual he will be greeted first by his dog. He is met by his son, however, and is obligated to turn the boy over to the fish. The latter raises the boy in his glass house at the bottom of the sea. When it comes time for the boy to marry, the fish helps him to choose a wife; but the boy disregards the fish's warning not to light any light in order to look at her on their wedding night, he strikes a match which falls on the girl's face, and in the morning he awakens in a desert. He finds his way to the house of three giants, where he takes refuge, but is warned not to enter either of two baths nor to touch a certain horse. While he is sweeping the stable one day, the horse talks to him and tells him he is his father, the fish. He instructs the boy to enter the two baths, which he does, and he emerges with a head of silver and a body of gold. The two of them flee from the house of the giants. They kill and skin a Negro whom they meet on the road, and the boy puts on his skin. They travel to a castle where the boy obtains work as a gardener, and the horse uses his magic power to produce flowers and fruit trees overnight. The king's three daughters are delighted with the Negro's talent, become very curious about him, and spy on him when he bathes. When they see his body of silver and gold, they fall deeply in love with him and want to marry him, much to the bewilderment and opposition of the king. Meanwhile, a war has developed between the forces of the king and the three giants, and the king's daughters have been promised in marriage to the slayers of the giants. The boy, in his disguise as a Negro and with the help of the horse, gets to the giants before any of the king's men and kills them one by one on three separate occasions, remaining unidentified throughout the three battles. He later reveals his identity, produces the three crowns that had been given the victors of the battles, and chooses the youngest daughter for his wife, saying that he will marry her for the second time, since they were already married before at the bottom of the sea.

Éste era una señora y un señor. El señor era un pescador. Y de eso se mantenía él, pescando pescado y vendiéndolo. Cuando una vez fue al mar a pescar y salió un pescado. —¿Qué andas haciendo, buen hombre (1)?

—¿Qué he de estar haciendo, buen pescado? Pescando para . . . mantenerme yo y mi esposa y mi familia.

—Mira, buen, buen señor, si me traes el primero que salga a encontrarte a tu casa, te hago rico.

—Está bien, . . . pescadito. Yo te voy a traer . . . lo que tú me pides.

Y como todo el tiempo salía el perrito a encontrarlo, . . . y ese día estaba el perrito dormido en la cocina porque tenía frío. Y el niño ya cumplió un año, y salió gateando. Y incontró a su papá. Y él dice: —¡Ay, hijo de mi vida! ¿Por qué salistes tú? Te tengo que llevar con el pescado, porque si no te llevo el pescado no me va a dar la vida.

Bueno, pos agarró al niño y se lo llevó. Y le dijo al pescado: —Pescado, aquí está el niño que me pediste, porque me salió a incontrar (2).

Dice: —Dámelo. Bueno, pos que se lo dio. Y luego se metió pa dentro. Se lo comió el pescado al niño. Y le dio seis sacos de puras monedas de oro, que el padre con eso se mantuviera toda la vida (3).

Y luego que se llevó el pescado al niño, fue y lo echó al mero fondo del mar onde tenía una casa. Y esa casa era de puro cristal, que podían vivir gentes que no fueran del mar (4, 5).

Y entonces el viejito, como tenía tanto dinero, y la tristeza de su hijo, se emborrachaban la señora y el señor todos los días. Todos los días tomaban. Y iba desmenudiendo el dinero. Se iba acabando el dinero. Y entonces luego el . . . el pescador, pos ya no pescó.

Y el, y el niño, llegaron . . . a tener quince años el niño al fondo del mar. Cuando luego le dijo el pescado: —Oyes, Juan, tienes que salir al . . . otro lado del agua. Y tienes que ir a ver a tus padres. Y luego que veas a tus padres entonces te vienes.

—Pues que sí, papá. Pos luego el pescado se comió aquel joven de quince años, . . . dieciséis años, porque él tenía un año cuando le llevó. Pos luego lo echó a . . . a la orilla del agua.

Y luego ya fue . . . a buscar a los viejitos. Y no los encontraba. Cuando luego una señora dijo: —¿Qué buscas, niño?

—Vengo a buscar a una señora y un señor, que el señor es pescador.

—Oooo, dice, —él ya tiene mucho tiempo que no es pescador. Él ya es un señor muy vago, muy borracho, y viven en la miseria. No tienen ni qué comer. Y no más anda pidiendo trago para poder tomar.

Entonces el niño fue y le llevó el dinero que quería la señora para que tomaran. Y luego le dijo la señora, la mamá: —Pos, no te queremos a ti porque no te tenemos amor. 'Tá bueno que te regreses para atrás.

Entonces él se fue muy triste, pero nada más de eso, pues no los quería a ellos. Quería más a su . . . papá pescado. Y luego cuando llegó, entonces el pescado estaba listo y se lo comió y lo volvió a bajar para dentro de . . . del fondo del mar.

Dice:—Oyes, hijo, ya tienes dieciséis años y es tiempo de que te cases. Te voy a buscar una . . . una novia. Pero te voy a poner muchas muchachas bonitas, bonitas, de las más bonitas que hay, para ver cuál te gusta (6). Pero no vayas a enamorarte no más a la primera vista. Yo te hago la seña.

—Pues que sí, papá.

Entonces le trajo muchas muchachas, como unas veinticinco muchachas, muy bonitas, bonitas. Y dice: —Ay, con ésta me quiero casar. ¡Qué bonita! Y el pescado le dicía que no. —Ay, pos ésta está más bonita. Y el pescado le dicía que no. Y luego, hasta que llegaron a la última. Y el pescado le dijo que sí. Entonces le dijo: —Niña, ¿quieres casarte conmigo?

Dijo: —Sí, a eso vine, a casarme contigo.

Dice: —¡Qué linda y qué bonita eres tú! Luego que pensaba que aquellas otras eran las más bonitas. Y ella no más se rio.

Y luego le hicieron una fiesta muy elegante. Y le dijo el pescado: —Mira, hijo, . . . cuando ya sea de noche y que se acuesten, no vayas a prender luz porque cae en la desgracia. No vayas a prender nada (7).

—No, papá.

Bueno, pos él, que estaba pensando en su esposa, que estaba muy linda, dice: —Yo quiero verla otro poquito. Yo no me espero para mañana. Pos agarró un . . . un fósforo y lo prendió. Y luego le vio la cara y la vio muy linda, linda. Y luego, se le cayó el fósforo . . . prendido, en la cara de la niña.

Pos luego se, . . . ya cuando amaneció, él amaneció en un desierto

(8, 9). Y el sombrero tirado cerca de un nopal. Y luego buscaba él al . . . al pescado, y no lo hallaba. Y luego vio una lucecita muy lejos, lejos, lejos. Y luego fue anda y anda, y luego llegó. Y tocó la puerta. Era una casa de unos gigantes.

Luego salió el gigante menor. Dice: —¿Quién toca?

Dice: —Yo soy.

—¿Qué buscas aquí? ¿No ves que te pueden comer mis hermanos (10)?

—No le hace. Yo vengo a buscar trabajo. Tengo mucha hambre. Lo que tú me quieras dar de comer, yo te hago trabajo. Te hago lo que tú pidas. Dame un trabajito. No seas malo.

—Ándale, pues. Vente a comer. Y él le dio de comer. Cuando en esto . . . le dijo: —¡Ay, escóndete, que áhi viene mi hermano! Tengo que hablar primero con él (11). Viene mi hermano que sigue de mí.

Y luego llegó. Y dice: —Hermano, hermano, huele a carne humana. Si no me la das te como a ti (12).

—¡Ay, mi hermanito! ¿Cómo quieres comerme a mí? ¿Cómo quieres comer carne humana? Si aquí no hay ni una mosca, fíjate, menos carne humana.

—Pos ya te lo digo.

Dice: —Mira, te tengo una res . . . para que te la comas.

Dice: —Y si no me lleno con la res, entonces te como a ti.

—No, hermanito, cómete esa res y verás.

Pos luego se comió el gigante . . . toda una vaca. Grandota la vaca (13). Dice: —Ay, qué satisfecho, qué lleno quedé. Que ni ganas me dan de carne humana.

Dice: —Hay algo que yo quería saber. Oyes, hermanito, aquí está un niño escondido, que tiene hambre. Pero si tú gustas lo tenemos aquí.

—Ay, pero, ¿si viene mi hermano el mayor, y si se lo come?

—O, no, hermanito. Pues lo escondemos y le preguntamos.

Bueno, pos que sí. Luego le dijo: —¿Cómo te llamas, niño?

—Pos, mi papá me puso Juan.

—Ándale pues, Juan. Dice: —Ay, áhi viene mi hermano el mayor. Viene a comer.

Y luego dijo el hermano más chico . . . de los gigantes, dice: —Mira, le voy a dar una res y un becerrito para que no le quede hambre, porque él tiene el estómago más grande. Bueno, pos que sí. Le hizo la res, y luego el becerrito. Y luego le dio de comer. Y luego le quedó otro poquito de hambre, y le dio el becerro. Y luego se lo comió todo (13).

Y luego dice: —Hermanos, a mí cuando yo entré me olía a carne humana. Pero no tuve tiempo de decirles que me los comía a ustedes porque tenía mucha hambre y me dio el olor de la carne que estaban haciendo (12). Y a ver. ¿Ónde está ése? Para . . . pa ver si me lo como mañana.

—No, hermanito, no te lo vayas a comer. Te prometo que todos los días te hacemos una o dos vacas pa que te las comas (14). Pero no te vayas a comer el muchachito porque, pos fíjate, . . . tiene más poca carne que un borrego. Pos, ¿qué . . . de qué te sirve?

—Bueno. Está bueno. Pues a ver, que venga. Bueno. Pues si luego ya vino. Y luego le dijo: —Mira, Juan, tú tienes que hacer todos los quehaceres, porque nosotros vamos a ir a trabajar (15). Pero sí te digo que no te vayas a meter a estos dos baños. Porque está prohibido (16). Y ni vayas a agarrar ese caballo, porque si agarras ese caballo te mata (17). Y si te metes a esos dos baños te mueres.

—Está bien, señor. Haré lo que usted me mande.

—Bueno. Pos quédate. Nosotros nos vamos.

Cuando el niño estaba barriendo la caballeriza, oyó que le decían: —Juan, Juan . . .

—Pos, ¿quién me habla? No, no veo a nadie que me hable.

—Juan, yo, tu papá. Juan, acuérdate lo que te dije, que no prendieras un, un fósforo, y lo prendistes y cayó en la cara de la niña.

—Sí, me acuerdo.

—Pues, yo soy el pescado, tu papá.

—¿Cómo puede ser que te haigas vuelto . . . caballo?

—O, porque esto es un encanto. Estaba en un encanto allí donde estábamos. Y por eso yo me hice . . . caballo (18). Bueno, pos mira. Báñate en este baño . . . del cuerpo pa abajo.

—¡Ay, no! ¡Que cómo me voy a bañar allí, si dicen que no me meta!

—Te digo que, que te bañes.

Pos se bañó. Y salió lleno de, de plata (19). Bueno, y luego le dijo: —Ahora, meta la cabeza al otro baño.

—Pero si, que ¡cómo la voy a meter, si dicen que si meto la cabeza me voy a morir!

—Te digo que la metas.

—Bueno. Pos, se le hizo de oro (20). El niño se hizo oro y plata.

Bueno, pos luego dijo: —Vamos. Porque si vienen y nos encuentran, mira que nos matan a ti y a mí (21).

Pos se fueron anda y anda, cuando luego vieron a un negrito. Dice: —Vamos a matar este negrito y le quitamos la zalea. Bueno, pos que luego lo mataron y le quitaron la zalea con mucho cuidado. Con mucho cuidad quitaron el pellejo del negrito. Y luego se lo puso él (22). Y luego ya se hizo él un negrito.

Dice: —Y ahora, ¿qué vamos a hacer?

Dice: —Mire. Vamos ir a aquel castillo que está allí, que tiene el rey tres hijas. Y una de ellas te tienes tú que casar con ella.

—¿Y cómo?

—Pos, bien. Hora verás. Yo voy a, . . . tú gritas que quién quiere tener flores, hora las siembras y mañana salen. Árboles frutales que ahora los siembras y mañana salen.

Bueno. Pos que el rey estaba muy triste porque no había ni una flor. Y el rey estaba muy triste porque no había ni una fruta. Pues luego empezó el negrito: —¿Quién quiere un jardinero, que plante los árboles ahora y mañana den . . . frutas (23, 24)?

Bueno. Pos que luego después dijo el rey: —Mira, si no me traes las flores para mañana te mato. Y si no traes la fruta que dices para mañana te mato. Pena de la vido o cinco balazos.

—Está bueno.

Pos ahora en ese tiempo le dieron el trabajo, . . . y luego el niño le dijo al caballo: —Papá, ¿cómo lo voy a hacer? ¿Cómo voy a plantar las flores ahora y mañana va a haber flores?

Pues, luego después el caballo dijo: —Tú, quédate bien. Que mañana te voy a arreglar todo (25, 26). Pos luego, cuando el niño se durmió, el caballo se levantó. Y empezó a . . . a escarbar, a poner las semillas. Y luego después, ya que plantó todo, entonces ya otro día los

. . . olores . . . de las flores, que las reinas no podían levantarse porque
. . . por tanto olor tan bonito.

Y luego dijieron: —Papá, papá, . . . papá, papá, ¿por qué has hecho tú tantas . . . cosas? Mira no más tantas flores. ¿De ónde compras-
tes las flores? Es un olor que parece que es un perfume.

Y dice: —No, este perfume lo, lo trajo el negro. El negrito fue el
que está haciendo eso.

Bueno, pos que luego después, . . . le dijo el rey: —Mira, cuando te
quieras bañar allá está el baño, para que te vayas a bañar.

—Sí, mi Sacarrial Majestad.

Bueno. Pues luego todas estaban admiradas con aquel . . . negrito
que plantaba las flores y luego luego salían, y luego plantaba los árboles y luego luego comían fruta otro día. Y luego dijo la hija más
chica: —Yo voy a ver cuando se baña ese negrito, a ver cómo se baña.
Pos luego después, ella fue y se sentó en un lugar donde no la mirara. Y
vio cuando el niño se quitó la zalea. Y lo vio que era de oro y de plata
(27). Dice: —¡Ay, qué niño tan chulo! Nunca había visto un hombre tan bonito como éste. Pos se quedó áhi. Se enamoró de él, que no
hallaba qué hacer ella del amor, de enamorada (28). Y luego . . . no
durmió. Y no más decía a las hermanas: —¡Ay, qué buen mozo el
negrito!

Y luego le dijo la hermana de en medio: —Jmm, ¿cómo te vas a
casar con un negro? Tan feos que son y tan prietos, y luego tan trom-
pudos. ¿Te vas a casar con un negro?

—O, sí, yo lo quiero mucho. ¿Cómo no me voy a casar con él (29)?

Bueno, pues que luego después la hermana quedó muy . . . pensa-
tiva. Porque estaba . . . la hermana chica que se quería casar con el
negrito. Dice: —Yo voy a ver qué virtud tiene ese negro. Ha de tener
alguna virtud porque, a ver, mi . . . mi papá le dio las flores . . . las
semillas, y otro día salieron frutas . . . y flores. Yo voy a ver qué, qué,
qué tiene este negro. Pos fue y lo vio en . . . y lo vio cuando . . . se metió al agua. Dijo: —Ay, pos éste no es el negrito. Éste es un . . . un
muchacho muy simpático, muy hermoso, mira no más. Bueno, pues
ella salió también enamorada (28). —Lástima que mi hermana lo vio
primero, que yo . . . quisiera casarme con él.

Y luego le dijo: —Papá, cuando tú me digas que me case, yo me caso con el negrito (29).

—Pos, ¿ya tú? Tu hermana la chica quiere casarse con el negrito. Tú también te quieres casar con el negrito. Pos, ¿cómo está eso . . . que quieren casarse . . . las dos con el negrito?

Bueno, pos que luego la hermana grande oyó. Dice: —Pos, ¿qué tiene ese negro . . . que ustedes lo quieren tan locas?

—Bueno. Si no más lo vieras te enamorabas también de él.

Bueno. Pos ésta les ganó. Cuando él se metió a bañar más temprano, esta muchacha no durmió . . . por ir a, a ver cómo se bañaba. Y luego que lo vio, pos también ella se enamoró (28). Pos las tres 'taban enamoradas del negrito. Dice: —No, yo le voy a decir a mi papá que me caso con él, porque yo soy la mayor y a mí me hace más caso mi papá. Y le dijo: —Papá, yo me quiero casar con el negrito (29).

—¿Cómo? Pos, si ya las tres quieren casarse con él. Ponle que sea de virtud él, pa que se tenga tres esposas.

Cuando luego en eso le llegó una carta, que iba a haber una guerra. Entonces luego dijo: —¡Válgame Dios! Estaba muy triste el rey porque iba a haber una guerra. Y iban a hallar cómo matar esos gigantes, porque eran los gigantes más malos del mundo. Entonces luego le dijo el . . . el papá: —Oye, ponme . . . un telegrama, para que vaya para el Rey Fulano que si quieren venir, porque tenemos que ir a . . . a acabar la guerra. Y, y esos tres que van a pelear con los . . . con los gigantes se van a casar con mis hijas. Los que los maten a . . . a los gigantes van a ser mis yernos (30). Pos que sí.

Cuando luego en eso oyó el caballo que, que iban a pelear. Y dijo: —Juan, Juan, ándale. Quítate la zalea. Que ya van a, a venir a pelear. Y luego Juan se quitó la zalea. Y luego se subió a caballo. Y luego después ya se fueron y pelearon y, y luego pues, mataron al gigante más chico (26). Y cuando los soldados del rey llegaron hasta la puerta, a, a irse en sus caballos, pues ya los habían . . . ya habían matado al gigante.

Y los otros dos gigantes ya se habían ido de escapada, porque dijeron: —O, aquí nos va a ganar este . . . este muchacho y este caballo. Nos van a ganar. Así es de que . . . vámonos.

Pues luego después, ya, ya se fueron. Y luego la, la muchacha estaba recontenta, contenta, porque habían matado al gigante chico. Y luego que vino el papá, le dijo: —Papá, ¿quién fue de los soldados quien mató al gigante? ¿Entre cuántos soldados?

—No, cállate, hija. Que fue un muchacho, que no lo alcanzaron a ver porque se despareció. No sabemos que si es viejito o es muchacho, . . . de qué color será no sabemos. Y era un . . . caballero muy, galope, que cuando pasó no distinguimos quién era (31).

Bueno. Entonces luego el caballo le dijo: —Juan, ponte ya la zalea, pa que no te, no te vayan a . . . desconocer.

Pues luego después ya . . . vinieron los reyes. Hicieron una junta, y dijieron: —Pos ya perdimos una de nuestras . . . de nuestros hijos. Ya no se van a casar con una de tus hijas. Ahora te tengo que dar esta corona.

—Pos, está bueno. Pos hora tengo que entregarla al que haya sido el que mató al gigante pequeño. Pues, sí. Pues luego ya pusieron la, la corona en un lugar que . . . el muchacho la agarrara. Entonces el muchacho estaba listo. Entonces fue el caballo y agarró la corona de . . . del rey, que ya había perdido una de las hijas.

Y luego le dijo la, la muchacha chica: —Papá, vamos, que yo me voy a casar con . . . con el que mató al gigante.

—Sí, hija, te vas . . . tú te vas a casar con él.

—¡Ay, qué bueno, yo lo quiero mucho!

—¿Y cómo sabes? ¿Cómo lo conoces?

—No, no más lo sueño. Yo, yo, digo. Bueno, pues estaba ella muy recontenta y las otras, pos, se iban a casar con los otros.

Y luego dijo la hermana grande: —Papá, pues, ¿que no quieres que yo me case con el muchacho?

—No, hija, porque es la corona más chica.

—Está bueno, papá.

Pos luego después ya el negrito empezó él a hacer sus jardines, a ponerles más flores misteriosas, que no las podía haber en el mundo aquellas flores y aquellos perfumes que entraban en la casa. Cuando luego recibió el . . . el rey otro telegrama, que iba a empezar la guerra. Y iba a venir más . . . más enojados los gigantes, que ya habían matado uno de los hermanos.

Cuando le dice el caballo: —Juan, ándale, apúrate, que quítate la zalea, porque vamos ir a, a ganar esa otra corona.

—Pos, que está bien, papá. Yo estoy listo. Entonces la . . . luego el . . . negrito se quitó la zalea, y ya se hizo . . . un joven muy hermoso. Y luego ya se fueron.

Entonces estaba el gigante de en medio. Entonces 'taban pélea y pélea y pélea muy duro para, para morir el gigante . . . de en medio. Cuando luego en eso se descuidó el gigante y le . . . y siempre entre el caballo y él, pero el que más lo mató fue el caballo, . . . lo mató al . . . al gigante (26). Bueno, pues que, cuando ya el rey iba llegando allá a la guerra, ya el . . . este Juanito y . . . y el caballlito ya se, ya se venían. Y no alcanzaron a verlos tampoco, porque estaban medio escondidos.

Bueno, pos que luego ya después llegaron a la casa y dijo: —Ya . . . ya ganó el mismo. El mismo que mató al . . . al gigante mató al otro.

Luego dijo la muchacha: —Pos hora, ¿cómo lo vamos a hacer? Dijo: —Yo . . . yo me voy a casar con él, dijo la muchacha de en medio.

Bueno, pues luego después le dijo . . . el papá: —No, hija, ¿cómo te vas a casar tú también con el muchacho ese, siendo de que tu hermana la chica fue la que, la que . . . se va a casar con el muchacho?

—Pos, no le hace, papá. Pos, que ella se case con otro rey y yo me caso con ese muchacho. Bueno, pos que luego después, estaban allí las dos, las otras llorando porque la que iba a ganar era la . . . la muchacha más chica. Pues luego después, esta muchacha . . . se, estaba muy contenta porque ya iba a ser la esposa del . . . muchacho de oro y plata.

Cuando luego el caballo le dice: —Ándale, Juan. Vas a la otra . . . a la otra guerra, del gigante mayor. Pero te voy a decir una condición. El gigante ese no hay quién lo mate, ni porque vengan muchas tropas. No hay quién lo mate al gigante, porque tiene muchas mañas. Él tiene la vida . . . en el pie derecho (32). Áhi le vas a dar un . . . con él con, con una daga en el pie o con la espada, y con eso lo matas.

Bueno, pos que así estuvo. Pos ya se fueron y luego entonces el caballo empezó a patear al . . . al gigante. Y luego le dice: —Ya, ya te estoy yo viendo. Yo pienso que tú eres el caballo que yo tenía encerrado. Ya, ya, ya estoy viendo, que yo pienso que este muchacho es el muchacho de oro y de plata. Pues, luego después el muchacho estaba peleando, cuando luego en eso le encaja la, la daga en el pie derecho. Y se murió el gigante.

Y luego dijo: —Hemos triunfiado. Hemos ganado la guerra. Hora sí, nadien puede quitarnos nada. Y entonces luego ya le dieron las otras dos coronas que le faltaban. Entonces dijo: —¿Pa qué quiero yo tantas coronas? No más con una tengo. Entonces las echó en un costal . . . las tres coronas.

Y luego después, estaban allá que, que no hallaban qué hacer luego las muchachas, que iban a hacer una invitación a los reyes, porque se iban a casar con los . . . príncipes. Y luego los . . . los príncipes 'taban muy contentos. Y luego dijo la muchacha chica: —Yo me caso con el negrito.

—O no, yo no te voy a dejar casarte con el negrito.

Entonces fue el negrito, muy triste, con el caballo. Dice: —Papá, no quiere que yo me case con ella.

—Cuando yo dé una patada vuelves a decir que sí te casas. Y si dice que no, doy otra patada. Son dos. Y si dice que, que no, doy la última. Son tres patadas (33). Entonces cuando te diga que no te quitas la zalea y le enseñas las . . . le enseñas las, las tres coronas. Pos que sí.

Dijo: —Mi Sacarrial Majestad, quiero que me dé la mano de . . . de su hija la más chica.

—O, no es posible que un negro se case con mi hija.

—Pues, que no, dice. —¿Qué pueda tener un negro que no pueda tener un blanco?

Dice: —Pos ya te digo, tú no puedes casarte con mi hija.

Entonces dijieron las otras: —Ya está bien. Me caso con él. Pos, ¿cómo estuvo eso? Un hombre no puede casarse con tres mujeres. No más con una.

Pues, él volvió a decir otra vuelta: —Mi Sacarrial Majestad, quiero que me dé la mano de su hija.

—Ya te dije que no. Tú no te puedes casar con mi hija.

Entonces el caballo dio otra patada.

—Mi Sacarrial Majestad, quiero casarme con su hija.

—No, ¿cómo te vas a casar con, con mi hija? No puede ser.

Bueno, pues que luego dio otra patada.

—Mi Sacarrial Majestad, quiero casarme con su hija.

—Primero muerto que dejarte casar con, con una de mis hijas.

Pues luego después le . . . se quitó la zalea delante del rey, y luego vio que era de oro y de plata. Y dijo: —¿No puede ser que tú hayas sido el que matastes . . . los tres gigantes?

Dice: —Sí. Y aquí traigo las tres coronas (34). Pero dos le doy, y con una me quedo.

Entonces luego la hija más chica le dijo: —Yo me caso con él.

Y dice: —Sí, con ella me quiero casar. Y luego le dijo: —Pues yo, yo me quiero casar por segunda vez, porque yo fui casado con ella en el fondo del mar. Es mi verdadera esposa (35, 36).

Pos luego ya se casaron (37). Y luego ya las otras también se casaron. Cada una se casó con . . . otros dos príncipes. Y ya así, pues, que se quedaron la familia todas casadas. Y vuelo por un caminito, vuelo por otro, cuénteme usted otra.

The story is basically that of Mt. 314, but with several divergent episodes. It is structured as follows: 314 Ib (unwittingly promised to fish for wealth, as in S241. Child unwittingly promised: "first thing you meet.") c (to fish's home at bottom of sea) + Hansen 302 II*e. Enchanted princess sleeps with youth. He strikes match to see her. Must seek her. + 314 IIa IIIa (the fish, in enchanted form) IVa Va (covers self with Negro's skin) c VIac (giant killer) Vd (she is discovered to be the princess he already married at the bottom of the sea).

Aarne-Thompson 314. The Youth Transformed to a Horse.
Hansen 314. The Youth Transformed into a Horse.
(1) B211.5. Speaking fish.
(2) S241. Child unwittingly promised: "first thing you meet."
(3) S221. Child sold (promised) for money.
(4) F725.3.3. Undersea house.
(5) F771.1.6.2. Glass house.
(6) H1301.1. Quest for the most beautiful bride.
(7) C312. Tabu: man looking at woman.
(8) C932. Loss of wife for breaking tabu.
(9) C952. Immediate return to other world because of broken tabu.
(10) G11.2. Cannibal giant.
(11) F531.5.1. Giant friendly to man.
(12) G11.2.1. Giant devours any person who fails to do his bidding.
(13) F531.3.4. Giant eats (drinks) a prodigious amount.
(14) G582. Giants appeased by feeding them.
(15) G462. Person as servant in ogre's house.
(16) C611. Forbidden chamber.
(17) B316. Abused and pampered horses.

(18) B318. Helpful animals transformed from other animals. [Fish to horse.]
(19) F521.3.4. Person with body of silver.
(20) C912. Hair turns to gold as punishment in forbidden chamber.
(21) G552. Rescue from ogre by helpful animals.
(22) K521.1. Escape by dressing in animal (bird, human) skin.
(23) K1816.0.3. Menial disguise of princess's lover.
(24) K1816.1. Gardener disguise.
(25) B184.1. Magic horse.
(26) B401. Helpful horse.
(27) H151.13. Disguised hero's golden hair discovered by spying princess.
(28) T91.6.4. Princess falls in love with lowly boy.
(29) T55.1. Princess declares her love for lowly hero.
(30) T68.3. Princess as prize to man who saves his country.
(31) R222. Unknown knight.
(32) Z311. Achilles heel.
(33) Z71.1. Formulistic number: three.
(34) H83. Rescue tokens.
(35) K1911.3. Reinstatement of true bride.
(36) T298. Reconciliation of separated couple.
(37) L161. Lowly hero marries princess.

> Grimm, no. 136.
> Mexico: Wheeler, nos. 84, 86, 87.
> United States: Boas, *JAF*, 35(1922), 67–73; Espinosa, *SFNM*, nos. 13, 14, 15, 24; Rael, nos. 164, 176, 230, 231, 232, 235, 236.
> Chile: Montenegro, p. 203; Pino Saavedra, nos. 21, 22, 23, 59, 245, 260.
> Dominican Republic: Andrade, no. 111, no. 102 (has Hansen 302 II*e).
> Ecuador: Carvalho Neto, no. 447.
> Puerto Rico: Mason-Espinosa, *JAF*, 38(1925), 584, no. 9b; 585, no. 9c; 586, no. 9d; 587, no. 9e; 588, no. 9f; 39(1926), 272, no. 21h.

68. El señor y la gallinita

(Recorded by Candelario Gallardo on December 2, 1966, in Oxnard, California)

A very poor man who always made many sacrifices in order to provide for his large family decides that just once he would like to know the feeling of a full stomach. He asks his wife to prepare a special lunch for him that he may take off into the countryside and have all to himself. To his dismay he runs into an old man who asks him to share his food. He refuses to do so and feels even more justified when he learns that the old man is God, for God is not just in his dealings with men. He provides some with wealth, while He condemns others to poverty. He is about to settle down once more to his meal, when he is approached by an old woman with whom he likewise refuses to share. When he learns that she is Death, however, he very willingly shares with her, exclaiming that Death does indeed treat all men equally.

Bueno, les voy a contar . . . este cuentecito también, aunque sea corto . . . el cuentecito. Pero pa que se diviertan, yo creo que . . . está bien.

Éste era un hombre . . . muy pobre. Tenía mucha familia, tenía diez de familia. Y él no alcanzaba. Pues se quedaba sin comer por darles a sus hijos. Su mujer muy pobre, completamente. Y él . . . nunca llenaba su estómago, por darle a su familia.

Hasta que un día dice: —Oyes, esposa mía, yo quisiera, dice, —que mi estómago se llenara, dice, —y irme a comer un almuercito que me prepares, dice, —al monte por allá, yo solito. Quiero yo satisfacer mi estómago.

Dice después: —Ándale, viejo. No más di qué, qué es lo que quieres.

Dice: —Yo quisiera una gallinita rellenada, con unas tortillas calientitas.

—Ándale, viejo, dice. —Ahorita te las preparo.

Pos luego luego le . . . le preparó la gallina, muy bien preparada, y unas tortillas calientitas, y áhi va al monte a comérselas todas.

Pues que iba a empezar a comerse . . . su comidita cuando viene un viejito. —Hombre, dice, —áhi viene este viejito, hombre. Y a poco quiere que le dé.

No, pues se llegó, . . . llegó el viejito. Dice: —¿Vas a comer?

—Sí, me voy a comer esta comidita. Sabe que . . . tengo deseo de comerme esta comidita, dice. —Tengo mucha familia y yo quiero que mi estómago, pos, se llene.

Dice: —¿No me vas a dar?

—No, dice, —no le doy. Yo quiero comérmela solito.

—No, dice. —Está bueno que me des.

—Pos, no, ya le digo, no le doy.

—¿No sabes quién soy yo?

—No, dice, —yo no sé quién sea usted.

—Que si yo soy Dios Nuestro Señor.

Dice: —Pos, menos le doy.

—¿Por qué?

—Porque tú, dice, —no tienes, . . . no, no eres parejo con la humanidad. A unos los tienes más ricos, los tienes muy ricos, y otros muy pobres. De modo es que yo soy muy pobre, me tienes muy pobre, que a veces no alcanzo . . . ni pa comer. Y por eso no le doy. Porque usted no es parejito con la, con la gente.

—'Tá bien, dice. —Entonces me iré.

No, que ya iba lejos Dios Nuestro Señor como le había dicho. Iba a comerse otra vez la comidita, cuando vido venir una viejita, hombre. —Home, áhi viene aquella viejita. A poco también quiere que le dé, hombre. Pues que ya llega, y la saluda.

—¿Vas a comer?

—Sí, me voy a comer esta comidita.

Dice: —¿No me vas a dar?

—No, dice, —no le doy nada. Que . . . pos yo quiero que mi estómago se llene. Dice: —Aquel viejito que . . . va allá dice que es Dios Nuestro Señor. Pero le dije que no era parejo con . . . toda la gente. A unos los tiene muy ricos y a otros muy pobres. Y por eso no le di . . . a Dios Nuestro Señor.

Dice: —¿Que no sabes quién soy yo?

—No, dice, —yo no sé quién sea usted.

Dice: —Yo soy la Muerte (1).

—¡Ay, caramba!, dice. —A usted sí le doy, porque usted sí la echa parejitos. Niños y viejitos, y todos. A usted sí le doy.

Y . . . a ella, sí le dio la . . . el almuerzo (2). Así es de que . . . pos, aquí termina estas platiquitas, este cuentecito cortito.

[Interviewer: —¿Quién le contó la historia?]

Es un cuento también del viejito [reference to Miguel Guevara, rancho La Cofradía, Guanajuato]. Es cuento también del viejito que nos . . . que nos platicaba él. Sabía cuentos chiquitos, sabía cuentos grandes. Y también fue . . . era historia del viejito. Así es de que si les gusta el . . . ese, ese cuentecito de la gallinita y el señor que se la comió, . . . y aquí termina.

Aarne-Thompson 332B* Death and Luck.
Hansen 332**A. Godfather Death.

The story is structured as indicated above, but the character Luck is replaced by God, and in Narrative 69 by two characters, God and the Virgin.

(1) Z111. Death personified. [An old woman.]
(2) J486. Death preferred above God and Justice. [Here, because Death is just.]

    Mexico: Robe, version in manuscript, from Jalapa, Veracruz; Toor, *Treasury*, pp. 492–494; Wheeler, nos. 152, 155; film *Macario*.
    United States: Rael, nos. 83, 85, 86.
    Chile: Guzmán Maturana, *AUC*, vol. 92, pp. 6-13.
    Puerto Rico: Mason-Espinosa, *JAF*, 37(1924), 325, no. 36.
    Spain: Curiel Merchán, pp. 15–16, 292–295; Sánchez Pérez, no. 53.

69. El señor pobre y la Muerte

(Recorded by Inocente Rocha on November 17, 1966, in Oxnard, California)

A very poor man with a large family asks his wife to prepare a lunch for him that he might take off into the countryside and eat all by himself. He encounters God and refuses to share the food with Him because it is God who ought to give to him and his family. He also refuses to share with the Virgin, for she will not intercede in his behalf to request food for his children. But when he encounters Death, he agrees to share his food, because Death is fair and treats all men equally.

Había un señor muy pobre, con muchos . . . hijos y familia, . . . unos diez. Y en seguida le dijo a la señora, dijo: —Esposa mía, hazme una cosa de alimento para alimentarme en el camino.

Cuando en el camino . . . iba, entonces encontró un señor. Le pidió alimento del . . . de lo que llevaba en su saca. Él le dijo: —No puedo darte parte, porque me vine para llenar mi estómago.

—Está muy bien, dijo. —Si te digo quién soy yo, me vas a dar.

Dijo: —¿Quién puedas ser? Pero dime quién eres.

Dijo: —Yo soy Dios.

Dijo: —Yo no podría darte a ti. Tú eres el que me había de dar para alimento de mis hijos. Se marchó adelante y el señor se despareció.

Al momento se fue siguiendo . . . y a la falda de un cerro la encontró . . . una joven. Y le dijo: —Buen hombre, dice, —¿adónde vas?

Dijo: —Voy a . . . ir a una parte sombría, a . . . tomar mi alimento.
Me vine por no darles a mis hijos.

—'Tá muy bien, dijo. —Si te digo yo quién soy, ¿me poderás dar?

Dijo: —Pueda ser que sí, pueda ser que no.

Dijo: —Bueno, entonces al momento yo te voy a decir. Pues, soy la
Virgen.

—¡Ay! dijo, —¡Madre Mía! Dijo: —Yo te podría dar, pero únicamente si podrías rogar a tu hijo que me diera a mí . . . para darles
alimento a mis hijos.

Dijo: —Márchate, pues, buen señor, para adelante.

En seguida, al tiempo más delante, encontró una . . . dicha señora,
ya muy viejita. Al mismo tiempo cuando ya . . . encontró, que ya la
encontró, le dijo: —Dame lo que llevas de tu alimento.

Dijo: —No puedo darte. Mira, ¿quién puedas ser tú? Encontré a
. . . a Dios y no le di. Encontré a la Virgen y no le di.

—¿Por qué?

Porque ellos tendrían que darme a mí, y no yo a ellos.

—Ay, buen hombre, si te digo yo quién . . . quién soy yo.

—¿Quién puedas tú ser?

—Pues yo soy la Muerte (1).

Dijo: —Sí, a ti sí te doy. Porque eres pareja con todos. Te llevas
viejos, . . . niños, roñosos, todos, enfermos, de todas clases de enfermedades. Pues, hora sí. Aquí semos compañeros (2). Y aquí se terminó.

Esa historia me la platicó un padre. Llamábase Agustín . . . García,
de Albuquerque, New Mexico.

See Narrative 68.

70. El señor y la gallina

(Recorded by Rafael Gudiño on May 3, 1966,
in Los Angeles, California)

A poor man who works very hard to provide for his family decides
that for once he would like to have a good meal all to himself. He has
his wife prepare a chicken, which he takes into the countryside to eat.
On the way he encounters God and the devil and refuses to share his

food with them, but he is moved to pity by Death who is very thin and seems terribly needy, and together they eat the chicken. In return for his kindness Death gives him a candle to replace his own life light, which he informs him is about to go out; but the man, in his haste, drops the candle and does not arrive in time to replace his own light.

Una vez había un señor muy pobre, que tenía como unos . . . nueve o diez hijos. Y él diario vivía trabajando y . . . lo que ganaba no le ajustaba, no le completaba para . . . darle de comer a su familia.

Y un día . . . dijo: —Bueno, dijo, —yo tengo ganas de comer un día solo una gallina, ¿verdad? Y le dijo a su esposa: —Mira, esa gallina me la matas y me la . . . arreglas, bien arreglada, y me voy a ir al campo a comérmela yo solo, donde no me pida nadie absolutamente.

Bien. Le mataron la gallina y se jue al campo. Iba por el camino cuando se encontró . . . un viejecito, ¿verdad?, . . . que le dijo: —Oye, dice, —¿no me das de comer? Y se cree que era Dios Nuestro Señor.

Que le dijo: —No, dijo, —pues, apenas tengo esta gallina para comérmela yo solo, un día en toda mi vida que quiero comerme esta gallina yo solo. ¿Y te voy a dar parte a ti? No.

Más adelante . . . se encontró un señor vestido de charro y bastante . . . bien, bien puesto, gordo y todo, que se cree que era el Diablo. Entonces le dijo: —Oye, ¿no me das un pedazo de tu gallina que traes allí?

Dijo: —Si el viejecito que me encontré atrás que estaba tan viejecito no le quise dar, ¿te voy a dar a ti que, que estás tan . . . fuerte y tan joven? Yo no te voy a dar a ti absolutamente nada.

Y siguió caminando. Más adelante encontró a la Muerte (1). Y le dijo, pues, que . . . que si le daba. Dijo: —Bueno, pues, plano, dice, —tú estás tan flaca que, que realmente . . . a ti sí te voy a dar un pedazo. Y se pusieron y se comieron la gallina entre la Muerte y, y ese señor (2).

Bien. Cuando ya terminaron de comer, que le dijo la Muerte, dijo: —Bueno, dijo, —mira, en agradecimiento de que me diste de comer, te voy a hacer un favor. Dice: —Mira, vete por esta vereda derechito, derechito hasta donde llegues donde haiga muchas velas. Se cree que esas velas era . . . una parte donde están las . . . vidas de nosotros comparadas con velas (3). Y que es, la que se va acabando, se apaga, pues, ése se va muriendo, ¿verdad? Dijo: —Bien llegando allí ves, como a las tres filas de velas, dice, —hay una muy chiquita que ya casi se está apagando. Dijo: —Ésa es la tuya. Vas, toma, te voy a regalar esta vela, . . . llegas, la prendes, y la pones allí.

Pero en el camino ese se le tiró la vela por ir de prisa. Y cuando llegó, pues, ya la velita estaba entre queriéndose apagar. Y entonces agarró otra vela de las que había por allí enteras y que, . . . pero apagadas, y fue y la prendió y . . . no le alcanzó a poner, porque allí cayó muerto porque . . . se congestionó con la gallina, que nunca comía.

The story is structured as AT 332B*, with the character Luck replaced by God and the devil, followed by E765.1.3. Life-lights in lower world.

See Narrative 68 for 332B*.

(1) Z111. Death personified. [An emaciated woman.]
(2) J486. Death preferred above God and Justice. [Here, above God and the devil.]
(3) E765.1.3. Life-lights in lower world.
        Mexico: Film *Macario*.
        Dominican Republic: Andrade, no. 229.

71. La Reina Isabel

(Recorded by Lola Cruz on December 8, 1966, in Los Angeles, California)

A king falls in love with a doll he sees in a window, which he takes to be a real girl, and is told that her name is Isabel. He requests her hand in marriage, promising to pay the owner, whom he takes to be a servant, a great deal of money and threatening her with death if she refuses. The frightened woman sets out to find a girl she can offer to the king and manages to trick a mermaid into trading her own beautiful daughter for the doll. The doll disintegrates in the water, and, when the mermaid discovers she has been tricked, she pronounces a curse on her own daughter who is to marry the king. She will have to suffer three punishments and marry three times. They have been married only three months when Isabel, the name given the mermaid's daughter, becomes mute. The king is very displeased, sends her away, and finds himself a new wife. The servants were very fond of Isabel,

however, and their continual praise of her arouses the jealousy of the
new wife, who insists on going to visit her to see what is so extraordinary about her. While she is there she observes Isabel cut off her
head, curl and comb her hair, and then replace her head more beautiful than ever, whereupon she rushes home to imitate her and succeeds
only in killing herself. When the king learns his wife is dead he goes
and brings Isabel back to live with him. It is only a short time, however, before she once again becomes mute, and he sends her away and
remarries a second time. The process repeats itself: the new wife goes
to visit Isabel, observes her fry fish in her hands, attempts to imitate
her, and is burned to death. Isabel is brought back to live with the
king, she very soon becomes mute and is sent away, and the king remarries a third time. This wife attempts to imitate Isabel in her bath
and drowns. With this third incident, the mermaid's curse is fulfilled,
Isabel explains to her husband what has happened and is reunited
with him to the delight of all, including the servants. Soon thereafter,
she presents the king with a daughter equally as beautiful as the doll
that disintegrated in the water.

Esta era una viejita muy pobrecita. No tenía . . . hijos. No tenía
hijas. Y tenía una muñeca de esas que están en el aparador [indicates
dolls on her dresser]. De ese tamaño, . . . como unas princesas. Y les
hacía vestidos a las gentes, para que . . . las cosiera, a las princesas.
Pos esta vez esta señora, que ya no tenía renta porque ya no podía
ella coser porque le faltaba la vista.

Y luego había un rey . . . que pasaba por allí. Y ese rey daba vuelta.
Y entonces fue a la carrera ella, y entonces compró material del más
fino. Y hizo un vestido muy elegante para la princesa. Un vestido
azul. Y luego paró la muñeca, . . . la paró en, en la ventana. Entonces
ella se puso detrás de la muñeca, y fingía la voz la viejita como una
muchacha muy jovencita.

Y entonces pasó el rey y la vio. Y la vio tan bonita. Y luego ella
hacía así como que se limpiaba la, la cara. Y luego la hizo a la muñeca,
porque él llegó allí, que tirara un pañuelo. Y el pañuelo cayó . . . abajo de, de, de la calle. Allí cayó en la calle, porque eran barandales
como de esos barandales que ponían de casa de dos pisos.

Bueno. Pues luego . . . el, el rey agarró el pañuelo y en el pañuelo
dicía "Isabel." Entonces se agachó la viejita a recoger el pañuelo y le
dice: —Oyes, señora, ¿ésa es tu patrona?

—¿Cómo se llama?

—Pos, se llama Isabel.

—¿Que ella no sale nunca a la calle?

—No, señor. Cuando no está acá parada, está sentada. Porque su mamá es muy delicada y su papá es muy delicado. Y no la dejan salir. Pero si usted quiere mandarle una cartita o un recadito yo se lo llevo.

—Está bien. Dale esta cartita. Y luego le dicía: "Mi querida Isabel: Desde el momento que recogí tu pañuelo yo te quiero y te adoro. Quiero que seas mi esposa."

Y luego ya después le mandó . . . la, la viejita le mandó otra notita hecha por la viejita . . . al rey. Le dicía: "Pues mi querido señor: Cuando usted guste, no les pida la mano a mis padres. Pero sí a la sirvienta. Con ella pídame y ella me dejará casar. Ella me lleva de la casa escondida de mis padres, porque si mis padres ven que me voy a casar . . . me matan."

Pues el rey tenía miedo de que la mataran, y nunca tocaba a la puerta sino que se quedaba allá abajo. Bueno, pues, entonces le dijo el rey a la viejita: —Si no me das a Isabel te mato.

Y luego se puso a llorar la viejita. Ya no hallaba qué hacer. Dice: —¿Qué haré, qué haré, qué haré?

Dice: —Mira, si tú me traes a Isabel . . . te doy dinero . . . para que comas todo el tiempo de tu vida.

Bueno, pues esta señora andaba casa por casa, a ver dónde se hallaba una muchacha . . . bonita como Isabel (1). Iba pasando por el río, por el mar. Estaba, . . . luego pasó cantando la viejita, porque tenía . . . una voz muy bonita, bonita la viejita.

Y luego salió una sirena. Y le dice: —Oyes. . . . Mitad de pescado y mitad de, de gente. Dice: —Oye, señora, ¿quién canta?

—Mi hija.

—¿Es tu hija? ¡Qué linda está! Está más bonita que mis hijas. Tengo . . . siete hijas. Pero de las siete tres son mitad de pescado y mitad gente. Y las otras . . . son . . . de, de, . . . tienen pies. ¿Quieres una?

Dice: —Quiero escogerla. Y luego se escogió. Luego vio una igualitamente a la muñeca. Cabellos de oro, los ojos azules, . . . y muy blanca. Y dijo: —Esta niña me la das. ¿Cómo se llama?

—¿Cómo quisieras ponerle?

—Pues, yo le quisiera poner Isabel.

Bueno. Pos se llevó a . . . se llevó a, a la . . . hija de la sirena. Cuando la viejita metió la muñeca allí se la dio a la sirena.

Y luego, como a los cinco minutos como la, la sirena se llevó al fondo del mar a la muchacha, pues se deshizo porque era de cartón. Se deshizo la, la muñeca. Entonces salió la sirena muy enojada. Dice: —Anda, vieja fea, me robastes a mi hija. Pero sé pa qué la quieres.

Dice: —¿Pa qué la quiero?

Dice: —Mira, mi hija la quieres para venderla. Te van a dar una cantidad de dinero. Dice: —Pero mira que . . . el rey . . . se tiene que casar tres veces. La primera vez tiene que cortarse la cabeza; la segunda vez tiene que frir pescado . . . en su mano; la tercera vez . . .tiene que . . . meterse al agua, a un . . . a un, una fuente, una cosa muy honda, honda, honda. Ésos son los tres castigos que le voy a dar a mi hija (2, 3, 4).

Bueno, pues no hizo caso la viejita. Y se fueron anda y anda las dos. Y llegaron al palacio. Y el rey ya muy contento, y la mamá del rey, y el papá.

Y dijo: —Ya te hallastes novia.

—Sí.

Y luego ya vieron, y era una muchacha tan bonita, que no había en todo allí . . . aquélla. Y ella era muy buena, buena con todas sus . . . criadas. La criada que le dicía que necesitaba alguna cosa, ella le daba.

Luego una de las criadas le, le dijo: —Ay, niña, mi mamá está muy mala y no tengo dinero.

—No te apures. Yo te doy el dinero que quieras. Y le dio el dinero que . . . que quería. Le dio más . . . que el dinero que ella quería.

Y luego el jardinero le dijo: —Ay niña, mi, mi esposa necesita dinero pa comprarles zapatos . . . a mis niños.

—No te apures. Yo te voy a dar el dinero. Y le dio más dinero, que le alcanzó hasta pa comprar una casita.

Y le decía: —Ay, que la Reina Isabel, que nunca nos falte, porque es muy, muy buena con todos nosotros.

Bueno. Que ella, cuando tenían tres meses de casados, la Reina Isabel se hizo muda. No hablaba. Luego llegó el rey y le dice: —Isabel, tenemos una, una salida, para ir a una visita. Ándale, alísate. Ponte el vestido más bonito que tengas, porque vamos ir.

No le contestó Isabel. Fueron a la fiesta, y Isabel muda, muda, muda, muda, que no contestaba.

Y luego dijo la mamá del rey: —No, no, no, yo no quiero que vivas con esa . . . mujer muda. Quiero que la lleves . . . onde la trajistes.

Pues el rey . . . llevó a la . . . muchacha a onde estaba la viejita. Pero ya la viejita se había muerto. Ya la viejita no estaba porque murió de puro miedo. Entonces luego ya . . . la muchacha, pues, empezó a arreglarse y hacer más bonito . . . la casita onde vivía.

Y entonces luego le dijo la mamá del rey. —Mira, tienes que . . . ir a, a buscar una novia.

Y se casó el rey . . . con otra. Y luego después, ya que se casó le dijeron los otros criados: —Mira, que necesito dinero.

—Trabaja. El que trabaja lo tiene, y el que no trabaja no lo tiene. Dice: —¡Qué mala!

Y luego le dijo el jardinero: —Niña, que mi . . . niña está enfermita. Que necesito una medecina para la enferma y no tengo con qué comprarla.

—Trabaja más. Si no trabajas no tienes dinero.

Entonces empezaron: —Mmm, ¿quién como la Reina Isabel? No hay otra. Y todos: —¿Quién como la Reina Isabel? No hay otra.

Y entonces dice: —¡Cómo me aburren con la Reina Isabel! Pos, ¿qué tiene la Reina Isabel que no pueda tener yo?

—Mmm, la Reina Isabel tiene lo que usted no tiene.

—Pos, ¿qué tiene ella?

—Cariño . . . y voluntad.

—¿Quién sabe dónde vive la Reina Isabel?

—Yo sé.

—¿Me llevas?

—Sí.

—Pues, no más se va el rey y nos vamos.

—Pues, luego se fueron . . . a donde vivía la Reina Isabel. Luego tocaron la puerta, y luego salió la criada. Dice: —¿Quién buscan?

—A la Reina Isabel.

Y luego la Reina Isabel . . . le dijo: —Dile que se espere.

—No, que si quiere entrar.

—Pues, que pase si quiere ver lo que estoy haciendo. Que entre. Bueno, pues que ya le presentó la, la señora, y luego le dice: —Espére-me. No quiero que platique conmigo hasta que no . . . haga yo lo que voy a hacer.

—¿Y qué va a hacer?

—Usted lo va a ver. Entonces le dijo a la criada: —Tráeme una charola; tráeme un cuchillo; tráeme un peine, un cepillo, y un enriza-dor.

Ya le trajo toda la . . . la, le trajo todo a la Reina Isabel la criada. Y luego se . . . agarró el cuchillo y se cortó la cabeza. Y la puso en la charola. Y luego agarró el cepillo y la empezaba a cepillar. Y luego agarró el peine y la empezó a peinar. Y luego agarró el enrizador y la empezó a . . . a, a enrizar. Y luego después la, ya la enrizó. Y luego se puso la cabeza pa tras (5). Dice: —Ahora, que hable de lo que quiera.

—No, no, no, no, no. ¡Qué le voy a hablar! Ya me voy, ya me voy, ya me voy. Y se fue y no le dijo nada.

Bueno, pues que luego llegó a su casa. Y le dijo a la . . . a las criadas: —Tráiganme una charola; tráiganme un peine, un cepillo, un cuchi-llo, y un enrizador.

Pues, luego le llevaron . . . llevaron todo. Un cuchillo agarran. Dijo una de las criadas, dijo: —Vamos a llevarle el cuchillo más, más filoso que haiga. Y le dieron más filo y se lo llevaron. No, pues no más se cortó la cabeza y murió la señora (6, 7).

Pues, luego llegó el esposo y dijo: —¿Qué pasó?

—Pos, que la señora está muerta.

—¿Qué le pasó?

—Pos, ella se degolló.

—¿Y cómo se degolló?

—Pos, ¿quién sabe? Nos dijo que le diéramos un cuchillo y se lo dimos. Dijo ella que el más filoso, y nosotros . . . se lo dimos. Y se cortó la cabeza.

—Válgame Dios. Isabel, estoy harto ya con Isabel. Vamos. Yo ahorita voy a ir con Isabel.

Luego tocó la puerta. Dijo: —¿Quién habla? ¿Quién manda abrir mis puertas? Que no se las abriré mas que sean órdenes del rey.

Dijo: —Pos yo soy el rey, y tienes que abrirme las puertas, Isabel. Pos ya le abrió la puerta, y luego ya le dijo: —Que vino . . . que vino mi esposa, y que . . . te vio que estabas . . . ¿haciendo qué?

—Nada. Yo me estaba peinando.

—¿Cómo?

—No sé. Yo me estaba peinando.

—¡Ay, Isabel, mira no más. ¡Dios sabe, tienes una voz más linda que nada! Vámonos.

—Bueno, pos si tú quieres te acompañaré. Y luego Isabel no dijo que no, sino quedó otra vez casada con . . . con él.

Pues luego los . . . los criados: —¡Ay, qué bueno que viene la Reina Isabel, y que ya no se vuelva a ir! Y que: —¡Mi Reina Isabel! Y luego . . . muchas flores, y luego le hicieron una fiesta muy grande.

Estuvo muy bien por cerca de seis meses Isabel. Cuando luego en eso le dice el rey: —Isabel, que vamos a ir a una fiesta. Arréglate. Y no le contestó. Isabel muda, muda, muda. —Isabel, te estoy hablando.

Y luego fue con la mamá. —Mamá, ya no me habla, ya no me contesta Isabel. No me quiere contestar. No sé qué es lo que tiene.

—Anda, hijo, no te apures, dijo. —Isabeles hay muchas en el mundo. Anda, búscate otra. Lleva ésta a su casa y búscate otra. Bueno, pos que la llevó a su casa.

Y luego se empezó a buscar otra. Y luego le dijo la, . . . le dijeron los criados: —Señora, pos que . . . queremos semillas pa plantar unas flores.

—¡Ay, Dios! Si no necesito jardín. Ustedes . . . no son tan buenos trabajadores. Y los voy a quitar de aquí a todos y voy a traer trabajadores nuevos.

Y empezaron a llorar todos los criados. Luego dicían: —Ay, si estuviera aquí la Reina Isabel no pasara esto. ¡Quién como la Reina Isabel! No hay otra.

—Pos, ¿qué tiene la Reina Isabel? ¿Qué tienen ustedes con la Reina Isabel? ¿Quién es ella?

—Mmm, pos si la viera.

—Pos, sí la veo. Llévenme.

Entonces la llevó una de las criadas . . . a la casa de la Reina Isabel.

Luego ya van tocando a la puerta. Y luego salió una de las criadas. Dice: —¿Quién habla?

—Pues, yo soy. Quiero ver a la Reina Isabel.

Y la criada le contestó: —Ahorita está ocupada. Está preparando la comida para comer.

Entonces luego le contestó la Reina Isabel: —¿Quién toca? ¿Quién es?

—Pos, es una señora que es la esposa del rey, y que . . . viene a buscarla. Quiere hablar unas palabras con usted.

—Pos, dile que pase y que me espere.

Entonces ya se sentó la señora en una silla, y luego le dijo a la criada: —Tráeme una . . . una botella de aceite, un pescado, un plato, un tenedor, un cuchillo. Y entonces ya la criada ya le arrimó los cubiertos. Y luego después, ya que estaba todo listo, agarró el aceite y se lo puso en la mano. Y luego le prendió juego [i.e., fuego] con una . . . con un cerillo. Y luego que ya le prendió con el cerillo puso el aceite en las manos y frió el pescado en sus manos. Y luego que ya estaba el pescado frito, . . . entonces lo vació en el plato. Y luego la señora le dijo: —Ahora, sí, señora, mientras que yo como puede usted hablar conmigo.

—O no, no, no, no. Ya me voy, ya me voy. Y se fue.

Y luego dijo la señora: —¡Qué fácil es lo que hace ella! Ahora que llegue a mi casa voy a hacer lo que hizo la Reina Isabel. Les voy a dar pruebas que yo soy . . . más que la Reina Isabel.

Cuando luego llegó a la casa, sin más le dijo a la criada: —Tráeme una caja de . . . cerillos y una, un cuchillo y un tenedor y un plato. Pos, todo le arrimó la criada. Y luego vació el aceite en las manos y le prendió juego. Y luego puso el pescado. Y se quemó toda. Toda se quemó la señora (7). Entonces la . . . la llama del aceite le corrió por todo el vestido y el cuerpo. Y cuando vino el señor . . . estaba hecha ceniza.

Y luego le dijo: —¿Ónde está mi esposa?

—Mmm, su esposa, señor, está . . . ahorita . . . muerta. Y no hay ni nada, ni huesos ni nada, porque es pura ceniza.

Y . . . y dijo: —Pos, ¿adónde fue?

—Ah, pues, fue a ver a la Reina Isabel.

—¡Oo, ya Isabel hizo otra cosa! Dice: —Ahorita voy a reclamarle.

Entonces fue a la carrera, en un caballo a galope. Y luego llegó a la casa de la Reina Isabel. Fue y . . . tocó la puerta muy recio, recio. Luego dijo . . . Isabel: —¿Quién mandáis? ¿Quién tocáis mis puertas? ¿Que me las quieres quebráis [*sic*]?

—Yo soy. Soy tu esposo. Soy el rey. Vengo a reclamarte. ¿Qué fue, qué fue lo que hizo mi otra esposa, . . . mi tercera esposa?

—O, pues, lo que hizo, que hizo lo que yo hice. Y yo no tengo la culpa y no me preguntes nada más.

Dice: —¡Ay, qué bonito hablas! Hablas más bonito que la otra vez que me estabas hablando. Vámonos para mi casa.

—O no, dice. —¿Cómo quieres que me vaya pa que me vuelvas a traer?

—No le hace. Vámonos. Yo te quiero mucho. Y se la llevó.

Y luego los criados le hablaron: —¡Ay, Reina Isabel, qué buena es usted! ¡Y qué bueno que ya volvió de vuelta!

Dice: —¿Qué les pasa? Usted tiene dos niños. ¿Se han enfermado?

—Sí, Reina Isabel.

—Pos, tengan este dinero. Llévelos con el doctor. Y tú, ¿qué le falta a tu familia?

—Pos, que necesitan ropa.

—Pos, toma este dinero. Cómprales ropa. Y tú, dice, ¿qué te pasa?

—Pos, que las plantas se secaron y quiero . . . que me des, que me des unos . . . centavos pa comprar semillas para . . . para las plantas. Pues, ya les dio todo el dinero que pidieron, y muy contentos. Y muy contenta estaba toda la gente.

Cuando . . . ya el rey se fue a la guerra. Entonces ella se quedó muy contenta. Y luego después el rey le dijo: —Voy a venir dentro de unos . . . cinco o seis meses. Pos 'taba muy contenta la reina con sus criados, que . . . la servían muy . . . muy tranquilos.

Cuando vino el rey de vuelta, entonces le dice: —Oyes, Isabel, te voy a llevar . . . allá donde ando. Y ya Isabel ya no le habló. Ya estaba muda. —Isabel, te estoy hablando. Que te voy a llevar allá a la guerra donde yo ando. Y no le habló Isabel. Muda, muda, muda. Dice: —No hay más. Que otra vez te tengo que llevar para tu casa. Ya hiciste, . . .

que sea la última vez. Ya no más. Ya te voy a llevar. Y ya si te llevo yo no te traigo. Bueno, pues, la agarró y se la llevó . . . para su casa.

Y luego después, estaba ella muy triste, cuando le dice la, la criada que tenía ella: —No se ponga triste, niña. Que algún día . . . Dios se va a acordar de usted, y la va a hacer muy feliz.

—Eso dices. Pos yo quiero mucho a mi esposo.

—Pues, sí. Pero alguna maldición ha de tener usted. Alguna maldición ha de tener usted. Por eso . . . no, no puede usted . . . estar feliz con su esposo.

—Pos, ¿quién sabe? Sea por Dios, y a ver qué nos pasa.

Bueno, pues luego le dijo la, la mamá del rey: —Hijo, ya tienes mucho que estás solo. ¿Por qué no te casas? Pa que puedas . . . tener bien el palacio.

—¿Y con quién me caso, mamá? Si todas se mueren, todas se matan.

—Pos, mira que ahorita vienen unas muchachas de muy lejos, unos reyes lejanos, y quiero que te cases con una de las hijas.

—Bueno, pues vamos. Y se casó . . . con una reina. Y a esa reina le faltaba un pie. 'Taba la reina coja, ésa con la que se casó. Y tenía una pata de palo. Pues luego el rey . . . siempre se casó, pero él no sabía. Y luego ya cuando se iba a . . . cuando ellos se iban a acostar vio que tenía la pata de palo, que se la quitó. Y dice: —Válgame, para . . . mal de mis males. Una muda y la otra coja. ¿Hora qué voy a hacer? Pues no hay, que tengo que aguantarla.

Y ella muy corajuda. A todos les, hasta les pegaba . . . a los criados. Y luego dicían, dicían los criados: —¡Ay, qué mujer tan mala, como nos trata! No hay como la Reina Isabel tan . . . buena.

Y ella se enojaba porque era muy celosa. —¿Qué tiene la Reina Isabel que no pueda tener yo?

—Jum, . . . que tiene sus dos pies, y hace todo lo que . . . lo que hace. Y todas las que van a verla, cuando vienen se matan.

—Jum, pues yo no había de matarme por una mujer. ¿Quién me lleva?

Y luego dijo una de ellas: —Yo la llevo con mucho gusto.

Y luego dijeron todas: —¡Qué bueno! Que si se va, viene y se muere, y ya nos quedamos contentos y viene la Reina Isabel pa tras.

Bueno. Pues la llevó. Entonces estaban tocando la puerta. Y salió la criada. —¿Quién es?

—Yo soy.

—¿Qué deseaba?

—Vengo a ver la Reina Isabel.

—Ay, señora, en este momento se va a bañar la Reina Isabel.

—No le hace. Quiero hablar con ella. Ella en el baño y yo platicándole.

Bueno, pos, . . . que pasó. Y luego que pasó estaba un, uno de esos como, como una, un baño, que era muy grande, como de unos veinte pies . . . de hondo. Grande, grande. O doscientos, no sé. Muy hondo. Y luego le dijo a la criada: —¿Quién tocaba?

—Esta señora quiere hablar, . . . la, la esposa del rey.

—Que pase y que me espere. Ahorita salgo.

—Pos, ahora, dice, —quiere hablar con usted.

—Espéreme un momento. Ahorita salgo. Dijo: —Tráeme una caja de polvo, una botella de perfume, un jabón muy oloroso, y tráeme una esponja, y tráeme un vestido . . . más bonito que tengo en el ropero. Pos le llevó el vestido bonito y . . . la esponja, el jabón, el polvo, y el perfume. Y se metió adentro del agua. Y cuando salió dentro del agua, . . . salió sin mojarse, . . . aperfumada y polveada . . . y peinada.

Dice: —No pueda ser de que esta mujer haga eso. Pues, ella, que es tan astuta, y yo que no soy nada astuta, . . . yo hago más. Y fue y les dijo a los criados: —A ver. Tráiganme unos doscientos hombres. Que sean albañiles.

—Aquí están, señora.

—Si aquélla tenía de doscientos . . . pies de, de hondo el tanque, yo quiero que me hagan un tanque . . . más hondo, más hondo, que con una . . . con un, . . . que se vea como el tamaño de un espejo adentro. Pos hicieron todo aquello que ella . . . lo que ella dijo. Entonces luego le dijo a la criada: —Tráeme . . . un perfume, la caja del polvo, mi vestido, y una esponja. Y se metió. Echó un clavado y se mató. Se pegó en la cabeza y se mató adentro. Después vinieron y la sacaron muerta (7).

Luego vino el rey. —¿Qué tienen? ¿Qué quieren sacar? ¿Quién hizo este tanque?

—Su esposa quiso que hiciéramos este tanque. Y ella nos dijo . . . que lo hiciéramos y que le diéramos un vestido, una botella de . . . de perfume, una caja de polvo, y se metió, y ya no salió.

—Pos, ¿adónde fue?

—Pos, con la Reina Isabel.

—Ahorita voy a ver a la Reina Isabel. Ya le dije que no.

Y tocó la puerta, que ya . . . hasta le quebró la puerta. Luego le dice la Reina Isabel: —¿Quién mandáis abrir mi puerta? ¿Quién quebró la puerta? Que yo no he dado permiso.

Dice: —Yo, tu marido. Vengo a reclamarte. —¿Qué es lo que has hecho con mis tres esposas?

—Yo no tengo la culpa de que ellas hagan . . . lo que yo hago.

Dice: —Isabel, ¿por qué haces todo esto?

Dice: —Porque yo no era la mujer con la que te ibas a casar. Tú te ibas a casar con una muñeca. Y una viejita le cambió la muñeca a mi mamá. Yo soy hija de una sirena. Y esa muñeca se deshizo en el agua. Y luego mi mamá, de coraje, nos . . . nos . . . echó la maldición. Que tres veces tenías tú que casarte. La primera vez me tenía yo que . . . cortar el pescuezo . . . y peinarme. La segunda vez me tenía que frir unos pescados en la mano con aceite. Y la tercera vez me tenía que . . . que bañar. Eso es todo.

Dijo: —Bueno. ¿Entonces ya no va a pasar nada?

—No. Vámonos.

—Pos, vámonos pues. Se fueron (8).

Dijo: —Pero para más de esto, tengo que llevar a mis criados, . . . y todo mis . . . gentes que tengo aquí. Y luego se llevó a los criados, y luego les dijo a los criados: —Señores y señoras, quiero que tengan una poquita de atención, . . . y a todos mis criados y mis criadas, los vean como hermanos. Pues que tantos ellos como ustedes han sido mis servidores del alma. Y como ustedes me quieren, yo también los quiero a ustedes.

Y luego la cigüeña vino y le trajo una niña. Pero ésa sí, era una niña tan bonita, como la muñeca . . . que se desbarató en el agua. Y vuelo por un camino, vuelo por otro, cuéntenme ustedes otro.

This tale does not seem to fit well into any given tale type. The two principal elements, the false or substituted bride [K1911] and the fatal imitation

[J2401], are found in Mt. 402 and Mt. 403, but both structure and detail are considerably different. On the basis of Mt. 403, which seems to be the closest, the following structure can be outlined: 403 IIIa (doll, taken to be live girl, is seen by king who falls in love with her) IVa (before marriage, stepmother throws doll into water) c (mermaid's daughter substituted) + Q556. Curse as punishment + J2401. Fatal imitation + K1911.3. Reinstatement of true bride.

(1) K1911. The false bride (substituted bride).
(2) B81.13.8. Curse by mermaid.
(3) Q556.12. Curse for stealing.
(4) Z71.1. Formulistic number: three.
(5) D1865.1. Beautification by decapitation and replacement of head.
(6) J2411.1. Imitation of magic rejuvenation unsuccessful.
(7) J2401. Fatal imitation.
(8) K1911.3. Reinstatement of true bride.

72. Antoñito Malverde

(Recorded by Candelario Gallardo on December 2, 1966, in Oxnard, California)

A young girl is badly mistreated by her stepmother but is aided in some of her tasks by a prince in the form of a bird named Antoñito Malverde. To escape the cruel treatment of the stepmother, she runs away from home and in her wanderings encounters a young man who is really the prince. They arrive at a palace where they are to spend the night, but she disregards his warning not to speak to him, kisses him as he sleeps, and breaks the spell. The palace disappears, and Antoñito Malverde announces that she will not see him again until she finds her way to Arboleras de Oro and Montañas de Cristal [the land of golden groves and glass mountains]. The girl disguises herself as a boy, sets off in search of Arboleras de Oro and Montañas de Cristal, and soon comes across three brothers fighting over the inheritance of their grandfather. She tricks them out of the three objects they are fighting over—a pair of magic flying boots, a food-producing napkin, and a magic stick that metes out blows—and continues on her way. She soon meets a hermit who says he is the Air and who aids her in her search for the mysterious land. They find it, the girl disenchants the prince, the king, and the queen by removing thorns from the heads of three birds, and she marries Antoñito Malverde. Meanwhile, the girl's father has made a pact with the devil in exchange for information about his daughter's whereabouts and has found his way to Arboleras de Oro and Montañas de Cristal. The girl sees him seated on the palace grounds day after day, takes an interest in him, and, upon talking with him, discovers he is her father. The stepmother also, with the assistance of the devil, finds her way to Arboleras de Oro and Montañas de Cristal, where, upon learning that her stepdaughter, the princess, is due to have a baby, she sets herself up as a midwife. At three successive births, she substitutes three cats and sends the princess's three children off to sea in boxes. The prince, in anger at his wife for producing cats instead of children, locks her up in a cage. The three children are retrieved from the water by a hermit who then raises them as his own; but on a visit to the city they are recognized as the children of the prince, and the hermit dies of sadness at losing them. The stepmother is called to the palace, and, thinking that the princess must be due to give birth again, she brings along a cat to substitute for the child. This serves as dramatic proof of her guilt, and she is sentenced to death.

Les voy a contar el cuento de un señor. Su provisión de este señor era la arriería. Se mantenía . . . con sus burritos, haciendo la vida. Él iba por allá, traía . . . pos, frutita, en fin, traía su fruta y la vendía. Era su provisión de este señor.

Este señor, se le murió su esposa, y quedó viudo. Y entre sus viajes de él, que iba a . . . hacer por allá, . . . pues éste se halló por allá una señora. Esta señora, pues, manifestaba, le manifestaba a él . . . una señora muy, muy noble, muy buena mujer. Y el señor, pues, también era muy bueno, ¿verdad? Muy trabajador. Y la señora, pues, también se le presentaba . . . muy buena mujer. Pero él no quería llevársela a su hija. Tenía una hijita que le había quedado de su señora. No quería llevársela, porque ya la hijita estaba grande, y no quería darle esas molestias a ella, y llevarle a otra mujer que no fuera su mamá.

Pero . . . en los viajes, tanto le rogaba la señora. —Ay, dice, —llévame a con tu hija, dice, —pobrecita, dice. —Cómo estará sufriendo la probrecita. Yo voy a ser su mamá. Llévame para allá. Pues el señor no quería porque, pos, ya la muchachita, pos, . . . ¿cómo le iba a llevar a su mamá que no era? Pero la señora, cuando ya se miraban, mmm, áhi está rogándole que la llevara a su tierra, que . . . para educarla a la, la niña.

Pues un día se resolvió el hombre. Dice: —Te preparas, y al regreso te voy a llevar para allá. Voy a dejar un burro vacante pa llevarte.

—Está bien. Pos, la señora con mucho gusto, ¿verdad? Hizo sus maletas y ya estaba esperando al señor . . . que viniera. Ya llegó. Dice: —Ya tengo aquí todos mis velices preparados pa que me lleves.

—'Tá bien. Áhi 'tá el burro vacante, dice, —para . . . para llevarte.

Pos se vinieron y llegaron donde estaba la . . . la niña, y luego luego la abrazó, y a beso y beso. —Pobrecita, dice, —mira no más, huerfanita de tu madre. Pero yo voy a ser tu madre. Pobrecita. Mira no más, tan simpática, tan bonita niña.

Bueno, la niña, pues, se encariñó con ella, ¿verdad? Dice: —Pos, qué buena mujer.

Y luego ya le . . . el hombre vino. —Hijita, dice, —a pesar de que tu madre se, se murió, dice, —aquí traigo esta mujer. Esta mujer es muy buena. La vas a reconocer como si fuera tu madre. Ella se ve encargada de todo, dice, —educarte, echarte a la escuela.

—Pos, 'tá bien, papá. Lo que tú digas.

Entonces el señor hizo su viaje . . . siempre a . . . a lo que iba. Traía su frutita pa venderla afuera . . . pa soportar su familia.

Y luego que ya tenía un día de camino el señor, le dice a la niña: —¿Con que usted no sabe hacer nada, niña?

—No, yo no sé hacer nada, dice. —Mi mamá, dice, —no quería ni que el aire me diera (1).

Dice: —Pos ahora sí, conmigo (2). Hora está . . . ese nixtamal, y me lo va a moler. Me va a echar unas tortillas, dice. —Y si no, ya verá (3). Luego le arrimó allí el maicito, el nixtamal, y el metate. Y luego áhi 'tá la niña, toda se trompezaba con la mano del metate. La niña toda herida de sus manitas. Y a llora y llora y llora. Porque . . . no podía hacer ese trabajo (4). Y llega la señora. —¿Qué pasó? ¿Ya está esa masa lista pa las tortillas?

—Señora, dice, —pos, no puedo. Mire mis manos cómo las tengo. No puedo hacer eso yo, señora.

Y que agarra una vara que tenía ya prevenida, ¿verdad? Y le da una . . . vareada, pero buena (5). A llora y llora y . . . voy y voy y voy y voy. ¡Uy, la golpeó mucho! Dice: —Ahora se va a ir al río. Y esta zalea prieta, me la pone blanca. Y la blanca me la pone prieta (6). Y si no lo hace le voy a dar otra más buena. Tenga. Váyase al río.

Y áhi va . . . la niña con aquellas zaleas. Y áhi está refriega y refriega con jabón. ¿Cuándo se volvían . . . la prieta blanca y la blanca prieta? Por más . . . lucha que le hizo, pos ¿cuándo se volvían así? Pos que áhi viene otra vez con sus zaleas. Le dice . . . la hechicera:

—¿Qué pasó?

—Señora, dice, —por más lucha que le hice . . . no pude.

Otra vareada buena. Y ya la mataba. —Ahora, tenga ese, ese . . . ese peso, . . . ese peso y va al pueblo. Y me trae veinticinco de carbón, y veinticinco de sal, . . . en fin, el peso. —Y me trae el cambio (4). ¿Qué cambio le iba a traer? Si todo lo gastaba . . . en el carbón y sal, y, y . . . y arroz, y en fin . . . todo de veinticinco. ¿Qué cambio le traía?

—¿Qué pasó con el cambió?

—Señora, pues no me dio.

Otra vareada buena. Home, ya la mataba. Pos que . . . dice: —Ahora, dice, con el carbón . . . me va a hacer una hoguera. Prenda el carbón, y que se haga . . . una hoguera. Y si me deja salir . . . una cosa que va a salir de la hoguera, la pura verdad, casi medio la mato (4).

Oooo, áhi está la niña apuradísima . . . prendiendo el carbón, y . . . una hoguera calientísima. Y le tapaba con el rebocito la niña. Le tapaba con el rebocito, porque le había indicado que iba a salir alguna cosa . . . de allí. Y ya le dijo que si dejaba . . . que si dejaba salir lo que iba a salir de la hoguera, pues casi la mataba. Y áhi está con el rebocito, tapando la hoguera, . . . a ver qué cosa salía. Pues, que de repente, que da un estallido el carbón y que . . . sale un pájaro (7). Y que pronto . . . le agarró un aloncito y no lo dejó ir.

Le dice el pájaro: —Suéltame.

Dice: —No te suelto. Porque esta señora me mata si te suelto, porque me indicó que no dejara salir . . . lo que iba a salir del carbón. Y si te dejo ir, me mata después.

Dice: —No te mata. Arráncame un . . . una pluma de mi alconcito, y no más dices tú: "Ven, Antoñito Malverde, sálvame de esta apuración y yo me casaré contigo." Y, yo, yo te salvo (8). Déjame ir. Y . . . ya lo que te digo. Arráncame una plumita de mi aloncito. Tonces la niña le . . . jaló, y le arrancó un . . . una plumita del aloncito, y voló el pájaro. Pero que . . . aquella plumita se la guardó (9).

Pos que viene, viene la señora. —¿Qué pasó? ¿Me dejó ir de lo que salió del carbón?

—Sí, señor.

—Señora, dice, —pos sí. Salió un pájaro y se fue, y no lo pude agarrar. Mmm, le dio una . . . que ya la mataba.

Tonces iba a ser día de su santo de la, de la señora. Y la encerró en un cuarto. Y le llevó un corte para un vestido, . . . y una mesa, tijeras, todo allí. Dice: —Ahora mañana va a ser día de mi santo. Y usted va a cortarme ese, ese, . . . me va a hacer un vestido . . . a mi cuerpo, y para mañana está listo porque me lo voy a poner (4). Mañana va a ser día de mi santo. Áhi está la . . . el lienzo, áhi está . . . lo que le compré, tijeras y máquina y todo. Y la encerró.

Pos, ¿qué vestido le iba a hacer, hombre? Si la niña era una niña que no sabía nada. Pos que áhi . . . 'tá, muy apurada la niña. Y acuérdase de la alita. Dice: —Yo voy a probar esta alita. Saca la alita. —Eh, Antoñito Malverde, sácame de esta apuración y yo me caso contigo.

Uy, dice, luego luego que vino por las paredes volando el pájaro: —¿Qué deseas?

Dice: —Pos, ¿qué voy a desear? Dice: —Que esta señora . . . quiere áhi un vestido, que va a ser el día de su santo para mañana y lo quiere listo muy temprano.

Dice: —Acuéstate. No te apures. Al amanecer está el vestido (10, 11). No, pos, que áhi va a dormir la niña.

Pero ya otro día sale el vestido, para su cuerpo de la señora. Y luego ya la niña . . . llega donde dormía la vieja y la despierta. —¿Qué pasó? Tú vas a, . . . tienes más poder que yo. Así es de que te voy a . . . casi te voy a matar. Le dio una, pero . . . buena.

Entonces dice: —No, no cabe duda, dice, —esta mujer me va a matar. Y un día se le huyó. Agarraba por tooooodo el río, anda y anda y anda y anda, y allá . . . se cansaba la niña. Cuando vido venir un joven . . . muy bien parecido. Ya se encontraron.

—¿Aónde va, niña?

Dice: —Voy perdida. ¿Y usted?

—También voy perdido. ¿Qué le pasa, niña?

Dice: —¿Qué me va a pasar? Dice: —Hay una señora que me quiere matar.

—¿Cómo que la quiere . . . ? Él ya sabía. —¿Cómo que la quiere matar?

—Sí, dice. Y le platicó lo pasado.

—Pues, vámonos, le dice el niño a la niña. —Vámonos perdidos los dos.

—Pos, vámonos. Ya tengo mi compañero.

Y áhi van . . . los dos, anda y anda y anda y anda y anda. Ya dice . . . el niño: —Vamos a llegar . . . a aquella casa. Aquella casa es mi casa. Que era una casa, un palacio, pero . . . bonito, bonito aquel palacio. Y entraron a palacio allí. Unas camas muy bonitas. Entonces . . . una cama así y una cama así. [Indicates arrangement.] Le dice Antoñito Malverde, . . . porque sí era . . . Antoñito: —En esta cama usted va a dormir, y yo aquí en ésta. Si usted despierta primero, no me vaya a hablar (12). Porque somos perdidos. Duerma usted aquí, dice, —y no vaya a despertarme.

Pues la niña no podía dormir. Estaba nerviosa. Y el niño estaba dormido, y 'taba muy hermoso el niño. Entonces en gratificación de que . . . pos iban de compañeros y él era muy bueno, se arrimó y le dio un beso (13). Y despierta el niño. —¡Híjole! Lo más encargado, lo más olvidado. Y no encontrarás a mí (14) . . . hasta Arboleras de Oro y Montañas de Cristal (15). Y se despareció el palacio.

Quedó en el monte, quedó en la selva la niña . . . sentada. Oooo, áhi 'tá muy apurada la niña. Dice: —Yo me voy . . . en siguimientos . . . de Antoñito Malverde (16), . . . que era, . . . se volvió un pájaro (17). Sus nagüitas las hizo calzoncitos, pantaloncito. Y le hizo un pantaloncito y se vistió de hombrecito con un sombrero. Y en . . . y en dirección de . . . donde voló el pájaro, áhi va, entre la selva, anda y anda y anda y anda y anda y anda y anda la niña.

Y encontró . . . unos, unos tres niños . . . peleándose. Estos niños, peleándose por la herencia de . . . de su abuelito. Y: —que no, que a mí me toca esto, y: —que a mí me tocan las botas, y: —que a mí me tocan. Todos querían las botas. Porque era un . . . unas botas viejas, . . . un . . . una servilleta, y un garrotito. Era lo que peleaban entre ellos. Todos querían las botas. No, que . . . pos áhi así.

Y luego, llega la niña. Dice: —¿Por qué se pelean, niños?

Dice: —Porque, por la herencia de mi abuelo. Dice: —Yo quiero las botas, éste también las quiere, y éste también las quiere. No nos podemos convenir.

Le dice la niña: —Bueno. Pues, ¿qué virtud tienen esas, esas botas? Las botas están muy viejas. La servilleta, pues, pueden hacer otra. Y el garrotito pues, 'tá todo roto, que aquí pueden encontrar otro.

—No, niña. . . . No, niña, éste es, . . . pos tienen virtud. Las botas no más les dice: "Vuelen botas, vuelen botas," y se le van en el viento (18). Y . . . y la servilleta no más le dice: "Componte servilletita," y se compone la comida que usted quiera (19). Y el garrotito no más le dice uno: "Componte garrotito," y áhi va echando garrotazos por todos lados (20).

—Aaa, dice, . . . dice la niña: —¿No quieren que se halle un juez? —Sí, sí. Usted va a ser el juez (21).

Dice: —Se agarran los tres de las . . . de la mano, y se van hasta aquel . . . hasta allá retirado, hasta aquella lomita. Y luego el que corra más recio, a ése le doy las botas. Y luego ya, a otro la servilleta, y a otro el garrotito.

Pos que así lo hicieron. Se fueron agarrados de manos, hasta donde les había dicho. Pos, mientras que iban ellos . . . a . . . hasta la lomita para correr, ella se puso las botas y agarró la servilleta y el garrotito, y le dice a las, le dice a las, a las botas: —Vuelen botas, vuelen botas, y áhiiiii, áhi va . . . elevada . . . en el viento (22). Y se fue a dirección donde se había ido Antoñito Malverde. Llegó a un monte. Dice: —Yo voy a calar la servilleta. Ya bajó a tierra. Dice: —Componte servilletita. Ay, que luego se. . . compuso la servilleta una comida muy . . . muy buena. Y comió.

Y luego, vido venir . . . un viejito . . . que era un, un hermitaño . . . que habitaba en la selva. Con unas greñotas hasta acá, hasta el pecho [indicates length]. Dice la, la niña, dice: —Aaa, aquí viene este viejito, dice. —¡Qué feo! No, pos que ya llega.

—¿Qué estás comiendo, hombre? Jovencito, ¿qué estás comiendo?

—Señor, yo estoy comiéndome esta comidita.

—Pero si . . . esta comidita, ¿quién te la preparó? Comida muy buena.

Dice: —Yo la preparo, señor.

—No, hombre. A ver, prepárame una comidita como ésa. Yo también traigo hambre.

No más le dice a la servilletita: —Componte servilletita. Mmmm, áhi 'tá otro . . . otra comida . . . elegantísima, buena. Comió el . . . muy bien el . . . el hermitaño.

—Bueno, dice. —En gratificación que me distes de comer, ¿qué misión llevas? ¿Para dónde vas? Dice: —Yo soy, . . . ¿tú no sabes quién soy yo?

—No, dice. —¿Quién eres tú?

—Yo soy el Aire. El Aire dondequiera se mete y dondequiera anda. Yo soy el Aire. ¿Y tú?

—Pues, ya le digo. Yo soy . . . una niña. No más que vengo . . . de hombrecito.

—¿Qué misión llevas?

Dice: —La misión que llevo es de que . . . vengo a ver si llego a Arboleras de Oro y Montañas de Cristal. Para allá se fue mi compañero Antoñito Malverde. Y me dijo que no lo encontraría hasta Arboleras de Oro y Montañas de Cristal. Y yo ese rumbo llevo. Así es de que, pues, si, si usted me puede ayudar, que usted es el Aire y ondequiera se mete y ondequiera anda, si usted me da razón de Arboleras de Oro y Montañas de Cristal, dígame qué tan retirado está.

—Mmmm, niña, dice, —ya sabes tú que yo soy de ondequiera ando y dondequiera me meto, y nunca he oído yo de esa . . . población de Arboleras de Oro y Montañas de Cristal. Pero en gratificación que tú me has dado de comer, nos vamos a aquel cerro que está muy altísimo, y a ver si vemos brillar, a ver qué es lo que miramos. A ver si de casualidad yo te puedo ayudar. Pues que . . . yo soy el Aire. Móntate en mis hombros.

—No, dice. —Si yo traigo modo de volar.

—¿Cómo?

—Sí.

Dice: —Entonces sígueme. Y áhi va el Aire, que hasta las alturas aventaja.

Y áhi va. —Vuelen botas, vuelen botas. Y áhi va atrás del Aire.

Y ya llegaron a la altura del, del cerro. Empezaron a, a ver por todos lados. No . . . ya dice: —Yo voy. Me esperas aquí. Voy a volar lo más que pueda, dice, —como yo soy el Aire. Voy a volar con toda la velocidad, a ver si de casualidad doy con esa . . . población. Me esperas aquí.

—Sí.

Pos que áhi va un aeronazo, pero fuertísimo, y llega donde . . . Arboleras de Oro y Montañas de Cristal. Y salieron las hechiceras, la gente hechicera.

—¡Ay Dios!, dice. —Que Arboleras de Oro, que nunca se había visto, dice, —el aeronazo que está haciendo en Arboleras de Oro y Montañas de Cristal.

—Mira no más, dice el Aire. —Aquí es. Y áhi va a regresar. Se regresó para atrás. Dijo: —Niña, dice, —ooo, dice, —está muy lejísimo. Está muy lejos, dice. —Quizá no puedas ir (23).

—No, dice. —Llego. Yo traigo aquí mis botas, que pueden volar también casi como tú.

—Bueno, que está bien. Entonces te voy a dar un consejo. Cuando llegues allá a ese Arboleras de Oro y Montañas de Cristal han de salir las hechiceras. Y te dicen, "Adelante, niño. Una taza de café o una comida. Véngase, niño, a comer." Y no vayas a aceptar eso, ni vayas a volcar para atrás, porque te quedas encantado. Así es de que éste es el consejo que te doy (24, 25).

—Pos, que está bien. Entonces áhi dice: —Vuelen botas, vuelen botas, y áhi va.

Pos sí llegó. Y ciertamente le decían: —Niño, niño, niño, niño, dice, —véngase a una taza de café, o una . . . comidita. Que pase a mi casa, y que se. . . .

Y ella no más decía: —Yo, a lo que vengo, vengo. Y yo a lo que vengo, ni a precio deshacía. Ni volteaba para atrás, como le había dicho el Aire. Y llegó a palacio. Llegó a palacio. Y luego, allí en palacio entró para dentro, y estaban unas jaulotas grandes. Y estaban unos pericos . . . ya, ya viejos, asina. —¡Mira, qué pericos, hombre! Yo creo que esto es encantado (26, 27). ¡Qué hechicera! Dice: —Yo creo que esto ha sido encantado.

Y luego ya . . . el perico habló, como hablan, ¿verdad? Dice: —Adelante, niña, dice. —Desencántenos. Sáquenos la espina de la cabeza (28). Que tenían una espina en la cabeza los . . . los pericos. Era el, el rey . . . y la esposa del rey, y la niña, una niña. Le sacó el . . . la espina, y áhi está el rey. Y le sacó la espina, era Antoñito Malverde . . . el jovencito.

Y luego a una hermana de . . . de Antoñito Malverde. Y luego luego Antoñito Malverde conoció a la niña. Y se desencantó toda la ciudad. —¡Híjole! Pues, que mira no más, hombre. Que ésta fue la que
nos . . . la niña que . . . sufría mucho, que por su madrastra.

Y el rey muy encantado con, con la niña. —No hay más que . . . pos
tú te vas a casar con Antoñito Malverde (29).

Pos áhi vamos a dejar, . . . hora vamos . . . atrás con el papá de la
niña. El papá llegó, . . . y la señora la encontró llora y llora y llora y
llora y llora. Y: —¡Ay Dios! Y que: —¡Válgame Dios, que se me perdió mi hija! Que tanto que la quería, y . . . y esto y lo otro.

Y . . . y luego el marido dice: —¿Dónde está?

Dice: —Pos no viene. Dice: —Se, se perdió.

—¿Cómo que se perdió?

—Sí, si no la hallo.

Pos que áhi está el hombre busca y busca a . . . a su hija, y no, imposible de hallarla también. Entonces . . . el señor empezó a vender los
burros. Y se los . . . y empezaba a la tomada . . . al vino. Y . . . y acabó,
. . . todos, todos los burritos se los tomó de vino. Y quedó muy pobre.

Y luego la, la hechicera . . . que era la señora, como tienen artes del
diablo, pues, puso . . . sus astucias, que a ver, que a ver dónde se, se
hallaba la niña. Y lo ya supo. Puso las astucias y imposible de dar con
ella. Estaba muy lejísimo. Por más que . . . lucha que le hacía la hechicera, no podía dar con Arboleras de Oro y Montañas de Cristal. 'Taba
muy lejos.

Entonces el papá de la niña . . . pos se obligó, pos iba a gritarle al
diablo . . . donde hacía cruz el camino. Y luego áhi está: —Diablo,
Diablo, y Diablo, preséntate aquí, Diablo. Dice: —Yo quiero a mi hija, que me digas en dónde está (30).

Y se le presenta un, un viejo con una gorra galona y un caballo
prieto (31). Le dice: —¿Qué tienes, viejo?

Dice: —Quiero que me digas en dónde está mi hija.

—Ooo, dice, —tu hija está muy lejos. 'Tá en Arboleras de Oro y
Montañas de Cristal. Es muy lejos.

—Pos ayúdame. ¿Qué puedo hacer?

—Bueno, dice, —dame tu alma.

—Sí, te la doy (32).

—Pos, móntate en el caballo, . . . en ancas de mi caballo y cierra los ojos.

Y así lo hizo. Cuando . . . cuando abrió los ojos, ya estaba allá. Ya estaba allá en Arboleras de Oro y Montañas de Cristal. Era una ciudad desencantada. Ya la había desencantado la . . . la niña. O, pos que ya llega allá. Una ciudad preciosísima. Preguntándole a la gente, ya estaba medio . . . estaba medio volviéndose ya loco, preguntándole a la gente que si no habían visto a su niña. —¿Cuál niña, pues, dice, —hombre?

—Pos, mi niña, que es Fulana de Tal.

—No, ¿cuál niña?

Y frente a palacio, pos estaba muy pobre y . . . y tenía frío, había un . . . una esquinita que daba luego luego el sol. Y el viejito ya muy andrajoso. Y se asoleaba allí en aquel rinconcito . . . frente a palacio. Y él agarraba solecito allí.

Y luego la . . . la niña . . . salía del, del balcón. Dice: —¿Quién será ese viejito que . . . ya tengo días que lo estoy viendo . . . en ese rinconcito agarrando sol? Y toditito se parece a mi padre. Entonces un día le decía a la guardia que tenían ellos allí: —A ver, dice. —Tráigame ese señor.

Y ya fue la guardia allí. Dijo: —Anda y habla a la princesa.

—¿Qué quiere, dice, —la princesa? Yo estoy muy andrajoso, dice. —Yo no puedo presentarme.

—Pos, no, yo no sé. Anda y habla. Pos que ya fue.

Dijo: —Oiga, dice, —mi hijito. Ya tengo días de verlo en ese rinconcito asoleándose. Platíqueme su vida. ¿Qué le pasa?

Mmm, se puso a llorar el viejito. Dice: —Tanto tiempo hace, dice, —que se me perdió mi niña, y . . . imposible de, de encontrarla. Hasta que me hallé obligado a hablarle al diablo. Y el diablo me trajo para acá.

—Y, ¿cómo se llamaba su, . . . cómo se llamaba la niña?

Dice: —No, mire, dice. —Yo, yo mi provisión mía . . . era la arriería. Y yo me hallé, bueno, tenía yo una niña y quedó huérfana. Y yo, entre mis viajes, dice, —me hallé una señora. Y la señora me rogó mucho a que la llevara onde estaba mi hija, dice. —Y esa señora, cuando ya

. . . regresé yo de mi, de mi arriería, ya no la encontré. Y la señora, pues, también estaba muy apurada. Ooo, se muere la pobre por su hija.

Entonces le dice: —Usted es mi papá.

—¿Cómo voy a ser yo su papá?

Dice: —Usted es mi papá. Ahora que está diciendo que está muriendo esa señora por mí, . . . y ya le contó lo de atrás, de la, . . . qué le hacía y todo eso. —Usted es mi padre.

Y luego ya vino Antoñito Malverde y vino el rey y la reina, y le contó que aquél era su padre. Ooo, luego luego, lo bañaron y lo vistieron de a pies a cabeza, y lo rasuraron, y ya no hallaban qué hacer con el papá de la niña, de la princesa.

Bueno, pos que luego . . . ya, ya iba a tener un, un bebito. Iba a tener un bebito.

Pero en esto vamos atrás con la hechicera. La hechicera . . . se le perdió su esposo. Y luego, no lo hallaba. Ya estaba en Arboleras de Oro y Montañas de Cristal. ¿Ónde lo iba a hallar? Entonces por más que puso sus astucias, no lo podía hallar. Entonces también fue a hablarle al diablo, . . . donde hacía cruz el camino. Y áhi está gritando la señora al diablo: —Diablo, y Diablo, dime dónde está mi viejo. Y: —Diablo, y —Diablo, dice (30).

Viene el Diablo . . . igualmente como se vestía (31). —¿Qué me das? ¿Tu alma?

—Sí, te la doy (32). A ver, ¿dónde está mi esposo?

—Móntate en mi caballo, . . . en ancas de mi caballo, y cierra los ojos.

Así, así lo hizo. Cuando abrió los ojos, ya estaba en Arboleras de Oro y Montañas de Cristal. Y como era hechicera, allí le valía su astucia, . . . que iba a tener un bebito la, la, la niña. Y luego enfrente de palacio, luego luego rentó un . . . cuarto. Luego luego puso un rótulo: "Partera Especialista en Niños."

Pues que ya Antoñito Malverde dijo al rey, dice: —Hombre, dice, —aquí está la, la doctora pa cuando se le ofrezca a mi esposa. Aquí está muy cerquita.

Pos sí, se le ofreció. Iba a tener el . . . el bebito. Y como el palacio estaba a orillas casi del mar . . . muy bonito. Iba a tener el primer bebito, cuando luego luego fueron y le hablaron a la señora. —Señora, dice, —pos, usted está en este trabajito. Así es de que vaya a sacar a, a mi esposa.

—'Tá bien. Entonces áhi va. Pero la, la señora era muy mala. Ya había criado un gatito, y luego luego se lo echó, como en México dicen el seno, . . . se lo echó en el seno, y áhi lleva el gatito . . . en el seno. Que: —A ver, ¿dónde está aquí la enferma? Que yo soy, soy Fulana y . . . qué sé yo qué.

—Pásese, señora. Aquí está.

—Déjenme solita con la enferma. Y sálganseme todos. Yo la voy a sacar aquí. Como el palacio estaba, ya le digo, como . . . a orillas del mar, . . . luego luego pos, en esas enfermedades casi ni se dan cuenta dicen, ¿quién sabe?, pos que tuvo el bebito. Y luego que tuvo el bebito, lo echó en una caja y lo echó al mar, . . . en una caja muy bien cerrada. Y lo echó al mar (33). Y luego ya dio orden que ya había salido aquella, aquella niña, aquella princesa de sus cuidados.

Y luego el rey y el príncipe: —¿Qué, qué hubo? ¿Niño o niña?

—Miren, un gato (34).

—Miau, miau. [Imitates cat.]

—¿Un gato?

—Pos un gatito fue el que tuvo.

—Pero, ¿cómo va a ser gato?

—Pos sí. Aquí está . . . a la prueba. Es un gato.

Mmmm, pues ya se desconsolaron. Dijo el rey, dice: —¿Quién sabe?, dice. —Serán los primeros . . . niños, dice. —No te alarmes. ¿Quién sabe? Tal vez al otro . . . sea niño. Y el rey lo conformaba a Antoñito Malverde.

Pa no alargarles, fueron tres niños. Y los tres, gatos que llevaba la señora . . . a meterle que eran gatos (34). Ella los echaba al mar muy bien cerrados en las cajitas y se iban al mar (33). Y puros gatitos, . . . le decía que tenía puros gatos. Pos que áhi están el rey y todos allí enojados con la . . . con la princesa. —Ooo, dice, —vamos a empaderar, dice, —a esta . . . a esta niña, dice. —La vamos a empaderar a la, a la esposa y le vamos a dar mal las comidas y casi ni agua le damos. La empaderaron, y ya está la niña empaderada (35). Y . . . y luego . . . y luego ya que la trataban muy mal, ya el papá . . . de la niña, ya hasta casi lo corrían. Lo echaba . . . de mal modo.

Y luego los niños se fueron al mar en sus cajitas. Y luego andaba un . . . un hermitaño, pescando. Él se mantenía con pescados . . . y animalitos que comía. Y tenía su cueva . . . el hermitaño. Y tenía una venada . . . con venaditos, y . . . casi luego a los venaditos se acababa la leche de la venadita. Y él comía . . . tomaba leche de la venadita . . . el hermitaño. Y estaba pescando. También pescaba. Y vido venir esas . . . esas tres cajitas en el mar, orillándose y orillándose las cajitas. Y luego con un remo que traía . . . el hermitaño remaba aquellas cajitas. Y luego las sacó (36). Dice: —Home, ¿qué será esto que traen estas cajitas? Pos eran los tres niños, vivos. ¡Mmm, pero hermosísimos aquellos niños! —Ooo, dice el hermitaño, —yo voy a crear [i.e., criar] estos niños (37). Al cabo, tengo la venada. Se los llevó a la cueva, y allí les daba leche de . . . de la venadita (38). Y los crió . . . a los niños.

Ya estaban grandecitos . . . y no conocían el pueblo ni la gente. Entonces les dice el hermitaño, . . . ya lo reconocían como su padre: —Hijos, dice, —voy a darles una vueltecita aquí por toda la selva, dice, —para que . . . miren el pueblo y vean la gente. Ustedes no conocen la gente. Y miran el pueblo. Y nos vamos a dar una vuelta.

Pos que áhi van . . . ya vestiditos de . . . pos de pieles de animalito. Y jue a darles una vuelta . . . pa el pueblo, onde almiradísimos aquellos niños, que miraban aquella ciudad tan bonita y la gente . . . y . . .

Pero en esto la gente luego luego: —¿Dónde hallaría este . . . este . . . hermitaño esos niños tan bonitos? Mira no más. Y luego fueron allá con el chisme con el rey. Ya dicen: —Mi rey, dice, —¿sabe qué?, dice. —El hermitaño que habita en . . . en, en la selva trae . . . trae tres niños . . . pero hermosísimos aquellos niños. Y muy pobrecitos, dice. —Los trae vestidos de piel . . . de animal.

Dijo: —Cuando los miren. . . . Luego mandó allí . . . a una guardia. Tiene su guardia el gobierno. Luego luego: —A ver, búsquenme el . . . el hermitaño. Y que me traigan esos niños para acá, para darles un regalito, que dicen que andan pobres.

No, pos luego fueron a buscarlo. Pos no lo pudieron hallar. Pos sólo allá dentro de la selva, sólo él sabía la entrada de la cueva. Pos él, sin saber, les dijo que fueran a dar otra vueltecita, que si les había gustado. Pues áhi van los niños. Pos que . . .áhi va con los niños. Y se los quitaron. Se los quitaron. Y de pesar, de pesar de, de, de sus niños, se murió . . . el hermitaño. Se jue a la cueva y allí se murió.

Y luego llevaron a los niños . . . y miraban el retrato de, de Antoñito Malverde, y miraban el retrato de los niños. Igualitos. Pos que ya el rey dice: —Home, dice, —a ver, tráiganme ese, ese . . . ese hermitaño, a ver dónde hubo esas cajas, . . . esos niños. Pos que áhi a la selva a busca y busca y busca y busca y busca y busca. Y dan con la cueva. Y el hermitaño ya estaba muerto. Ya estaba muerto . . . llenitito de flores, . . . ya por Dios. Pero había dejado escrito . . . de qué manera . . . de qué manera hubo sus niños, onde todo decía, cómo había sacado sus niños y todo. Y luego, áhi traen al hermitaño . . . a darle un sepulcro. ¡Pero elegantísimo! Y enterraron al hermitaño. Pero allí estipulaba . . . de qué modo había . . . habido esos niños.

Tonces miraban el retrato de Antoñito Malverde, y miraban el retrato de los niños. Igualitos. Dice el rey: —Aquí hay una confusión. A mí se me hace que esta señora, . . . nada de gatos, sino que eran niños (39). Pos que allí estipulaba . . . el papel que había dejado el hermitaño. Luego luego ya mandan traer a la . . . a la señora, la partera. Y áhi viene con otro gato. Creía que era otro niño. [Laughs.]

Y luego luego dice: —Déjenme solita, déjenme solita.

Y luego el rey le dice: —Oiga, señora, usted me va a decir la verdad. Usted sabe que palabra del rey nunca vuelve atrás (40). ¿Qué me dice? ¿Jueron niños los que tuvo mi nuera, o jueron gatitos?

—No, señor, pos gatitos. Ya vido usted.

Y áhi no más que . . . que hace: —Miau, miau [imitates a cat], el gato que llevaba otra vez en el seno.

Dice: —¿Qué le tantea, señora? Ya trae otro gatito, ¿no?, creyendo que es otro niño. Jum. Palabra de rey no vuelve atrás. Enciérrenme esta señora . . . en el cuarto, y échenle pólvora, y préndale juego [i.e., fuego] . . . para que explote. Y así lo hicieron. De modo es que . . . le echaron a un cuarto, le echaron pólvora, y le prendieron. Reventó allí. La mataron (41, 42).

Así es de que . . . éste es el cuento . . . de . . . de la hechicera. Así es que si les gusta, pues, pueden oírlo. Está algo larguito, . . . para que se diviertan y, pero quién sabe les dé soñito si lo ponen muy noche. Pero si les gusta, pues no le hace que se desvelen. Y . . . y aquí termina el cuento . . . de la hechicera.

The tale is structured as follows: S31. Cruel stepmother + H1010. Impossible tasks + H1023.6. Task: washing black wool (cloth, cattle) white + 432 Ia IIIa + 425 IIIc² IVb (from children) cd Vb (by removing thorn from head) + M211.9. Person sells soul to devil in return for granting of wishes + 707 IIa (wicked stepmother substitutes cats) b (hermit) c IIIa (to see the city) IV ac.

 (1) L55. Stepdaughter heroine.
 (2) S31. Cruel stepmother.
 (3) H934.3. Tasks assigned by stepmother.
 (4) H1010. Impossible tasks.
 (5) L55.1. Abused stepdaughter.
 (6) H1023.6. Task: washing black wool (cloth, cattle) white.
 (7) D641.1. Lover as bird visits mistress.
 (8) B501. Animal gives part of body as talisman for summoning its aid.
 (9) D1021. Magic feather.
(10) B450. Helpful birds.
(11) B313. Helpful animal an enchanted person.
(12) C400. Speaking tabu.
(13) C121. Tabu: kissing supernatural husband.
(14) C932. Loss of wife (husband) for breaking tabu.
(15) F751. Glass mountain.
(16) H1385.5. Quest for vanished lover.
(17) D150. Transformation: man to bird.
(18) D1521.1. Seven-league boots.
(19) D1472.1.8. Magic tablecloth supplies food and drink.
(20) D1401.1. Magic club (stick) beats person.
(21) D832. Magic objects acquired by acting as umpire for fighting heirs.
(22) D1520.10. Magic transportation by shoes.
(23) H1232. Directions on quest given by sun, moon, wind and stars. [Here, only the wind.]
(24) C331. Tabu: looking back.
(25) G263. Witch injures, enchants or transforms.
(26) F768.2. City of enchanted people.
(27) D157. Transformation: man to parrot.
(28) D765.1.2. Disenchantment by removal of enchanting pin (thorn).
(29) L162. Lowly heroine marries prince.
(30) G303.6.1.2. Devil comes when called upon.
(31) G303.7.1.1. Devil rides on black horse.
(32) M211.9. Person sells soul to devil in return for granting of wishes.
(33) S331. Exposure of child in boat (floating chest).
(34) K2115. Animal-birth slander.
(35) S430. Disposal of cast-off wife.
(36) R131.10. Hermit rescues abandoned child.
(37) N856.1. Forester as foster father.

(38) B535. Animal nurse.
(39) S451. Outcast wife at last united with husband and children.
(40) M203. King's promise irrevocable.
(41) Q261. Treachery punished.
(42) Q414. Punishment: burning alive.
Aarne-Thompson 432. The Prince as Bird.
Boggs 432.
Hansen 432. The Prince as Bird.
   Mexico: Robe, *Mexican Tales*, no. 65; Wheeler, nos. 88, 90.
   United States: Campa, *WF*, 6(1947), 326, no. 2; Espinosa, *SFNM*,
      nos. 13, 36; Paredes, no. 34; Rael, nos. 112, 113.
   Chile: Laval, *Carahue*, no. 9; Pino Saavedra, no. 58.
   Cuba: Portell Villá, no. 100 (parallels the origin of the bird from
      the forbidden cage).
   Dominican Republic: Andrade, no. 123.
   Puerto Rico: Mason-Espinosa, *JAF*, 39(1926), 312, no. 4.
   Spain: Hernández de Soto, *BTPE*, vol. 10, p. 201, no. 16; p. 209,
      no. 17.
Aarne-Thompson 425. The Search for the Lost Husband.
Boggs 425.
Hansen 425. The Search for the Lost Husband.
Grimm, no. 127.
   Mexico: Córdova, no. 2; Robe, *Mexican Tales*, nos. 60, 61, 62, 63;
      Wheeler, no. 90.
   United States: Campa, *WF*, 6(1947), 326, no. 2; Espinosa, *JAF*,
      24(1911), 402, no. 2; Espinosa, *SFNM*, nos. 13, 16; Paredes, no.
      34; Rael, nos. 153, 154, 155, 156, 157, 166.
   Argentina: Chertudi, 1st series, no. 45 (425A).
   Chile: *AUC*, vol. 92, pp. 67–74; *BTPE*, vol. 1, pp. 126–136; Gon-
      zález, *AFCH*, 3(1951), 97–100; Laval, *Cuentos populares*, nos.
      12, 13, 14, 15, 16; Pino Saavedra, nos. 43, 44, 45, 250; Vicuña
      Cifuentes, pp. 185–190 (4 versions); *RCHG*, I, p. 100.
   Dominican Republic: Andrade, nos. 117, 152, 182, 183 (425A).
   Ecuador: Carvalho Neto, no. 44.
   Puerto Rico: Arellano, nos. 63, 64, 82 (425A); Mason, *JAF*,
      27(1914), 179, no. 15; 39(1926), 291, no. 21; Mason-Espinosa,
      JAF, 38(1925), 607, nos. 12, 12a; 610, no. 12c; 39 (1926), 628,
      no. 21f; 292, no. 21y.
   Spain: Ampudia, no. 1; Cortes Vázquez, nos. 44, 45; Curiel Mer-
      chán, pp. 82–88, 142–144, 167–169; *BTPE*, vol. 2, pp. 25–37;
      Espinosa, *Castilla*, nos. 111, 112, 113; Espinosa, *Cuentos*, nos.
      126, 127, 128, 130; *El folklore frexnense y bético-extremeño*, pp.
      17–18, 89–96, 239–244, 244–268; Henderson, p. 9; Hernández de
      Soto, *BTPE*, vol. 10, p. 139, no. 9; p. 159, no. 12; p. 217, no. 18;
      p. 242, no. 20; Sánchez Pérez, nos. 45, 92.
   Venezuela: Monroy Pittaluga, *AFV*, I, p. 366.
Aarne-Thompson 707. The Three Golden Sons.
Boggs 707.
Hansen 707. The Three Golden Sons.
Reid, "A Comparative Study of a Spanish Folktale . . . *Los siete infan-
   tes.*"

Thompson, *Folktale*, pp. 120–122.
Grimm, no. 96.

> Mexico: Mason, *JAF*, 27(1914), 200–203; Robe, *Mexican Tales*, nos. 91, 92, 93, 94, 95; Wheeler, nos. 70, 73, 74, 76.
> United States: Campa, *WF*, 6(1947), 326, no. 2; Espinosa, *SFNM*, no. 9; Rael, nos. 123, 124, 125.
> Chile: Kössler-Ilg, pp. 118–122; Laval, *Cuentos populares*, I, no. 13 (and pp. 283–284); Lenz, *RFC*, 3(1912), 57–76; Pino Saavedra, nos. 95, 96, 261.
> Dominican Republic: Andrade, nos. 60, 61, 62.
> Ecuador: Carvalho Neto, no. 45.
> Panama: Riera Pinilla, nos. 24, 25.
> Puerto Rico: Arellano, nos. 60, 61, 62.
> Spain: Ampudia, nos. 6, 19, pp. 68–69 (variant of no. 19); Caballero, *Cuentos, oraciones*, p. 31; idem, *Cuentos y poesías populares andaluces*, pp. 31–43; Cortes Vázquez, no. 26; Curiel Merchán, pp. 63–67, 284–286; Espinosa, *Castilla*, nos. 138, 139, 140, 141; Espinosa, *Cuentos*, nos. 119, 129; *Folklore andaluz*, pp. 305–308; *La gran conquista de Ultramar* (*BAE*, XLIV); Hernández de Soto, *BTPE*, vol. 10, p. 175, no. XIV; Menéndez Pidal, p. 342; Soupey, p. 115; Wolf, 152.

Rank, *Myth of the Birth of the Hero* (contains a psychological study of Mt. 707).

73. Blancaflor

(Recorded by Candelario Gallardo on December 2, 1966, in Oxnard, California)

A prince falls in love with Blancaflor through hearing his parents talk of her and decides to kidnap her and marry her. Posing as a merchant, he gets her to come aboard his ship to see his wares and then sets sail with her captive on the ship. His servant, José, who understands the language of the birds, overhears a conversation of several gulls, and thereby learns of two threats to the lives of the prince and Blancaflor, as well as the means of preventing their deaths. Upon reaching shore, José is to kill a horse offered to the prince by a handsome Negro, which will thus prevent the death of the prince; later, when Blancaflor falls dead at a dance, he is to revive her by placing four drops of wax in the form of a cross over her heart. These things take place, but the prince becomes furiously jealous when he sees what appear to be José's inappropriate attentions to Blancaflor as he is reviving her, and he orders José executed. José's last words are to assert his innocence, after which he turns into stone. The prince and Blancaflor, in deep remorse, vow that they would give anything to see José returned to life. Some years later, after three sons have been born to them, José tells the prince that, if he will kill his sons and bathe him in their blood, he will return to life. The prince agrees to do so, and José is restored to life. Then, after miraculously replacing the severed heads of the three sons, the prince tests Blancaflor, asking her if she would agree to kill her own sons in return for bringing José back to life, and she refuses. The prince says that he has already done it, that José is alive once again, and that he miraculously revived the sons also.

Voy a contarles este cuento . . . de un . . . adulto, muy ancianito. Él nos los contaba para que todos los niños nos divirtiéramos. Y así es de que como yo, también yo estoy ancianito, así quiero complacerlos a los que lo oyen. Y así como nos los contó el ancianito se lo voy a ofrecer.

Así es de que . . . ésta era una reina que se llamaba Blancaflor. Esta reina era muy hermosa, muy bonita. Su pelo quebrado, sus ojos grandes, azules, su boquita chiquita. Bueno, todas las cualidades tenía la reina. Muy bella. Y sus padres estaban orgullosos de su hija, que era muy hermosa.

Así es de que . . . había también en un reinado un príncipe. Este príncipe también era muy, muy simpático, muy . . . muy bonito, muy generoso. Y también sus padres eran reyes. Y sus papás conocían muy bien a Blancaflor, que era muy hermosa. Y ellos platicaban. Dicía:
—Quisiera que . . . que nuestro hijo se casara con Blancaflor. Porque la pura verdad, es muy . . . muy hermosa. Eso dicían los papás de este príncipe.

Pero el príncipe oía todas las versiones de sus padres, que había una . . . una reina que se llamaba Blancaflor, que era muy hermosa. Así es de que este príncipe estaba muy enamorado de ella, y sin conocerla (1).

Pero un día este príncipe, pues, dice: —Yo me voy a ir hasta donde está Blancaflor. Pero para esto necesito yo, dice, —mandar hacer una poca de vajilla pa írsela a ofrecer a la reina. Entonces le dice, le dice a José el criado: —Oye, José, ¿tú no has oído a mis papás, que hay una reina que . . . se llama Blancaflor, que es muy hermosa y muy bonita?

—Hombre, sí, dice, —sí, los he oído yo al rey y a la reina . . . que
. . . es muy hermosa Blancaflor.

—Bueno, dice, —sabes que vamos por ella. Nos vamos a ir perdidos hasta donde está la reina.

—Pos, como usted mande, príncipe (2).

Dice: —Pero pa esto, dice, —anda . . . a todos los plateros del pueblo. Manda . . . manda hacer una vajilla de puro oro y plata, para irnos de mercaderes donde está Blancaflor.

Tonces mandaron hacer la vajilla, ¿verdad?, de puro oro y plata,
muy hermosa la vajilla. Y se embarcaron . . . rumbo al reinado donde
vivía Blancaflor. Entonces le dice al tripulante del barco, dice: —Mire, dice, —vamos a ir por la reina Blancaflor. Y usted se va a poner
muy listo. Cuando ya nosotros entremos con la reina al barco usted le
da toda la velocidad al barco, porque nos la vamos a secuestrar (3).

—'Tá bien, príncipe.

Así lo hicieron. Entonces echaron un . . . una poca de vajilla en una
charola de puro . . . de pura plata, la cosa más hermosa. Se la fueron a
ofrecer a la reina él y José. Entonces llegaron a palacio. Y andaba . . .
una niña en el balcón.

Le dice el príncipe: —Ándale, José. Háblale, dice. —Allá anda la
reina. ¡Mira no más qué hermosa!

Entonces José le, le decía: —Niña, niña, niña, ¿no comprará, dice,
—esta poca de vajilla?

Dice: —Señor, señor, dice, —voy a avisarle a la reina. Yo nada más
soy la criada.

Dijo el príncipe: —Mira no más, dice. —Si ésta es la criada, tan
hermosa y tan bonita, pos la reina, ¿cómo estará?

Entonces jue a avisarle la criada a la reina. —Por acá . . . por aquí
le hablan unos mercaderes, niña. Pos fue.

Oooo, que va viniendo. Tan hermosa, tan bonita que el príncipe
hasta los ojos se le querían salir. Y: —Niña, niña, ¿no comprará una
poca de vajilla?

—Sí, dice. —La necesito.

—Bueno, dice. Entonces ya se la enseñó.

Pero nada más que es muy poca vajilla. Yo necesito bastante.

—Niña, dice, —pues yo en mi barco tengo la . . . suficiente vajilla, pa si gusta ir al barco, pues vamos.

Y ya . . . dice la reina, dice: —Bueno, me espera un poquito, dice. —Sí, cómo no.

Entonces ya se arregló la . . . la reina, y se jue con ellos al barco. Pero ya como el tripulante estaba muy . . . ya, ya le había avisado, el príncipe le había avisado, cuando entraron al barco desenganchó el, el barco, y que le dio toda la velocidad que pudo el tripulante.

Y luego aquel príncipe: —Mire, niña, y que aquí está esto, y a ver si le gusta esto, y a ver si este otro, y . . . y mire, aquí está esto . . . más bonito. Pos, entreteniéndola, pos, ¿verdad?, porque el barco caminaba.

Entonces cuando ya hicieron el trato de la vajilla: —Bueno, dice, —pos entonces voy a traer para llevar la vajilla. Cuando quiso salir . . . del barco, no más cielo y agua. Dijo: —¡Ay, Dios, príncipe! ¿Qué ha hecho conmigo?

—No se apure, señorita, dice. —Yo también soy rey. Yo soy hijo del rey. Y especialmente vengo por usted. Así es de que no se apure.

Bueno, tanto le fue avisando hasta que la sedució. Luego que ya la sedució ya . . . iban muy contentos . . . ya platicando. Ya, pos, ¿qué hacía pos la reina, pos, verdad?

José, que era el criado, se sentó en la piramíde [*sic*] del barco. Y vido para arriba. Y áhi arriba del piramíde iban . . . iban tres gaviotas. Y como este José . . . ese don le había dado Dios de entenderles a los pájaros, ellas iban platicando allá arriba (4, 5).

Dicía una . . . una gaviota: —Ay, Dios, dice, —la hija del rey va hurtada. Pero cuando llegue a tierra se le presentará . . . un hombre de color con un caballo muy fino y una cabalgadura muy bonita. Pero . . . al tiempo que acepte el caballo el príncipe, cairá muerto y no gozará a Blancaflor. Eso dijo la primer gaviota (6, 7).

Y luego dice la otra gaviota, dice: —Pero si José que lo acompaña al momento le mata el caballo, entonces sí gozará a Blancaflor (8).

Y luego dice la otra . . . gaviota: —Pero cuando esté en las bodas y que estén . . . pues . . . con aquel gusto, que andan bailando, entonces en la pieza que estaba tocando la orquesta, "Olas del Danubio," cairá muerta Blancaflor (9). Entonces si José que lo acompaña, al momento que cae muerta Blancaflor, le descubre el seno y le pone en el corazón cuatro gotas en cruz en el corazón entonces vivirá Blancaflor (8).

Entonces andaba bailando, agitada Blancaflor, y cae muerta. Pero aquel José, como estaba listo, luego luego fue y le, le descotó su pecho y le puso cuatro gotas . . . en cruz en el corazón (10, 11, 12).

Pero en eso llega el príncipe. Y halló a José poniéndole esas cuatro gotas de . . . de cera en el corazón, y entonces se enceló mucho el príncipe. Dice: —¿Qué pasó?

—Príncipe, pues sabe que cayó muerta Blancaflor. Y yo, . . . por eso le estoy poniendo aquí cuatro gotas de cera en el corazón en cruz.

—¡Qué cruz ni qué nada! dice. —Te voy a matar. Mira no más lo que has hecho con mi esposa (13).

—Pos, está bien, príncipe. Lo que usted . . . guste.

Entonces ya le formaron el cuadro, el rey enojadísimo, el papá del príncipe. —No, dice, —hay que matarlo. Entonces lo iban a matar, cuando dice: —¿Qué mercedes pides?

—Bueno, dice, —yo quiero hablar unas palabras aquí ante el público, y aquí ante Blancaflor y ante el príncipe.

—Pos diga, dice. —¿Qué palabras son?

Dice: —Mira, príncipe, si usted hubiera aceptado el caballo, al tiempo de usarlo con su . . . con su esposa que iba a ser, entonces hubiera cáido [*sic*] usted muerto, y no hubiera gozado a Blancaflor. Pero como la, la reina, al tiempo de matar el caballo, dijo, "Déjelo, príncipe," dice, "él sabe lo que hace," tonces ya se . . . ya el príncipe, pues lo que ella dice, ¿verdad? Dice: —Cuando usted estaba en las bodas y que andaban bailando . . . angustiosamente, muy gustosos, en el vals "Olas del Danubio," cayó muerta Blancaflor. Pero como yo estaba allá al pendiente, lo que las gaviotas me habían dicho, entonces yo le estaba haciendo la curación. Así es de que así es, príncipe. Y . . . y se volvió una estatua . . . de piedra, José. Invisiblemente se volvió una piedra . . . con ojos y todo, pero de piedra (14).

Oooo, entonces toditita la gente hincada allí de rodillas. El príncipe, pos, apuradísimo. Blancaflor también. Lloraban los dos. Él . . . los papás, que eran del príncipe, . . . toda la gente lloraba . . . por ver a José hecho piedra. Y dice: —Ay, dicían todo el tiempo.

Luego que tenían tiempo ya de casados. Todos los días casi iban allí a persignarse ... con José, que era la piedra. Dicía Blancaflor: —Ay, dice, —qué diera yo, dice, —por ver a José como enantes era. Yo daría todas mis riquezas, todo lo que tengo, por ver a ... a José como enantes era.

Dice el príncipe: —Yo también acepto eso, dice. —Yo daría todo lo que tengo por ver a José como enantes era. Y así era todos los días ... que se persignaban. Y cada vez que se acordaban iban y le gritaban allí a él.

Hasta que un día, ... Blancaflor era muy ... muy devota. Iba a rezos y iba a misa. Y un domingo se jue Blancaflor a misa. Y el príncipe se fue a llorarle, diciéndole que ... pidiéndole a Dios que le concediera ese milagro ... de ver a José como enantes era, y llorando, pidiéndole de corazón que ... que le concediera Dios ese milagro. Hasta que la piedra le respondió, ... José.

Dice: —¿De veras me quieres, dice, —de ... verme como enantes era?

—Sí, José, sí, te quiero ver. Tú eres, de todas mis riquezas tú eres el dueño. Y Blancaflor también acepta eso.

—Bueno, dice, —príncipe, ... voy que no hace una cosa.

Dice: —¿Qué cosa?, dice. —Dime.

Entonces ya tenían tres hijitos Blancaflor y el príncipe.

Dice: —¿Cómo no hace una cosa?

Dice: —¿Qué?

—Voy que no degüella a sus hijos (15).

Dice: —Los degüello. Cómo no.

Dice: —Pos ándale. Los degüellas y paras la sangre en una ... una cosa, una charola, y calientita la sangre, me das un baño desde la cabeza hasta los pies. Y entonces me verás como enantes era.

—Lo voy a hacer.

Tonces los niños andaban así jugando, ¿verdad?, allá en la mesita. Y él ya los iba a degollar. Ya estaba preparado ... el cuchillo y todo. Entonces le ... al más grandecito le vendó los ojos y luego le estiró el pescuecito, y luego con la cuchilla le ... mochó el pescuezo. Y luego paró la sangre en una bandeja. Y luego vino el otro, y ... y el otro.

Bueno, los tres. Y los degolló y paró la sangre en una charola (16). Y luego calientita, jue y le dio el baño de sangre desde la cabeza hasta los pies. Y áhi está José (17).

Dice: —Has cumplido tu promesa. Aquí estoy como enantes era.

—Ay, José, dice. —Degollé a mis hijos.

Dice: —No te apures, hombre. Ahorita, ¿ónde están los niños? Ya fueron allí y sí, ciertamente, pos áhi estaban . . . degollados. Entonces le dice José: —Anda, pos, dice, —pasa a la otra pieza y no salgas, dice, —hasta que yo te hable.

Entonces agarra las cabecitas, ¿verdad?, y el cuerpecito y los pegó. Y luego dijo: —Váyase a ver a su papá. Y áhi va, ya como si no le hubiera pasado nada. Y así a los tres. Les hizo la misma operación y áhi van los muchachitos igualmente. Como si no les hubiera pasado nada (18, 19).

Y luego ya dice: —Venga, príncipe, para acá. Que le hablan sus niños. ¡Hombre, qué caray, igualitos, hombre!

Y entonces el príncipe dice: —Tú eres un santo. Le dice: —José, dice, —vamos a calar a . . . a Blancaflor. No tarda en venir de misa, y le vamos a decir que . . . que ella desea, pues que verte como enantes eras, le voy a decir que si no degüella a sus hijos. Escóndete, José. Áhi viene.

Ya se escondió. Ya vino muy contenta Blancaflor. —Oye, Blancaflor, dice, —¿qué dieras tú por ver a José como enantes era?

—Ya te dije . . . que daría todas mis riquezas, todos mis bienes. Y llorando: —Yo quiero ver a José como enantes era.

Dice: —Voy que no haces una cosa.

Dice: —¿Qué cosa, príncipe?

Dice: —Voy que no degüellas a tus tres hijos (15).

—¡Ay, dice, —sí no! Eso sí no, príncipe. Sí no los degüello.

—Ay, dice a Blancaflor, —yo te voy a decir, pues yo los degollé.

Y pega el grito: —¡Cómo que los degollastes!

—Sí. Pero no te vas a asustar. Dice: —Este José es un santo. Yo los degollé, mire, y le di un baño desde la cabeza hasta los pies, y . . . y vas a ver. José, ven para acá. Y va viniendo. Va viniendo José como enantes era.

—Pero, ¿qué pasó?, dice Blancaflor.

Dice: —Pos lo bañé con la sangre calientita. Le di un baño desde la cabeza hasta los pies, y . . . aquí tienes a José . . . como enantes era.

Y . . . y así es de que si . . . aquí les conté este cuento, ¿verdad? Si es de que les gusta, pues, pueden oírlo, ¿verdad? Pero yo se los conté como . . . el ancianito ese viejito, yo se los conté. Por eso sé los cuentos. Si les parece y lo quieren oír y quieren divertirse, ya yo se los conté.

Y aquí se termina el cuento de Blancaflor.

The story is structured as follows: 516 I*c (hearing his parents speak of her) IIa IIIa**7 (Prince will disappear when he mounts horse unless someone kills it) a**9 (If prince dances with princess she will die unless someone puts four drops of wax in form of cross over her heart) IVabcd Vac.

   Aarne-Thompson 516. Faithful John.
   Boggs 516.
   Hansen 516. Faithful John.
(1) T11.1. Love from mere mention or description.
(2) P361. Faithful servant.
(3) K1332. Seduction by taking aboard ship to inspect wares.
(4) B216. Knowledge of animal languages.
(5) B215. Bird language.
(6) B143. Prophetic bird.
(7) M352. Prophecy of particular perils to prince on wedding journey.
(8) N452. Secret remedy overhead in conversation of animals (witches).
(9) T175. Magic perils threaten bridal couple.
(10) R169.4.1. Rescue of bride from mysterious perils by hidden faithful servant.
(11) D1766.6. Magic results from sign of cross.
(12) E79. Resuscitation by magic.
(13) N342.1. Faithful servant guarding master's wife from danger falsely condemned for betraying his master.
(14) D231. Transformation: man to stone.
(15) H1558. Tests of friendship.
(16) S268. Child sacrificed to provide blood for cure of friend.
(17) D766.2. Disenchantment by application of blood.
(18) E783.1. Head cut off and successfully replaced.
(19) E30. Resuscitation by arrangement of members.
   Thompson, *Folktale*, pp. 111–112.
   Grimm, no. 6.
      United States: Espinosa, *SFNM*, no. 46 (last part); Rael, no. 205.
      Chile: Montenegro, p. 215 (last part); Pino Saavedra, nos. 81, 82.
      Dominican Republic: Andrade, no. 124.
      Puerto Rico: Arellano, nos. 81a, 81b.
      Spain: Fernández de los Ríos, p. 140; Hernández de Soto, *BTPE*, vol. 10, p. 225, no. 19.

74. La esposa infiel

(Recorded by Candelario Gallardo on November 25, 1966,
in Oxnard, California)

A husband and wife feel such great love for each other that they make a vow that, whenever one dies, the other will be buried alive with the dead spouse. When the wife dies, the husband's enthusiasm for the agreement diminishes; he has himself buried with her but stays alive by breathing through a reed that emerges above ground. As they lie buried the husband observes how a rat revives his dead love with a flower, and he uses the same flower to resuscitate his wife. They call to the gravediggers through the reed and are freed by them. When they go to the priest to whom the husband had given his life savings, thinking he would have no further use for his money, the priest returns part of the money, but says that the couple must leave town permanently in order not to prove an embarrassment to him, as he had already said masses for them. The couple set off on their journey into exile, and soon the husband becomes weary and decides to rest at the side of the road. While he sleeps, a rich and powerful captain spots the wife from afar, approaches, and succeeds in enticing her to accompany him to his land to live there as his wife. When the husband awakens he is informed by a shepherd about what has happened, and the shepherd tells him how to reach the land of the captain, giving him his own clothes as a disguise. The husband finds his way there and succeeds in getting an appointment as an attendant to the governor's wife, who is really his own wife. The latter soon tells her new-found husband, the governor, that she is displeased with the attendant, and the governor plots to get rid of him by planting a stolen article on him and then condemning him to death. The husband, disguised as the shepherd, however, still carries with him the magic flower, and he arranges to have himself resuscitated after death. He escapes and manages to find employment in the service of a king, whose daughter soon falls in love with him and is determined to have him as her husband. He is forced to reveal his situation in explanation of why he cannot marry the princess, whereupon her father immediately plans a visit to the land of the governor in order to see what can be done. Once there, he demands to see all marriage licenses, and, upon discovering that the governor himself is not legally married to the woman he is living with, the legal wife of the man his daughter wants to marry, he orders them both executed, thus making it possible for his daughter to marry the man she has chosen.

Voy a dedicar a la Señorita Miller un cuento que ella, pues, desea tener en . . . sus libros.

Este cuento es, es de un borreguerito, que le . . . pasó a él en su vida. Había . . . había un señor, un matrimonio, que se querían mucho. Y cuando ellos estaban platicando sus pláticas de ellos eran: —Ay, si tú te murieras, ¿qué hiciera yo?

—Aaa, dice, —si tú te morías, yo me moría también. Y todo eso, pues, eran sus pláticas de ellos . . . todas las noches.

Entonces le dice el hombre: —¿Que me quieres mucho?

—Ooo, dice, —te adoro.

—Bueno, dice. —¿Cómo no hacemos una cosa?

—A ver. ¿Qué?

—Si yo me muero, tú te mueres también. Yo me entierro junto contigo si tú te mueres. Entonces hicieron un juramento: el que se muriera primero, el otro que estaba vivo moría también. Se enterraba junto con . . . con ella (1).

Pero como a la señora le tocó la suerte . . . de morir, dice: —¡Ay, caray!, dice. Ya la señora ya se murió. Y dice: —Yo, pues, pues ya hicimos ese juramento. Pues yo también me voy a enterrar junto con ella.   . .

Entonces ya los que estaban haciendo allí la sepultura, la fosa, les dice: —Háganla anchita, dice, —porque yo también me voy a morir. Me voy a enterrar áhi junto, dice, —porque hicimos un juramento con mi esposa, que . . . si se muriera primero, dice, —me enterraba también . . . allí junto con ella.

Entonces los, los que estaban haciendo el hoyo lo hicieron anchita. Y . . . y él también se enterró (2). Pero éste jue vivo. Entonces jue a . . . a . . . por ahí, quién sabe dónde, se halló una pipita, y luego la . . . la echó pa arriba para resollar, para agarrar respiración. Y . . . por allí resollaba. Pos tenía oxígeno. Y no . . . no estaba muerto.

Entonces . . . vido salir de un rinconcito un, un ratoncito . . . que andaba para ahí y para acá y para ahí y para acá (3). Y luego vido una ratita que estaba muerta. Era su compañera. Y iba y corría y le besaba el piquito, y . . . y se metía al agujerito, y andaba loco el . . . ratoncito, por su ratita. Entonces . . . el ratoncito tanto corrió por ahí, que se halló una florecita. Y . . . y ahí va y lleva al piquito la florecita. Se la

. . . se la pone en la boquita a la ratita. Y que revive la ratita, con la florecita que le puso en las narices (4, 5, 6). Y entonces corrieron los dos y se metieron al . . . al hoyo y dejaron la florecita.

Y el hombre, viendo el que estaba muerto vivo allí: —Por Dios, dice. —Esta florecita tiene . . . tiene virtud. Yo voy a acercarla a mi esposa. Entonces agarra la florecita y se la pone en la . . . en la boca a la esposa. ¡Y que revive, hombre (6, 7)!

Entonces, oía: —Pues, ¿en dónde me tienes?

—Pues, que, ¿no sabes que te moriste, tamién? Y estoy enterrado aquí porque hicimos el juramento.

—¿Y ahora, qué hacemos?

Dice: —O, dice, yo voy a hablar para arriba, dice. —Yo aquí tengo una pipita que sale para arriba. Y . . . y luego ya dice: —Sepulturero, . . . sepulturero.

Y entonces los que andaban allí cuidando el panteón, los que hacían los hoyos, dice: —¿No será un fantasma?

—No, dice, —será, . . . parece que los que enterramos ayer.

—Pos, vamos a ver.

Y luego ya . . . gritaba éste: —Sepulturero, . . . sepulturero.

Y, y luego ya. —¿Qué, qué pasa?, dice. —¿Qué, están vivos?

—Sí, sí, estamos vivos. Échennos para afuera.

Entonces agarran las palas los que andaban allí en . . . haciendo los hoyos para enterrar los muertos y, y los sacaron. —Pos, ¿qué pasó?

Dice: —Hombre, dice, —pos sabes que ya vivimos. Y él le contó la historia que había pasado con los ratoncitos.

—Bueno, está bueno.

Pero, . . . y este, este individuo, cuando ya se murió la esposa, le llevaron . . . tenían unos ahorros. Aquel dinerito que, que tenían ellos, pues, ya le llevaron a . . . al señor cura. —Señor cura, dice, —aquí están estos centavitos, dice. —Pos yo . . . ya . . . me, me voy a morir también. Le contó la historia cómo había pasado.

—O, dice, —está bueno. Éstos te sirven a ti pa las misas gregorianas. Son sesenta misas (8). Y para que . . . se vayan al cielo, con las sesenta misas se van a ir derechitos al cielo.

—Está bien.

Pero luego que ya vivieron, el hombre, pos, estaba pobre. Fue por el dinerito. Entonces ya . . . dice el padre, dice: —No, dice. —Pos, ¿si a cuál dinero?, dice. —Ya lo . . . ya no más queda la mitad, porque la otra mitad, pos, ya la emplié.

—Pos, 'tá bien. Era lo que quería . . . conformarse, pues, con . . . con la mitad.

Entonces le dice el cura, dice: —Te me vas a ir del pueblo . . . perdido, dice, —onde no . . . onde no te vean . . . aquí los del pueblo. Porque si saben que viven, dice, —hasta a mí me puede ir mal. Me pueden hasta matar. Y tú te me vas perdido.

Entonces, pos, ya vino con la mujer. Dice: —¿Sabes qué?, dice. —Nos vamos a ir perdidos. Porque el señor cura así lo dispone. Y, y nos vamos a ir perdidos. Así es de que . . . échanos ropita en los velices, y nos vamos a ir.

Entonces así lo hicieron. Se fueron por la orilla del mar, anda y anda y anda y anda y anda. Ya se cansaba la señora. Dice: —Mira, la esposa le dice. —¿Ves aquel árbol que está allá a orilla del mar? Está muy bonito, dice. —Allí vamos a descansar. Llegaron a aquel árbol . . . tan bonito aquel árbol que estaba a orilla del mar. Y el hombre iba, pues, con sueño. Entonces el hombre se acostó en las faldas de la, de la esposa, y empezó a dormirse. Y se durmió. Y él, . . . ella allí, pues, contemplándolo en su sueño a su esposo.

Pero en el mar venía, un, un barco . . . con gobierno. Entonces como el capitán trae los anteojos viendo a ver qué . . . qué mira, a ver qué hay, entonces echó los anteojos pa onde estaba aquel árbol. Y áhi estaba . . . la esposa. Ahí estaba la señora, muy bonita mujer. Le dice . . . a los que lo manejaban, dice: —Dale recio, dice, —al barco, dice. —Allá está una . . . muchacha muy preciosa. Bueno, pos sí. Le dieron . . . bastante gasolina a . . . al barco y llegaron allá. Y luego ya llega el capitán. —¿Quihúbole? ¿Qué está usted haciendo aquí, señorita?

—Señor, dice, —vamos de camino.

—Pero, ¿es posible, dice, —que usted vaya de camino, y cara de trampa?, dice. —Mire cómo anda. Viene no más como la trae el, el hombre, . . . falta de ropa y luego tan . . . con, con hambre. ¿Qué es de usted este señor?

—Señor, es mi esposo.

—No, dice. —Vámonos conmigo. Yo soy capitán del gobierno y tengo dinero y tengo . . . mucho poder. Vámonos conmigo. Yo voy a ser su esposo. Yo la quiero pa . . . para mi esposa.

—No, señor. Yo tengo aquí mi esposo. Yo no puedo dejarlo.

Pues tanto le platicó el capitán que la sedució. Entonces dice: —¿Y cómo le hacemos?, dice. —Él está aquí, pues, en mis faldas.

—No, dice, —usted no más me dice que sí, y yo hago . . . lo a un ladito.

—Bueno, pues entonces está bien. Entonces el capitán, pues, no más lo hizo a un lado, y . . . y áhi va la señora con el capitán al barco. Y áhi van (9).

Llegaron allá a la isla donde estaban. Ooo, pues era un laberinto. Que el capitán, que qué bonita mujer, y que qué bonita muchacha y que se, y que se va a casar el capitán y, ooo, el gobierno allí, un laberinto que hacían. Pues que . . . bien.

Entonces, . . . no, que despertó el, el . . . el esposo. Empezó a llora y llora porque no hallaba su esposa. Y: —Ayayay. Y: —¿Dónde está mi esposa? Y: —¿Dónde estás, esposa mía? Y a llora y llora y llora y llora, porque a pesar de que era . . . orillas del mar, había selvas y . . . y monte como, una selva pues.

Entonces un borreguerito que cuidaba sus borregas estaba escondido . . . onde . . . 'taba viendo toditita la . . . todo lo que decía, todo lo que hizo, el capitán, . . . y todo lo que decía . . . el señor por su esposa. Entonces sale el borreguero y le dice: —¿Por qué llora, hombre?

—¿Cómo por qué, señor?, dice. —A mí me robaron, o, —¿Dónde está mi esposa? ¿Dónde está?, dice. —¿La comería alguna fiera?

—Nada de fiera, dice. —Áhi vino un capitán, dice, —en un barco, dice. —Y . . . y él estuvo, . . . le hizo el amor y se la llevó. O, pues más lloraba . . . más lloraba aquel señor. Y luego le dice el borreguero: —Ya no llore, señor. Yo le voy a dar el camino, dice, —pa que vaya . . . allá onde está su esposa (10). Dice: —Pero para esto, dice, —necesita que me, que cambiemos de ropa. Usted me da su vestido y yo le doy mi vestido de borreguero. Usted se viste de borreguero y . . . y yo le . . . le enseño el camino (11).

Pos así lo hicieron. Entonces se fueron a . . . se fueron el borreguerito y el señor, y él le enseñó el camino. Como pudieron, . . . como pudo pasó, deteniéndose de ramas y . . . y como que nadando y agarrándose de . . . balsas de . . . agua, y en fin él pasó.

Y luego que ya pasó para allá, . . . no, dice, luego luego se vino uno de los soldados. Dice: —Hombre, viene un borreguero, dice. —¿Qué quedrá? ¿Quihubo, borreguerito? Pos, ¿qué andas haciendo tú aquí?

Dice: —Hombre, pues vengo a solicitar trabajo.

—Mm, pos aquí trabajo no hay, borreguerito. Aquí lo que hay es puras armas, para ir a echar . . . pues, balazos. Así es de que si quieres solicitar las armas yo te puedo arreglar . . . te puedo arreglar el trabajo.

—Sí, sí, las agarro.

Pos que ya fueron para allá con el capitán. —Mi capitán, dice, —aquí el borreguerito solicita las armas.

—Mm, dice, —pero pos, para eso, dice, —necesita que sea bueno. Yo tengo aquí personas que cada . . . los que quieren solicitan trabajo. Si son buenos, les doy. Si no, no les doy.

Pos que sí. Luego luego trajeron un . . . un hombre que lo escalaba. Y luego luego le dieron un . . . un arma, una espada, al borreguerito y otra al que lo escalaba. Mmm, pues, luego luego el borreguerito se lo echó. Le ganó.

Dice el capitán: —Éste es de los míos. Éste sí es bueno. Pero este hombre, dice, —no lo voy a llevar por allá, que lo maten, dice. —Se lo voy a llevar a mi esposa para que . . . lo mande, . . . que haga . . . los mandatos.

Pos que ya lo llevaron a ella (12, 13). —Mira, le dice, —mira, aquí te traigo este borreguerito para que tú lo, lo . . . lo que tú quieras. ¡Cómo, cómo, . . . cómo se mirarían! Si ellos se conocían. El borreguerito conocía a su esposa y la esposa conocía al borreguerito. ¡Cómo creen que haigan sufrido! Pos así estaban . . . calladitos ¿no?

Llegaba el capitán. —¿Cómo te ha tratado el borreguerito, esposa?

—Ooo, dice, —muy bien. Muy bien me ha tratado.

—Bueno, dice, —vale que siga así.

Y luego a poquito ya le volvió a decir: —¿Cómo te ha tratado el borreguerito?

—Eh, si vieras que ya . . . casi ya me está cayendo gordito.

—Bueno, dice, —pos si te cae gordo ya el borreguerito, que ya no lo, ya no lo quieres muy bien, pos lo vamos a fusilar.

—Ay, ¿cómo lo vas a fusilar?, dice. —Él no ha hecho nada.

—No, dice, —para . . . esto, dice, —le voy a echar mi centillo de oro en la bolsa sin que él se dé cuenta. Y lo . . . yo sé de qué manera voy a hacerlo (14).

El borreguerito andaba áhi afuera . . . descuidadamente. Agarra el centillo el . . . el capitán, y se lo echa. Sin que él sintiera, se lo echó a la bolsa. Y luego hizo el barrullo el capitán. —A ver, dice, —se me perdió mi centillo de oro. Y así es de que al que lo halle, lo voy a fusilar. Forme toda la tropa.

Entonces el capitán, el capitán le dice: —Mira no más, dice. —Después de que yo creía que tú eras un hombre de bien, te hallé yo mi centillo de oro (15). Así es de que . . . yo te voy a fusilar por lo que hicistes. Entonces ya le . . . iban a . . . formar el escuadro para fusilarlo. Y le dice el capitán: —¿Qué mercedes pides?

Dice: —Señor, dice, —yo quisiera que . . . que me dejara hablar con, con el soldado que me consiguió el trabajo.

—Ándele, dice, —vaya . . . vaya a hablar allá con él.

Y entonces le dice: —Me van a fusilar, compañero. Pero cuando ya me afusile, . . . te voy a dar este, esta florecita. Y . . . y cuando las . . . a la una, las dos de la mañana, cuando tú quieras, me la pones en las narices y yo revivo.

—Está bien, dice. —Así lo haré.

—Aquí está la florecita. Agarró la flor y la guardó.

Entonces ya dice el capitán: —¿Ya, ya habló?

—Sí, señor, dice, —ya.

—Hora, sí, a fusilarlo. Tonces lo . . . lo afusilaron, y luego el capitán se arrimó y en la cabeza le dio el tiro de gracia.

Y luego el que le consiguió el trabajo: —Mi capitán, hágame el favor de que yo vele . . . el borreguerito, onde yo sé, solo por áhi, onde vaya y llore yo solo por allá.

—Ándele, sí. Cárguelo, cárgueselo, lléveselo onde usted quiera.

Entonces ya como . . . cuando él lo estaba velando, como a las doce de la noche, le, agarra la florecita y se la pone en . . . en las narices.

¡Hombre, que revive (6)! Dice: —¡Ooo, qué cara, hombre! Pues, de veras, esta florecita tiene virtud. Pero hora, hora, hora me mata a mí el . . . el capitán.

—No, dice. —Mira, te vas a ir por donde yo te dije . . . que estaba el camino. Y yo le voy a decir que te enterré.

—Bueno, está bien.

Entonces el borreguerito, como . . . había llegado, sabía el camino, ...pasó al otro lado. Y como enantes, en aquellos tiempos eran puras guerras y puros reyes, éste se fue anda y anda y anda y anda. Y . . . y llegó a una ciudad. Pasó a solicitar otra vez trabajo . . . con los reyes que eran antes, que puras guerras había. Y ya solicita el trabajo con el rey. Dice: —Hombre, dice, —pues 'tamos en guerra, dice. —Si quieres agarrar . . . las armas, dice, —sí, dice, —tal vez hay trabajo.

—Sí, sí, las agarro, mi rey.

—Está bien. Entonces ya . . . le dio trabajo. Y dice: —Tú no vas a las armas por allá, dice. —Estás muy joven, dice. —Tú, lo que vas a estar aquí. Tengo una hija, dice. —Tú le vas a atender a mi hija.

—'Tá bien.

Entonces . . . tanto tiempo el borreguerito era muy simpático y muy honrado. Pues . . . aunque le gustaba la, la muchacha. Pero nunca le dicía nada. Y la muchacha estaba enamorada de él (16). Pero . . . a veces quería dicirle y a veces no quería dicirle.

Hasta que un día se determinó la muchacha y le dice: —Bueno, borreguerito, dice, —¿que no sabe usted de que yo . . . estoy enamorada de usted (17).

—Ay, señorita, dice, —sí, comprendo el cariño, dice. —Me comprendo el cariño que usted me tiene, dice, —pero, pos que voy a ser serio con usted, señorita, dice.

—No, dice, —yo me caso con usted.

Dice: —Pero yo no puedo casarme.

—¿Por qué?

—Dice: —Yo soy casado.

—Pero, ¿cómo?

—Sí, sí, soy casado.

—¿Y su esposa?

Entonces dice: —Mire, señorita, le voy a decir. Un capitán que dicen que está en la isla . . . por áhi, una isla, dice, —ése se llevó a mi esposa. Se llevó a mi esposa en, . . . y luego yo, pues, . . . yo me quedé así. Y no puedo yo casarme con usted. Y . . . dicen que ese capitán . . . pos, era muy malo. Me mató, pero . . . [laughs], resulta de que . . . yo, pos, con una florcita que . . . que traía, me la puso el compañero en la nariz, y yo reviví, señorita. Pero yo no puedo casarme. Yo soy casado.

No, pues, luego que le dijo el borreguerito, dice: —No importa eso. Si yo lo arreglo. Con su padre.

Entonces ya . . . llega el papá que era el rey. Dice: —¿Cómo estás, hija? ¿Cómo te ha tratado el borreguerito?

—Papá, dice, —sabes que, . . . no te vas a enojar.

—¿Por qué, mi hija?

Dice: —Sabes que estoy muy enamorada . . . del borreguerito. Es un muchacho muy bueno. Dice: —Yo quiero casarme con él. Dice: —Pero me dice que él es casado, papá.

—¿Cómo que es casado?

—Sí. Pero mira, papá, dice, —dicen que el capitán le traicionó su mujer . . . su esposa. Y . . . y él no puede casarse.

—Pero, pos, . . . lo tenemos en la mano, hija. Yo soy el rey. Mando a toda la región, todo el . . . reinado. Entonces . . . dice, puso un telegrama . . . a la isla. Dice: "Prepárese, mi capitán," dice, "porque va a ir el rey . . . con su familia. Y así es que quiero que esté listo."

Ooo, luego luego, el capitán hizo un laberinto. Que va a venir el rey con su familia. Y adorno áhi en el campo y todo eso y . . . música. Y luego llega el rey allá con su familia. —A ver, mi capitán, ¿cómo ha estado?

—Bien, mi rey.

—Y la tropa, ¿cómo está?

—Pos, bien.

—Y bueno, dice el rey, dice, —todas estas mujeres que están aquí, . . . ¿están legalmente con sus . . . con sus esposos?

—Pues, yo creo que sí.

—Fórmelas, fórmelas.

Entonces ya se formaron todas las . . . los esposos con sus mujeres, y empezaron a sacarlos de uno por uno, a ver si estaban legalmente.

Pos que sí, que sí, que sí, todas estaban legalmente. Y luego le dice el rey: —A ver, usted, mi capitán. Usted también tiene su esposa. Tráigame usted su acta de matrimonio, a ver si está legalmente.

—Aa, que mi rey, que . . .

—No, no, no, no. Palabra del rey no vuelve atrás (18). Tráigame su acta de matrimonio.

¿Cuál, cuál, cuál acta de matrimonio? Pos tenía, pos si se la llevó, . . . pos no era su esposa. Entonces . . . pos ya le declaró que no tenía.

—Palabra del rey, lo vamos a fusilar. Los vamos a fusilar (19, 20).

Luego luego formaron el cuadro, ¿verdad? Y luego . . . ¡ponte! . . . los mató (21).

Dice: —Hora, sí, mi hija, está libre usted para que se case con el borreguerito (22). Y así jue la historia que pasó del borreguerito.

The story is constructed as follows: 612 Iab II a (mouse uses flower) III*a (they abandon the husband) *b (husband is falsely accused of theft and executed) IV a *a^1 (he enters service of another king, whose daughter wishes to marry him) b (killed) *d (he marries second king's daughter).

Aarne-Thompson 612. The Three Snake Leaves.
Boggs 612.
(1) M254. Promise to be buried with wife if she dies first.
(2) S123.2. Burial of living husband or wife with dead spouse.
(3) B437.2. Helpful mouse.
(4) B512. Medicine shown by animal.
(5) E181. Means of resuscitation learned.
(6) E105. Resuscitation by herbs (leaves.) [Here, by a flower.]
(7) E165. Resuscitation of wife by husband giving up half his remaining life.
        [The last part of the motif is not present.]
(8) Z71.13. Formulistic number: sixty.
(9) K2213.5. The faithless resuscitated wife.
(10) N841. Shepherd as helper.
(11) K1816.6. Disguise as herdsman (shepherd, swineherd, etc.).
(12) K1813. Disguised husband visits his wife.
(13) K1831.2. Service in disguise.
(14) K2213.3. Faithless wife plots with paramour against husband's life.
(15) K2127. False accusation of theft.
(16) T91.6.4. Princess falls in love with lowly boy.
(17) T55.1. Princess declares her love for lowly hero.
(18) M203. King's promise irrevocable.
(19) Q241. Adultery punished.
(20) Q261.2. Treacherous wife punished.
(21) Q411.4. Death as punishment for treachery.
(22) L161. Lowly hero marries princess.
        Mexico: Parsons, JAF, 45(1932), 307, no. 15; Robe, *Mexican Tales*,
            no. 85.
        United States: Rael, no. 227.   Spain: Thoms, p. 29, no. 4.

75. Los dos compadres

(Recorded by Angel Flores on July 14, 1967, in Oxnard, California)

A rich man and a poor man are traveling in the sierra. The poor man has brought no food for the trip, and when he asks his companion to share his food the latter agrees to do so only on the condition that the poor man, in return for the favor, will allow him to put out his eyes. Because of his great hunger, the poor man agrees to the condition, and he is then abandoned by his companion, who is thankful to be rid of him. He climbs a tree under which some robbers subsequently hold a meeting, and he thus overhears that the remedy for the blindness of a king in a nearby city is to be found in the leaves of the very tree in which he is sitting; and also that, in another city, where the people are dying of thirst, the place to find water is in the palace of the king himself. After the robbers leave, the man uses the leaves to restore his own sight, then goes and restores the sight of the blind king, and is rewarded with great riches. The rich man is very surprised to see that his companion has not only found his way back home, but has also become extremely wealthy; and, desiring to discover his secret, he succeeds in getting himself taken along on the next trip. Believing that the key to discovering his secret is to get his now very rich friend to do to him what he had originally done to him, to put out his eyes, the man does not bring any food for the trip, agrees to let his eyes be put out in exchange for some food from his companion, and is thus left blind. Meanwhile the companion goes off to accomplish the second of the two remedies he had overheard from the robbers. He digs a well right in the king's palace, water gushes forth, and the town is saved. Once again he is rewarded with great wealth. Meanwhile, the blind companion has climbed the same tree, and the robbers have once again met to exchange news of their findings. One of them reports that the king's eyesight has been restored with the leaves of that very tree and that water has been found for the town where the people were dying of thirst. When the tree is mentioned, they look up and see the blind man hiding there, and, believing he is the one who stole their secrets, they bring him down and kill him on the spot.

Bueno. Voy a contarles un cuento. Espero que los divierta y les guste un poco.

Éste eran dos compadres que uno era muy pobre y el otro era muy rico. Y de la pobreza que él tenía le dijo al compadre que lo llevara un día a sus viajes que tenía él a su . . . a otros pueblos. Y el compadre le acectó [i.e., aceptó] llevarlo con él. Pero de tan pobre que era pues no llevó comida, y el compadre rico llevó su comida en el camino. A los pocos días que tenían caminando le entró mucha hambre a uno de ellos y se puso a comer.

El compadre pobre, pues, lo miraba nada más y estaba con mucha hambre diciéndole que le diera que comer. Y el compadre rico le dijo que, que sí le daba que comer, pero que tenía que hacer un pacto con él . . . de sacarle un ojo. Y el compadre de pronto no acectó.

Luego después, a los dos, tres días de caminar le volvió a dar hambre al compadre y le volvió a pedir la comida. Le dijo que sí se dejaría sacar el ojo, pero que le diera de comer. El compadre acectó y le sacó el ojo y le dio la comida.

Entonces caminaron más. Y volvió el compadre a pedirle de comer a él. Y él le dijo que si almetía [i.e., admitía] sacarle el otro ojo que él le daba la comida. Pues sí. Le sacó el ojo. Y ya que le sacó el ojo entonces el compadre lo aventó, para dejarlo a media sierra donde iba él a . . . a traer sus viajes (1).

Luego siguió él caminando. Ya no miraba. Encontró un árbol, y allí se subió él arriba (2). Cuando a medianoche llegaron unos ladrones. Y él escuchó los pasos de ellos, y se asilenció pa oír a ver qué cosas decían (3).

En seguida oyó que estaba diciéndoles el . . . el jefe de ellos que qué cosas habían mirado en los pueblos, de uno al otro. Y le contestó uno que él lo que había mirado en una ciudad que la gente se estaba muriendo de la sed. Y que solamente en el palacio del rey podrían sacar el agua. Que era la única parte que había (4).

Luego le preguntó al segundo que qué cosa había encontrado él en su gira, en su camino. Le contestó el otro que él, en tal parte, había un rey que estaba ciego de los ojos, y que solamente con las hojas del árbol donde estaban podría aliviarse (5, 6).

Y el individuo que estaba arriba, que le sacaron los ojos, estaba escuchando lo que ellos estaban platicando. Entonces terminaron su reunión ellos.

Y le dijo: —Pues no. Vamos a guardar el dinero y vamos a seguir, dice, —a ver qué suerte nos toca. Seguimos, dice. Y fueron donde tenía la piedra.

Entonces el jefe de ellos le habló y le dice: —Ábrete, sésamos (7). Y abrió la piedra para los lados. Y vaciaron el dinero que traían, que habían robado (8). En seguida se fueron.

Y el compadre pobre estaba arriba con los ojos sacados. Pero luego que ellos se fueron, tomó unas hojas del árbol y se talló en un ojo. Y él . . . sintió que miró al momento (9). Entonces agarró más y volvió a tallarse en el otro ojo. Y lo que hizo, se bajó del árbol, agarró unas hojas, y se fue a donde había oído de la ciudad que el rey estaba ciego de los ojos.

Se fue, y llegó a con una viejita al pueblo. Y estaba el pueblo muy triste. Entonces preguntó que por qué estaba la ciudad muy triste. Le contestó la viejita que el pueblo estaba de luto porque el rey estaba ciego. Y por eso el pueblo estaba de luto. Entonces él contestó que si el rey almetía que lo curara que él podría curarlo, regresarle su vista.

Luego la viejita corrió a avisarle que había un hombre que podría curarle la vista, y que volvería a ver. Entonces el rey ordenó a uno de sus mozos que fueran a traerlo. Y fue. Lo llevó a su casa y le dijo que si él podría curarlo. Y le dijo que sí, que él lo curaba a modo de que él volviera a mirar.

Dice: —Bueno, si tú me curas y yo vuelvo a mirar, yo te regalo la mitad de mi riqueza, dice, —pa que tú te la lleves (10).

Pues, bien. Lo curó y el rey volvió a su . . . estado de mirar (11, 12). Cuando estaba aliviado, ordenó que se le hiciera un banquete al que lo curó. Luego le ordenó a uno de los mozos que le cargaran cinco mulas de dinero para que se las llevara a su casa (13, 14).

Pues él, contento, se las llevó a su casa. Llegó. . . . Entonces el compadre rico que le sacó los ojos tuvo mucha almiración de que, cómo había regresado, siendo que él en la sierra le había sacado los ojos y lo había dejado a modo de que se muriera y que ya no volviera, para que ya no lo enfadara.

Entonces le dijo que cómo era que volvió a ver y regresó con tanto dinero a su casa.

Entonces le contestó él: —No, compadre, dice. —Tengo que volver otra vez.

Entonces le dijo: —Compadre, dice, —si vas, quiero que me lleves contigo.

Pues sí, acectó él, y lo volvió a llevar. Entonces lo llevó a él. Y este individuo, por la envidia, no llevó comida, para modo de que le hiciera la misma que él le había hecho, de sacarle los ojos.

Se hizo en el camino que le dio mucha hambre para que le sacara los ojos. Entonces él vino y le dijo que sí le daba de comer pero que se dejara sacar los dos ojos. Entonces él acectó, de sacarle los dos ojos. Bueno, pues, ya él siguió su camino. Jue y le sacó los dos ojos (1), y volvió a donde estaba él en el árbol de antes (2).

El siguió su camino, y se fue a la otra ciudad donde estaba el otro rey, que estaba la gente muriendo de sed. Preguntó a uno de los . . . vivientes del pueblo. Y le contestó que la gente no tenía agua para tomar. Que por eso la gente estaba muriendo. Y que el rey daba una cantidad de dinero porque le sacara el agua de donde fuera, fuera . . . en su propio palacio o . . . en otro lado. Y él le dijo que sí él le sacaba el agua, pero debía de ser en su palacio de él mismo. Y él acectó. Hizo un hoyo en el palacio y ahí brotó el agua (11).

Entonces el rey le dio la mitad de su dinero que tenía por agradecimiento de que había vuelto a . . . sacar el agua para que la gente tomara (10).

Cuando él regresó a su pueblo halló la novedad de que el compadre no regresaba.

Entonces el compadre, donde lo dejó, volvió a subir al árbol donde había subido él. Cuando llegan unos ladrones. Hicieron su reunión en el árbol mismo. Y luego le preguntó que qué cosa habían oído, qué cosa habían visto.

Y le contestó uno, dice: —Yo, lo único que sé . . . que en el pueblo, en la ciudad donde yo le platiqué que el rey estaba ciego, pues alguien ya fue a curarlo. Y lo curaron con la misma hoja de este árbol.

Luego le dice el otro, dice: —Pues, también en el pueblo, dice, —donde yo fui, ya alguien sacó el agua en el palacio del rey.

Entonces cuando dijeron que sacaron el agua, y el rey otro volvió a mirar con las hojas de ese mismo árbol, uno de ellos miró para arriba.

Y lo miraron que estaba arriba (15). Entonces subió uno a bajarlo con tanto coraje, siendo de que lo agarraron y lo destrozaron entre todos por el mismo capricho de que les había jugado traición (16).

The story is structured as follows: 613 Ic II*c (robbers) III abc IV.

Aarne-Thompson 613. The Two Travelers (Truth and Falsehood).
Boggs 613.
Hansen 613. The Two Travelers (Truth and Falsehood).
(1) M225. Eyes exchanged for food.
(2) F1045. Night spent in tree. Hero goes into tree and spends the night.
(3) N451.1. Secrets of animals (demons) accidentally overheard from tree (bridge) hiding place. [Secrets of robbers.]
(4) N452.1. Remedy for lack of water in certain place overheard from conversation of animals (demons). [Conversation of robbers.]
(5) N452. Secret remedy overheard in conversation of animals (witches). [Conversation of robbers.]
(6) D1500.1.4. Magic healing plant.
(7) N455.3. Secret formula for opening treasure mountain overheard from robbers (Open Sesame).
(8) N512. Treasure in underground chamber (cavern).
(9) D1505.18. Tree restores sight.
(10) Q112.0.2. Half of property as reward. [Half of wealth.]
(11) H963. Tasks performed by means of secrets overheard from tree.
(12) D2161.3.1. Blindness magically cured.
(13) Q94. Reward for cure.
(14) Z71.3. Formulistic number: five.
(15) N471. Foolish attempt of second man to overhear secrets (from animals, demons, etc.). [From robbers.]
(16) Q261. Treachery punished.
Christiansen, "The Two Travelers," FFC 24, p. 18.
Libro de los gatos, no. 28.
Grimm, no. 107.
Mexico: Mason, *JAF*, 27(1914), 189, no. 19; Robe, *Mexican Tales*, no. 126; Wheeler, nos. 130, 131, 132.
United States: Rael, no. 262.
Chile: Pino Saavedra, no. 72.
Dominican Republic: Andrade, nos. 120, 121.
Puerto Rico: Mason-Espinosa, *JAF*, 37(1924), 181, no. 19; 281, no. 8; 291, no. 91; 39(1926), 295, no. 21; 334, no. 20; 354, no. 45.

76. El rancherito y las tres piedras

(Recorded by Candelario Gallardo on December 15, 1966, in Oxnard, California)

A king who is worried that his great wealth is frightening away potential suitors for his daughter sends out a decree announcing a search for the richest man and offering a prize of his daughter's hand in marriage. Word of the contest reaches a very poor rancher whose total wealth consists of one hundred sheep and a donkey. He decides that he, too, will try his luck at winning the princess for his wife, and he sets off toward the city with his flock of sheep. On three successive nights he finds three stones that give off an extraordinary light, and, unaware of their great value, he tosses them into his saddlebags. When he arrives at the royal palace he takes his place in line with the other suitors to present his wealth for the king's consideration, but he is treated as a drunk and a vagrant and is repeatedly thrown out of the line by the police. Nevertheless, he is determined, and so he spends the night on the doorstep in order to be the first in line the next day. The king is angered at the apparent mockery of the poor man's meager presentation, and he locks him up to await execution. On three successive nights he uses the three stones to provide light and thus attracts the attention of the princess who sends her servants to ask him to sell her the stones. He gives her two of them and offers the third in exchange for a promise to marry him. The princess recognizes the value of the stones, finds the man rather attractive, and so agrees to the condition. She then gives him all of her money and jewels in order to assure his being the richest of all. Meanwhile, the king has already selected the richest man, and he announces this to his daughter; but she reminds him of the poor man in the chapel and has him brought out to reassess his wealth. This time he presents the three stones, whose value easily places him beyond all competition, and the stones, together with the princess's money and jewels, win him the hand of the princess in marriage.

Este cuento que voy a contarles es de un rey. Este rey tenía una hija. Y esta hija, pos tal vez no le tocaba a ella ser casada todavía, porque ya era una señorita ya . . . mayor. Y en vista de que . . . pues, ni novio tenía ni nada, pues el rey y la reina estaban muy . . . pos, algo apurados.

Pero un día se le ocurrió al rey, le dice a la reina: —¿Sabes qué se me ha ocurrido?

—¿Qué cosa?, dice.

—Yo . . . yo quiero poner unos decretos a todos los países pa ver . . . de todas las personas, el que salga más rico, pos, se casa con nuestra hija, dice (1, 2). —Pos que . . . pos aquí, tú sabes, no ha tenido

novio porque pues tú sabes que semos muy ricos y . . . y el puesto que
ocupamos. Y tal vez un pobre, pues no se enamore de nuestra hija. Y
así poniendo unos decretos a todos los países que vengan los ricos a
manifestar su riqueza, y el individuo que salga más rico, pos él se casa
con nuestra hija.

Pues así lo hizo el rey. Puso unos decretos a todos los países y, pues
luego luego emprendieron sus, sus viajes los ricos, y a llevar todos sus,
sus capitales al reinado a . . . con el rey a ver si . . . les tocaba la feliz
suerte de casarse con, con la hija del, del rey.

Pero también hubo un, hubo un rancherito que tenía sus cien borreguitas y tenía una burrita. Y dice: —Hombre, dice, —pues yo también lo voy a hacer. Yo también voy a hacer el viaje, dice, —a ver si
me toca la suerte de casarme con la hija del rey (3). Pos llevo yo mis
cien borregas y mi burra. Pos este, este muchacho les avisó a sus papás
y, pos, los papás le hicieron, lo juzgaron, . . . no, pues luego le echaron
un, le echaron un lonch y áhi va con sus borreguitas, por toda una
selva . . . a dirección donde estaba aquel reinado.

Pues que se le hizo . . . se le estaba haciendo noche, . . . y luego pos
él no llevaba ni lámpara ni nada, ni, ni una velita, ni, casi ni cerillas ni
nada. Y se le iba a hacer noche por la, por la selva, por el camino que
llevaba. Pero más delante vido . . . una lumbre que iluminaba. Dice:
—Allá está un rancho, dice. —Allá voy a . . . quedar al rancho, dice.
Pos no. Llegó a onde estaba esa luminaria, y era una piedra que iluminaba (4, 5). Entonces él allí, pues se quedó. Dice: —Hombre, esta
piedrita me puede servir, dice, —pa cuando se me haga noche. Pos yo
me ilumino con esta piedrita. Llevaba sus arganitas el, el, el hombre.
Tonces agarró la piedra y se la echó a la arganita y siguió la ruta, . . .
caminando por la misma selva.

A más delante se le hizo, se le volvió a hacer noche. Y también era
otra piedra, otra iluminaria. Era otra piedra. Así es de que este muchacho, pues no las dejaba. Se las echaba a sus arganitas. Y ya más delante, pos, sucedió igualmente. Otra piedra, más grande. Pero este muchacho no sabía qué contenía . . . aquellas piedras. Esas piedras eran
muy finísimas. Eran unos carburos . . . muy finos, de valores de . . .
miles y miles y miles de . . . dinero, de pesos (6). Así es de que el

muchacho no sabía que . . . no más las cargaba porque aluminaban.

Pues que éste llega allá a la ciudad. Y andaba una viejecita, pues, barriendo la calle. Y ya le saluda: —Buenos días, viejita.

—Buenos días, señor.

Dice: —¿Qué tiene de nuevo por aquí?

Dice: —O, dice, —pues 'tán llegando muchos ricos, dice, —a . . . porque el rey quiere que, . . . el, el, el rico que salga más rico, él se casa con la hija del rey. Y aquí todo el pueblo está adornado, está muy bien barrido, regado, y muy decorado que está el, el pueblo. Y usted, dice, —¿va a pasar por aquí por onde ando barriendo?, dice. —Me va a ensuciar todo.

—No, dice, —dígame dónde está un mesón . . . aquí, dice.

—Áhi adelantito, señor, está el mesón.

Dice: —¿Me permite pasar?

—Sí, dice. —Pase.

Pues que ya llega al mesón. Y ya encerró sus borreguitas en un departamento que le . . . le rentó allí al, al dueño del mesón. Y empezaron ya a platicar.

—¿Qué tiene de nuevo usted aquí, señor, en su pueblo?

Dice: —Hombre, lo nuevo que hay es de que 'tán llegando muchos ricos de todas ciudades. Y . . . y el que salga más rico de todos, dice, —se casa con la hija del rey.

Dice: —¿Y me puede decir dónde está ese . . . ese palacio, ese castillo?

—O, dice, —venga para acá. Salieron a la calle y vieron la aglomeración de gente. Dice: —Allí onde está aquella aglomeración de gente, dice, —allá es el palacio. Dice: —¿qué, va a ir . . . ustéd también para . . . ?

Dice: —Home, pues sí. También vengo a lo mismo. Áhi traigo mis borreguitas y mi burra, dice, —pues a ver si me toca suerte.

Se rio el hombre, dice: —Ándele pues, amigo, a ver si le toca suerte.

Y si áhi va. Se fue allá y agarró cola áhi entre tanta gente. Y el polecía lo sacaba del cuello. —Quítese de áhi, amigo. No esté ensuciando. Pos ya lo hacía pa tras, y él siempre hacía cola. No, pos, ya se . . .

se llegó la hora aquel día que ya, pues, cerraban la puerta, ¿verdad? Y él no alcanzó.

Y llega con el dueño del mesón. —¿Qué pasó, amigo? ¿También alcanzó?

—No, señor, dice. —Me agarró el polecía y me echó pa tras, dice. —Yo no, no alcancé.

Dice: —Pues mañana se va tempranito, amigo.

—Pos yo mañana voy a dormir allí, a frente a la puerta.

Pos así lo hizo. Se fue muy tempranito. Se fue allí a dormir . . . pegadito a la puerta. Cuando ya el señor que . . . apuntaba allí, pues, todos los bienes que . . . que los ricos presentaban allí, vido allá aquel hombre que estaba allí, pos se puede decir que acostado.

Y dice: —¿Qué está haciendo usted aquí? Creía que sería algún borracho. —¿Qué está haciendo usted aquí, amigo?

—Bueno, dice, —pues yo vengo aquí también a ver si me toca la suerte, dice, —de casarme con la hija del rey, pues así lo anunció.

Entonces ya llamó al rey, dice: —Venga para acá. Dice: —Mire, también éste viene también a lo mismo, a casarse con su hija de usted. Y, dice, —pos quién sabe traiga dinerito.

—Palabra del rey no vuelve atrás (7). Dígale que qué capital trae.

—A ver, amigo, ¿qué capital le sumo? Presente usted.

—Bueno, yo traigo mis cien borregas y traigo mi burra.

—¿En dónde los tiene?

—Cerca, en el mesón.

Entonces fueron a valuar las borregas. Fue un valuador allá a valuarlas. Y las való a peso. De modo es que fueron cien borregas, cien pesos. Y la burrita flaquita, pues . . . cinco. De modo es que son ciento cinco.

Y ya llegaron a con el rey. —Pues ya, dice, —son cien pesos. Valuamos las borreguitas a peso. Son cien. Y una burrita flaca que trae . . . la valuamos a cinco pesos. De modo es que son ciento cinco.

—Bueno, dice, —pasen este individuo para acá. Lo voy a encapillar. Y terminando yo . . . que el individuo salga más rico de todos, lo voy a fusilar a presencia de todos.

Pues si ya, ya encerraron, encapillaron al rancherito. Pero no le arrimaron allí ni una luz ni nada. Oscura la capilla. Y, y luego dice el rancherito: —Home, dice, —aquí no le arriman aquí ni una luz ni nada, dice. —Pero no le hace, dice. —Yo traigo mis arganitas, dice. —Traigo una luz. Entonces sacó el carburo más chiquito sobre la mesa, y se iluminó toditita la . . . donde estaba encerrado, la capilla.

Dicen las criadas: —Niña, niña, dice, —el rancherito se está ardiendo.

—A ver, dice. —Corran, dice. —No se esté ardiendo.

Ya fueron las, las criadas allí, y se asomaron por la . . . chapa de la puerta.

Dice: —Niña, dice, —pos si es una piedra que tiene sobre la mesa.

—Aa, pues vaya, díganle que si, que si me hace el favor de vendérmela.

Entonces ya, ya fueron las criadas y le, le tocaron. [Informant knocks on the door next to him.]

Dice: —¿Quihubo? [Imitates rustic speech.]

—Rancherito, dice la niña que si no le vende esa piedrita que tiene usted sobre la mesa.

—Dígale a la niña que no se la vendo, que se la regalo.

Pues ya fueron allá las criadas. —Niña, dice que no se la vende, que se la regala.

—Bueno, está bien.

Entonces la . . . a la . . . segunda noche, volvió a suceder igual. Otra, la segunda piedrita la puso y se iluminó más. Y ya le dijieron: —Niña, niña, dice, —¿el ranchero ya tiene otra piedra tal vez? Dice: —Mire cómo está la . . . la capilla.

—Vayan. Díganle que me venda esotra piedrita.

Ya fueron. [Informant knocks again.] —¿Quihúbole?

—Señor, rancherito, dice la niña que si no le vende esotra piedra que tiene sobre la mesa.

—Dígale que no se la vendo, se la regalo.

Pos allá iban las criadas. —Niña, dice que no se la vende, que se la regala.

La tercer noche volvió a pasar igual. El carburo más grande lo puso sobre la mesa, y las ráfagas salían por la chapa de la puerta y hasta se iluminaba el castillo.

Entonces manda la . . . manda a las criadas: —Díganle que si me vende esa piedra, pero que ahora sí le ponga precio. Porque ya me regaló dos. Y ahora, pues, que me regale esotra. . . .

Ya fueron las criadas. Y le dijo: —Rancherito, rancherito, dice, —dice la niña que si no . . . le vende esotra, esotra piedrita.

—Dígale que no se la vendo, se la regalo. Que en cabo, en mi tierra hay como pedregal. Entonces: —Pero dígale que con una condición: que se case conmigo.

Pues ya fueron allá las criadas y le dijieron: —Ay, niña, dice que no se la . . . no se la vende. Que en su tierra hay como pedregal. Pero que se la regala con una condición: que usted se case con él.

Entonces como . . . la, la niña tiene sus consejeras, llamó a sus consejeras. Las consejeras dijieron: —¡Qué! Pos el muchacho, pos, aunque sea muy, pos 'tá muy jovencito, muy simpático, y . . . y ya muy rico. Con esas piedras que trae sale más rico de todos. Dígale que sí, niña.

Pos aceptó la niña. Pero . . . la niña . . . le dice al rancherito: —Mire, rancherito, usted no sabe lo que, lo que traía en sus arganitas. Son unos carburos muy finos . . . de . . . millones de pesos. Y usted se va a, los va a presentar con mi papá. Y, y, pero por las dudas, le voy a dar todas mis alhajas, todo mi dinero, para que . . . la presente allí, allí con mi papá. Y usted va a salir, después usted va a salir más rico de todos (8).

Pos lo mandó . . . lo mandó bañar y lo vistió muy bien. Lo, lo rasuró, y . . . y le compró un vestido, pues muy elegante. Pero para poder salir a presentar su riqueza . . . le . . . ya estaba preparado el rancherito, muy bien arreglado. Y luego con su gabancito embrocado, y el sorbete y, y gabán, y las arganitas acá debajo [laughs], de modo es que, pos estaba curioso el ranchero, ¿no?

Pues que ya . . . ya, ya un individuo había salido más rico de todos. Y ya le dijo: —Éste va a ser tu esposo.

Entonces le dice: —Papá, ¿y el rancherito que tienes tú encapillado?

Ya dice: —O, señores, dice, —a presencia de todos ustedes voy a fusilar un rancherito que se vino aquí, pues . . . pues a burlarse, tal vez de . . . mi familia o de mí. Y a presencia de todos ustedes lo voy a fusilar.

Pues que áhi viene el rancherito, y . . . a presentar sus riquezas. Los carburos los traía en las arganitas. Y, y . . . luego mandaron traer un aparejo allí y lo rellenaron de puros billetes y todas las alhajas, y los carburos que traía en las arganitas. Y ya, pues dice: —A ver, rancherito, usted traía cien borregas. Son cien pesos. Una burrita la valuaron a cinco pesos. Son ciento cinco. Así es de que, ¿usted trae algo por áhi más?

—Pues aquí traigo mis arganitas, señor.

—A ver, dice, —preséntelas.

Entonces sobre la mesa puso el carburo más chiquito. Ooo, pues ascendió luego luego muchos . . . miles de pesos. Y luego el otro. Ooo, se empezaron a ver los ricos unos con otros. Y luego puso el otro. Y ya dijo el rey, dice: —Rancherito, ya es suficiente. Ya es suficiente, dice. —Tú salistes más rico de todos con esas . . . carburos tan finos que . . . que presentastes.

Dice: —No, aquí traigo mis alhajas.

—Ooo, dice. Unas alhajas de . . . muchísimo valor. Pero esas alhajas eran de la, de la hija del rey. Y . . . y luego ya se empezaron a ver los . . . los ricos unos con otros, y se empezaron a salir. Y luego ya, pues, muy avergonzados que aquel otro pobre les había ganado. Y luego . . . trajo el aparejo, y luego con la navaja sacaba los billetes y los confetió a los ricos y les echaba los billetes. Los confetió. Y él se casó con la hija del rey (9). Y aquí termina el cuento.

This tale seems to be an incomplete version of Mt. 621. The only requisite here for winning the princess in marriage is wealth; the element of the louse skin is absent. Equaling or surpassing the wealth of the king does enter into some versions of Mt. 621, as for example in Wheeler, no. 6. The manner in which the poor shepherd wins the princess, by giving her the precious stones he has found in exchange for her promise to marry him, is similar to Mt. 425 Va, in which the bride uses three jewels to recover her husband. The story is structured as follows: T68. Princess offered as prize + H1311. Quest for the richest person + 425 Va (lowly hero uses 3 jewels to win princess's hand) + L161. Lowly hero marries princess.

Aarne-Thompson 621. The Louse Skin
Boggs 621.
Hansen 621. The Louse Skin.
(1) H1311. Quest for the richest person.
(2) T68. Princess offered as prize.
(3) L113.1.4. Shepherd as hero.
(4) F800. Extraordinary rocks and stones.
(5) D1645. Self-luminous objects.
(6) D1645.1. Incandescent jewel.
(7) M203. King's promise irrevocable.
(8) H151.1. Attention drawn by magic objects: recognition follows.
(9) L161. Lowly hero marries princess.
   Grimm, no. 212.
      Mexico: Córdova, no. 8; Paredes, no. 37; Robe, *Mexican Tales*, nos.
         86, 87; Wheeler, nos, 6, 7.
      United States: Rael, nos. 10, 16.
      Argentina: Chertudi, 2nd series, no. 70 (has incident like the 3
         nights, 3 objects that attract princess and that he gives her on
         agreement he may sleep with her).
      Chile: Lenz, *RFC*, 1, 360–362; Pino Saavedra, nos. 73, 74, 75.
      Puerto Rico: Arellano, no. 30; Mason-Espinosa, *JAF*, 35(1922), 19,
         no. 63; 20, no. 63a; 21, no. 64.
      Spain: Ampudia, nos. 134, 135; Cabal, pp. 15–19; Caballero, *Cuen-
         tos, oraciones*, 62–65, 137–144; Espinosa, *Castilla*, 131; Espinosa,
         Cuentos, nos. 9, 10, 11; Sánchez Pérez, p. 90.

77. El hermano rico y el hermano pobre

(Recorded by Candelario Gallardo on July 28, 1967, in Oxnard, California

A rich man devises a scheme for getting rid of his poor brother who
is always asking him for money. He takes him on a walk into the
woods and, knowing that the poor man has brought no food for the
journey, he offers to feed him only if he will let his eyes be put out.
The poor man's hunger is so great that he agrees, and he is then left
blind and alone in the woods. He climbs a tree for protection from the
wild animals and overhears the cure for his blindness as well as the
magic words to open up a treasure cave from a group of robbers who
meet under the tree. He uses the formula "ábrete sésamo" to get into
the cave and takes home a fortune in gold. He borrows his brother's
measure to see how much money he has acquired and, when he returns
it, a piece of gold is left stuck in the measure, and in that way his
brother learns of his newly acquired wealth. He persuades him to take
him into the woods, in the hope of finding the same treasure, which

the now rich brother agrees to do. He lets his own eyes be put out in return for food, climbs the same tree, overhears the same secrets from the robbers, and gets into the cave. But while he is there the robbers return; thinking he is the one who has been stealing from them, they hang him from the tree, which is, as the informant says, God's way of punishing the brother's envy.

Vamos a contar un cuento de dos hermanos. Uno estaba muy rico y otro muy pobre. Y el pobre, pues, lo molestaba mucho, porque pues, él tenía la necesidad de que . . . el hermano le prestara dinero, . . . para comer y sostener su familia. Pero de tantas molestias que tenía, el hermano rico dice: —Hombre, dice, —pues este hermano, dice, —pues tanto préstame y préstame dinero, dice, —pues me va a acabar mi dinero. Así es de que le dice un día a su esposa: —Yo voy a perder aquí a mi hermano, dice, —a ver de qué manera le hago, a ver de qué manero lo . . . dejo por allá en, en la sierra perdido. Y así lo hizo.

Entonces le dice: —Hermano, dice, —¿cómo no hacemos una gira? Vamos, dice, —a ver si hallamos una fortuna por áhi, por allá. Y también te haces tú rico.

Dice: —Hermano, pues, ándele, vamos.

Entonces hicieron el viaje. Y, y el hermano llevaba muy buen lonche. Y el otro pobre, pues, ¿qué llevaba? Nada de lonche que llevaba. Pues, ¿qué llevaba? Pues muy pobre.

Entonces el pobre dice: —Hermano, dice, —ya me anda de hambre.

Dice: —Pues, yo te voy a dar de comer, hermano, solamente con una, con una condición.

—¿Qué condición, hermano?

Dice: —Pues, que te saques un ojo, hermano.

—Pero, ¿cómo me va a sacar un ojo, hermano, para darme de comer?

Dice: —Pues, áhi tú lo sabes. Sólo así te puedo dar de comer.

Pues, tanto era el hambre que tenía el hermano. —Pues, ándale, pues, hermano. Sácame el ojo.

Le sacó un ojo. Siguieron caminando, y, y otra vez ya le andaba de hambre al, al pobre. —Hermano, dice, —dame de comer. Pero ya me sacastes un ojo, y me vas a sacar el otro, dice.

—Pues, solamente así, hermanito, te doy de comer.

Y entonces le sacó el otro y quedó ciego. Pues, así lo quería, así lo deseaba él, para dejarlo en la montaña, pues, ciego (1).

Entonces luego que ya lo hizo ciego, él se regresó a su casa. Y el cieguito se fue como pudo, tentaleando, un tronco de un árbol. Y éste, de miedo, que tal vez sería que se le iba a comer algún animal, alguna fiera, se subió arriba del árbol. Y allá estaba, en el árbol (2). Cuando oyó un ruido, que venían, venían los ladrones. Era habitación de ladrones.

Entonces ya, ya le dice el capitán: —Bueno, dice, —pues, aquí vamos a hacer la, todo esto que juntamos aquí, todo este dinero que, que robamos, ellos robaban, —pues lo vamos a poner aquí en la cueva (3).

Entonces el cieguito oyendo todas esas versiones. Entonces se fue el capitán, y dice a la, a la piedra que cubría la, la cueva onde ponían el dinero, le dice: —Ábrete sésamo (4). Entonces se abrió aquel enorme peñasco que tenía, que cubría la cueva. Entonces ya metieron todo el dinero en la cueva, y, y luego ya les dice el capitán: —Tú, ¿qué supistes en el pueblo?

Dice: —Bueno, dice, —yo supe que con estas hojas del árbol, mira la gente (5, 6).

Entonces el cieguito agarró un puño de hojas y se limpió los ojos, y vido (7, 8).

Entonces ya todos los ladrones se fueron. Hicieron la repartición y se fueron.

Entonces el cieguito se bajó y le dice: —Ábrete sésamo. Y se abrió aquella enorme . . . peñón que cubría la, la cueva. Entonces vido mucho dinero, oro y, y, y mucho oro había. Entonces éste dice: —Pues yo me voy a ir a mi casa a traer unos burros, unas mulas, aunque sean prestados, pos, yo estoy muy pobre.

Consiguió por áhi unos burros, y vino. Y se cargó lo que pudo. Entonces ya llegó a la casa con su esposa, dice: —Mira, mira, vieja, dice, —ya me . . . Dios me socorrió, con este dinero. Entonces dice: —Anda, dice, —con el hermano, a que nos preste la medida. A ver qué tanto es.

Pues que ya fue la esposa, le dice: —¿Cómo no nos hacen el favor de prestarnos la medida onde miden ustedes su dinero?

—Sí.

Agarró la medida de a . . . de cinco litros, que así es la medida. Así es el nombramiento de la medida.

Entonces ya trajo la medida, y midieron todo el dinero que traía. Pos, era bastante, ¿verdad?

Entonces cuando ya fueron a entregar la medida, pos de casualidad se fue pegada una onza de oro en el asiento de la medida. Entonces la señora le dice: —¿No era que tu hermano está muy pobre? Dice: —Ya midieron el dinero que, que tienen. Y mira en el asiento de la medida viene esta onza de oro pegada (9).

—¿Cómo le haría mi hermano?, dice. —Si yo lo, lo hice ciego en la montaña. ¿Cómo le haría, ciego? Así es de que, yo le voy a preguntar.

Dice: —Hermano, dice, —¿cómo lo hicistes? Te prestamos la medida, y . . . en el asiento de la medida venía una onza de oro. ¿Te hallastes alguna fortuna?

—No, hermano. Yo . . . me pasó esto. Ya le 'tuvo platicando cómo se había, cómo había visto la, las hojas del árbol, y que se había limpiado los ojos, y que había visto, y que habían venido los ladrones, y que habían hecho las cuentas, y el capitán echó en la cueva todo ese dinero. Dice: —Como yo oyí, dice, —que dicía el capitán "ábrete sésamo," entonces se abrió una peña. Y yo así también dije: —Yo me voy a bajar del árbol y le voy a decir "ábrete sésamo." Entonces se abrió la piedra, y vido muchísimo dinero. —Y así jue, hermanito. Así es de que me tienes ahora, pues, también con una fortuna.

Entonces el hermano, el más pobre, pos se hizo pobre, se hizo pobre. Dice: —Hermano, ahora yo soy el pobre. Hora, cómo no vamos a onde hicistes esa fortuna, dice, —a ver si Dios también me socorre.

—Sí hermanito, pos, vamos. Cómo no.

Entonces ya fue . . . fueron por el camino. Y ya fue la vice versa, que el otro le hizo, ¿verdad?, que lo hizo ciego. Dice: —Hermanito, dice, —ya me anda de hambre, dice.

—Pues, sácate un ojo, hermanito, pa darte de comer.

Entonces, pues, se sacó el ojo. A poco de camino . . . : —Ya me anda otra vez de hambre, hermanito.

—Pues, sácate el otro ojo.

Y entonces ya le sacó los dos. Lo hizo ciego (1). Entonces ya se fue también al tronco del árbol. Y se subió, por las fieras, pues había muchas fieras que se podían comérselo (2).

Y entonces vino el capitán, . . . el capitán. Y luego ya dice: —Pues, hay que repartir el dinero que robamos. Ya lo repartieron.

Y luego ya dice: —Hombre, dice, —yo voy a limpiarme los ojos con, con las hojas del árbol. Porque oía decir los ladrones que las hojas del árbol tenían virtud, y que limpiándose con las hojas veía la gente (6). —Entonces yo voy a hacerle el cale. Agarró un, un puño de hojas y se limpió los ojos. Y vido (7, 8).

Cuando el capitán decía: —Ábrete sésamo. Y se abrió la, la piedra (4).

Entonces luego que ya se fueron los ladrones todos, entonces él se bajó. Mmmm, también halló muchísimo dinero. Veía mucho dinero.

—Con razón mi hermano se hizo rico. Mira no más cuánto dinero hay aquí.

Pero le tocó la mala suerte que cuando andaba robando cayeron los ladrones (10). Le dijeron: —Mira. Aquí, este hombre es el que nos estaba estafando el dinero. Y, y lo agarraron, y lo mataron. Lo colgaron del árbol, para ejemplo de los demás. Y quedó colgado (11).

Así es de que este cuento, . . . pos le tocó la mala suerte al hermano, que . . . por la envidia. Por eso no consta tener . . . no ser envidioso (12). Dios lo castigó, y, y . . . y así lo, lo hicieron, pos, lo colgaron del árbol.

Y hasta aquí se acaba el cuento.

The story is structured as follows: 613 Ic II*c (robbers) IIIae + 676. See Narrative 75 for Mt. 613.

Aarne-Thompson 676. Open Sesame.
Boggs 676.
Hansen 676. Open Sesame.
(1) M225. Eyes exchanged for food.
(2) F1045. Night spent in tree. Hero goes into tree and spends the night.
(3) N512. Treasure in underground chamber (cavern).
(4) N455.3. Secret formula for opening treasure mountain overheard from robbers (Open Sesame).

(5) N451.1. Secrets of animals (demons) accidentally overheard from tree
     (bridge) hiding place. [Secrets of robbers.]
(6) N452. Secret remedy overheard in conversation of animals (witches).
     [Conversation of robbers.]
(7) D1500.1.4. Magic healing plant.
(8) D1505.18. Tree restores sight.
(9) N478. Secret wealth betrayed by money left in borrowed money-scale.
(10) N471. Foolish attempt of second man to overhear secrets (from animals,
     demons, etc.). [From robbers.]
(11) Q413.1. Hanging as punishment for theft.
(12) Q302. Envy punished.

Thompson, *Folktale*, pp. 68–69.
Grimm, no. 142.

> Mexico: Boas, *JAF*, 25(1912), 223; Parsons, *JAF*, 45(1932), 350–
> 352, no. 5; Radin, *El folklore de Oaxaca*, no. 102; Robe, *Mexican
> Tales*, nos. 124, 125.
> United States: Espinosa, *JAF*, 24(1911), 424; Rael, nos. 343, 344,
> 345.
> Chile: Montenegro, p. 103; Pino Saavedra, nos. 90, 91.
> Dominican Republic: Andrade, nos. 144, 145, 146.
> Puerto Rico: Mason-Espinosa, *JAF*, 37(1923), 276, no. 5.
> Spain: Curiel Merchán, pp. 39–42; Espinosa, *Cuentos*, no. 175.

78. El pájaro que habla

(Recorded by Lola Cruz on December 8, 1966, in Los Angeles, California)

Three princesses are seated together sewing one day, when three
kings, having stopped near their house to get out of a rainstorm, overhear their conversation. The eldest says that if she were to marry the
king she would make for him a suit of clothes that would fit in a nutshell; the second princess says she would make a cape that would fit
in the shell of a pine nut; and the youngest says she would give him
three children: two sons with hair of gold and silver, and a daughter
with a star on her forehead. The kings decide to marry the princesses
and see if each keeps her promise. The two older sisters make the
clothing they promised; but when the youngest gives birth to her first
child, they become jealous, substitute a newborn puppy, and send the
child floating down the river in a box. A lonely hermit, who has been
bemoaning the fate that denied him any children to whom he could
leave his inheritance, notices the box floating down the river, retrieves
it, and is delighted to find a child with hair of gold. Meanwhile, the
king has ordered his wife locked up in a cage with the puppy she supposedly gave birth to. At two subsequent births, the jealous sisters
substitute a kitten and a pig and send these children as well down the
river into the hands of the same hermit. The wife is left in the cage

with her three "offspring," a dog, a cat, and a pig, while the hermit raises the children as his own. Fifteen years later the sisters become curious about the fate of the children, and they consult a magic mirror that tells them that they are doing well. The sisters ask how they might succeed in killing the girl and are told that they must entice her into going to seek the speaking bird, the magic fruit tree, and the fountain of a thousand colors. They engage a witch to go and suggest this to the girl by telling her that these things are more beautiful than what she already has. The witch is successful, and the girl's brothers vow to find and bring back to their sister the bird, the tree, and the fountain. They are unsuccessful, for they fail to heed a warning not to respond to anyone who calls them, and they are turned into stone. The girl herself then goes and is successful, for she ignores all attempts to distract her. She disenchants a whole population of kings and queens by sprinkling them with water from the fountain of a thousand colors and by using a feather from the tail of the speaking bird. A banquet is planned in celebration of the event, and the girl's father and her aunts and uncles are among the guests. A special dish, a cucumber with a pearl inside, taken from the magic tree, is served to the father, to which he reacts by commenting that it is impossible for a cucumber to have a pearl in it. The bird replies that neither can a woman give birth to dogs, cats, and pigs. The curious king demands an explanation of the comment, and his three children are brought before him, the sons with hair of gold and silver and the daughter with a star on her forehead, exactly as promised by his wife. The family is reunited, and the wicked aunts are condemned to death.

Éste eran tres reyes . . . y tres reinas, tres princesas. Y las tres princesas 'taban sentadas . . . bordando, en un día de . . . de agua. Cuando luego los tres reyes pararon allí junto a la casa de ellas pa resistir el agua (1). Y después dijo la, la, la princesa mayor: —Si yo me casara con el rey fulano, le . . . hacía un vestido . . . que cupiera en hueco de una . . . nuez.

Y luego dijo la . . . la de en medio: —Y si yo me casara con el rey . . . más chico, le hacía una capa que cupiera en hueco de un piñón (2).

Y luego después la chica dijo: —Y si yo me casara con el rey más chico, yo le daría tres hijos: un hijo con cabello de oro (3) y . . . una niña con lucero en la frente (4) y otro niño con el cabello de plata (5).

Bueno. Pos que los reyes oyeron esta historia y les dijeron a sus, . . . uno al otro: —Pues, vámonos casando con ellas, a ver si cumplen lo que nos han dicho. Pues luego les dijieron que si se casaban con ellos y dijieron que sí.

Y luego la más grande le hizo el vestido . . . al rey . . . que cupo en el hueco de una nuez. Y la otra le hizo la capa que cupo en el hueco de un piñón.

Y la otra se esperó hasta que la cigüeña vino . . . al año de casados. . . . Luego dijo la, la hermana, las dos hermanas: —Oyes, no vamos a usar doctor.

Y luego le dijo el . . . el, el rey: —Manda traer un doctor para que venga . . . venga a aliviar a mi esposa.

Dicían: —No, no necesita doctor. Aquí estamos nosotras para . . . asistirla a ella (6). Y luego éstas fueron y buscaron un . . . un perrito . . . que estuviera recién nacido. Y trajieron el perrito y luego le taparon el hociquito para que no llorara y lo pusieron en una cajita. Y luego, y . . . mandaron hacer una cajita de cristal. Y luego cuando ya la señora dijo que iba a tener su niño, entonces luego le quitó pronto a la carrera, una le quitó el niño y la otra le, le puso el perrito (7). Y luego lo llevaron a . . . a tirar al niño aquel. Lo echó en un río (8, 9).

Y estaba un viejito diciéndole a Dios Nuestro Señor: —¡Ay, Diosito santo, Padre Mío! ¿Cómo nunca me has dado un hijo ni una hija . . . ni una nadie, ni un amigo ni nadie para dejarle toda mi herencia? Tanto dinero que tengo yo y no hay a quién dejárselo. Cuando luego en eso vio una . . . una cosita que, que brillaba. Dice: —Ay, tengo dinero y luego más dinero que viene. Pos, ¿qué voy a hacer con tanto dinero? Cuando llegó hasta enfrente de él la agarró, la cajita (10), dijo: —¡Ay, qué precioso niño, qué hermoso con el cabello de oro! ¡Válgame, qué niño tan lindo! Lo sacó, dijo: —Bendito Dios, te doy las gracias por este niño que me has dado, que me has mandado. Yo, que tenía . . . miedo de morirme y no tener a quién dejarle mi herencia (11).

Cuando luego en eso entró el rey, y le preguntó . . . a las . . . a las cuñadas: —¿Qué fue lo que tuvo mi esposa? ¿Una niña o un niño?

Y luego el perrito empezó: —Gua, gua, gua, gua. [Imitates dog.]

—¡Ay!, dice, —¡Jesús de mi vida! ¿Qué es esto . . . un perro? No puede ser de que una mujer tenga perros.

—Bueno, pos, ¿quién sabe? Éste es tu hijo.

Luego dice: —Luego que se alivie tienen que ponerla en una . . . en una jaula con su perro. Y en las noches que se venga a . . . allá a la cama (12).

Pues luego a la carrera le hicieron su jaula . . . una silla, y luego el perro con su collar . . . pa que estuviera el perro junto de su madre. Y el perro quería mucho a la señora. Y le aventaban desperdicios de . . . de, de lo que comía el rey. Se los aventaban allí pa que comieran tanto la señora como . . . el perrito.

Pues luego en eso, en una . . .temporada que pasó, entonces luego el viejito estaba sentado con el niño, y dijo: —Mira, hijito, cuando el niño tenía un año, —aquí te recogí en este río. Y que gracias a Dios que te ha mandado a ti.

Cuando luego en eso estaba, allá en la casa del rey, empezó la señora que tenía . . . unos dolores, que se sentía muy mala. Y luego le dijo el . . . rey, a las cuñadas: —Hora sí, está bueno mandar traer un doctor.

—No, no, no cuñadito. ¿Pa qué quieres doctor? Si nosotras estamos para . . . servirte, y eso. No tienes tú que buscar doctor. Nosotras podemos estar aquí.

—Bueno.

Pues, luego en eso ella anduvo viendo, a ver qué, qué, qué había nacido primero para ponérselo a la señora. Y era un . . . era un . . . un gatito, que estaba . . . nacido. Y luego después ya se lo trajieron. Y luego . . . ya cuando . . . el esposo le preguntó a las cuñadas que qué había tenido su esposa, dijo: —O, tuvo un gato (7).

Y empezó el gato: —Miau, miau. [Imitates cat.]

Dijo: —No puede ser de que una mujer tenga perros y gatos.

Cuando luego en eso aventaron a la niña en una cajita de cristal (8, 9). Y estaba el viejito allí con su bebito, con su niñito. Estaba . . . acariciándolo. Cuando luego vio relumbrar la cajita de vuelta, y dijo: —¡Ay, esta caja está muy brillosa! ¿Qué tendrá? Mira, hijo, más dinero que te . . . que te mandó Dios. Cuando sacó la caja, va viendo una

niña muy hermosa (10). Dijo: —¡Ay, qué hermosura! Mira, mi hijito, una hermanita que tienes. Esta hermanita te va . . . a cuidar todo el
tiempo.

Bueno, pos que ya la, ya la juntó. Y . . . y luego la señora, mamá de
los niños, pos ya estaba con su perro y su gato en la jaula. Pos que el, el
rey había destinado que aquella señora debía de estar amarrada con
una cadena ella áhi también, junto con sus hijos. Y las hermanas estaban muy contentas porque ellas estaban haciendo todo este mal.

Y luego . . . ya cuando vuelto del año, estaba el viejito con su niña
y su niño y diciéndoles, ya el niño tenía dos años y la niña tenía un
año . . . :—Miren, hijos, aquí los saqué de este río. Y qué bendito el
cielo y Dios que me los ha tráido para tenerlos aquí.

Cuando luego la señora . . . allá en el palacio resultó con los dolores. Y luego le dice a la, a las cuñadas: —Ay, sáquenme de aquí,
porque ya voy a dar a luz. Ojalá Dios quiera que ahora sí sea un niño,
. . . que no sea animal. Bueno, pos que luego ya la llevaron y dijeron al
rey que su esposa iba a tener . . . otra criatura.

Pues luego ya la sacaron y la llevaron. Y luego dijo: —Pos, trae un
doctor.

—Ya te dije que pa qué quieres doctor. Que, que nosotras . . . podemos servir de doctoras. Pos luego trajieron, fueron ellas a buscar y
hallaron un puerco. Y luego le quitaron el niño aquel (8, 9), y le pusieron el puerquito (7).

Y luego ya le dijo el señor: —¿Qué tuvo mi esposa?

—Jum, aquí está.

Y empezó el puerco: —Cui, cui, cui, cui. [Imitates pig.]

—¡Ay, válgame Dios, si fue un puerco! No puede ser que una mujer tenga perros, gatos, y puercos. Ay, nada más, que la lleven a su
jaula. Y la llevaron, y al puerco le pusieron un . . . una batea, pa que
se . . . se volcara con el lodo allí . . . allí donde la tenían presa.

Pos luego las cuñadas estaban muy contentas. —¡Qué bueno! Que si
se muere mi hermana nosotras nos quedamos con el castillo. Porque
eran unas señoras muy invidiosas

Bueno, pos luego el . . . el viejito estaba allí, contándoles un cuento
. . . a los dos niñitos. Cuando luego ya ven que viene otra, otra cajita.

—Miren, hijitos, áhi viene . . . otra cajita. Vamos a sacarla . . . a ver quién es (10). Bueno, pues que ya vio un niño, y le dijo: —¡Ay Diosito, ya no queremos más! Ya con los tres hijos que me has mandado . . . con ésos tengo. Y luego dijo: —Ay, niños míos, ahora les voy a poner un nombre a cada uno. El primero se va a llamar José; la, la niña, María; y el, y el chiquito se va a llamar Juan. Para que así distinguirlos y hablarles como debo de, de llamarlos.

Y luego la señora allá estaba con aquella . . . tristeza que, que no sabía cómo Dios en lugar de darle criaturas le dió . . . perro, gato, y puerco. Pues ella lloraba y lloraba sus amarguras. Y luego dijo el rey: —Desde hoy . . . nunca serás mi esposa, nunca llegarás a mi cama. Nunca tendré que verte ni de día ni de noche. Aquí vas a estar hasta todos los días de tu vida, hasta que te mueras. Y ella siempre estaba con sus hijos, porque los quería mucho, porque creía que ella los había tenido, esos animalitos.

Pos luego después, ya cuando ya pasaron quince años, las dos . . . mujeres vieron un espejo y dijieron: —Espejito, espejito de virtud, con la virtud que Dios te ha dado, quiero que nos des razón . . . de los tres hijos de mi . . . de mi hermana, . . . qué fin tienen (13).

Dijo: —Mmmm, cállate la boca. Si tus . . . tres sobrinos están rebién. El señor está ya muy viejito. Ya está para morirse. Y luego . . . les tiene todo lo que la niña quiere. Porque la niña es la reina, y ella todo lo que ella quiere, todo . . . se lo dan sus hermanos . . . y su papá.

Dice: —¿Con qué puede morirse ella?

—Ooo, pues ella se puede morir no más con . . . con decirle del . . . pájaro que habla, y el árbol que da fruta, . . . y el agua de mil colores (14).

Mmm, pos luego fue ésa con una bruja y le dijo a la bruja: —Oyes, anda tú . . . y dile a . . . a la niña que vive en tal parte, que es mi sobrina, que su casa de ella no es tan bonita como donde está . . . el pájaro que habla, el agua de mil colores, y el árbol que da fruta.

—Pos que sí. Pos luego en eso . . . fue la bruja y tocó a la puerta.

Dice:—¿Quién es? ¿Qué deseaba?

Dice: —¿Ónde 'tá tu hermanita?

—Áhi adentro está. ¿Qué deseaba?

—Quiero ver su jardín. Quiero ver su . . . su . . . de esas cosas cómo tiene ella.

—Pase, pase. Ella es una niña que . . . le desea todo lo mejor para ella. Y cuando hay otra cosa en el mundo, ella se nos muere.

Pues ya fue la . . . la bruja y vio. Y le preguntó a la niña: —Oyes, ¿tú estás muy contenta con todo lo que tienes?

—O sí. Si hay otra cosa más bonita en el mundo yo me muero.

—No, no, no. Tú, tú, te falta otra cosa aquí.

—¿Qué me falta?

—Jum, . . . pos te falta el árbol . . . el árbol que da fruta (15) y el agua de mil colores (16) y el pájaro que habla (17).

—¿Y dónde están?

—O, pos, eso está lejos. Tiene que ir.

Tonces dijo . . . José, dijo: —Mira, hermanita, no te pongas triste. Yo voy a, a traerte ese árbol. Entonces . . . dice: —Mira, toma. Te doy esta navaja. La entierras en el suelo y la sacas. La entierras en el suelo y la sacas todos los días . . . una vez. Y cuando la entierres y ves que no quiere salir, es de que estoy muerto (18).

—Está bien, hermanito.

Pos se fue. Y luego estaba áhi un viejito . . . que era hermitaño. —¿Adónde vas, buen niño (19)?

—¿Adónde he de ir, buen señor? Voy a traer el pájaro que habla, y . . . y la fuente de mil colores, . . . y la, y el árbol que da fruta.

—Mmm, niño, ni esperanzas que llegues, porque si te hablan te vas a quedar encantado. Y si te quedas encantado, pos, te vuelves piedra (20, 21). No . . . y si te hablan, no voltíes. Si oyes caballos, no voltíes (22).

—No. ¡Qué voy a voltear!

Bueno, pos éste siguió andando y andando y andando, y le decían: —José, José.

—No he de voltear. No he de voltear.

—José. Y luego oía los tropellos de caballos.

—No he de voltear.

Y luego oyó una muchacha, que le dijieron: —José, José, tu hermana está muy triste. Y volteó pa tras. Y se volvió piedra. Y se fue corre y corre y corre la piedra. La piedra se fue corre y corre hasta que llegó . . . abajo.

Y luego después la niña metió la navaja y la sacó, y luego la metió otro día y ya no salió. Y luego se puso a llorar. Y le dijo . . . el hermanito . . . más chiquito: —¿Por qué lloras, hermanita? ¿Qué tienes?

—Ay hermanito, ¿cómo no voy a llorar? Nuestro hermano se nos ha muerto.

—¿Cómo sabes que se nos ha muerto?

—Porque él me dio una navaja pa que la enterrara y la sacara, y no quiere salir. Dice: —Yo acabo de hacer la lucha.

Entonces el hermano empezó a hacer por sacarla y no la pudo sacar. Se quedó enterrada. Dice: —No te apures, hermanita. Yo voy. Toma. Te doy esta navajita. La cierras y la abres todos los días, y si ves que la cierras y no se puede abrir, es que yo estoy muerto (18).

—'Tá bueno, hermanito. Dios que te ayude.

Bueno, pos se fue andando. Y luego incontró al viejito otra vuelta. —¿Adónde vas, buen niño (19)?

—¿Adónde he de ir, buen señor? Voy a, a, a traer a mi hermanita el árbol que, que da fruta, el pájaro que habla, y la, y la pila de mil . . . colores.

—Ooo, niño, hace poco tiempo vino un niño, y áhi tienes, que le dije que no volteara, y volteó y se volvió piedra.

—Aa, dice, —pues yo no volteo (22). Yo voy a ir.

Pos, siempre se . . . se fue anda y anda y anda, . . . un poquito más que el otro hermano. Luego le hablaban: —Juan, Juan. Y no volteaba. Luego oyó música, oyó cantos, oyó . . . que estaba, que iba a llover, y no volteó. Y luego oyó que lo llaman: —Juan, tu hermana está muy triste. Volteó y se hizo . . . pos, piedra (20, 21). Y se fue rueda y rueda y rueda y rueda y rueda, y cayó hasta bien abajo.

Bueno, pos que luego después la hermanita abrió la navaja y la cerraba, y luego la, la abrió, la cerró, y no pudo abrirla. Dice: —Ay, mi hermanito también ya se murió. ¿Qué voy a hacer yo? Y luego se fue . . . se fue ella . . . allá a andar. Se puso unos pantalones y una . . . y una mascada en la cabeza. Y luego se fue ella.

Cuando luego le salió el viejito. —¿Adónde vas, buena niña (19)?

—¿Adónde he de ir, buen señor? Voy a traer mi pájaro que habla, y mi . . . pila de, de agua de mil colores, y voy a traer mi árbol.

—¿Cómo dices que tú . . . ?

—Pues bien, señor, porque yo sé que los voy a traer.

—No, niña, si hace días se fue un niño y se volvió piedra. Luego volvió otro niño y se volvió piedra.

Dice: —Aa, pues, ésos son mis hermanos. Pero ahora voy yo (23).

Pos, dijo: —Mira, si te hablan, no voltíes. Si oyes que están cantando, no voltíes. Si oyes que vienen caballos, no voltíes. Si oyes . . . mucha agua, no voltíes (22).

—Está bien.

Pues luego la niña se fue anda y anda, y le hablaban: —María, María. Y no volteaba. Y luego, ya . . . caballos. Y no volteaba. Oía voces. No volteaba.

Y luego ya . . . estaba allá, y luego le dijo el pájaro (24): —Arráncame una pluma de mi cola. Entonces le arrancó la, la, la pluma. Y luego iba a voltear pa tras. —No voltíes, no voltíes. Porque si volteas, . . . te vuelves piedra. Entonces luego después agarró la pluma y la metió en la, la fuente . . . de mil colores y empezó a echar gotitas, gotitas de agua. Y se empezaron a levanter reyes (25, 26). Se empezaron a levantar reyes (27).

Y entonces luego dijo, dijo: —Y ahora, ¿cómo me llevo este . . . este árbol?

—No te apures. Entre todos lo llevamos. Y luego, llevamos también la, la fuente . . . y el pájaro. Entonces el pájaro, ella lo llevó.

Entonces le hicieron . . . mucha fiesta a la niña porque había vuelto a todos los reyes. Y le dieron muchos regalos. Y luego hicieron invitaciones. Y entre las invitaciones que hicieron le cayó una invitación a . . . a su papá y a sus tíos de, de ella . . . y a las tías, a las dos tías. Entonces luego le dijo el . . . el pájaro: —Mira, . . . pon todos los platos, pero un plato especialmente. Y agarra . . . un pepino del árbol, y ponle al rey que está allí. Entonces ella hizo lo que el pájaro le dijo. Tonces agarró el pepino y se lo puso.

Comieron. Y, y luego le puso el pepino al señor. Y luego le dijo . . . dijo el rey: —No puede ser de que un pepino tenga perla.

Y luego dijo el pájaro: —Y no puede ser de que una mujer tenga perros, gatos, y puercos.

—¿Qué dices?

—Lo que dices tú.

—Ah, pues, yo digo que no puede ser de que un pepino tenga perla.

Dijo:—Yo también digo que no puede ser de que una mujer tenga perros, gatos, y puercos.

—¿Por qué dices?

—Porque tu esposa está en una . . . enjaulada. Y está con los que no son sus hijos. Sus hijos aquí los tienes, que son estos niños y la niña. Destápate la cabeza, niña. El lucero en la frente (28). —Destápate tú, niño. Oro en la cabeza. —Destápate tú, niño. Plata en la cabeza (29). —Éstos son los tres niños que te ofreció tu esposa. Cuando estaba ella cosiendo, bordando, te dijo que si tuviera tres hijos te los daba. Dos niños y una niña. Un niño con el pelo de oro, una niña con lucero en la frente, y otra . . . y otro niño con el cabello de plata. Y tú tienes esa señora castigándola injustamente.

Entonces luego dijo . . . el perico, el pájaro: —Lo que debes hacer . . . es de, de, de buscar dos caballos y poner a las señoras . . . de una pata en unos caballos brutos. Entonces luego . . . andaban buscando quién tenía caballos brutos.

Y luego dijo el pájaro: —Yo sé dónde están, y yo se los traigo aquí. Pegó vuelta el pájaro, y vuela y vuela y vuela y vuela. Y se trajo a los caballos a piquete. Y luego ya que estaban allí amarró . . . agarraron a la, a una de un caballo y a otra de otro caballo. Y luego el caballo corrió, y luego ya se, se despedazaron ellas a, a puros pedacitos de, de todo lo que . . . las arrastraban (30, 31).

Pues luego después, . . . fueron al palacio y sacaron a las . . . a la señora que estaba en la jaula. Y luego le dijo: —Aquí están tus hijos.

Le dijo: —Madre mía, tú eres nuestra madre. Que nuestras tías nos habían tirado en el agua, y un viejito nos recogió cuando nos fuimos.

Dice: —Bendito sea el cielo que nos ha . . . me han traído a mis tres hijos que yo le ofrecí a mi esposo. Y ya la sacaron de la jaula. Y a los animalitos no los tiraron porque la señora los quería mucho, . . . porque ella los quería como sus propios hijos (32).

Y vuelo por un camino y vuelo por otro, cuénteme usted otro.

The story is structured as follows: 707 Ia (three children: son with golden hair, daughter with star on forehead, son with silver hair) b IIa (dog, cat, pig) b (hermit) c IIIbcd (old man) IV abc.
See Narrative 72 for Mt. 707.

  (1) N455.4. King overhears girl's boast as to what she should do as queen.
  (2) F821.2. Dress so fine that it goes in nutshell. [Suit.]
  (3) F555.1. Gold hair.
  (4) F545.2.1. Gold star on forehead.
  (5) F555.2. Silver hair.
  (6) K2212. Treacherous sister.
  (7) K2115. Animal-birth slander.
  (8) S142. Person thrown into the water and abandoned.
  (9) S331. Exposure of child in boat (floating chest).
(10) R131.10. Hermit rescues abandoned child.
(11) N856.1. Forester as foster father.
(12) S430. Disposal of cast off wife.
(13) D1323.1. Magic clairvoyant mirror.
(14) D1311.2. Mirror answers questions.
(15) H1333.1. Quest for marvelous tree.
(16) H1321.1. Quest for Water of Life.
(17) H1331.1.4. Quest for speaking bird.
(18) E761.4.1. Life token: knife stuck in tree rusts. [Here, knife stuck in ground cannot be removed; then, knife cannot be opened.]
(19) N843. Hermit as helper.
(20) C961.2. Transformation to stone for breaking tabu.
(21) G263.2.1. Witch transforms to stone.
(22) C331. Tabu: looking back.
(23) R158. Sister rescues brother(s).
(24) B450. Helpful bird.
(25) E64.9. Resuscitation by magic feather.
(26) E80. Water of life.
(27) F768.2. City of enchanted people.
(28) H71.1. Star on forehead as sign of royalty.
(29) H71.2. Gold (silver) hairs as sign of royalty.
(30) Q261. Treachery punished.
(31) Q416.2. Punishment: dragging to death by a horse.
(32) S451. Outcast wife at last united with husband and children.

Religious Tales

79. El muchacho y la hostia

(Recorded by Candelario Gallardo on December 15, 1966, in Oxnard, California

A couple who cannot afford to support their son send him off to work as a shepherd. The people for whom he works decide they are not raising the boy properly and that he ought to attend mass, and so he is told to go to the church and to do what he sees others doing. Instead of consuming the Host at communion, he carries it home with him and, following the advice to imitate what he saw at church, he proceeds to say mass for his herd of sheep. Others observe this activity, see the sheep kneeling and the boy singing, and they bring the priest to observe. When they look into the hollow of the tree, where the boy had put the Host, they find a golden image of Christ. The priest feels the boy is chosen by God, and he takes him on as his sacristan. At the church the boy takes pity on the figure on the crucifix, covers it up with his own coat, and attempts to feed it. Discovering this, the priest decides the boy is mentally unbalanced and returns him to his parents, to whom he gives a monthly pension for his support. But the boy becomes ill, gradually wastes away, and finally dies. He is taken straight to heaven, perhaps, as the informant suggests, because he was so good.

Voy a . . . a contarles otro cuentecito para que se diviertan áhi. Si es de que les gusta, pues lo pueden oyir, y se pueden . . . se pueden divertir.

Éste era un, un muchacho, pues muy, muy buena gente. Y porque, como dicen los sacerdotes, . . . cuando uno quiere buscar su esposa, dicen, "Busquen el árbol que dé fruta buena. Porque si el árbol da fruta mala, todo el tiempo la da; y si el árbol da fruta buena, todo el tiempo da buena fruta." Así . . . el papá y la mamá eran unas almas de Dios, y así salió el muchacho. Muy buena gente . . . un alma de Dios. Pero los papás estaban muy pobres y no podían soportarse . . . pues, ellos. Estaban muy pobrecitos.

El muchacho luego ya fue creciendo y ya, pues, dijeron: —Pues, hay que conseguirle trabajo a este, a este muchacho, dice, —pa podernos soportar. Y . . . y ya fueron con un ranchero para que lo ocupara.

Y ya le hablaron al ranchero: —Señor, dice, —aquí venimos con este muchacho, a ver si nos lo ocupa por áhi, a ver en qué . . . puede servirle.

Ya dice el, el del rancho, dice: —Hombre, dice, —pues yo . . . yo lo puedo ocupar aquí, dice, —a que me cuide las borregas. Me falta un borreguero. Así es de que si él quiere cuidar las borregas pues yo lo ocupo.

—Pues que sí.

—Bueno, ya déjenmelo aquí.

Pos este muchacho . . . era muy buen pastor. El tenía las borregas muy gordas . . . muy bien cuidadas. Las bajaba al río onde estaba un río tan más bonito, con una agua muy clarita, muy bonito. Y en los ríos había unos . . . unos sabinos, unos árboles enormes, por toda la orilla del río. Y allí había un árbol que tenía un hueco en el tronco. Y a él le gustaba porque tenía ese hueco . . . el árbol. Y le gustaba mucho al borreguero. Y bajaba sus borreguitas al agua. Y luego que les daba agua pos él se dormía, a descansar un rato en la sombra de aquel árbol. Las borreguitas también tenían calor. Rodeaban el árbol y allí ellas . . . pues, descansando también.

Pos así 'tuvo mucho tiempo, cuando el ranchero, el patrón de él, le dice a su esposa, dice: —Estamos incurriendo con este muchacho, dice, —no más cuidando borregas, dice, —y no oye misa. Así es de que era bueno mandarlo que, que oiga misa.

—Pos sí. Está bien.

Luego le dijeron: —Oye, muchacho, . . . vas a dejar áhi las borregas enredadas y, y vas a misa al pueblo. Te metes allí a onde 'tén llamando las campanas, y onde 'té entrando mucha gente. Y tú también entras allí. Es la iglesia. Y todo lo que hagan allí, te pones muy bien cuidado, dice, —y lo que hagan allí, tú también lo haces.

—Está bien, señor. Se fue a, al pueblo a misa. No, pos 'taban llama y llama las campanas, que fueran a misa todos los fieles. Y él se metió luego luego. Y se metió a frente al altar . . . allí hincado. Bueno. Cuando ya se llegó la hora de dar la comunión el padre, él se ponía muy al pendiente. Y venía dando la comunión. Y el padre, pues, también le dio la comunión a él. Pero él no se la comió. El se la sacó de la boca y se la echó a la bolsa. Dice: —Todavía yo no me la como.

Entonces . . . pues ya terminó la misa, y ya se fue pa su rancho. Y ya le dice el patrón: —¿Oyistes misa, muchacho?

—Sí, dice, —cómo no. Todo, dice, —todo lo que hizo él, también yo lo hice.

—Bueno, echa afuera tus borregas.

Y las echó al . . . donde las pasteaba. Y luego ya . . . luego ya que llegó al hueco del sabino a darles agua allá al río a las borreguitas, se fue, como a la orilla del río había muchas flores, trajo muchas flores y colocó en el hueco del sabino, colocó aquella hostia. Y la rodeó de puritas flores. Y luego áhi está haciendo las . . . las reverencias como el padre. Alzaba las manos y todo lo que hacía el padre, toditito. Si, ¡qué bien aprendió, home (1, 2)! Y . . . y luego ya que terminaba, dice, pues ya . . . ya descansaba.

Pero de tantos . . . días que empezó a hacer esto, las borreguitas, ya sería por Dios, sería por . . . por instinto, ya las borreguitas se hincaban también al derredor del, del árbol. Y él, luego luego se iba allí a hacer todo lo que hacía el padre, allí en el hueco donde estaba la hostia. Y todas las borreguitas hincadas allí (3).

Entonces . . . había un, un camino que . . . que pendía al pueblo. La gente se fijaba que estaban aquellas borregas hincadas, y les llamaba la atención. —Mira, todas esas borregas hincadas áhi en derredor del árbol. Pos vamos a, vamos a darle parte al patrón. Ya fueron a, a con el patrón. —Señor, dice, —¿sabe qué?, dice. —Las borregas se hincan al derredor del, del árbol. Yo . . . venemos a avisarle a usted, dice: —El muchacho canta en el hueco del sabino y hace las . . . hace las reverencias del padre. Así es de que . . . 'tá curioso eso. ¿Cómo no lo espía?

Tonces ya el patrón se vino por allí, se escondió, y luego ya vido venir el borrero [sic]. Y luego luego bebieron agua las borreguitas y, y se jueron al árbol y se hincaron. Y luego él se fue luego luego a cantar allí y a hacer las reverencias que hacía el padre. Y el patrón viendo. Cuando ya terminó todo, dijo: —Oye, muchacho, ¿qué . . . cómo enseñastes tú a las borregas a hincarse?

—No, dice. —Yo no las enseñé. Ellas solitas, ellas solitas se hincan.

Dice: —Y tú, ¿qué tienes áhi en el hueco del árbol?

Dice: —Pues ése es mi pan.

—¿Cuál pan?

—Pues, ¿que no se acuerda cuando jui a misa que me dijo usted que me fijara, que todo lo que hacía . . . hiciera yo. Pues él le dio pan a los demás, y yo . . . también me dio pan. Pero yo no me lo comí. Yo me lo eché a la bolsa. Y éste es el pan que tengo yo aquí. Le puse flores, también él tenía muchas flores.

Tonces el patrón ya se arrimó al hueco del . . . del sabino, y vido . . . vido un Cristo (4). Y luego ya el patrón fue a darle parte al cura. Dice: —Señor cura, sabe que . . . yo mandé para acá mi borreguero a que oyera misa. Y yo, pues como era un muchacho inorante, le dije que se fijara, que todo lo que . . . viera hacer que él también hiciera. Y él, resulta de que cuando vio, cuando dieron la hostia, dice que es pan, que no se comió su pan, que se lo echó a la bolsa, y que ese pan lo tiene en el hueco del sabino. Y ya yo jui a ver, dice, —y es un Cristo.

—Hombre, dice, —pues mañana vamos a espiarlo.

Se jue el patrón y el, y el señor cura, a espiar al borreguero. Sí, pues luego . . . vino con sus borregas, y tomaron agua las borregas, y luego luego a hincarse en derredor del árbol. Y él luego luego a cantar y a hacer las reverencias que el padre hacía. Y, y el señor cura y el patrón allí cuidándolo.

Luego que ya terminó ya jueron a hablar con él. Dice: —Oyes, muchacho, dice, —¿pues qué . . . cómo . . . cómo haces tú que se hinquen las borregas? ¿Cómo hicistes?

—No, dice, —ellas solitas se hincan. Solitas se hincan, dice.

—¿Y tú?

—Bueno, dice, —yo aquí hago lo que . . . lo que el padre hizo allá en la iglesia. Él les daba, les dio pan allá a los señores y señoras. A mí también me dio. Y yo no me comí mi pan. Yo me lo guardé en la bolsa. Así es de que este pan áhi lo tengo. Yo les doy misa a mis borregas. Les doy su misa. Y así es de que . . . el señor cura fue y se asomó. No . . . pues era un Cristo ya bien hecho. Un Cristo de oro, muy bonito.

Entonces ya dice: —No, dice, —pues este, este muchacho, dice, —es por Dios. Yo lo voy a recoger. Y este árbol, dice, —lo voy a prohibir aquí, dice, —y hacer . . . pos . . . pos más bien una capilla allí onde está el árbol. Ya era por Dios allí. Se llevó al muchacho. Dice: —Tú vas a vivir aquí de, de sacristán. Vas a llamar aquí a todos los fieles pa que vengan a misa. Das la primer campanada y la primer llamada, y luego la segunda, dos campanadas, y luego la tercera, tercer campanada, dice, —y ya después repicas que ya se terminó.

Aaa, este muchacho agarra la campana y áhi está a dale y dale y dale y dandandandandandan. Sale el señor cura. —No tanta, hijo.

—No, dice, —pues si con una no oyen, dice. —Pos yo por eso doy muchas campanadas, pa que . . . los que están dormidos.

—Aaa, está bueno.

Tonces ya así lo hacía el . . . el muchacho. Y luego . . . un día le dice el señor cura: —Oyes, muchacho, dice, dice, —anda a sacudir los santos que están allá, dice. —Tengo un cuarto, dice, —donde están todos los santos viejos. Pues, a sacudirlos. Han de tener mucho polvo.

Pues que áhi va el muchacho donde estaba aquel . . . aquellos santos. Y estaba un Cristo grandote. Y usted sabe que, pues los Cristos están encueraditos, ¿no? Entonces lo vido. —¡Ay, dice, —qué frío pasarás! Dice: —Mira no más, ni tata cura no te da ni una frazadita ni una camisa ni nada. Dice: —¡Qué frío pasarás encueradito, pobrecito! Te voy a dar mi gabán. Entonces se quita el gabán y se lo embrocó al Cristo. Dice: —Y yo creo que no te da ni de comer tampoco, dice, —porque estás muy flaquito. Dice: —Pero mañana, dice, —te voy a traer mi comida pa que tú te la comas. Pos sí.

Cuando ya lo llamaron a comer, pues, él se guardó la comida y, y jue a darle al Cristo, hombre. Con una cuchara le daba la sopa. Y lo tenía todo mantecoso [laughs] al Cristo. Así es de que el señor cura fue allá a visitarlo. Pues ya iba el Cristo allí con gabán, y áhi el Cristo todo mantecoso allí, . . . que . . . el muchacho le daba de comer (5).

Dice el padre: —¡Ooo, qué muchachito éste! Tal vez que está, pues, no está bien de los sentidos.

Entonces ya, ya fue y le dice a su mamá y a su papá, dice: —Van a recoger a su muchacho, dice. No le dijo por qué ni nada. El padre dice: —Ya yo le voy a dar un . . . una pensión mensualmente, y . . . para que se, se pueda mantener el muchacho, dice. —Y ustedes también, pues alcanzarán. Y así lo hizo el padre. Le dio una pensión para que se mantuviera. Pero el muchacho, pues, como no estaba, pues, muy bien . . . se fue . . . enfermando, se fue enfermando, y tal vez Dios se lo llevó porque era un muchacho bueno. Se murió. Se fue derechito al cielo.

Aquí termina el, el, el cuentecito, pa que se diviertan si es de que les gusta. Y si no les gusta, pues, pues no. Y, áhi queda.

The tale, as told by this informant, starts with an incident in the nature of Boggs *1690, the fool who is sent to mass, causes commotion there, and commits various foolish acts. The detail, however, is not the same, the tone being, in fact, much more serious. The boy's saying mass for his sheep, in imitation of what he saw the priest do in church, takes on the nature of a religious miracle, for the sheep kneel before the sacrament, and the latter miraculously turns into a golden image of Christ. Perhaps this illustrates a strong attraction to miracle legends or a preference, on the part of the informant, for a more serious treatment of the sacred topic of the mass. I have not found a parallel to this first part. The second part is Mt. 767. Food for the Crucifix.

The story is structured as follows: Boggs *1690 + V35.1.1. Horse kneels before stolen sacrament [here, it is sheep who kneel] + V35.1.2. Sacred image miraculously appears on stolen sacrament [here, the sacrament actually turns into a sacred image] + 767.

(1) J2461.1. Literal following of instructions about actions.
(2) J2400. Foolish imitation.
(3) V35.1.1. Horse kneels before stolen sacrament. [Here, sheep.]
(4) V35.1.2. Sacred image miraculously appears on stolen sacrament. [Here, host actually becomes golden statue of Christ.]
(5) Q172. Child taken to heaven: offers food to crucifix. [Here, on earth.]
     Boggs *1690.
     Hansen *1690. Fool is sent to mass. . . .
         Mexico: Wheeler, no. 170.
         Dominican Republic: Andrade, nos. 7, 9, 26.
         Puerto Rico: Arellano, no. 116; Mason-Espinosa, *JAF*, 34(1921), nos. 4, 4a, 4b, 4d, 4e, 4f, 25, 25a, 25b, 54, 55, 56.
         Spain: Espinosa, *Cuentos*, no. 184.
     Aarne-Thompson 767. Food for the Crucifix.
     Boggs *767.
         Mexico: Wheeler, no. 44.
         Chile: Pino Saavedra, no. 109.
         Spain: Alfonso el Sabio, *Cantigas*, no. 353.

Romantic Tales

80. Como la sal y el agua

(Recorded by Lola Cruz on December 8, 1966, in Los Angeles, California)

A king calls his three daughters to him and asks them how much they love him, to which the youngest replies that she loves him as she does salt and water. The king is angered at this apparent lack of affection, and he orders her killed and her eyes brought to him as proof of the deed. The servants, however, are fond of the girl, and they kill a dog instead, present the king with the dog's eyes, and send the girl off to make her own way. After wandering a great distance she comes upon the cave of a band of thieves, hears the magic words to which the door opens, and lives on food that she takes from them in exchange for doing their housekeeping. They finally find her out but treat her very kindly. A wicked witch hears her singing one day and decides to kill her with a pair of enchanted shoes so that she can then enter the cave and steal the thieves' riches. The girl agrees to try on the shoes and immediately falls into a deep sleep. The thieves, thinking she is dead, put her into a crystal coffin ornamented with gold and silver, give her a magic wand, and set her afloat on the sea. She is retrieved from the water by a poor coal merchant and regains consciousness when the shoes are knocked from her feet. She repays him with the richly ornamented coffin and sets off again, having used the magic wand to make herself appear very ragged and dirty in order to attract less attention. She buys three gems from a man she meets on the road and finally arrives at a palace where she asks for charity and is lodged in the chicken shed. Using the magic wand and the extraordinarily beautiful light of the gems, she makes herself very beautiful and her surroundings very elegant; she is observed by the king, the queen, and the prince on three successive nights. The latter falls deeply in love with her; they marry and plan a wedding banquet to celebrate. All the royalty for miles around, including the girl's mother and father, attend the banquet, and special instructions are given to serve her parents food without salt or water. They are displeased with the meal, the daughter reveals her identity, and they readily recognize the true compliment she paid them in saying she loved them like salt and water.

Éste era un rey, que tenía tres hijas. Y luego el rey les dijo a las hijas, . . . llamó a sus tres hijas para ver a cómo lo querían. Y luego le preguntó a la hija mayor: —Oyes, hija, deseamos saber tu mamá y yo cuánto nos aprecias, cuánto nos quieres.

Luego la hija mayor le dijo: —Pos, ay, papá, . . . hay tantos . . . composturas, tanta ropa y tantos lujos, tantos . . . diamantes que nos gustan a nosotros, pero más te queremos a ti y a mi mamá.

—Está bien.

Otra era la hija . . . menor [i.e., la de en medio]. Le dijo: —Hija, deseamos saber tu mamá y yo qué tanto nos quieres, qué tanto nos . . . aprecias.

Pos luego después le dijo la, la hija de en medio, dijo: —Pos, papá, hay muchos perfumes, hay muchas . . . flores que adoramos, y muchas cosas en el mundo que queremos nosotros, pero más los quiero a ustedes.

—Está bien, hija.

Llama a la chocoyota. La chocoyota quiere decir la hija menor, la más chiquitita. Ésa es chocoyota. Bueno. Pos que luego ya mandaron traer a la . . . a la hija . . . más chiquita y le dijo: —Oye, hija, deseamos saber tu mamá y yo qué tanto nos quieres, qué tanto nos aprecias.

—Pues, papá, yo los quiero como la sal y el agua (1).

Dice: —¿Cómo que nos quieres como la sal y el agua?

—Sí, papá.

Bueno, pos que luego ya . . . le, le dijo al, al criado que hacía de mayordomo que llevara a matar a su hija, y que de señas le trajiera los ojos y el dedito de la mano derecha. Pos luego después el, el señor llevó su escolta, el viejito, y dijo: —Ay, niña, tan buena que es usted con nosotros, ¿cómo va a ser posible de que la mátemos [*sic*]? No puede ser que la mátemos a usted que es muy buena con nosotros.

—Hagan lo que mi padre ha dicho. Mi padre ha dicho que . . . que me maten y tienen que matarme. Cuando en eso el perrito iba detrás de ella. No la dejó.

Y luego uno de los criados le dijo: —No, señor, no la matemos. Vamos matando . . . al perrito, porque el perrito tiene los ojos del color de la niña (2).

—Pos, está bueno. Entonces matamos al perrito y lo sepultamos. Lo mataron al perrito y le . . . le quitaron los ojos. Y los pusieron en una cajita. Y luego le cortaron el dedo chiquito a ella, de la mano derecha, y se lo pusieron en . . . una cajita también, áhi donde estaban los ojitos (3). Y luego dijo: —Bueno, ya, niña . . . vete . . . por donde tú quieras porque no podemos llevarte, porque si te llevamos, entonces el rey nos mata a nosotros.

Dice: —Sí. Mira, váyanse ustedes y yo me voy a ver por ónde llego.

Cuando luego en eso llegaron con el rey y le dijieron: —Tus órdenes, . . . mi Sacarreal Majestad, tus órdenes están cumplidas. El dedito de la niña y los ojitos aquí los tienes.

Dice: —Qué bueno que se ha . . . hecho lo que yo he mandado, porque esa niña dijo que nos quería como la sal y el agua.

Cuando luego en eso estaba la niña anda y anda y anda y ya se moría de hambre y de sed. Y se puso junto de una piedra . . . allá a descansar, cuando oyó un tropello de caballos. Y eran unos . . . ladrones. Era la cueva de los siete ladrones (4). Y luego entonces uno de los ladrones dijo: —Ábrete sésamo. Y se abrió (5, 6). Y entonces entraron ellos. Y se . . . acostaron. Y luego la niña, titiritiando de frío, se quedó afuera.

Y luego otro día que amaneció: —Ábrete sésamo. Y se abrió (5).

Y luego cuando ellos salieron dijieron: —Ciérrate sésamo. Y se cerró el sésamo.

Y luego la niña . . . se, se puso muy lista y luego dijo: —Ábrete sésamo. Y se abrió el sésamo (5). Y luego entró y comió, . . . lavó los trastes, barrió, lavó la ropa, tendió las camas, . . . y planchó, a todos les planchó, y hizo todo lo que quiso . . . allí. Estuvo muy contenta. Cuando ya vio que ya era hora de que iban a venir los dueños de la casa. Entonces salió, dijo: —Ábrete sésamo (5). Y se abrió el sésamo, y entonces ya se salió . . . la niña.

Y luego vinieron los bandidos y dijieron: —¡Ay, mira, Dios de mi vida! ¿Quién ha venido aquí a limpiar esto (7)? Parece que es un ángel del cielo. Que ha de haber dicho Dios Nuestro Señor: "Estos hombres 'tán solos. No tienen mujer, no tienen quien les, quien les haga la limpieza," y, y era . . . ha mandado un ángel a que nos haga todo, un ángel del cielo. Porque Dios se compadece de los que no pueden hacer las cosas. Bueno, pos luego ya comieron con la comida que la niña les hizo, y se cambiaron de limpio. Y luego ya estuvieron muy contentos.

Y luego le dijo el capitán de los ladrones, le dijo a uno: —A ver, ¿quién se quiere quedar aquí para que vea . . . a ver quién viene?

Pues dijo uno: —Yo me quedo.

Dice: —Pero no te vayas a dormir.

—No, no me duermo.

Luego se fueron los . . . demás, y quedó él solo. Y luego dijo: —Pos hora yo me voy a arrimar mi comida y una botella de vino . . . para . . . alcanzar a ver a . . . a ver quién es. Pero en ese tiempo él se tomó todo el . . . toda la botella . . . y se emborrachó. Y luego se durmió.

Pues luego cuando entró la niña y que dijo: —Ábrete sésamo (5), pues ya no podía ver él, . . . de nada, porque estaba dormido. Y luego la niña . . . empezó a barrer, a limpiar, a volver a lavar la ropa que se habían quitado. Tendió las camas y hizo la comida y comió ella, y luego, . . . y arregló todo y se apuró y se fue.

Cuando vinieron los, los bandidos, dijieron: —Ábrete sésamo (5).
Y se abrió el sésamo. Y luego le dice, . . . luego entonces en ese tiempo
dispertó él.

Y luego dijo: —Oyes, ¿quién vino?

—Ay, mi capitán, pos áhi tiene usted. Aquí no vino nadie. Sabe
usted que en una parpareada que yo di, mire que todo se arregló listo.
Nadien, nadien entró.

—Mmmm, ya es como yo digo, que es un ángel del cielo que ha de
haber venido . . . a limpiarnos, a barrernos, a hacer toda la limpieza.

—Pues sí. Vámonos a comer y luego nos acostamos. Luego ya comieron la comida que les hizo ella. Unas comidas muy elegantes de las
que hacen los reyes. Pero como ellos tenían todo allí, pues ella, no se
le dificultaba nada.

Pues luego en eso . . . ya se levantaron otro día, y le dijo: —¿Hora
tú te vas a quedar?, le dijo al otro.

—O, sí, mi capitán. Yo sí voy a, voy a, no voy a parparear. Y a ver
quién veo.

—Está bueno. Pos luego después ya . . . empezaron a arreglar y se
fueron.

Cuando luego en eso . . . la niña vuelve a venir. Y ya el otro ya estaba dormido tamién. Y luego dice: —Ábrete sésamo (5). Y ella no se
había fijado que había alguien. Entonces luego limpió, arregló y hizo
otra diferente comida y hizo distintas comidas cada vez de que iba. Y
luego ya después lavó, planchó y luego hizo su comidita y luego se llevó poquita comida para cenar ella allá onde estaba.

Bueno, pos que luego ya llegaron los bandidos. Y dijo: —¿Qué hay,
. . . amigo?

—Pos nada, mi capitán. Pos, no más me agaché a prender un cigarro, y cuando ya . . . ya volteé, mire que ya se apareció todo.

—Ah, pues no cabe duda que es un ángel que ha venido a hacernos
la limpieza.

—Pos sí, mi capitán. Yo sé que ha de haber sido un ángel.

Dice: —Bueno. Ahora váyanse ustedes. Y mucho cuidado, no los
vayan a agarrar. Hora yo me quedo.

Y luego dijo: —Pero, capitán, arrímese una botella.

Dijo: —No, yo no quiero botella, no quiero nada. Bueno. Él no agarró botella. No más agarró comida para comer y . . . y se escondió.

Y luego oyó que dijieron: —Ábrete sésamo, una voz muy dulce (5).

Y dijo: —Ay, alguien ya viene. Y entonces vio la niña que entró. Y vio cuando luego se puso un delantal que ella traiba. Y luego entonces en seguida barrió, lavó los trastes, tendió las camas, lavó y planchó. Y luego se puso a hacer comida. Y luego que ella hizo la comida comió. Y luego les dejó la mesa servida.

Y luego . . . luego dijo, . . . cuando se iba la niña entonces él le habló y dijo: —Niña, de parte de Dios te pido de cuál mundo eres. ¿Eres de éste o eres del otro (8, 9)?

Dijo: —Ay, señor, soy de este mundo, mas que tenía mucha hambre, . . . y he venido aquí a hacer . . . a granjiar mi comida haciendo los quehaceres . . . para comer. Pero no me llevo nada. No más me llevo un poquito de comida para comer yo . . . en el resto de la noche.

Dice: —Bueno, desde ahora en adelante aquí te vas a quedar. Aquí tienes . . . todo. Platícame tu historia. Entonces ya le platicó la historia de lo que le había pasado, que sus padres la habían mandado matar porque los quería como la sal y el agua. Pos luego le dijo: —Mira, ya va, ya vienen áhi los muchachos. Y vas a tener mucho cuidado con ellos.

—Sí, sí, señor.

Cuando luego en eso vinieron los bandidos. —Ábrete sésamo. Y se abrió el sésamo (5). Y entraron. Dice: —Ay, mi capitán, pero, ¿qué tiene aquí? ¡Mira no más qué cosas tan bonitas tiene usted!

—Pos sí, es el ángel del cielo que ha venido a hacernos el quehacer.

—¡Ay, mi capitán! ¿Y cómo la vio?

—Pues bien, yo no me dormí. Yo estuve listo y la vi cuando entró. Y la vi cuando hizo todo, todo el quehacer. Y hasta comida nos hizo.

Luego empezaron: —Es para mí.

—No, que es para mí.

—No, que es para mí.

Dijo: —No, nadien aquí. Ni yo porque soy el capitán, ni ustedes porque son mis . . . mis trabajadores. Tienen que respetarla.

—Pues sí, mi capitán.

—Pos hora tienen . . . traigan una aguja. Trajieron una aguja y se picaron una vena del brazo todos, y luego llenaron un vasito de sangre. Y luego ella, la niña, también. Le dijo: —Ahora con esta sangre la tenemos que tomar un trago cada uno para ser hermanos. Pos así lo hicieron. Y después ya la quisieron como una hermana, ya no la quisieron como . . . una desconocida (10).

Y luego le . . . le dijo el capitán a la niña: —Tú eres la dueña de la casa. Y tú vas a hacer aquí . . . todo, todo lo que yo te mande. Y, y tú no tienes que dejar que nadien te, te moleste.

—Pues, que sí, señor.

Dijo: —Y ahora, más de esto, . . . toma . . . todos estos vestidos para que te los pongas. Y luego áhi está este cuarto muy elegante para que duermas en él. Bueno, pos ella se quedó muy contenta, porque tenía . . . unos vestidos muy preciosos y un cuarto donde dormir sin frío y con comida.

Pos luego en esto, estaba ella cantando unas canciones muy bonitas, bonitas, cuando oye una, una bruja. Andaba juntando leña por allí, y oye y le dice al esposo: —Oyes, ¿estás oyendo esa niña que está . . . esa voz que está cantando?

—Sí.

—Pos esa voz no me . . . no se me figura una gente de, de pueblo. Se me figura una gente de palacio, una reina, una princesa. Vamos a ver. Bueno, pos luego después la bruja se arrimó . . . allá a la, a oír cantar. Y entonces la bruja empezó a arrimarse más, más, y más onde oía el canto tan hermoso. Y luego tocó . . . la puerta.

Y luego la niña salió y dijo: —Ábrete sésamo. Y luego se abrió el sésamo (5).

Y luego llegó la, la . . . señora esa bruja, y le dijo: —Buenos días, buena niña.

—Buenos días, señora. ¿Qué deseaba?

—Ay, niña, pues que mire, que nosotros no tenemos dinero, no tenemos esto, no tenemos lo otro.

Entonces luego dijo: —Buenos pues, . . . entonces yo les voy a dar aquí . . . un poco de dinero. Y no vengan a molestar, porque si vienen a molestar mis hermanos se van a enojar.

—Está bien, buena niña. Entonces se entró ella y sacó . . . todo lo que abarcaba su delantal, de puras onzas de oro.

Y luego la bruja dijo: —¡Ay, qué bueno está esto! Hora con esto vamos a hacerle unos zapatos que estén embrujados pa que se muera, y entramos a robar. Bueno, pues luego empezaron a trabajar . . . ellos, a hacer los zapatos. Empezaron a trabajar a hacer los zapatos con . . . con la brujería (11).

Pues luego le dijo, . . . tocaron otra vuelta otro día la puerta y luego dijo ella: —Ábrete sésamo (5). ¿Qué deseaban, señores? ¿Qué, se les acabó el dinero?

—No, niña pero en recompensa de que usted nos dio . . . este dinero venimos a traerle estos zapatitos. Póngalos.

—No, no, no, yo tengo muchos zapatos . . . que me han dado mis hermanos y no puede usted . . . darme los zapatos.

—Bueno, no se los damos. No más mírenselos. Con que se los miren, con eso tenemos. Pues luego se puso la niña . . . por no estar hablando, . . . se puso los zapatitos. Y cuando se puso los zapatitos la niña cayó . . . cayó muerta (12, 13). Y luego después . . . entraron . . . esa viejita bruja y el viejito, y . . . empezaron a ver, y de tanto que vieron no agarraron nada, nada, nada porque se asustaron de ver tanta cosa que había.

—Y luego vinieron los hermanos. Y luego dijieron: —Ábrete sésamo (5).

Dijo: —No, pues, ¿cómo se va a abrir el sésamo si está abierto? Estamos descubiertos. ¿Qué pasó? Ay, pues nuestra hermana, que está muerta, que se ha caído muerta, mira no más.

Bueno, pos luego después . . . ya le pusieron un vestido muy elegante. Y luego dijieron: —Vamos a enterrarla.

—No, no, ¡qué enterrarla ni qué nada! Vamos a hacerle un . . . una caja de puro cristal (14), cubierta de oro y de plata, con las barras de oro y de plata (15, 16).

—Pos, está bueno. Pos luego hicieron las varillas . . . de oro y de plata . . . para cubrir . . . las pegaduras de, del cristal de la caja.

Y luego le dijo: —Ay, tengo que darle esta varita de virtud, que estas varitas nadien las tiene porque es la última que nos robamos. Vamos a ponerle esta varita a la niña. Pues le pusieron la varita de virtud, y la pusieron en la caja (17). Y luego la pusieron en la, en el agua para que se la llevara el mar a ver hasta dónde iba a llegar.

Cuando en ese tiempo iba pasando un . . . carbonero, que era un hombre muy pobrecito, pobrecito. Y traiba unas burritas cargadas de carbón. Y luego le, y luego le dijo: —¡Ay, qué chula caja viene! ¡Ay, parece un tesoro! Luego él desató las . . . mulas y, y tiró el carbón, y agarró el . . . el mecate y lazó la, la caja y la sacó (18). Y al tiempo que él sacó . . . le dio un golpe a la caja cuando, cuando estaba él, . . . se le salen los zapatitos a la niña. Y cuando abrió la caja se sentó la niña (19).

Dice: —¡Qué bueno que me has, . . . que me ha salvado, buen señor!

—¿Qué te pasó, buena niña?

—Pos, no me acuerdo. Dice: —Yo estoy muy lejos de mis hermanos. Una señora y un señor me pusieron unos zapatos y no, no me acuerdo. No más me caí, y es todo lo que yo me puedo acordar. ¡Ay, dice, —mira lo que traigo aquí! ¡Una varita de virtud!

—Ay, buena niña, si la ven los . . . los hombres, la van a matar o le van a hacer una cosa.

—Mira, buen señor, no tengo con qué pagarte, pero te pago con la caja. Anda, consigue otros . . . mulas pa que te lleves todos los vidrios. Puedes venderlos porque son muy finos. Y el oro y la . . . y la plata puedes venderla y sacas mucho dinero, que te puedes quitar de pobre.

—Está bien, buena niña. Voy a hacer eso.

Bueno, pos luego ya la niña dijo: —Pues, ¿qué hago, qué hago para andar, . . . que no me vayan a hacer nada? Luego dijo: —Varita, varita de virtud, por la virtud que Dios te ha dado, quiero que me pongas muy mocosa . . . y muy greñuda y muy mugrosa, muy cochina, que nadien se me arrime (20, 21).

Luego pasaron unos arrieros y le dijieron: —¿Adónde vas, muchacha?

—¿Adónde he de ir, buenos señores? Voy a buscar . . . el palacio del rey, . . . del palacio primero que encuentre.

—Pues, ¿qué vas a hacer allá? Allá no van muchachas roñosas como tú . . . mugrosas. ¿Cómo te llamas?

—María Moco, señor.

—Pues, ¿ni lo niegas? Porque estás tan mocosa que hasta tú misma

te pones ese nombre. Dice: —Válgame, pues. Vete. Toma estos . . .
veinticinco centavos y vete (22).

—Está muy bien, señor. Ya me voy. Bueno, pues se fue anda y anda
y anda y anda y anda, cuando pasan unos . . . otros hombres, más ca-
trincitos.

Y le dijo: —¿Adónde vas, muchacha?

—Voy a la casa del rey, señor.

—¿Cómo te llamas, muchacha?

—María Moco, señor.

—Ay, ¿ni lo niegas? Mira no más, tan . . . cochina y tan atascada
que andas. Dice: —A ver, ahora, toma estos cincuenta centavos para
que . . . te ayudes en el camino y vete. Áhi derecho derecho encuentras
la casa del rey.

—Está muy bien señor. Muchas gracias. Luego ya juntó . . . setenta
y cinco centavos.

Y luego se fue anda y anda y anda, cuando vio pasar unos condes,
unos reyes, unos . . . más elegantes. Y le preguntaron: —¿Dónde vas,
muchacha?

—A la casa del rey, señor.

—¿Cómo te llamas?

—María Moco, señor.

—¿Ni lo niegas? Estás muy cochina que ni lo niegas cómo te llamas. A ver, muchacha, toma este peso. Se lo aventaron. —Para que te
ayudes en el camino.

—Está muy bien, señor.

Bueno, pos que luego se fue . . . más pa adelante, y se encontró un
viejito. Dice: —¿Adónde vas, buena niña (23)?

Voy a . . . buscar la, la casa del rey, señor.

—Cómo te llamas?

—María Moco, señor.

—Pues, toma, niña, estas tres piedritas . . . por este dinero que traes
(24). Toma estas tres piedritas. En una ocasión que las puedas . . .
prenderlas . . . pa alumbrarte. Ésta es una azul, una colorada y una
blanca (25, 26). Y estas piedritas te pueden servir de mucho. Y dame
esos centavos que traes pa comprar mi comida.

—Sí, señor. Aquí están. Uno setenta y cinco.

Bueno pos, luego se fue. Llegó a la casa del rey y le dijo a la criada:
—Señora, señora, deme una tortillita o deme una comidita o déjeme
entrar a dormir aquí.

Dice: —No, tú no puedes entrar aquí. Te vas a emporcar todo.

—Dígale a la reina y al rey que si no me dan permiso de quedarme
aquí.

Y luego fue. —Señora, señora, aquí está una . . . una muchacha.

—¿Qué clase de muchacha es? Al poco viene aquí por mi esposa.

—No, señor, es una muchacha muy mugrosa, . . . muy mocosa. Y
quiere un lugarcito.

—Ah, pues acabamos de matar todas las gallinas. Ponla en el gallinero. Entonces luego . . . :—Áhi, dale un petatito y dale una . . .
un pedazo de garra, y áhi que se quede en el gallinero (27).

—Está bien, señora.

Pues luego ya le dieron el petatito y un . . . una . . . cobija toda rompida y un . . . y una garra y una almohada. Entonces ella se sentó allí
en su gallinerito. Y luego ya como . . . cuando vio que eran las doce de
la noche . . . entonces dijo: —Varita, varita de virtud, por la virtud
que Dios te ha dado, quiero que me pongas una cama muy elegante
con unos pabellones muy finos y unos vestidos muy elegantes (21).
Quiero que me los pongas aquí. Y luego agarró una de las piedritas,
la piedrita azul, y la . . . y la iluminaba.

Y luego entonces luego ya . . . entraba a los ojos del, del príncipe,
que no podía dormir porque no se casaba porque no había con quién.

Y luego dijo: —¡Ay, qué luz viene tan bonita! ¿De dónde vendrá
esa luz? Y se asomó . . . y ya vio que venía del gallinero. Entonces fue
poco a poquito, poco a poquito, . . . y luego ya vio que era una reina.
Dijo: —¡Ay, ésta es una reina! Es más elegante que ni mi mamá y más
elegante que mis familiares (28, 29). ¡Mira no más qué cosas tan pre-
ciosas! Bueno, pues áhi se quedó hasta que amaneció y se fue él a su
cuarto.

Entonces luego ya . . . se levantaron todos y, y sirvieron comida. Y
luego le dijo la, la criada: —Mi Sacarreal Majestad, ¿qué es lo que doy
de comer a la muchacha?

—Dale de lo que sobre de las mesas. De eso que coma, porque es el desperdicio de las gallinas.

—Sí, señora.

Y luego dijo el muchacho: —No, no, no, no. Que le lleven mi . . . mi desayuno. Ella tiene que comer mejor que yo.

—¿No puede ser que tú comas mejor que la, que la . . . muchacha?

—Sí, ¿cómo se llama, mamá, esa joven?

—Se llama María Moco.

—¡Ay, pues yo me casaría con María Moco si ustedes quisieran. Y estaba triste, triste el muchacho porque no querían que platicara con ella.

Cuando luego el papá le dijo: —¿Por qué no quieres comer, hijo?

—Porque no quieren darle de comer a María Moco. Porque yo quiero que coma María los manjares que me toquen a mi.

—O, no. Tú no puedas . . . dejar de comer porque coma esa mocosa.

—Sí, papá.

—Pues luego en la noche dijo la, . . . ya llegó la noche y dijo la niña: —Varita, varita de virtud, por la virtud que Dios te ha dado, quiero que me pongas ahora la cama más elegante que la de anoche y unos vestidos muy preciosos, muy elegantes (21). Cuando luego en eso prendió, puso la piedrita colorada y . . . y era un deslumbre.

Dijo [el rey]: —¡Válgame Dios! dice. —El sol tan . . . tan noche. No puede ser éste sol que haiga venido aquí. Dice: —Voy a ver. Ahora también tengo curiosidad de ir a ver a . . . a la muchacha que mi hijo no quiere comer porque quiere que . . . que María Moco coma la comida de él. Y luego fue al gallinero el señor, el rey, y vio aquella princesa tan bonita. —Lástima de que mi hijo la, la vio. Si mi hijo no la hubiera visto yo me había casado con esa princesa tan preciosa y tan bonita. Ya mi esposa, ya me cansó.

Bueno, pos luego empezó el esposo con la esposa: —Oyes, . . . yo quiero que la . . . que la muchacha esté aquí adentro, de, de la casa.

—No puede ser de que ella venga aquí a la casa con nosotros. Ella es una . . . muchacha muy pobre. Y luego: —Es María Moco, ¿y no ves cómo está, toda mocosa? Y luego se asomó la señora, y la vio titiri-

tiando de frío. Y la vio muy pobrecita, pobrecita y muy mugrosa, mugrosa.

Bueno, pos luego después dijo en la noche la señora: —Pues yo, . . .
¡qué tentación tienen éstos, mi hijo y mi esposo, de que María Moco
venga para acá . . . conmigo! Pos luego después ella se puso a velar.

Y luego la . . . la niña empezó: —Varita, varita, varita de virtud,
con la virtud que Dios te ha dado, quiero que me pongas una cama
que la reina nunca la haiga visto, y unos vestidos muy preciosos que la
reina nunca los haiga visto. Y se le puso todo muy bonito (21). Y
luego prendió la, puso la piedrita blanca.

Y luego ya la reina se asomó y dijo: —¡Ay, qué bonito! ¡Qué . . .
qué luz tan preciosa, que nunca la he visto yo en mi vida! ¿Qué será?
Voy a ver. Entonces viene por el, el gallinero. Y fue y incontró a la
niña y dice: —¡Ay, no está esa niña! No es María Moco. Ésta es una
reina, es una princesa. ¿De ónde vendría esta princesa?

Bueno, pues que luego él dijo, . . . estaba enfermo, y luego le dijo:
—¿Por qué estás enfermo, hijo?

—Porque no me dejas casar con María Moco.

—Bueno. Si tanto la quieres, sí, quiero que te cases con ella. Arrí-
mense todos los criados, y dígale a María Moco que vamos ir por ella.

Entonces dijo el hijo: —No, mamá. Yo quiero que pongan alfombra . . . desde el gallinero hasta el palacio.

Ya después . . . le dijo: —María Moco, te quieren allá en palacio.
Que vayas.

—Ay, pero ¿cómo voy a ir con estas trazas así, tan mugrosa y tan
. . . mocosa como estoy?

—No le hace. Así te quieren. Mi mamá y mi papá quieren que
vayas. Y los criados te están esperando.

—Está bien. Pues dice:—Espérame un momentito. Y luego dijo:
—Varita, varita de virtud, por la virtud que Dios te ha dado, quiero
que me des . . . un vestido muy elegante, que ninguna de las princesas
lo haya estrenado. Quiero ser la única moda que . . . que haiga . . . usado este, este vestido. Pues ya le trajo un vestido muy elegante, muy bonito . . . de puros diamantes. Entonces ya fue subiendo al palacio.

Y luego ya le dijo la reina: —Pos, ya estás aquí. Pos, te vas a casar
con mi hijo (30). Y vamos a hacer las invitaciones.

Y luego hicieron todas las invitaciones . . . para los reyes, todos los reinados, todos, hasta que llegó una invitación al papá de . . . de ella. Y luego . . . vinieron y luego ya los conoció que era su papá y su mamá.

Y luego les dijo a los criados: —Miren, a esa señora y ese señor quiero que le . . . no le den . . . sal ni agua en la comida, le hagan la comida seca . . . y la comida sin sal. Bueno, pues que le hicieron una comida especialmente a ellos sin sal y sin agua.

Pues luego dijo, . . . no comían. Todos comían y solamente esos dos no comían. Y luego se arrimó, dijo: —Ay, señores, ¿qué, no les gustan . . . los, las comidas? Miren no más qué criados, qué comidas les fueron a traer. Y probó la comida. Y dice: —O, ésta, le falta sal. Y le falta agua también. De veras que sin la sal y sin el agua no se puede vivir. Y luego les preguntó a todo el reinado que estaba allí: —¿Quién puede vivir sin la sal y sin el agua?

—Nadien.

—¿Y quién prefiere mejor la sal y el agua? Y todos se alzaron las manos, que todos. Entonces le dijo la niña a su papá: —Pues, padre mío, yo soy tu hija. Tú me mandastes matar, . . . y . . . y los criados no me mataron. Mataron a mi perrito. Y mi dedo chiquito fue el que te llevaron. Se quitó el guante y luego le vieron el dedito mocho.

Y luego le, le preguntaron todos los reinados —¿Y por qué te mandó matar?

—Porque yo les dije que los quería como, . . . que los quería yo como la sal y el agua (1).

Dice: —Ay, es una injusticia, porque sin la sal y sin el agua nadien puede vivir. Porque la sal es para el bautismo y el agua también.[120] Y luego tenemos que comer en la comida sal, y cocerla con agua. Porque una comida que se coce sin agua y sin sal no sabe a comida. No sabe a nada.

Y así es de que ellos se fueron avergonzados, y ya se quedó ella con su esposo. Vuelo por un caminito, vuelo por otro, cuénteme usted otro.

I have found no parallel version involving the combination of these three tale types, although 923 and 510 is a common blend. The tale is structured as

___

[120] In Catholic churches, the holy water is salted. See Moya, "Superstitions and Beliefs," p. 42.

follows: 923 + 510 Icd + 709 IIa (father orders her killed; dog's eyes sub-
stituted) b (she wanders to robbers' cave) IIIa (witch) *e (bewitched shoes)
IVb V*c (coal merchant finds her, shoes knocked off, and she revives) + 510
IIIc V VI.

 (1) H592.1. Love like salt: value of salt.
 (2) K512. Compassionate executioner.
 (3) K512.2.0.2. Eyes of animal substituted as proof for eyes of children.
 (4) Z71.5. Formulistic number: seven.
 (5) D1552.2. Mountain opens to magic formula (Open Sesame).
 (6) N455.3. Secret formula for opening treasure mountain overheard from
     robbers. (Open Sesame.)
 (7) N831.1. Mysterious housekeeper.
 (8) E545.19.2. Proper means of addressing ghosts.
 (9) E451.4.1. Ghost asked to identify itself in the name of God.
(10) P312. Blood-brotherhood.
(11) F823. Extraordinary shoes.
(12) G263. Witch injures, enchants or transforms.
(13) D1364. Object causes magic sleep. [Shoes.]
(14) F852.1. Glass coffin.
(15) F852.2. Golden coffin.
(16) F852.3. Silver coffin.
(17) D1254.1. Magic wand.
(18) N856. Helpful forester.
(19) D1978.3. Waking from magic sleep by removal of enchanting instru-
     ment. [Shoes.]
(20) K1816. Disguise as menial.
(21) D1473.1. Magic wand furnishes clothes.
(22) N841. Shepherd as helper.
(23) N825.2. Old man helper.
(24) D822. Magic object received from old man.
(25) F800. Extraordinary rocks and stones.
(26) D1645. Self-luminous objects. [Stones.]
(27) L132. Pig-sty abode for unpromising hero (heroine). [Here, chicken
     shed.]
(28) H151.1. Attention drawn by magic objects: recognition follows.
(29) H151.6. Heroine in menial disguise discovered in her beautiful clothes:
     recognition follows.
(30) L162. Lowly heroine marries prince.
     Aarne-Thompson 923. Love Like Salt.
     Boggs 923.
     Hansen 923. Love Like Salt.
        Mexico: Reid, *JAF*, 48(1935), 113, no. 4; Robe, *Mexican Tales*, nos.
           112, 113; Wheeler, no. 54.
        United States: Boggs, *NMFR*, 2(1947–1948), 20–23 (+510); Es-
           pinosa, *Hispania*, 23(1940), 130, no. 2 (+ 510); Post, *UAHB*,
           5(1934), 48–50; Zunser, *JAF*, 48(1935), 159, no. 3.
        Chile: Guzmán Maturana, *AUC*, XCII, pp. 40–49.
        Puerto Rico: Arellano, no. 82; Mason-Espinosa, *JAF*, 39(1926),
           300, no. 21ff.
        Spain: Cortes Vázquez, p. 72, no. 25; Curiel Merchán, pp. 346–348,
           358–361; Espinosa, *Cuentos*, nos. 107, 108 (+510); Giner Ari-

vau, *BTPE*, VIII, pp. 175–179 (+510); Menéndez Pidal, *Poesía popular*, p. 341; Sánchez Pérez, no. 87.

Aarne-Thompson 709. Snow-White.

Boggs 709.

Hansen 709. Snow White.

Grimm, no. 53.

> Mexico: Robe, *Mexican Tales*, no. 96; Wagner, JAF, 40(1927), 125–131; Wheeler, no. 68.
>
> United States: Rael, nos. 121, 122, 141, 142, 143.
>
> Chile: Pino Saavedra, nos. 98, 262.
>
> Dominican Republic: Andrade, nos. 194, 209.
>
> Puerto Rico: Arellano, nos. 84, 85; Jijena Sánchez, no. 44; Mason-Espinosa, *JAF*, 38(1925), 517, no. 2a (= Jijena Sánchez); 519, no. 2b; 520, no. 2c; 521, no. 2d; 522, no. 2e; 524, no. 2f; 525, no. 2g.
>
> Spain: Ampudia, no. 29; Espinosa, *Castilla*, nos. 52, 53; Espinosa, *Cuentos*, nos. 115, 116; Sánchez Pérez, no. 61.

Aarne-Thompson 510. Cinderella and Cap o' Rushes.

Boggs 510.

Hansen 510. Cinderella and Cap o' Rushes.

Grimm, nos. 21, 65.

Morosoli, "A Theoretical Reconstruction of the Original Cinderella Story."

Woods, "A Study of the Cinderella Story in the Spanish Folklore of New Mexico and Colorado."

> Mexico: Boas, *JAF*, 37(1924), 354, no. 5; Mason, *JAF*, 25(1912), 192, no. 2; Mendoza, *San Pedro Piedra Gorda*, pp. 413–415; Robe, *Mexican Tales*, nos. 68, 69, 70; Wagner, *JAF*, 40(1927), no. 23; Wheeler, nos. 56, 57 (510); 76 (510A); 49, 51, 52 (510B).
>
> United States: Espinosa, nos. 4, 5, 6, 7; Rael, nos. 106, 107, 108, 109, 111, 113, 114, 115, 237 (510); 116, 117, 118, 119 (510B).
>
> Argentina: Chertudi, 1st series, no. 49 (510A); 2nd series, no. 52 (510A).
>
> Chile: *BTPE*, vol. 1, pp. 114–120; Dufourcq, pp. 68–74 (510B); Laval, *Carahue*, II, no. 9 (510A); Lenz, *AUC*, vol. 8, no. 1; Pino Saavedra, nos. 53, 97, 254 (510A), 54, 55 (510B); Saunière, *RCHG*, 1, no. 17.
>
> Costa Rica: Lyra, pp. 87–97.
>
> Cuba: *AFC*, vol. 4, pp. 251–255 (510A); vol. 5, pp. 61–65 (510A, 510B); Portell Vilá, no. 21.
>
> Dominican Republic: Andrade, nos. 150, 163, 164, 165 (510A); 116, 166, 167, 168, 169 (510B).
>
> Puerto Rico: Arellano, no. 86; Boggs, *JAF*, 42(1929), 157–159 (510A); Jijena Sánchez, no. 4; Mason-Espinosa, *JAF*, 38(1925), 506, no. 1; 507, no. 1a; 508, no. 1b; 509, no. 1c; 511, no. 1d; 512, no. 1e; 513, no. 1f; 515, no. 1g (510A); 572, no. 8a; 574, no. 8b; 576, no. 8c; 577, no. 8d; 579, no. 8e; 581, no. 8f; 39(1926), 267, no. 21 (510B).
>
> Spain: Ampudia, nos. 31 (510A), 32 (510B); Cabal, pp. 30–35, 36–40 (510A); Curiel Merchán, pp. 241–247, 257–261, 265–267; Espinosa, *Cuentos*, no. 108 (510A + 923), 109, 110 (510B); Giner Arivau, *BTPE*, vol. 8, pp. 175–179 (923 + 510).

The Stupid Ogre

81. Juan Tonto

(Recorded by Lola Cruz on December 8, 1966, in Los Angeles, California)

Juan Tonto is sent to take care of the butcher shop one day because his grandmother is sick, and he sells all the meat on credit to a pack of dogs. His brother is disgusted with him and tells him to go clean up the yard and to take the pig [*puerca*] with him; but Juan Tonto misunderstands and brings a door [*puerta*]. The two brothers then climb a tree to escape from a band of robbers, and Juan Tonto drops the door on their heads, knocking them out. The police come and arrest them, and the brothers get the stolen money as a reward. Back at home once again, Juan bathes his ailing grandmother in boiling water and, not realizing he has killed her, tries to feed her some chicken. When his brother returns and sees what has happened, he tells Juan to go for the priest, but Juan brings back a whole string of miniature cardboard priests. His brother tells him he's absolutely useless, and they part ways. Juan Tonto arrives at a town where there is a princess who has never laughed, and he makes her laugh at some ridiculous clothing that he puts on, thus winning her hand in marriage. He then decides that he wants to present his wife with a castle, and so he sets out to seek work and gets a job caring for pigs. He sells the pigs for a castle, having first cut off their tails and buried them in the mud, making the owner believe that they simply sank into the ground. He then takes work making adobe bricks, at which he is very skilled, and wins a second castle from his wealthy boss by getting him to accept a wager that he is married to a princess and that she will bring him his lunch. The princess is very happy that she is able to laugh again, Juan Tonto is pleased at having become a millionaire with two castles, and they live happily ever after.

Ésta era una viejita . . . que tenía dos hijos. Y estos dos hijos eran nietecitos, porque quedaron huérfanos de papá y mamá y ella los crió. Y uno de ellos era tontito, que era el más chico. Se llamaba Juan. Y el otro no me acuerdo cuál era el nombre de él.

Pero de todos modos la señora le dijo al hermano mayor que pusiera una carnicería con los réditos que ella tenía ahorrados. Y luego puso la carnicería. Y luego un día estaba la señora mala, la, la viejita. Y luego le dijo: —Anda, Juan, anda, quédate en la carnicería mientras de que . . . tu hermano viene a . . . a llamar el doctor.

Pos luego le dijo: —Ándale, hermanito, que dice mi . . . mi abuelita que vayas y yo me quedo en la carnicería.

—Sí. Mira, tengo carne que trajieron nueva, y . . . y todos los que vienen a comprar y no traen dinero, les das la carne y no más les apuntas.

—Pos sí.

Pero como era tan tonto no sabía cuáles eran los perros. Y le dijo: —Gua, gua.

Le dijo: —Aa, quieres dos kilos de carne. Ahorita te los voy a dar. Y luego le dio los dos kilos de carne. Y luego después ese perro salió con la carne en el hociquito. Y luego se vino todo el bonche de perros. Y a todos les dio la carne. —Pos, que páguenme. Aa, bueno, se lo pongo en la cuenta. Se los pongo en el bill (1).

Pos luego vino el hermano. Y él recontento. Dice: —Anda, hermanito, te vendí toda la carne.

—¿Y el dinero?

—Pos no me lo dieron.

—¿Y a quién se la vendistes?

—Mira. Áhi va uno muy contento, saboreándose.

—Anda, animal. Ése es un perro. ¿Cómo vas a . . . a decir tú que ése es una gente? Tú no sirves para nada. Ándale. Mira, vamos al corral a limpiar la yarda.

—Sí, vamos a limpiarla.

Y luego le dice: —Ah, mira, aquí está esta puerca. Tráetela . . . para . . . a limpiar el corral. Entonces él no agarró la puerca. Agarró una puerta. Y le dijo: —Juan, ¿qué vas a hacer?

—Pues, no me dijiste que me trajera la puerta?

—No la puerta. La puerca (2).

Y luego se subieron en un árbol porque venían unos . . . bandidos. Y no hallaba cómo, cómo subir la, la puerta pa arriba del árbol. Y le dice: —Juan, ¿qué estás haciendo?

—Pos, subiendo la puerta pa que no se la roben.

Dice: —Déjala acá. Y entonces al oír los bandidos, que estaban, que no hallaban ni qué hacer. Y les cae la puerta . . . encima de la cabeza (3). Y cuando vinieron los . . . estos . . . polecías, agarraron los bandidos.

Y entonces luego dijeron: —Gracias a ustedes, que les dieron un tortazo en la cabeza a los bandidos, y soltaron todo el dinero. Entonces también le dijeron al señor que habían robado. Luego el señor les dio el dinero.

—Mira, dice, —ya nos pagaron los perros la, la carne. Porque todo el dinero que me dieron de los bandidos.

Dice: —Ahora, mira. Tú te quedas en la casa y yo voy a dar una vuelta, y bañas a mi mamá. Le coces su gallinita y le das . . . que coma. Pos, que sí.

Pues ese . . . cristiano trae y baña a la señora en agua hirviendo, agua muy caliente, caliente, caliente. La metió y la viejita se quemó y se, y se murió (4). Entonces luego la sentó, la, la vistió, y luego la sentó en una silla. Y le dijo: —Abuelita, mira, te estás riendo. Estás contentita. Aunque no hablas pero te estás riendo, abuelita. Qué bonita, mi viejita, que te estás riendo. Te voy a traer tu gallinita. Y luego le dio una cucharada de caldo . . . a la viejita y otra a él. Y luego dijo: —Mamá, ¿qué, no quieres comer hoy? Entonces dice: —Come. Dice: —¡Ay, qué dura estás, mamá! Estás más dura que la gallina. Entonces dijo: —No quieres comer. Yo me la como. Bueno, pues, se la comió la gallina el . . . el muchacho.

Luego vino el . . . hermano. —Juan, ¿ya bañastes a mi mamá?

—Mm, cállate la boca. Está recontenta. Fíjate, hasta un cigarro tiene en la boca. Ya le hice su gallinita y su caldito.

Y luego entró el hermano. —Pero si cristiano, mi abuelita está muerta.

—No, está bien. ¡Qué está muerta! Está bien. Mírala.

—Anda al mercado, tráeme el padre. Allá está en frente al mercado. Está en la iglesia. Allá está el padrecito.

Y en ese tiempo . . . era día de que . . . venden unos padrecitos de . . . que forman una cabecita de garbanzo. Y entonces ése . . . fue y trajo un montón de padrecitos. Y los formó. Desde muy lejos formó los padrecitos hasta la puerta de la casa. —Ya, Juan, ¿trajistes el padrecito?

—Ooo, sí, pues, áhi 'tán parados. Es que no quieren ni andar.

—A ver. Voy a traerlos. Luego fue el, el hermano a ver dónde estaban. Pos, así chiquitos, ¿ónde los iba a ver?

Dijo: —Ay, hermanito, vas a pisar a todos los padrecitos. Si viene un bonche de padrecitos. Mira, con diez centavos me dieron un montón.

—¿Cómo?

—Sí. Míralos.

Dice: —Tonto. Ésos no son padrecitos que confiesan ni que dan la, la comunión ni, ni nada. Ésos son unos de estos de cartón . . . y garbanzo. ¿No te digo? Tú no sirves para nada. Dice: —Hora, mira. Ya se murió mi abuelita. Tú agarras por un camino y yo agarro a otro. Entonces se separaron los dos. Ya que se murió la abuelita se separaron.

Entonces sale un viejito. Dice: —¿Adónde vas, buen cristiano?

—¿Adónde he de ir, buen señor? Voy a buscar . . . la vida y a ver qué consigo.

Dice: —Mira, a la tierra que fueres, haz lo que vieres.

Y . . . pues, había un señor, . . . había una reina en ese pueblo, que su . . . que el papá la quería casar (5). Y no la podía casar porque la reina no, no se casaba ni se reía (6). Estaba todo el tiempo triste, triste, triste. Le traiba payasos y no se reía. Porque si se reía la reina era feliz el rey. Le traiba muchas cosas y no se reía la reina. Nunca . . . en veinte años, nunca se reía la reina. Pues, luego el muchacho vio un señor muy catrín, . . . con una levita y un sombrero . . . de, de esos sombreros altos. Pues este muchacho vio un chiquigüite. Pero esos chiquigüites son como un . . . forma de canasto. Así como éste. [Indicates wastebasket.] Y luego se lo puso en la cabeza. Y luego agarró un costal y se lo puso. Y lo cortó, en medio del costal acá atrás, pa que sirviera de levita. Pos luego pasó por allí y agarró un palito como bordón. Así le hacía el . . . palito. Y áhi está la reina, que se desmorecía de risa (7).

Y luego dice el rey: —¿Qué, mi hija se ha reído? ¿Quién . . . qué ha visto, qué ha visto?

—Mira, papá, ¡qué gracioso! Mira, papá, ¡qué chistoso! Hasta se enfermó la reina de la risa que le dio, porque hacía veinte años que nunca se reía esa reina. Dice: —Papá, si tú quieres yo me puedo casar con él.

Entonces ya le hablaron. Dijo: —Oyes, muchacho, ¿cómo te llamas?

—Juan Tonto, señor. Porque así me dice mi hermano, Juan Tonto.

—Bueno, dice, —yo quiero saber una cosa, . . . si tú te quieres casar con mi hija.

—Pues, como usted guste y mande, señor. Estoy para hacer lo que usted diga.

Ya dice: —No, pues mira qué mugroso. Váyase. ¿Qué, no te has bañado en toda tu vida?

—No, señor. No más me quito la, la mugrita no más con un papelito, y es todo.

Entonces dijo: —Vénganse aquí los criados, los veinte criados. Y luego métanmelo . . . siete días en el baño todo el día. Y lo rascan con un cepillo o con una piedra, pa que se le caiga toda esa mugre que tiene.

Y luego se bañaba y se ponía la misma ropa. Y luego le dijo: —No, no. Póngase esta ropa que le dio el . . . el rey.

Dice: —No, ésta es ropa tan fina que se me puede salir hasta roña.

Dice: —No. Le digo que se ponga esa . . . esa ropa.

Pues se puso la, la ropa de, . . . que le había dicho el rey. Y luego cuando la reina lo vio muy bonito, dice: —Ay, papá, este muchacho está muy precioso, muy bonito. Y lástima que sea . . . tontito. Pero siempre me caso con él.

Bueno, pos que luego hicieron una boda, y se casaron (8). Y luego después le dicen, le dice el rey: —Hora, son [i.e., hijo], te voy a dar este castillo.

Dice: —Sí. Pero yo quisiera darle un castillo a mi esposa. Pero voy a ponerme a trabajar.

—¿Dónde vas a trabajar?

—Pos, a ver dónde ando.

Trabajó primero en un lugar . . . que era de marranas y vacas. Dijo: ¿Cóme me haré, dijo, —cómo me haré rey?, dijo.

Y luego dijo: —Oyes, Juan, mucho cuidado con las colas de los . . . puercos. Y que no se vayan a atascar en el lodo.

—No, patrón. Y estuvo piensa y piensa y piensa aquel muchacho toda la tarde, a ver qué hacía . . . con aquellos puercos. Eran más de diez mil puercos. Pues, luego . . . se le ocurrió a la cabeza . . . hacer una tabla grande, grande, grande, y enterrarla en el suelo . . . muy hondo. Y luego con un hilito, . . . a todos los puercos les mochó la cola. A todos los puercos les mochó la cola. Y, y luego las amarró de allí del, del palo que había puesto.

Entonces luego vino el patrón. Y luego escondió los puercos.

—Oyes, Juan, ¿y los puercos?

—¡Ay, patrón! Fíjese, pues, sabe usted que por tanto que llovió los puercos con la trompa hicieron hoyo y se metieron. Y, y mírelos. No más la cola tienen de afuera. Y como la cola estaba enredada entre alambre, pos no se podía salir. Y luego cuando el rey les jaló . . . a una cola, pos se vino otro pedazo de la cola. Y luego todas las colas allí, todas sacadas (9).

Bueno, pues, dijo: —¡Ay, Juan, mira no más! Tú no sirves ni para cuidar puercos. Los dejastes hundir.

Y entonces fue a otro pueblito. Y le dijo a un, a un, . . . le dijo un rey: —Oyes, muchacho, ¿qué quieres por esos puercos? Nunca había visto yo un puerco sin cola.

—Ah, señor, estos puercos son de mis dueños.

—Dámelos.

—No, ¡Qué se los voy a dar!

—¿Qué quieres? ¿A mi hija?

—No, señor. Si yo soy el esposo de una reina. ¿Cómo dejar esa reina y . . . casarme con otra?

—Pues, ¿qué quieres?

—Yo, todo lo que quiero, . . . déme su casa, su castillo.

—Trato hecho. Te doy mi castillo. Pues le dio un castillo, un palacio.

Pues luego después dijo: —Ahora, sí, yo tengo mi . . . castillo. Bueno, pos hora . . . después, voy a ver qué más hago.

Pos se fue . . . anda y anda. Y luego encontró un camino y . . . unos trabajadores estaban acomodando adobe para hacer una casa. Y dijo: —¿Qué están haciendo, muchachos?

—Anda, estamos haciendo estos adobes, pero no sabemos cómo.

—Mmm, yo sé hacer eso.

—¿Cómo te llamas?

—Juan Tonto.

—Ni tan tonto, porque sabes hacer . . . cómo se. . . . A ver, hazlos.
Y hizo uno. Y les gustó. Y el patrón también.

Dice: —Pos, quédate, muchacho, a trabajar aquí.

Pos, se quedó el muchacho a trabajar allí, cuando luego les dice:
—Mmm, yo soy el esposo de, . . . yo soy esposo de la reina.

—No puede ser que un . . . greñudo, mugroso sea esposo de una
reina.

Pos que oyó el rey, el dueño de aquel . . . casa que estaban haciendo.
—¿Qué tiene ese loco?

—Pos, dice que es esposo de . . . esposo de la reina.

—A ver.

—Sí. ¿Cuánto apuestan a que mi esposa viene a traer mi lonch?

—No puede ser de que una reina venga a traerte lonch.

—Mmm, hasta un beso me va a dar.

—Pos, a ver, vamos a ver. Pos que si viene tu esposa te doy mi castillo, aunque me quede yo en éste que estoy haciendo (10, 11).

Pos, luego a la noche se fue y le dijo a la esposa: —Oyes, tienes que
llevarme mi lonch.

—¿Cómo?

—Sí. Tienes que ir con toda tu escolta y en la calexa más elegante
que tú tengas, y el vestido más bonito que tú tengas. Y me llevas el
lonch, el almuerzo. Y me llevas comida al trabajo.

—Pos, lo que tú digas, mi vida, le dijo la reina.

Pues luego entonces, a las doce oyeron . . . un tropel de caballos y
soldados, una escolta que venía atrás de la reina. Como era reina tenía
. . . soldados atrás de ella. Cuando luego en eso vio . . . vio una polva-
dera. Y dicen: —¡Ay, qué carro tan . . bello, tan lujoso!

Entonces dijo uno de los trabajadores: —Pos, es la esposa de Juan
Tonto.

—No, no puede ser que tan elegante sea su esposa. . . . .

Bueno. Y luego le pusieron una alfombra pa que se bajara la esposa, para que no se emporcara el . . . pie, los pies. Pues luego ya se bajó
y le dio un beso. Y luego ya se sentaron a comer en la . . . un pedazo de

comida para él y otro para ella. Comieron en el mismo plato. Y luego
. . . le mandaron traer al rey, y ya el rey vio. Estaba la esposa con, con
Juan.

Dice: —No cabe duda que ahora voy a estar en la calle. Tú ganas-
tes, Juan. Toma el palacio. Y ya juntó dos palacios.

Bueno, pos que luego ya . . . pensó Juan, dijo: —Pos ahora, ¿pa
qué, pa qué trabajar?

Luego le dice la esposa: —¡Ay, Juan! Eres tan virtuoso que tú, con
tu mirada hasta la gente, se ríe la gente que no se ríe. Mira, yo tenía
veinte años que no me ría, y no más te vi y hasta unas carcajadas eché
que hasta me enfermé.

Dice: —Si no fuera por mi . . . por mi mal que tengo yo en la cabeza no tuviera tanto palacio ni fuera el más millonario . . . de los
reyes. Mira no más. De los puercos, de las colas de los puercos me hice
un castillo; a, a mi abuelita la maté en el agua hirviendo; a, a mi hermano le vendí toda su carne, y no me la pagaron, . . . la que [*sic*] nos
lo pagó . . . son los, los bandidos que iban alcanzando cuando una, una
tabla se me cayó. Dice. —Pos hora vamos a vivir muy felices.

Y es todo lo que sé.

The story is structured as follows: 1642 IIa + 1009 + 1653 B + 1013 +
559 Iab (funny clothing) + 1004I + N2.5. Whole kingdom (all property) as
wager.

 (1) J1852. Goods sold to animals.
 (2) K1413. Guarding the door.
 (3) K335.1.1.1. Door falls on robbers from tree.
 (4) K1462. Washing the grandmother—in boiling water.
 (5) T68. Princess offered as prize.
 (6) H341. Suitor test: making princess laugh.
 (7) H341.3. Princess brought to laughter by foolish actions of hero.
 (8) L161. Lowly hero marries princess.
 (9) K404.1. Tails in ground.
(10) N12.1. Wager: raja's daughter will bring servant dinner in field. [Here,
      worker is married to a princess, who will bring him his lunch in the
      field.]
(11) N2.5. Whole kingdom (all property) as wager. [Here, a castle.]
      Aarne-Thompson 1642. The Good Bargain.
      Boggs 1642.
      Hansen 1642. The Good Bargain.
      Thompson, *Folktale*, p. 203.
            Puerto Rico: Arellano, no. 120; Mason-Espinosa, *JAF*, 34(1921),
                150, no. 2; 181, no. 41.
            Spain: Espinosa, *Cuentos*, no. 185.

Aarne-Thompson 1009. Guarding the Store-Room Door.
Hansen 1009. Guarding the Storeroom Door.
    Mexico: Wheeler, nos. 171, 173.
    Argentina: Aramburu, *Hazañas*, p. 16.
    Cuba: Portell Vilá, no. 53.
    Spain: Espinosa, *Cuentos*, no. 184.
Aarne-Thompson 1653B. The Robbers under the Tree.
Boggs 1653B.
Hansen 1653B. The Robbers under the Tree.
    Mexico: Robe, *Mexican Tales*, nos. 115, 132; Wheeler, nos. 159,
        171, 173.
    United States: Brunner, *TFSP*, 31(1962), 9, no. 1; 13, no. 4; Pare-
        des, no. 62; Zunser, *JAF*, 48(1935), 170, no. 24.
    Argentina: Chertudi, 2nd series, no. 83 (1653A), no. 84 (1653B);
        Renca, pp. 113–116.
    Chile: Guzmán Maturana, *AUC*, vol. 92, pp. 74–80; Pino Saavedra,
        no. 165.
    Cuba: *AFC*, vol. 4, pp. 256–259; vol. 5, pp. 67–70; Portell Vilá, nos.
        23, 53.
    Dominican Republic: Andrade, nos. 7, 9, 26.
    Puerto Rico: Arellano, no. 116; Mason-Espinosa, *JAF*, 34(1921),
        160, no. 11; 162, no. 14; 204, no. 54, 54a; 205, no. 55; 207, no.
        56.
    Spain: Ampudia, no. 42; Boira, II, p. 313 (1653A); Espinosa, *Ca-
        stilla*, p. 363; Espinosa, *Cuentos*, no. 184 (1653A).
Aarne-Thompson 1013. Bathing or Warming Grandmother.
Hansen 1013. Bathing or Warming Grandmother.
    Mexico: Parsons, *JAF*, 45(1932), 304, no. 14; Radin, *IJAL*, 12
        (1946), 166, no. 9; Robe, *Mexican Tales*, nos. 114, 115, 117;
        Wheeler, nos. 171, 172.
    Chile: Pino Saavedra, no. 165.
    Puerto Rico: Arellano, no. 121.
Aarne-Thompson 1681B. Fool as Custodian of Home and Animals.
[Hansen **1704, **1706A; 1537**E]
    Mexico: Robe, *Mexican Tales*, no. 132.
    United States: Paredes, no. 62.
    Cuba: Portell Vilá, no. 53.
    Dominican Republic: Andrade, nos. 1, 2, 3, 4, 6.
    Puerto Rico: Arellano, no. 119; Mason-Espinosa, *JAF*, 34(1921),
        160, nos. 10a, 11.
Aarne-Thompson 559. Dungbeetle.
Boggs 559.
    Mexico: Paredes, no. 37; Wheeler, nos. 166, 167, 168.
    United States: Espinosa, *SFNM*, nos. 68, 69; Rael, nos. 314, 316;
        Zunser, *JAF*, 48(1935), 166, no. 10.
    Argentina: Chertudi, 1st series, no. 72.
    Panama: Riera Pinilla, no. 62.
    Puerto Rico: Mason-Espinosa, *JAF*, 34(1921), 163, no. 18; 191, no.
        50.
    Spain: Espinosa, *Cuentos*, nos. 177, 178; Sánchez Pérez, no. 96.
Aarne-Thompson 1004. Hogs in the Mud; Sheep in the Air.
Boggs 1004.

Hansen 1004. Hogs in the Mud; Sheep in the Air.

Mexico: Aiken, *TFSP*, 12(1935), 49, no. 16; Gamio, *Población*, vol. 2, p. 314, no. 12; Mendoza, *ASFM*, 6(1945), 431, no. 4; Parsons, *JAF*, 45(1932), 306, no. 14; Robe, *Mexican Tales*, no. 114; Toor, *Treasury*, p. 530; Wheeler, nos. 148, 149, 150.

United States: Espinosa, *JAF*, 27(1914), nos. 13, 14; Rael, no. 284.

Argentina: Aramburu, *Hazañas*, p. 52; Chertudi, 1st series, no. 64; 2nd series, no. 75; Gil Rojas, pp. 89–90.

Bolivia: Costas Arguedas, pp. 156–157; *Khana*, II, p. 136.

Chile: Coluccio, *Folklore de las Américas*, p. 175; Laval, *Pedro de Urdemalas*, no. 12; Pino Saavedra, nos. 163, 164, 194.

Guatemala: Recinos, *JAF*, 31(1918), 474–475, 476–478.

Puerto Rico: Mason-Espinosa, *JAF*, 34(1921), 162, no. 16; 172, no. 32.

Spain: Ampudia, no. 44; Cabal, pp. 174–181; Espinosa, *Cuentos*, nos. 163, 165.

Venezuela: Pereda Valdés, *AVF*, 4–5, no. 1, p. 223.

Thompson N2.5. Whole kingdom (all property) as wager.

Mexico: Foster, *UCAAE*, 42(1945), no. 39; Robe, *Mexican Tales*, no. 109; Wagner, *JAF*, 40(1927), no. 7; Wheeler, no. 166.

United States: Campa, *WF*, 6(1947), no. 1; Espinosa, *SFNM*, nos. 25, 26, 28.

82. Pedro de Ordimalas y Juan de Buen Alma

(Recorded by Candelario Gallardo on December 2, 1966, in Oxnard, California

Pedro de Ordimalas bathes his sick mother in boiling water and, unaware that he has killed her, attempts to feed her a chicken he has prepared especially for her. When his brother, Juan de Buen Alma, arrives home and sees what Pedro has done, he says they must flee from the house in order not to be arrested. He tells Pedro to bring along the pig [*puerca*], but Pedro misunderstands and brings the door [*puerta*]. They come across a group of robbers, and in order to get out of sight they climb a tree, door and all. Pedro is soon unable to support the door any longer, and he drops it on the robbers, sending them running in terror. When the two brothers sit down to eat the feast left behind by the robbers, another robber comes along and asks for food. They cut out his tongue and send him running off, babbling sounds that make the fleeing robbers think he is the devil pursuing them. Pedro and Juan soon run out of money, but Pedro manages to sell a fake money tree to a pair of mule drivers who happen by. When they arrive at a city they part ways to seek jobs on their own, and Pedro obtains work from a priest, telling him his name is Así ["thus"]. He robs the priest of his money one night as he is sleeping and blackens his face with soot.

When the priest awakens in the morning and receives no response to his calls for the boy he goes outside, unaware of the soot on his face, and asks people if they have seen Así, producing the humorous additional meaning, "Have you seen me like this?" The startled people answer that they have not and finally advise the priest to look in a mirror. Pedro and Juan do not meet again, and Pedro dies shortly thereafter, possibly, as the informant speculates, in punishment for his mistreatment of the priest.

Ésta era una viejita que tenía dos hijos. Uno se llamaba Juan y otro se llamaba Pedro de Ordimalas. Este Pedro de Ordimalas, pues, no estaba muy bien de su sentido, ¿verdad? Y . . . y se enfermó su mamá, muy enferma, y no hallaban qué hacerle porque estaban muy pobres. Entonces los vecinos de allí de su barrio decían: —Miren, . . . curen a su madre. Háganle esto.

—¿Qué cosa le podemos hacer?

Dice: —Pongan agua calientita y le dan un baño, . . . porque tal vez la flu la . . la mamá. Y le dan un baño, y le cocen un pollito, y le dan su caldito y , y van a ver cómo se desalivia.

Bueno. Entonces, . . . entonces Juan le dice a Pedro: —Pedro, me voy a traer leña . . . al monte, pa calentar el agua. Y le damos el baño . . . a mi mamá y . . . le cocemos un pollito pa que coma caldito.

Entonces se fue . . . Juan a traer la leña, y Pedro se quedó cuidando a su . . . mamá. Entonces éste no esperó a Juan, sino que se fue por allá a las casas a conseguir leña. Y luego en una tina puso el agua y le echó juego [i.e., fuego], mató el pollito, y en un lado puso el pollo a que se cociera. Y . . . y cuando estaba ya caliente el agua, jue y trajo a la viejecita.

Pos que ya ni miraba . . . la viejecita, y ¡que la zampa en el agua caliente! Ooo, pos la viejita, pos luego luego . . . pos se murió, ¿verdad? La coció (1). Y como estaba, pues, juera del sentido Pedro, dice: —¡Qué aliviada estás, madre! Dice: —Mira no más, hasta te estás riendo . . . con la . . . curación. Y . . . luego luego fue y se la llevó abrazada y . . . y la sentó en la cama. Y le puso una almohada por uno y otra almohada por otro lado. Y luego la peinó . . . a la viejita. Decía Pedro: —¡Ah, qué aliviada estás, madre! Pues estaba riéndose, dice:

—Hasta se está riendo. Dice: —Ahorita te voy a traer una piernita del pollito. Y luego fue allá y le trajo una piernita . . . y, y se la puso en la boca a la viejita. Dice: —No puedes comer todavía, dice, —pero yo te lo voy a meter ahí pa cuando tengas [laughs], cuando quieras . . . comértela te la comes.

Bueno, pues que . . . ya llega, llega Juan. —Ándale, Pedro, tráete la tina pa calentar el agua.

—No, home. Si ya hasta la bañé. Dice: —Fíjate, áhi está riéndose. Y está comiendo una piernita de pollito.

—¿Cómo asi? Jue a verla Juan. —¡Ay, dice, —qué cosas has hecho! Dice: —Ya, pos, sí, que ya matastes a mi madre.

—Home, ¿cómo la voy a matar? ¿No ves que acá está, comiendo pollo?

—Ah, ¡qué Pedro éste! Dice: —Vámonos de aquí, dice, —porque el gobierno . . . nos va a hacer cúmpleces.

Allí enterraron a la viejita. Hicieron un hoyo y allí la enterraron. No . . . pos luego hicieron el viaje a, pos a huir, pues. Ya fue . . . y iba ya. . . retirado. Tenían un, un, un puerquito . . . una puerquita gorda, una puerquita muy gorda, que la usaban . . . pa sus gastos de la mantequita. Y luego cuando ya iban, pues, ya retirados del camino le dice Juan . . . a Pedro: —Pedro, hombre, ¿sabes qué se quedó?

—¿Qué cosa se quedó?

—Hombre, anda, tráeta la . . . la puerca, hombre.

—Horita voy. Y éste no entendió que la puerca, sino que la puerta. Áhi va a desclavar la puerta, ¿verdad?, como pudo con el martillo. Y la desclavó, y áhi viene cargado con la puerta.

—¿Qué pasó? Pos, ¿qué trajistes?

—¡Ay, qué . . . ! La puerca, la puerca. Dice: —Pos, hora en castigo, cárguesela. Ande, vámonos. Y áhi va Pedro con la puerta cargada (2).

Ya llegaron por allá a un monte. Había un árbol muy grande, muy frondoso, que era . . . onde . . . asistían los ladrones. Estos ladrones robaban, y tenían una mesa onde comían y onde hacían sus cuentas, sus reparticiones de lo que robaban. Y . . . comidas muy buenas. Y luego, . . . llegó con la puerta Pedro . . . y Juan. Y: —Ay, dice, —éstos son ladrones, dice. —Vámonos subiendo el árbol.

—Pos vamos. Y áhi va Pedro, como pudo, con . . . con la puerta Pedro, pa arriba del árbol.

Y allá jueron y . . . áhi entre las ramas estaban cuando llegan los ladrones luego luego con el cargamento de dinero. —Vamos a hacer cuentas y a repartirnos. Pero antes de esto ya vamos comiendo. Unas comidas, pero buenas. Y aquéllos que tanta hambre tenían que hasta se saboreaban . . . Pedro y, y Juan, viendo comer allí.

Pues que, . . . dice Pedro: —Juanito, hermanito, dice, —ya no aguanto esta puerta. Se me quiere caer.

—No la dejes caer, dice, —porque aquí los ladrones nos matan.

Pos . . . dice: —Ya no aguanto. Pues . . . que de repente ya no la aguantó. De repente no la aguantó. Suelta la, la puerta Pedro y áhi va arruuuuu, . . . quebrando ramas y todo (3).

Dicen los ladrones: —¡El gobierno! ¡Vámonos! Vámonos. Aquí está el gobierno. Y corren todititos. Se fueron del árbol, de allí onde estaban. Dejaron dinero, dejaron comida, dejaron todo y se jueron todos los ladrones.

Y luego ya dice Pedro, dice: —A mí me anda de hambre. Yo voy a bajar, dice.

—Pues yo también, dice. —Ya me anda de hambre.

Se bajaron allí. Ooo, pues, unas comidas excelentes, ¿verdad? Y áhi 'tán a come y come y come y come cuando . . . vieron uno . . . otro ladrón que se asomaba y asomaba y asomaba. Como ese árbol, . . . que asistían ladrones, eran otros ladrones. Era un ladrón desvalido que también quería llegar allí a comer. Y luego, pos, Pedro dice: —Pásese, amigo. Pase a comer.

—Home, dice, —sí, traigo hambre también. Dice: —Mire, dice, —qué comida tan excelente. Mire qué jalea tan, tan buena.

Agarra el cuchillo y le, y le taja una rebanada de jalea. Dice: —Abra la boca. Y abrió la boca aquel ladrón que . . . desvalido, y que le atraviesa el cuchillo. Que le . . . mocha la lengua. Y luego áhi va . . . "leroleroleroleroleroleroleroler," . . . pa onde se habían ido toda la . . . parranda de, de ladrones.

Y luego ya dice: —¡Áhi viene el diablo!, dicían los otros ladrones. Más corrían . . . los ladrones, con aquél que iba "lerolerolero," pos con la lengua mocha, . . . y "lerolero."

Entonces . . . luego que ya, ya se jueron, dice: —Home, ¿ahora, qué vamos a hacer?

—Vamos, vámonos a llevar un poco de dinero, a ver hasta ónde alcanzamos. Pos que así lo hicieron. Se echaron un poco de dinero a la bolsa, y áhi van.

Pero como . . . pos hacían gastos y todo, . . . pero ya es cuento, pues, ¿verdad?, . . .se les terminó el, el dinerito. Y ya . . . se les acababa. Dice, dice Pedro, dice: —Ya, ya se nos está acabando el dinero. Dice: —Yo voy, en este árbol que está aquí, dice, —yo voy a, a quitarle todas las ramas verdes que tiene y voy a pegarle un poco de dinero con cera a todas las ramitas. Lo voy a pegar. Y voy a hacer un pozo y le voy a echar agua. Así lo hizo. Peló todas las hojas verdes y lo dejó pelón. Y luego ya puso con cera . . . todos los pesos, y hizo el pozo y áhi está. Y le hizo un tanque al . . . al árbol, y échele y échele agua y échele y échele agua y échele, y échele agua. Cuando vinieron . . . vieron venir un cargamento de mulas de . . . con dinero. Los arrieros traían todo ese dinero. Dice: —Aaa, vienen los arrieros con dinero. Dice: —Yo les voy a decir que, que este árbol da dinero (4).

Tonces ya pasaron los arrieros. —¿Quihúbole?

—Pues, este árbol da dinero. Mira no más cómo está, cómo brilla, dijo Pedro.

—¿Sí?

—Es nuestra mantención. Este árbol, dice, —da dinero. Dice: —No más le echa uno agua, dice, —y da dinero. Como ahorita, dice, —ya, ya no tardo en cortarlo. Y luego ya le vuelvo a echar agua, y vuelve a dar más dinero.

—Home, ¡qué bueno está!, dice, —Véndanos ese arbolito.

—O, no quisiera yo venderlo, dice. —Pos, es nuestra mantención. No nos apuramos de trabajar. No más le echamos agüita, y . . . y áhi está el dinero.

—¡Hombre, véndanoslo!

—Bueno, dice, —pos si, ¿no me han de dar una carga de dinero?

—Sí, se la damos.

Le dieron la carga de dinero [laughs], ¿verdad? Y luego uno se quedó echándole agua. . . . Y luego ya bulló el árbol, cayó todo el dinero, lo recogió, y luego échele y échele agua y échele y échele agua y échele y échele y échele agua. . . . Pos que . . . lo que pasó que enfrondeció aquel árbol. Echó unas ramas muy verdes, muy bonito, y nada de dinero. [Laughs.]

Dice: —No cabe duda. Nos engañaron. Bueno, ¿qué remedio? Ya se fue y le dijo: —No, hombre, nos engañaron, dice. —Yo, échele y échele agua y todo, y lo que pasa que mira no más qué árbol tan bonito se puso. Nos engañaron. Está bien.

Entonces llegaron a una ciudad Pedro y Juan. Dice: —Tú te vas por este, por esta calle, y yo me voy por estotra. Y cuando yo busque trabajo y que nos encontramos nos avisamos pa visitarnos. Pero tú te vas por esta calle, y yo por esta otra. Pos que así lo hicieron.

Entonces Pedro se jue . . . a todos los que, a toda la gente, que si no tenían trabajo, que si no tenían trabajo. Y no . . . no tenemos trabajo y no tenemos trabajo.

Entonces jue a dar . . . jue a dar con un, con el señor cura. Y el cura le dijo: —¿Qué andas haciendo tú, muchacho?

—Ando buscando trabajo.

—¿No hallas trabajo?

—No, dice, —no hallo.

—Bueno, dice, —a mí me falta un hombre pa que me cuide las mulas. Tenía . . . muchas mulas el señor cura. —Yo quiero un, un hombre que . . . me . . . pastoríe las mulas. De modo es que si quieres trabajar conmigo yo, yo te doy trabajo.

—Bueno, pos que sí. Cómo no.

Bueno, pues, ya se quedó allí. Le dice el señor cura: —Bueno, dice, —para esto, ¿cómo te llamas tú?

—Señor cura, dice, —yo me, . . . no le dijo que se llamaba Pedro, dijo, —yo me llamo Así (5).

—¿Es tu nombre, Así?

—Sí, es mi nombre, dice.

—Bueno, no más que yo cuando te diga Así me contestas.

Dice: —Pos, cómo no, dice. —Es mi nombre.

—Está bueno.

Pos que ya se quedó allí con el señor cura. En todo lo que se le ofrecía: —Así. Ooo, se viene corriendo.

—¿Qué se le ofrece? Pues que esto, que lo otro que. . . . Pos, ya él . . . ya entendía. Y así, pues, luego lo hacía.

Pos hizo ya con, con la larga. Cuando éste andaba por allí . . . muy, con mucha confianza, que le daba mucha confianza el señor cura, el señor cura, . . . tenía él dinero. Tenía dinero. Dice Pedro, dice: —Aquí está en la velita del señor cura. Dice: —Yo lo voy a tantear. Él ya sabía dónde tenía él todo el dinero. Y un día . . . estaba muy dormido el señor cura cuando entra, entra . . . Pedro. Dice: —Aaa, cómo está dormido el señor cura, dice. De modo es que él miraba dónde tenía la caja de dinero. Y luego se jue por allá . . . y trajo, . . . pos que allí en México le dicen tizne. Se embarró las manos de tizne . . . Pedro, y fue a hacerle cariños al señor cura. Dice: —Ya me voy a ir, señor cura. [Laughs.] Áhi te quedas, dice. —Y muchas gracias por el tiempo que estuve yo aquí. Y, y lo tiznó todo de la cara . . . al señor cura. Y luego fue y le . . . se llevó aquel dinero.

Y . . . cuando ya se levantó el señor cura le gritaba: —Así. Que lo quería . . . pa un mandado. —Así. Pos, ¿cuál Así? Si ya se había ido con el dinero. Luego que no le contestó salió afuera. Y, y le gritaba: —Así, Así. Llegó con unos familiares allí. —¿No me han visto Así?

Dijieron los . . . la señora, dice: —Señor cura, dice, —nunca lo hemos visto así. [Laughs.]

—Pos, ¿quién sabe?, dice, —ya se haiga ido este perdido.

—Señor cura, no lo hemos visto así.

—Pues ya les digo . . . que no lo hallo. Tal vez se. . . ya se fue pa su tierra.

—Señor cura, quiero que se mire en el espejo.

—¿Por qué?

Dice: —Porque no lo hemos visto así.

Pos, que se va a ver en el espejo. —¡Válgame Dios!, dice el señor cura. —Este muchacho . . . ya me hizo una travesura (6). Pos, así le hizo. Le, le tiznó toda la cara, ¿verdad?

Pos, que nunca se vieron más . . . con Juan. ¿Quién sabe qué vida tendría . . . Juan? Y a poco . . . Pedro, por allá se fue. Se fue a un rancho. Se enfermó, y ya sería . . . por Dios, el castigo que le mandó . . . Dios, por lo que le hizo al señor cura, . . . a poquito ya después se

murió. Y áhi termina . . . este cuento. Así es de que es el cuento de
Pedro de Ordimalas . . . y Juan . . . de Buen Alma.

The story is structured as follows: 1013 + 1009 + 1653B + Hansen
1539**A + J2496 + X459.

(1) K1462. Washing the grandmother—in boiling water.
(2) K1413. Guarding the door.
(3) K335.1.1.1. Door falls on robbers from tree.
(4) K111. Pseudo-magic treasure-producing objects sold. [Tree.]
(5) J2496. "I don't know" thought to be a person's name. [Here, hero's name
      is "Así."]
(6) X459. Jokes on parsons—miscellaneous. [Blackening of his face, which
      then leads to ridicule in the form of a play on words. See J2496.]

See Narrative 81 for Aarne-Thompson 1013, 1681B, 1009, 1653B; Hansen
1706A, 1537E.

Hansen 1539**A. Rascal sells tree to shepherds, claiming that it drops
  money every other day.
Thompson, *Folktale*, pp. 165–166.
Grimm, no. 61.
    Mexico: Aiken, *TFSP*, 12(1935), 47, no. 15; Mendoza, *ASFM*, 6
      (1945), 429, no. 2; Robe, *Mexican Tales*, no. 132; Toor, *Treasury*,
      pp. 530–531; Wheeler, no. 148.
    United States: Espinosa, *JAF*, 27(1914), 133, no. 14; Rael, no. 279.
    Argentina: Aramburu, *Hazañas*, p. 168.
    Chile: Laval, *Pedro de Urdemalas*, no. 1; Pino Saavedra, nos. 186,
      193.
    Guatemala: Recinos, *JAF*, 31(1918), 476–478.
    Puerto Rico: Cadilla de Martínez, *Cuentos*, no. 18; Mason-Espinosa,
      JAF, 24(1911), 179, no. 38; 183, no. 42.
Blackening the priest's face: Wheeler, no. 19, the priest blackens Pedro's
  face.

III. Biographies of Informants

Informant's name: Isaura Benicia.
Age: About 35.   Sex. F.
Resides: West Los Angeles, California. Resides at the above address
    on weekends, and at the home of the family for whom she
    works, in the San Fernando Valley, during the week.
Occupation: Domestic.
Education: Fourth grade. Literate. Speaks no English.
Area of Mexican background: Born in San José del Carmen, Jalisco.
    Lived there until age ten, and then in Guadalajara.
Residence in the United States/California: Has been living and work-
    ing in Los Angeles since 1963.
Dates recorded: 5/15/66.
Narratives: 3, 4, 7, 13, 25.

Informant's name: Elisa Contreras.
Age: 28.   Sex: F.
Resides: Culver City, California.
Occupation: Housewife. Husband is a commercial gardener.
Education: Sixth grade. Reads and writes with some difficulty.
    Speaks no English.
Area of Mexican background: Rancho Los Guapos, Sánchez Román,
    Zacatecas.
Residence in the United States/California: Has lived in the West
    Los Angeles area and in Culver City, California, since 1959.
Dates recorded: 5/17/66.
Narratives: 20, 50.

Informant's name: Lola Cruz.

Age: 56.   Sex: F.

Resides: West Los Angeles, California.

Occupation: Housewife. Her husband, informant Luis Cruz, is retired, but was formerly agricultural worker and construction laborer.

Education: No formal schooling. Taught herself to read and write, and does so with considerable difficulty. Speaks only isolated words and phrases in English, but understands somewhat more.

Area of Mexican background: Born in El Paso, Texas, in 1910, and lived there for four years. From 1914–1918 she lived in Mexico City.

Residence in the United States/California: After her initial four years in El Paso, Texas, the informant returned to the United States at age eight and lived in numerous towns in Texas, in a migratory fashion due to the nature of her father's employment with the railroads. In 1925, at age fifteen, she came to California to work the crops around Fresno and also lived for a time in the Lone Pine area where the family's livelihood depended principally on the maintenance of a herd of goats, together with working the crops. She lived for a time in San José, and has been living in West Los Angeles since about 1930.

Dates recorded: 5/19/66, 5/20/66, 5/23/66, 11/8/66, 12/8/66.

Narratives: 17, 18, 23, 24, 26, 28, 30, 37, 47, 60, 63, 66b, 67, 71, 78, 80, 81.

Informant's name: Luis Cruz.

Age: 60.   Sex: M.

Resides: West Los Angeles, California.

Occupation: Retired. Formerly agricultural worker and construction laborer. Husband of Lola Cruz.

Education: No formal schooling. Taught himself to read and write, but does so only with considerable difficulty. Speaks only isolated words and phrases in English.

Area of Mexican background: Born in San Julián, Jalisco, in 1905,

and subsequently lived in rancho del Saltillo, Villa Obregón
   (formerly Cañadas), Jalisco.
Residence in the United States/California: Came to California in
   1926 and was employed as a crop worker in the Fresno area.
   Lived briefly in San José, and then came to Los Angeles and
   worked as a construction laborer. Has been living in West Los
   Angeles since about 1930.
Dates recorded: 5/19/66, 5/20/66, 11/8/66.
Narratives: 21, 27, 38, 48.

Informant's name: Juana Esquer.
Age: About 60.   Sex.   F.
Resides: Venice, California.
Occupation: Domestic.
Education: No formal schooling. Speaks broken English.
Area of Mexican background: Alamos, Sonora, until age twelve.
Residence in the United States/California: Has been living in Cali-
   fornia since 1946, and lived in other areas of the United States
   prior to coming to California; was disinclined to offer details.
Dates recorded: 6/2/66.
Narratives: 14.

Informant's name: Ángel Flores.
Age: 35.   Sex: M.
Resides: Oxnard, California.
Occupation: Canning factory worker.
Education: Grade school. Speaks no English.
Area of Mexican background: Acapulco, Guerrero.
Residence in the United States/California: Total of eleven years.
   Two years in various states (including Indiana, Michigan, Loui-
   siana, Kansas, and the Northwest) working the crops and doing
   factory work; nine years in California.
Dates recorded: 7/14/67.
Narratives: 75.

Informant's name: Francisco Flores.
Age: About 55.   Sex: M.
Resides: Venice, California.
Occupation: Manual laborer.
Education: (No definite information.)
Area of Mexican background: Rancho La Playa, Sánchez Román,
    Zacatecas.
Residence in the United States/California: Has lived in California
    for four years, and resided in other states prior to coming here,
    but did not offer details.
Dates recorded: 6/2/66.
Narratives: 62.

Informant's name: Rosa Flores.
Age: 62.   Sex: F.
Resides: Venice, California.
Occupation: Unemployed widow.
Education: (No definite information.)
Area of Mexican background: Born in rancho La Playa near Tlal-
    tenango, Zacatecas, in 1904.
Residence in the United States/California: Resided for a short time
    in Chicago, Illinois, where her daughter, informant Amalia Her-
    nández, was born. Had arrived in Los Angeles from Mexico only
    ten days prior to my interview with her.
Dates recorded: 5/31/66.
Narratives: 59

Informant's name: Alfonso Domínguez Franco.
Age: 54.   Sex: M.
Resides: Valle de Guadalupe, Jalisco. Was visiting his mother, in-
    formant Petra Franco, at the time of the interview.
Occupation: Farmwork.
Education: Elementary. Speaks no English.
Area of Mexican background: Valle de Guadalupe, Jalisco.
Residence in the United States/California: Does not reside in Cali-

fornia, but was in Los Angeles for a one-month visit with his mother when I interviewed him.

Dates recorded: 11/15/66.

Narratives: 1, 6.

Informant's name: Petra Franco.

Age: 80.   Sex: F.

Resides: Venice, California.

Occupation: Retired. Widow.

Education: No formal schooling. Reads and writes with considerable difficulty. Speaks no English.

Area of Mexican background: Lived all her life in the colonia San Juan Bosco, Valle de Guadalupe, Jalisco, except for one year in Ocotlán, and four years in Guadalajara.

Residence in the United States/California: Has been living in Venice for nine years.

Dates recorded: 11/15/66.

Narratives: 15, 45, 57.

Informant's name: Candelario Gallardo.

Age: 75.   Sex: M.

Resides: Oxnard, California.

Occupation: Retired. Worked the crops in various locations in California.

Education: Fourth grade. Literate. Speaks very limited, broken English.

Area of Mexican background: Pueblo Nuevo, Guanajuato.

Residence in the United States/California: Has been in California since 1926, and during the early part of this residence made frequent visits to his home and family in Guanajuato.

Dates recorded: 11/25/66, 12/2/66, 12/15/66, 7/16/67, 7/28/67.

Narratives: 64, 65, 66, 68, 72, 73, 74, 76, 77, 79, 82.

Informant's name: Ismeria Garay.

Age: 46.   Sex: F.

Resides: Los Angeles, California. Lives at the home of her employer
    for whom she works as a domestic.
Occupation: Domestic.
Education: Fourth grade. Reads and writes with considerable diffi-
    culty. Speaks no English.
Area of Mexican background: Born in Pánuco, Sinaloa. At age
    twenty-two went to live in Mexicali, Baja California.
Residence in the United States/California: Has been living in Los
    Angeles under the employment of the same family for two years.
Dates recorded: 10/12/66.
Narratives: 2, 5, 41.

Informant's name: Guadalupe Gómez.
Age: 36.   Sex: F.
Resides: Venice, California.
Occupation: Housewife.
Education: No formal schooling. Occasionally attends some English
    classes at night school.
Area of Mexican background: Born on hacienda La Llave, Valle de
    Guadalupe, Jalisco, and lived only in Jalisco, prior to coming to
    California.
Residence in the United States/California: Has been living in the
    Los Angeles area for thirteen years.
Dates recorded: 11/10/66.
Narratives: 55.

Informant's name: Juana Gómez.
Age: 61.   Sex: F.
Resides: Venice, California.
Occupation: Housewife. Widow of a railroad worker.
Education: No formal schooling. Reads and writes with considerable
    difficulty. Speaks no English.
Area of Mexican background: Valle de Guadalupe, Jalisco.
Residence in the United States/California: Lived for five years
    (1929–1934) in Wyoming, where her husband worked for the

railroads; returned then to Jalisco. Has been living in Venice for nine years.

Dates recorded: 11/12/66.

Narratives: 22, 33, 46, 56.

Informant's name: Rafael Gudiño.

Age: About 35.   Sex: M.

Resides: West Los Angeles, California. Resides at the above address during the week and spends weekends with his family in Tijuana, Mexico.

Occupation: Commercial gardener.

Education: Elementary. Literate. Speaks almost no English.

Area of Mexican background: Born in the barrio El Alto, Tizapán, Jalisco; spent his early childhood there and in Mazamitla, Jalisco. When he was eight years old the family went to Guadalajara, where he lived until 1962. Brief period of residence in Tijuana, in the state of Baja California, Mexico, in 1962, prior to coming to California.

Residence in the United States/California: Has been living and working in Los Angeles since 1962.

Dates recorded: 5/3/66.

Narratives: 51, 54, 70.

Informant's name: Amalia Hernández.

Age: 35.   Sex: F.

Resides: Venice, California.

Occupation: Housewife. Husband is a commercial gardener.

Education: Third grade. Speaks no English.

Area of Mexican background: Born in Chicago, Illinois; family returned to Mexico one month later and lived in the rancho Los Guapos, Sánchez Román, Zacatecas. At age eighteen she came to Fresno, California, for several months, and then returned to Zacatecas where she married and lived for four more years.

Residence in the United States/California: Significant residence in

the United States dates from age eighteen, when she spent several months working as a grape picker and waitress in Fresno, California. After a four-year interlude of Mexican residence, she went to live in McAllen, Texas, for nine years and has now been living in Venice, California, since 1962.
Dates recorded: 5/16/66.
Narratives: 19, 36, 49.

Informant's name: Elvira Higuera.
Age: About 55.   Sex: F.
Resides: Venice, California.
Occupation: Housewife. Husband is a commercial gardener.
Education: Had eight consecutive years of schooling and several years beyond that, marked by many moves and interruptions. Speaks no English.
Area of Mexican background: Born in rancho Chicorato, near Capirato, Sinaloa. Lived all of her life, prior to coming to California, in Sinaloa.
Residence in the United States/California: Has been in Los Angeles since 1964.
Dates recorded: 10/31/66.
Narratives: 10, 16, 29, 31, 40, 52.

Informant's name: Socorro Higuera.
Age: 24.   Sex: F.
Resides: Venice, California.
Occupation: Factory work with a company called "Shirt Design."
Education: Seven years of schooling in Sinaloa. Currently in her first year of studying English at Venice High School.
Area of Mexican background: Born in Pericos, Sinaloa. Lived only in Sinaloa, prior to coming to California.
Residence in the United States/California: Has been in Los Angeles since 1964.
Dates recorded: 10/31/66.
Narratives: 32.

Informant's name: Josefina Márquez.
Age: About 50.   Sex: F.
Resides: Santa Paula, California.
Occupation: Housewife (widowed). The family owns a bakery in
    Santa Paula, and she occasionally helps out there.
Education: Elementary. Literate. Speaks rather good, although
    heavily accented, English.
Area of Mexican background: Born in Miami, Arizona; lived there
    until age ten, when the family moved to San Juan de los Lagos,
    Jalisco. Spent most of her youth there, except for a brief resi-
    dence in Zacatecas.
Residence in the United States/California: Born in Arizona and
    lived there ten years. Returned to the United States in 1946 at
    about age 30, took up residence in Santa Paula, California, and
    has been living there for twenty years.
Dates recorded: 5/7/66.
Narratives: 9, 35, 53.

Informant's name: Hugo Massa.
Age: About 24.   Sex.   M.
Resides: Hollywood, California.
Occupation: Service station attendant.
Education: Currently studying hotel management in Los Angeles;
    plans to return to Chichén Itzá, Yucatán, to manage his uncle's
    hotel.
    Reads and writes; understands and speaks some Mayan; very
    good English.
Area of Mexican background: Mérida, Yucatán.
Residence in the United States/California: One and one-half years
    in Los Angeles.
Dates recorded: 3/27/66.
Narratives: 34.

Informant's name: Praxedis Ramírez.
Age: About 45.   Sex: F.

Resides: Venice, California.

Occupation: Housewife.

Education: Elementary. Speaks no English.

Area of Mexican background: Born in McPherson, Kansas. Lived nineteen years in Mexico, mostly in Valle de Guadalupe, Jalisco, with some residence in Coahuila.

Residence in the United States/California: After several initial years in McPherson, Kansas, she returned to the United States nineteen years later and lived for a time in Arizona and new Mexico. Came to California in 1950.

Dates recorded: 10/31/66.

Narratives: 8.

Informant's name: Inocente Rocha.

Age: 70.   Sex: M.

Resides: Oxnard, California.

Occupation: Retired. Worked thirty years as a lemon picker, including fifteen years as foreman, for a company in Oxnard; did odd jobs and railroad work in various other states.

Education: Several years of formal schooling, interrupted by the revolution.

Area of Mexican background: Born and lived in rancho El Lobo, San Francisco del Rincón, Guanajuato.

Residence in the United States/California: Has been in the United States for sixty years, during which time he lived in many different places, including Chicago, Illinois, St. Louis, Missouri, Kansas City, Kansas, and various areas of Texas and New Mexico. Motivation was to see the country; supported himself by doing odd jobs and working for the railroad. Came to California in 1915, and has lived most of the time since then in Oxnard.

Dates recorded: 11/17/66, 11/21/66.

Narratives: 11, 12, 69.

Informant's name: Tecla Rocha.

Age: 84.   Sex: F.

Resides: Oxnard, California.

Occupation: Retired. Wife of informant Inocente Rocha. Tells
    with amusement of having been employed for one week at a
    wiener factory in Oxnard.
Education: Several years of primary schooling. Reads with some dif-
    ficulty. Speaks only very few words in English.
Area of Mexican background: Born in rancho Seco, near Jalpa de
    Cánovas, Guanajuato, and later lived in León, Guanajuato.
Residence in the United States/California: Has been living in Califor-
    nia since 1915, and most of that time in Oxnard.
Dates recorded: 11/21/66.
Narratives: 42.

Informant's name: Raquel Rodríguez.
Age: 42.   Sex: F.
Resides: Los Angeles, California.
Education: One year of primary school. Reads and writes only with
    great difficulty. Speaks no English.
Area of Mexican background: Born in Tepeaca, Puebla, and lived
    nine years there, followed by residence in Atlixco, Puebla, and in
    Mexico City, and two years in Tijuana, prior to coming to Cali-
    fornia.
Residence in the United States/California: Has been in Los Angeles
    since 1960.
Dates recorded: 11/7/66.
Narratives: 58.

Informant's name: Ana María Romero.
Age: 72.   Sex: F.
Resides: Oxnard, California.
Occupation: Retired widow; lives on a pension. Once did domestic
    work.
Education: About the equivalent of a secondary education at a
    school called La Amiga de la Obrera.
Area of Mexican background: Chihuahua, Chihuahua.
Residence in the United States/California: Went to live in El Paso,
    Texas, at age seventeen (1911); moved to Oxnard in 1945.

Dates recorded: 12/3/66.
Narratives: 44, 61, 66a.

Informant's name: Alicia Salinas.
Age: 28.   Sex: F.
Resides: West Los Angeles, California.
Occupation: Housewife.
Education: Sixth grade. Reads and writes. Speaks no English.
Area of Mexican background: Born and lived in Tlaltenango, Zacatecas, until age eighteen; subsequently lived in Guadalajara, Jalisco.
Residence in the United States/California: Has lived in Los Angeles since 1963.
Dates recorded: 5/26/66.
Narratives: 43.

Informant's name: Teresa Sánchez.
Age: 50.   Sex: F.
Resides: West Los Angeles, California.
Occupation: Domestic.
Education: Reads and writes well. Speaks some English.
Area of Mexican background: Daughter of a Hopi Indian woman and a Spaniard. No background of residence in Mexico.
Residence in the United States/California: Born in Flagstaff, Arizona, and has lived in Los Angeles since 1956.
Dates recorded: 5/24/66.
Narratives: 39.

IV. Appendixes

1. Index of Tale Types

(From Antti Aarne and Stith Thompson, *The Types
of the Folktale* [Helsinki, 1961])

2. Index of Motifs

(From Stith Thompson, *Motif-Index of Folk Literature*, 6 vols. [Bloomington, Indiana, 1955–1958])

Motif No.		*Tale No.*
D1865.1.	Beautification by decapitation and replacement of head.	71
D1978.3.	Waking from magic sleep by removal of enchanting instrument. [Shoes.]	80
D2072.	Magic paralysis. (Person or thing rendered helpless.)	18
D2135.2.	Magic air journey from biting an ear.	66
D2161.3.1.	Blindness magically cured.	75
D2176.3.2.	Evil spirits exorcised by religious ceremony.	18, 51, 52
E30.	Resuscitation by arrangement of members.	73
E63.	Resuscitation by prayer	8
E64.9.	Resuscitation by magic feather.	78
E79.	Resuscitation by magic.	73
E80.	Water of life.	78
E105.	Resuscitation by herbs (leaves). [Here, a flower.]	74
E121.4.	Resuscitation by saint.	8
E165.	Resuscitation of wife by husband giving up half his remaining life. [Last part not present.]	74
E181.	Means of resuscitation learned.	74
E242.	Ghosts punish intruders into mass (procession) of ghosts.	24
E265.1.	Meeting ghost causes sickness.	20, 24, 39
E265.2.	Meeting ghost causes madness.	20
E266.	Dead carry off living.	24, 41
E275.	Ghost haunts place of great accident or misfortune.	26
E279.2.	Ghost disturbs sleeping persons.	25, 26, 27
E281.	Ghosts haunt house. (It is sometimes hard to tell whether haunters are supposed to be ghosts or familiar spirits of some kind.)	25, 26, 27
E291.	Ghosts protect hidden treasure.	47, 48, 49 50
E291.2.1.	Ghost in human form guards treasure.	44
E332.3.3.1.	Vanishing hitchhiker.	28, 29, 30 31
E351.	Dead returns to repay money debt.	19, 20, 22
E352.	Dead returns to restore stolen goods.	21
E371.	Return from dead to reveal hidden treasures.	20, 43
E401.	Voice of dead heard from graveyard.	19
E402.	Mysterious ghostlike noises heard.	25, 49, 50
E411.	Dead cannot rest because of a sin.	21, 23
E411.0.2.1.	Return from dead to do penance.	23
E421.1.1.	Ghost visible to one person alone.	19, 20, 21

Motif No.		*Tale No.*
F473.2.1.	Chair rocked by invisible spirit. [Here, the *duendes* spin the cradle.]	53
F473.2.3.	Spirit puts out lights.	25, 49
F473.3.	Poltergeist mistreats people.	25, 26, 27, 52, 53
F473.5.	Poltergeist makes noises.	25, 26, 52
F482.2.1.	Brownies dressed in green.	53
F482.3.1.1.	Farmer so bothered by brownie that he decides he must move to get rid of annoyance.	54, 55
F482.5.3.	Brownies tease.	53
F482.5.4.	Helpful deeds of brownie or other household spirit.	53, 54
F482.5.5.	Malicious or troublesome actions of brownies.	51, 52, 53, 55, 56, 57
F521.3.4.	Person with body of silver.	67
F531.3.4.	Giant eats (drinks) a prodigious amount.	67
F531.5.1.	Giant friendly to man.	67
F545.2.1.	Gold star on forehead.	78
F555.1.	Gold hair.	78
F555.2.	Silver hair.	78
F601.	Extraordinary companions.	66
F601.3.	Extraordinary companions betray hero.	66
F610.	Remarkably strong man.	66
F611.1.1.	Strong man son of bear who has stolen his mother.	66
F611.3.1.	Strong hero practices uprooting trees.	66
F612.2.	Strong hero kills (overcomes) playmates: sent from home.	66
F626.	Strong man pulls down mountains.	66
F661.	Skillful marksman.	66
F725.3.3.	Undersea house.	67
F751.	Glass mountain.	72
F768.2.	City of enchanted people.	72, 78
F771.1.6.2.	Glass house.	67
F800.	Extraordinary rocks and stones.	76, 80
F821.2.	Dress so fine that it goes in nutshell. [Suit.]	78
F823.	Extraordinary shoes.	80
F835.2.1.	Iron club so heavy that five men can hardly lift it.	66
F852.1.	Glass coffin.	80
F852.2.	Golden coffin.	80
F852.3.	Silver coffin.	80
F942.1.	Ground opens and swallows up person.	60

3. Vocabulary

Los Angeles Spanish	*Spanish or English Form*
Afusile	Fusile
Áhi	Ahí
Ahoy	Hoy
Ajuera	Afuera
Almetía	Admitía
Almiración	Admiración
Almiradísimos	Admiradísimos
Aluminaban	Iluminaban
Amá	Mamá
Andulante	Ambulante
Aónde	Adónde
Apá	Papá
Apalladero	Lodazal
Aprevénganse	Prevénganse
Arboleras	Arboledas
Asilenció	Silenció
Asina	Así
Barra	English: bar
Bendecido	Bendito
Bill	English: bill
Block, -s	English: block, -s
Boggie	English: buggy
Bonche	English: bunch
Cabresto	Cabestro
Cáida	Caída
Cairá	Caerá
Cale	Hacer el cale. "To try."
Calexa	Calesa
Candada	Candado
Casamento	Casamiento
Centillo	Cintillo
Cercas	Cerca
Chiquigüite	Basket
Chirrioniza, Chirrionaza	A beating with a whip called a *chirrión.*
Ciéniga	Ciénaga
Cláxon	Claxón
Coce, -n	Cuece, -n

Los Angeles Spanish	*Spanish or English Form*
Companía	Compañía
Confetiar	To make confetti of; cut into small pieces
Cuega	An exclamation
Cúmpleces	Cómplices
Desalivia	Alivia
Desfiende	Defiende
Desmenudiendo	Disminuyendo
Despareció	Desapareció
Despuésn	Después
Destendiera	Extendiera
Devertir	Divertir
Diatiro	De a tiro
Dicía	Decía
Dijieron	Dijeron
Dispertó	Despertó
Dispierto	Despierto
Dizque	Dice que
Empaderar	Emparedar
Enantes	Antes
Endividuos	Individuos
Enduendado	Possessed of *duendes.*
En junto	Junto
Ensistió	Insistió
Espíritos	Espíritus
Frir	Freír
Fuertísimo	Fortísimo
Fuerzudo	Forzudo
Galona, una gorra galona	A wide brimmed hat, such as a ten-gallon hat.
Grandodototes	From "grandote." Augmentative.
Graniento	Granoso
Güesos	Huesos
Haiga	Haya
Home	Hombre
Hora	Ahora
Horita	Ahorita
Impidía	Impedía
Incontrar	Encontrar
Incontró	Encontró

Los Angeles Spanish	*Spanish or English Form*
Inorante	Ignorante
Invidiosas	Envidiosas
Jue	Fue
Juera	Fuera
Jueron	Fueron
Jui	Fui
Lonch, lonche	English: lunch
Malino	Maligno
Mamases	Mamás
Mátemos	Matemos
Medecina	Medicina
Mero	Casi
Mono	Patron saint
Muncho	Mucho
Nadien	Nadie
Nagüitas	Enagüitas
Naiden	Nadie
Onde	Donde
Ondequiera	Dondequiera
Oyí, -a	Oí, -a
Oyir	Oír
Oyistes	Oíste
Pa	Para
Pader	Pared
Parpareada	Parpadeada
Parparear	Parpadear
Paseyito	Paseíto
Pastoríe	Pastorée
Permetía	Permitía
Platicadera	Confused sound of voices.
Poderás	Podrás
Polecía, -s	Policía, -s
Polvadera	Polvareda
Porfisión	Profesión
Pos	Pues
Pucharon	English: pushed
Quedrá, -ía	Querrá, -ía
Quihubo, quihúbole	A greeting, similar to *¿qué tal?*
Raide	English: ride
Rastorjito	Rastrojito

Los Angeles Spanish	*Spanish or English Form*
Redumbo	Retumbo
Ría	Reía
Rocear	Rociar
Rompida, -os	Rota, -os
Sacarrial Majestad	Sacra Real Majestad
Sedució	Sedujo
Semos	Somos
Siguimientos	Seguimiento
Soportar	Frequently used to mean *sostener*.
Soterráneo	Subterráneo
Suidad	Ciudad
Tamién	También
Tascado	Atascado
Titiritiando	Titiritando
Tonces	Entonces
Traiba, -as, -an	Traía, -ías, -ían
Trampa	English: tramp
Triunfiado	Triunfado
Trompezaba	Tropezaba
Tropellos	Atropellos
Try	English: try
Tupiate	Basket
Való	Valoró
Vamos ir.	Vamos a ir
Vareada	A beating with a rod called a *vara*.
Velices	English: Valises
Venemos	Venimos
Vía, -n	Veía, -n
Vido	Vio
Voltié	Volteé
Voltíes	Voltées
Yarda	English: yard

Aarne, Antti, and Stith Thompson. *The Types of the Folktale*. Folklore Fellows Communications 74. Helsinki, 1961.

Abreu Gómez, Ermilo. *Leyendas y consejas del antiguo Yucatán*. Mexico City: Ediciones Bota, 1961.

Aiken, Riley. "A Pack Load of Mexican Tales." *TFSP*, 12(1935), 1–87.

Alfonso X, el Sabio. *Cantigas de Santa María*. Edición de la Real Academia Española. Madrid, 1889.

Álvarez, José S. *Cuentos de Fray Mocho*. Buenos Aires: La Cultura Argentina, 1920.

Ampudia. SEE Llano Roza de Ampudia.

Andrade, Manuel J. *Folk-lore from the Dominican Republic*. Memoirs of the American Folk-lore Society, 23. New York: The American Folk-lore Society, 1930.

Aramburu, Julio. *El folklore de los niños:Juegos, rondas, canciones, cuentos, leyendas*. Buenos Aires: El Ateneo, 1944.

———. *Las hazañas de Pedro de Urdemalas*. Buenos Aires: El Ateneo, 1949.

Arellano. SEE Ramírez de Arellano.

Ávila, María Teresa. *Flora y fauna en el folklore de Santiago del Estero*. Tucumán, Argentina: Impr. M. Violetto, 1960.

Barakat, Robert A. "Aztec Motifs in 'La Llorona.'" *SFQ*, 29(1965), 288–296.

———. "The Bear's Son Tale in Northern Mexico." *JAF*, 78(1965), 330–336.

Bascom, William. "The Forms of Folklore: Prose Narratives." *JAF*, 78 (1965), 3–20.

Bataillon, Manuel. "Dr. Andres Laguna, Peregrinaciones de Pedro de Urdemalas; muestra de una edición comentada." *Nueva revista de filología hispánica*, 6(1952), 121–137.

Beardsley, Richard, and Rosalie Hankey. "A History of the Vanishing Hitchhiker." *CFQ*, 2(1943), 13–25.

———. "The Vanishing Hitchhiker." *CFQ*, 1(1942), 303–335.

Blake, Mary. "Notes and Queries." *JAF*, 27(1914), 237–239.

Boas, Franz. "Notes on Mexican Folklore." *JAF*, 25(1912), 204–260.

———. "Tales of Spanish Provenience from Zuñi." *JAF*, 35(1922), 62–98.

———, and Herman K. Haeberlin. "Ten Folktales in Modern Nahuatl." *JAF*, 37(1924), 345–370.

Boggs, Ralph S. "Bibliografía del folklore mexicano." *Boletín bibliográfico de antropología americana* (Instituto Panamericano de Geografía e Historia, México, D.F.), 3, no. 3(1939): 1–122.

———. *A Comparative Survey of the Folktales of Ten Peoples*. Helsinki: Suomalainen Tiedeakatemia, Academia Scientiarum Fennica, 1930.

———. *Index of Spanish Folktales*. Folklore Fellows Communications 90. Helsinki, 1930.

———. "Seven Folktales from Porto Rico." *JAF*, 42(1929), 157–166.

———. "To Love Like Salt: A New Mexican Folktale." *NMFR*, 2(1947–1948), 20–23.

———, et al. "Mapa preliminar de las regiones folklóricas de México." *Folklore américas*, 9(1949), 1–4.

Boira, R. *El libro de los cuentos*. 3 vols. Madrid: Arcas y Sánchez, 1862.

Bonaparte, Marie. *The Life and Works of Edgar Allan Poe: A Psychoanalytic Interpretation*. London: Imago, 1949.

Bosquet, Amélie. *La Normandie romanesque et merveilleuse: Traditions, légendes et superstitions populaires de cette province*. Paris and Rouen: J. Techener, 1845.

Bourke, John G. "Popular Medicine, Customs, and Superstitions of the Río Grande." *JAF*, 7(1894), 119–146.

———. "La Virgen Suadanda [*sic*]." *Scribner's Magazine*, ca. 1894.

Brinton, Daniel G. "Nagualism: A Study in Native American Folklore and History." *Proceedings of the American Philosophical Society*, 33 (1914), 211–231.

Brunner, Theodore B. "Thirteen Tales from Houston County." *TFSP*, 31 (1962), 8–22.

Burgos, Fausto. *Aventuras de Juancho el zorro*. Buenos Aires: Raigal, 1953.

Burma, John. *Spanish-Speaking Groups in the United States*. Durham: Duke University Press, 1954.

Busk, Rachel Harriette. *Patrañas; or, Spanish Stories, Legendary and Traditional*. London: Griffith and Farran, 1870.

Cabal, Constantino. *Los cuentos tradicionales asturianos*. Madrid: Voluntad, 1924.

Caballero, Fernán. *Cuentos, oraciones, adivinas y refranes populares e infantiles*. Leipzig: Brockhaus, 1878.

———. *Cuentos y poesías populares andaluces*. Leipzig: Brockhaus, 1866.

————. *Spanish Fairy Tales*. New York: International Book Co., [n.d.].

Cadilla de Martínez, María. *Raíces de la tierra: Colección de cuentos populares y tradiciones*. Arecibo, Puerto Rico: Tipografía Hernández, 1941.

Campa, Arthur L. "Spanish Traditional Tales in the Southwest." *WF*, 6(1947), 322–334.

Campbell, Joseph. *The Hero with a Thousand Faces*. New York: Pantheon, 1961.

Canal Feijóo, Bernardo. *Ensayo sobre la expresión popular artística en Santiago*. Buenos Aires: Impresora Argentina, 1937.

Cañete de Rivas Jordán, María del Tránsito. *De nuestra tierra: Consejas, cuentos y leyendas*. Tucumán, Argentina: Imp. de la Penitenciaría, [n.d.].

Cano, Rafael. *Del tiempo de ñaupa (Folklore norteño.)* Buenos Aires: L. J. Rosso, 1930.

Carrillo Dueñas, Manuel. *Historia de Nuestra Señora del Rosario de Talpa*. Guadalajara, 1959.

Carvalho Neto, Paulo. *Cuentos folklóricos del Ecuador*. Quito: Editorial Universitaria, 1966.

Chapiseau, Félix. *Le Folk-lore de la Beauce et du Perche*. Paris: J. Maisonneuve, 1902.

Chertudi, Susana. *Cuentos folklóricos de la Argentina*. Buenos Aires: Instituto Nacional de Filología y Folklore, 1960 (1st series). Buenos Aires: Instituto Nacional de Antropología, 1964 (2nd series).

Christiansen, Reidar Th. *The Migratory Legends*. Folklore Fellows Communications 175. Helsinki, 1958.

————. *The Tale of the Two Travelers, or The Blinded Man*. Folklore Fellows Communications 24. Hamina, 1916.

Claudel, Calvin. "Tales from San Diego." *CFQ*, 2(1943), 113–120.

Colgrave, Bertram. "A Mexican Version of the 'Bear's Son' Folk Tale." *JAF*, 64(1951), 409–413.

Colorado: A Guide to the Highest State. Writer's Project, American Guide Series. New York: Hastings House, 1941.

Coluccio, Félix. *Folklore de las Américas, primera antología*. Buenos Aires: El Ateneo, 1949.

Concolorcorvo [Calixto Bustamante Carlos]. *El Lazarillo de ciegos caminantes desde Buenos Aires hasta Lima, 1773*. Buenos Aires: Ediciones Argentinas Solar, 1942.

Córdova, Gabriel. "Magic Tales from Mexico." M. A. thesis, Texas Western College, University of Texas, 1951.

Cortes y Vázquez, Luis L. *Cuentos populares en la ribera del Duero*. Salamanca: Centro de Estudios Salmantinos, 1955.

Costas Arguedas, José. *Folklore de Yamparáez.* Sucre, Bolivia: Universidad de San Francisco Javier, 1950.

Cox, Marian Roalfe. *Cinderella.* London: Folk-lore Society, 1893.

Crawford, Roselle. *Survival of Legends: Legends and Their Relation to History, Literature, and Life of the Southwest.* San Antonio: Naylor Co., 1952.

Creighton, Helen. *Bluenose Ghosts.* Toronto: Ryerson Press, 1959.

"Cuentos de animales en el folklore de Tucumán." *BATF*, Año II, vol. 1, nos. 21–22 (January–February 1952).

Curiel Merchán, M. *Cuentos extremeños.* Biblioteca de Tradiciones Populares. Madrid: C. Bermejo, 1944.

Cuscoy, Luis Diego. *Folklore infantil: Tradiciones populares.* Vol. 2. La Laguna de Tenerife, Spain: Instituto de Estudios Canarios, 1943.

Dalyell, Sir John Graham. *The Darker Superstitions of Scotland.* Glasgow: R. Griffin and Co., 1835.

Dean, C. M. "A Comparative Study of Certain Spanish-American Folktales." M. A. thesis, Indiana University, 1929.

De Huff, Elizabeth. *Say the Bells of Old Missions.* St. Louis, Mo., and London: B. Herder Book Co., 1943.

Dobie, J. Frank. "Charm in Mexican Folktales." *TFSP*, 24 (1951), 1–8.

———. *Tongues of the Monte.* Boston: Little, Brown, 1947.

Dorman, Artell. "Speak of the Devil." *TFSP*, 29 (1959), 142–146.

Dorson, Richard M. "Andrew Lang's Folklore Interests as Revealed in 'At the Sign of the Ship.' " *WF*, 11 (1952), 1–19.

Draghi Lucero, Juan. *Las mil y una noches argentinas.* Mendoza: Ediciones Oeste, 1940.

Dufourcq, Lucila. *Noticias relacionadas con el folklore de Lebu.* Santiago, 1943.

Durán, Agustín. *Romancero general.* BAE, vols. 10 and 11. 2 ed. Madrid: M. Rivadeneyra, 1859–1861.

Edmonds, I. G. *Trickster Tales.* Philadelphia: Lippincott, 1966.

Eells, E. S. *Tales of Enchantment from Spain.* New York: Harcourt Brace, 1920.

Espinosa, Aurelio. "Comparative Notes on New Mexican and Mexican Spanish Folk-Tales." *JAF*, 27 (1914), 211–231.

———. *Cuentos populares españoles.* 3 vols. Madrid: Consejo Superior de Investigaciones Científicas, 1946–1947.

———. "New Mexican Spanish Folk-Lore." *JAF*, 23 (1910), 395–418.

———. "New Mexican Spanish Folk-lore III: Folk-Tales." *JAF*, 24 (1911), 397–444.

———. "New Mexican Spanish Folk-Lore III: More Folk-Tales." *JAF*, 27 (1914), 105–147.

————. "Spanish Folk-tales from California." *Hispania*, 23(1940), 121–144.

Espinosa, Aurelio M. [hijo]. *Cuentos populares de Castilla*. Austral, no. 645. Buenos Aires: Espasa-Calpe, 1946.

————. "Spanish and Spanish-American Folk Tales." *JAF*, 64(1951), 151–162.

Espinosa, José Manuel. *Spanish Folktales from New Mexico*. Memoirs of the American Folk-lore Society, 30. New York: The American Folk-lore Society, 1937.

Fábulas de Esopo. Reproducción en facsímil de la primera edición de 1489, edición de la Real Academia Española. Madrid: 1929.

Feijóo, Padre. "Sobre la multitud de milagros." In *Cartas eruditas*. Clásicos Castellanos, 85. Madrid: Ediciones de "La Lectura," 1928.

Fernández de los Ríos, A. *Tesoro de cuentos*. Madrid: San Martín, 1875.

Folklore andaluz. Seville: Francisco Álvarez y Cía., 1882–1883.

El folklore frexnense y bético-extremeño. Fregenal, Spain: El Eco, 1883–1884.

Folktales from the Patagonia Area, Santa Cruz County, Arizona. Collected by Patagonia Union High School. Tucson: University of Arizona, 1949.

Foster, George. *Culture and Conquest: America's Spanish Heritage*. Viking Fund. Publications in Anthropology, no. 27. New York: Wenner-Gren Foundation for Anthropological Research, 1960.

————. *Empire's Children: The People of Tzintzuntzan*. Smithsonian Institution. Institute of Social Anthropology, Publication 6. Mexico City: Impr. Nuevo Mundo, 1948.

————. "Nagualism in Mexico and Guatemala." *Acta americana*, 2 (1944), 85–103.

————. "Sierra Popoluca Folklore and Beliefs." *UCAAE*, 42(1945), 177–250.

————. "Some Characteristics of Mexican Indian Folklore." *JAF*, 58 (1945), 225–235.

————. "Treasure Tales, and the Image of the Static Economy in a Mexican Peasant Community." *JAF*, 77(1964), 39–44.

Fraiberg, Selma. "Tales of the Discovery of the Secret Treasure." In *The Psychoanalytic Study of the Child*, vol. 9, pp. 218–241. New York: International Universities Press, 1954.

Franco, Luis. *Biografías animales*. Buenos Aires: Peuser, 1953.

Freud, Sigmund. *The Standard Edition of the Complete Psychological Works of Sigmund Freud*. 24 vols. London: Hogarth Press, 1953–.

Gaer, Joseph. *The Lore of the New Testament*. Boston: Little, Brown, 1952.

Gamio, Manuel. *The Mexican Immigrant: His Life Story.* Chicago: University of Chicago Press, 1931.

———. *Mexican Immigration to the United States.* Chicago: University of Chicago Press, 1930.

———. *Número, procedencia y distribución de los inmigrantes mexicanos en los Estados Unidos.* Mexico City: Talleres Gráficos Editorial y Diario Oficial, 1930.

———. *La población del Valle de Teotihuacán (México).* Vol. 2, pt. 5. Mexico City: Dirección de Talleres Gráficos, 1922.

Garibay, Ángel María. *Épica Nahuatl.* Mexico City: Universidad Nacional Autónoma, 1945.

Garnica Ornelas, Richard. "Folk Tales of the Spanish Southwest." M. A. thesis, University of Southern California, 1962.

Garza, Humberto. "Owl Bewitchment in the Lower Río Grande Valley." *TFSP,* 30(1961), 218–225.

Gil Rojas, Andrónico. *Los tipos de mi fogón.* Santiago del Estero, Argentina: Stechert-Hafner, 1962.

Giner Arivau, L. *Contribución al folklore de Asturias: Folklore de Proaza.* *BTPE,* vol. 8, pp. 101–308. Madrid: Librería de Fernando Fé, 1886.

González, Abertano. "Cuatro cuentos populares de Nirivilo." *AFCH,* 3 (1951), 91–103.

González, Jovita. "Folklore of the Texas-Mexican Vaquero." *TFSP,* 6 (1927), 7–22.

González Casanova, Pablo. *Cuentos indígenas.* 2d ed. Mexico City: Universidad Nacional Autónoma de México, Instituto de Investigaciones Históricas, 1965.

González Obregón, Luis. *Las calles de México.* 7th ed. Mexico City: Ediciones Bota, 1947.

———. *México viejo.* Mexico City: Editorial Patria, 1945.

Goodspeed, Bernice. *Mexican Tales.* 4th ed. Mexico City: American Book and Print Co., 1950.

Goodwyn, Frank. "Another Mexican Version of the 'Bear's Son' Folk Tale." *JAF,* 66(1953), 143–154.

La gran conquista de Ultramar. Edición de Pascal de Gayangos. *BAE,* vol. 44. Madrid: M. Rivadeneyra, 1858.

Griffith, Beatrice. *American Me.* Boston: Houghton Mifflin, 1948.

Grimm's Fairy Tales. Translated by Margaret Hunt and Rev. James Stern. New York: Pantheon Books, 1944.

Guerra, Fermina. "Mexican Animal Tales." *TFSP,* 18 (1943), 188–194.

Guerrero Román, Rebeca. "Folklore de la antigua provincia de Colchagua, VI. Cuentos." *RCHG,* 62(1929), 206–239.

Guirao, Ramón. *Cuentos y leyendas negros de Cuba*. Havana: Ediciones "Mirador," [1942].

Guzmán Maturana, Manuel. "Cuentos tradicionales en Chile." *AUC*, vol. 92, no. 14, pp. 34–81; no. 15, pp. 5–78.

Hankey, Rosalie. "California Ghosts." *CFQ*, 1(1942), 155–177.

Hansen, Terrence L. *The Types of the Folktale in Cuba, Puerto Rico, the Dominican Republic, and Spanish South America*. University of California Publications, Folklore Studies, 8. Berkeley and Los Angeles: University of California Press, 1957.

Hark, Ann. *Hex Marks the Spot, in the Pennsylvania Dutch Country*. Philadelphia and New York: J. B. Lippincott, 1938.

Hartt, Don V., and Harriett C. Hartt. "Cinderella in the Eastern Bisayas: With a Summary of the Philippine Folktale." *JAF*, 79(1966), 307–337.

Hawes, Bess Lomax. "La Llorona in Juvenile Hall." *WF*, 27(1968), 153–170.

Henderson, B., and C. Calvert. *Wonder Tales of Ancient Spain*. London: Allan, 1924.

Hendricks, George. "Four Southwestern Legends. *WF*, 27(1968), 255–262.

Hernández de Soto, Sergio. *Cuentos populares de Extremadura*. BTPE, vol. 10, pp. 1–301. Madrid: Libería de Fernando Fé, 1886.

Hernández Suárez, Dolores. "Cuentos recogidos en Camagüey." *AFC*, 4 (1929), 251–269; 5(1930), 61–70.

Hiester, Miriam W. "Tales of the Paisanos." *TFSP*, 30(1961), 226–243.

Hilka, Alfons, and Werner Söderhjelm. *Die Disciplina Clericalis des Petrus Alfonsi*. Heidelberg: Carl Winter, 1911.

Hinckle, Catherine J. "The Devil in New Mexican Spanish Folklore." *WF*, 8(1949), 123–125.

Horcasitas Pimentel, Fernando. "Textos modernos de 'La llorona,' " *Mesoamerican Notes* (Department of Anthropology, Mexico City College), no. 1(1950), pp. 34–52; no. 2(1950), pp. 53–67.

Hudson, Wilson M. "Another Mexican Version of the Story of the Bear's Son." *SFQ*, 15(1951), 152–158.

Hurt, Wesley R. "Spanish-American Superstitions." *El Palacio*, 47(1940), 193–201.

Jacobs, Joseph, ed. *The Fables of Aesop* [Caxton, 1484]. 2 vols. London: D. Nutt, 1889.

Janvier, Thomas A. *Legends of the City of Mexico*. New York: Harper and Brothers, 1927.

Jijena Sánchez, Rafael. *De la tradición popular en América: Los cuentos de Mama Vieja*. Buenos Aires: Versol, 1946.

———. *Perro negro en el folklore*. Buenos Aires: Dolmen, 1952.

Jiménez Borja, Arturo. *Cuentos peruanos.* Lima: Lumen, 1937.

————. *Cuentos y leyendas del Perú.* Lima: Instituto Peruano del Libro, 1940.

Jones, Louis C. "Hitchhiking Ghosts in New York." *CFQ,* 3(1944), 284–292.

————. *Things That Go Bump in the Night.* New York: Hill and Wang, 1959.

Jones, William. *Finger-Ring Lore.* 2d ed. London: Chatto and Windus, 1898.

Juan Manuel. *El libro de los enxemplos.* Edición de Gayangos. *BAE,* vol. 51, pp. 443–542. Madrid, 1960.

Keller, John E. *Motif-index of Mediaeval Spanish Exempla.* Knoxville: University of Tennessee Press, 1949.

Khana: Revista municipal de arte y letras (La Paz). Vol. 2, no. 31–32 (1958).

Kirtley, Bacil F. " 'La llorona' and Related Themes." *WF,* 19(1960), 155–168.

Knust, Herman, and Adolf Birch-Hirschfield. *Juan Manuel, el libro de los enxiemplos del Conde Lucanor et de Patronio.* Leipzig: Dr. Seele, 1900.

Koessler-Ilg, Bertha. *Cuentan los araucanos.* Buenos Aires, 1954.

Krappe, Alexander. *The Science of Folklore.* New York: Norton Library, 1964.

————. "The Story of Phrixos and Modern Folklore." *Folklore,* 34 (1923), 141–147.

Laval, Ramón A. *Contribución al folklore de Carahue.* 2 vols. Madrid: V. Suárez, 1916; Santiago: Imprenta Universitaria, 1921.

————. *Cuentos de Pedro de Urdemalas.* Santiago: Imprenta Cervantes, 1925.

————. *Cuentos populares en Chile.* Santiago: Imprenta Cervantes, 1923.

Leddy, Betty. "La llorona Again." *WF,* 9(1950), 363–365.

————. "La llorona in Southern Arizona." *WF,* 7(1948), 272–277.

Lenz, Rudolfo. "Estudios araucanos." *AUC,* vol. 7(1895–1897).

————. "Un grupo de consejas chilenas." *RFC,* 3(1912), 1–152.

El libro de los gatos. Ed. crítica por John Esten Keller. Madrid: Consejo Superior de Investigaciones Científicas, 1958.

Lipschultz, Robert J. "American Attitudes toward Mexican Immigration between 1924–1952." M. A. thesis, University of Chicago, 1962.

Lizano, Víctor. *Leyendas de Costa Rica.* San José, Costa Rica: Editorial Soley y Valverde, 1941.

Llano Roza de Ampudia, Aurelio de. *Cuentos asturianos.* Madrid: Caro Raggio, 1925.

————. *Del folklore asturiano.* Madrid: Talleres de Voluntad, 1922.

Loomis, C. G. "Legend and Folklore." *CFQ*, 2(1943), 279–297.

——. "The Miracle of Ponderosity." *CFQ*, 3(1944), 41–44.

Loorits, Oskar. *Livische Maerchen- und Sagenvarianten*. Folklore Fellows Communications 66. Helsinki: 1926.

Lucero-White Lea, Aurora. *The Folklore of New Mexico*. Santa Fe: Seton Village Press, 1941.

Lyra, Carmen. *Los Cuentos de mi Tía Panchita*. San José, Costa Rica: Imprenta española, Soley y Valverde, 1926.

Macario. A Clasa Films Mundiales Production, 1960. Released in the United States by Azteca Films. Producer: Armando Orive Alba. Based on a story by Bruno Traven.

Mason, J. Alden. "Folk-Tales of the Tepecanos." *JAF*, 27(1914), 148–210.

——. "Four Mexican-Spanish Fairy Tales from Azqueltán, Jalisco." *JAF*, 25(1912), 191–198.

——. (Edited by A. M. Espinosa). "Porto-Rican Folk-Lore: Folk-Tales." *JAF*, 29(1916), 423–504; 34(1921), 143–208; 35(1922), 1–61; 37(1924), 247–344; 38(1925), 507–618; 39(1926), 227–369; 40(1927), 313–414; 42(1929), 85–156.

McKenzie, Kenneth. "An Italian Fable: Its Sources and History." *Modern Philology*, 1(1903–1904), 497–525.

Mendoza, Vicente T. *Lírica infantil de México*. Mexico City: El Colegio de México, 1951.

——, and Virginia R. Mendoza. *Folklore de San Pedro Piedra Gorda, Zacatecas*. Mexico City: Secretaría de Educación Pública, 1952.

Mendoza, Virginia Rodríguez Rivera de. "Las brujas en el folklore de México." *ASFM*, 6(1945), 475–484.

——. "Los cuentos de Pedro de Urdemalas en Tlaxcala." *ASFM*, 6(1945), 429–432.

——. *El informante, elemento humano en la recolección folklórica*. Mexico City: Editorial Libros de México, 1958.

——. "La Llorona." *Previsión y seguridad* (Monterrey, Mexico), 14(1950), 225–228, 230, 232, 234.

——. "El nahual en el folklore de México." *ASFM*, 7(1951), 123–138.

Menéndez, Gabriel. *Leyendas y tradiciones yucatecas*. Mérida: Editorial Yucatanense "Club del Libro," 1951.

Menéndez Pidal, Juan. *Poesía popular*. Madrid: García, 1885 .

Miles, Elton R. "Christ in the Big Bend." *TFSP*, 27(1957), 171–179.

Miller, Walter S. *Cuentos mixes*. Instituto Nacional Indigenista. Biblioteca de Folklore Indígena, 2. Mexico City, 1956.

Monroy Pittaluga, Francisco. "Cuentos y romances tradicionales en Cazorla." *AVF*, 1, no. 2, pp. 360–380.

Montenegro, Ernesto. *Mi tío Ventura: Cuentos populares de Chile.* 2d ed. Santiago: Nascimento, 1938.

Morales, Ernesto. "Leyendas del zorro." *Azul: Revista de ciencias y letras,* 1, no. 6(1930), 5–22.

Morel-Fatio, Alfred. "*El libro de los enxiemplos por a.b.c.* de Clemente Sánchez de Valderas." *Romania,* 7(1878), 481–526.

Morosoli, Sabina K. "A Theoretical Reconstruction of the Original Cinderella Story." M. A. thesis, Stanford University, 1930.

Morote Best, Efraín. "Dios, la Virgen, y los santos (en los relatos populares)." *Tradición* (Cuzco, Peru), Año III, vol. 5, nos. 12–14(1953), 76–104.

Moya, Benjamin S. "Superstitions and Beliefs among the Spanish-Speaking People of New Mexico." M. A. thesis, University of New Mexico, Albuquerque, 1940.

Muñoz Camargo, Diego. *Historia de Tlaxcala.* 2d ed. Mexico City: Ateneo Nacional de Ciencias y Artes de México, 1947.

Negrón Pérez, Porfirio. "Origen de la Xtabay." *Yikal Maya Than* (Yucatán), 5, no. 58(1944), 134–136.

La novena de San Ramón. Mexico City, 1889.

Olivares Figueroa, Rafael. "Cuentos zoquetes." *Onza Tigre y León,* 9, no. 97(1947), 10–11.

———. *Folklore Venezolano, II. Prosas.* Caracas: Ministerio de Educación Nacional, Dirección de Cultura, 1954.

Olrik, Axel. "Epic Laws of Folk Narrative." In *The Study of Folklore,* pp. 129–141. Englewood Cliffs, N. J.: Prentice-Hall, 1965.

Palacios, Enrique Juan. *Huaxtepec y sus reliquias arqueológicas.* Mexico City: Secretaría de Educación Pública, 1930.

Palma, Ricardo. *Tradiciones peruanas completas.* Madrid: Aguilar, 1957.

Panzer, Freidrich. *Studien zur germanischen Sagengeschichte. I. Beowulf.* Munich: C. H. Beck, 1910.

Paredes, Américo. *Folktales of Mexico.* Chicago: University of Chicago Press, 1970.

Parochetti, JoAnn S. "Scary Stories from Purdue." *Keystone Folklore Quarterly,* 10(1965), 49–57.

Parsons, Elsie C. "Folklore from Santa Ana Xalmimilulco, Puebla, México." *JAF,* 45(1932), 318–362.

———. "Zapoteca and Spanish Tales of Mitla, Oaxaca." *JAF,* 45(1932), 277–317.

———, and Franz Boas. "Spanish Tales from Laguna and Zuñi, New Mexico." *JAF,* 33(1920), 47–72.

Pauer, P. S. "Folk Tales from Mexico." *JAF,* 31(1918), 552–553.

Pearce, T. M. "The Bad Son (*el mal hijo*) in Southwestern Spanish Folk-lore." *WF*, 9(1950), 295–301.

Pereda Valdés, Ildefonso. *Cancionero popular uruguayo*. Montevideo: Editorial Florensa y Lafon, 1947.

————. "Personajes folklóricos." *AVF*, 4–5(1957), 219–229.

Pérez, Soledad. "Mexican Folklore from Austin, Texas." *TFSP*, 24(1951), 71–127.

————. "The Weeping Woman." *TFSP*, 26(1954), 127–130.

Pérez Serrano, Manuel. "El duende y la Matlacihua." *ASFM*, 5(1944), 35–40.

Pineda Giraldo, Roberto. "La chama, un mito guajiro." *RF*, no. 2(December 1947), 113–126.

Pino Saavedra, Yolando. *Cuentos folklóricos de Chile*. 3 vols. Santiago: Instituto de Investigaciones Folklóricas "Ramón A. Laval," 1963.

Pitt, Leonard. *The Decline of the Californios: A Social History of the Spanish-Speaking Californians*. Berkeley: University of California Press, 1966.

Portell Vilá, Herminio. "Cuentos populares cubanos." 125 Cuban folktales in manuscript.

Post, Anita. "Southern Arizona Spanish Phonology." *UAHB*, 5, no. 1 (1934), 48–50.

Qvigstad, J. *Lappische Märchen- und Sagenvarianten*. Folklore Fellows Communications 60. Helsinki, 1925.

Radin, Paul. "Cuentos y leyendas de los zapotecos." *Tlalocán* (Sacramento, California), 1(1943), 3–30, 134–154, 194–226.

————, and Aurelio Espinosa. *El folklore de Oaxaca*. New York: G. E. Stechert, 1917.

————. (Edited by A. M. Espinosa). "Folk-Tales from Oaxaca."*JAF*, 28 (1915), 390–408.

————. "Zapotec Texts: Dialect of Juchitan Tehuano." *IJAL*, 12(1946), 152–172.

Rael, Juan B. "Cuentos españoles de Colorado y de Nuevo Méjico." *JAF*, 52(1939), 227–323; 55(1942), 1–93. Published as *Cuentos españoles de Colorado y de Nuevo Méjico*. 2 vols. Stanford: Stanford University Press [1957].

Ramírez de Arellano, Rafael. *Folklore portorriqueño*. Madrid: [Avila, Tipografía y encuadernación de S. Martín] 1926.

Ramos, José Ernesto. *Voces de Talpa*. Guadalajara, 1951.

Recinos, Adrián. "Cuentos populares de Guatemala." *JAF*, 31(1918), 472–482.

Redfield, Margaret Park. *The Folk Literature of a Yucatecan Town*. Carnegie Institution, Contributions to American Archaeology, no. 13. Washington, D.C., 1937.

Reid, John T. "A Comparative Study of a Spanish Folktale . . . Los siete infantes." M. A. thesis, Stanford University, 1930.

————. "Seven Folktales from Mexico." *JAF*, 48(1935), 109–124.

Renca, folklore puntano. Bueno Aires: Instituto Nacional de Filología y Folklore, 1958.

Riera Pinilla, Mario. *Cuentos folklóricos de Panamá.* Panama City: Departamento de Bellas Artes y Publicaciones del Ministerio de Educación, 1956.

Riva Palacio, V. *Tradiciones y leyendas mexicanas.* New York: T. Nelson and Sons, 1927.

Robe, Stanley L. "Four Mexican *exempla* about the Devil. *WF*, 10(1951), 310–315.

————. Manuscript version of Hansen 332**A. [In Robe's collection.]

————. *Mexican Tales and Legends from Los Altos.* Berkeley and Los Angeles: University of California Press, 1970.

Robinson, Cecil. *With the Ears of Strangers.* Tucson: University of Arizona Press, 1963.

Ruiz, Juan. *Libro de Buen Amor.* (Ducamin edition.) Paris: A. Picard et fils, 1901.

Ruiz, Ramón E. "Hijos olvidados: La historia del pueblo de descendencia mexicana en los Estados Unidos de Norteamérica." *América indígena*, 12(1952), 121–130.

Sahagún, Fray Bernardo de. *Historia general de las cosas de Nueva España.* Mexico City: P. Robredo, 1938.

Samaniego, Félix María. *Fábulas en verso castellano.* 2 vols. Madrid, 1902.

Sánchez Pérez, José. *Cien cuentos populares.* Madrid: Editorial SAETA, 1942.

Saunière, S. de. "Cuentos populares araucanos y chilenos." *RFC*, 7(1918), 3–282.

Sébillot, Paul. *Contes espagnols.* Paris: Libraire d'Education de la Jeunesse, 1900.

Serrano Martínez, Celedonio. "Pedro de Urdemalas en la narración tradicional en Guerrero." *ASFM*, 6(1945), 415–428.

Shoemaker, Henry Wharton. *Pennsylvania Mountain Stories.* Reading, Penn.: Reading Times, 1910.

Sinninghe, Jacques R. *Katalog der niederländischen Märchen-, Ursprungssagen-, Sagen-, und Legendenvarianten.* Folklore Fellows Communications 132. Helsinki, 1943.

Sojo, Juan Pablo. "Cuentos folklóricos venezolanos." *AVF*, 2, no. 3 (1953–1954), 175–189.

————. "Folklore literario. Folklore anímico." *BIF*, 2, no. 3(1955), 77–96.

Sonnichsen, Charles L. "Mexican Spooks from El Paso." *TFSP*, 13(1937), 120–129.

Soupey, M. *Contes et légendes d'Espagne*. Paris.: Nathan, 1925.

Storm, Dan. "The Little Animals of Mexico," *TFSP*, 14(1938), 8–35.

Suddeth, Ruth E. *Tales of the Western World: Folktales of the Americas*. Austin, Texas: Steck, 1953.

Sydow, C. W. von. *Selected Papers on Folklore*. Copenhagen: Rosenkilde and Bagger, 1948.

Szövérffy, J. "From Beowulf to the *Arabian Nights*." *Midwest Folklore*, 6(Summer 1956), 91–92.

Thompson, Stith. *The Folktale*. New York: Dryden Press, 1951.

————. *Motif-Index of Folk-Literature*. 2d ed. 6 vols. Bloomington: Indiana University Press, 1955–1958.

————. *Tales of the North American Indians*. Cambridge, Mass.: Harvard University Press, 1912.

Thoms, W. J. *Lays and Legends of Various Nations; Illustrative of Their Traditions, Popular Literature, Manners, Customs and Superstitions. Lays and Legends of Spain*. London: Cowie, 1834.

Tolman, Ruth B. "Treasure Tales of the Caballos." *WF*, 20(1961), 153–174.

Toor, Francis. *Three Worlds of Peru*. New York: Crown Publishers, 1949.

————. *A Treasury of Mexican Folkways*. New York: Crown Publishers, 1947.

Tully, Marjorie F., and Juan B. Rael. *An Annotated Bibliography of Spanish Folklore in New Mexico and Southern Colorado*. Albuquerque: University of New Mexico Press, 1950.

Valdés, Ignacio de Jesús. *Cuentos panameños de la ciudad y del campo*. Panama City, 1928.

Vicuña Cifuentes, Julio. *Estudios del folklore chileno: Mitos y supersticiones*. Santiago: Editorial Nascimento, 1947.

————. *Prosas de otros días*. Santiago: Prensas de la Universidad de Chile, 1939.

Wagner, Max L. "Algunas apuntaciones sobre el folklore mexicano." *JAF*, 40(1927), 105–143.

Wallrich, William J. "Five *bruja* tales from the San Luis Valley." *WF*, 9(1950), 359–362.

————. "Spanish American Devil Lore in Southern Colorado." *WF*, 9 (1950), 50–55.

Warren, Nina. *Old Spain in Our Southwest*. 2d ed. Chicago: Rio Grande Press, 1962.

Wheeler, Howard T. *Tales from Jalisco, Mexico.* Memoirs of the American Folk-Lore Society, 35. Philadelphia: American Folk-Lore Society, 1943.

Wolf, Fernando José, and Conrado Hofman. *Primavera y flor de romances.* 2d ed. In Menéndez y Pelayo, *Antología de poetas líricos castellanos,* vols. 8–9. Madrid: Hernando y Compañía, 1912.

Woods, Barbara Allen. *The Devil in Dog Form: A Partial Type-Index of Devil Legends.* University of California Publications, Folklore Studies, 2. Berkeley and Los Angeles: University of California Press, 1959.

Woods, Margreta J. "A Study of the Cinderella Story in the Spanish Folklore of New Mexico and Colorado." M. A. thesis, Stanford University, 1948.

Yáñez, Agustín. *Yahualica.* Mexico City, 1946.

Zunser, Helen. "A New Mexican Village," *JAF,* 48(1935), 125–178.